STEPHANIE
DENNE

RUINOUS SECRETS

4
BLACKTHORN
SAGA

Published in Canada by Amethyst Corvid Press, Ontario, Canada.

Ruinous Secrets.
First Edition.
ISBN: 978-1-7381014-1-2
Stephanie Denne.

See more books by Stephanie Denne at https://stephaniedenneauthor.com
Editing by Kelly Schaub

Cover Design by Stephanie Denne

For My Lily...

You were the best girl, and life will never be the same without you.

Mama will never forget you.

I love you always.

A Message from the Author

This book contains content that may be unsuitable for certain readers. To learn more about content warnings in the author's work, please visit her website:
https://www.stephaniedenneauthor.com/content-warnings

This story features a character who struggles with undiagnosed ADHD. Please read responsibly for your mental health if this is something you would be uncomfortable with.

The events and reactions to the world through their eyes are not the only way ADHD can manifest itself. I based much of Riley's take on the world, and her own inner struggles, on my own personal struggles, past experiences in my time with the same diagnosis, and coping mechanisms in dealing with the world. No two people are alike, and we won't all share the same struggles. There are symptoms not expressed, and some symptoms heightened that may be subdued for you or another, as happens with anyone on the neurodivergent spectrum.

When reading, know that if your experience is not the same, it is not a dismissal of how you face the world, but merely how this character's own mind works.

You are seen. Your struggles and triumphs are valid.

I hope in reading a character that perhaps shares in some of your experiences, or faces struggles of her own, you can relate and possibly get a sense of peace in that.

For those who do not face these types of struggles, hopefully this will help you better understand anyone you may know that navigates life the way Riley does, and that you are able to take something away from that.

Happy reading!
– Stephanie

Some secrets were best left in the dark, in a place where hearts and lives existed bound by barbed wire. Where with one wrong move, the truth of those secrets would slice through and leave nothing but ruin.

PLAYLIST

The Birthday Massacre – Under Your Spell
Snow Patrol – Run
Fleurie – Hurts Like Hell
Three Days Grace – Over and Over
The Pretty Reckless – Make Me Wanna Die
Bad Omens – Just Pretend
Noelle Johnson – Broken
Two Feet – ADHD
Two Feet – Love Is a Bitch
My Darkest Days – Perfect
The Pretty Reckless – You
Alec Benjamin ft. Alessia Cara – Let Me Down Slowly
Rhys Lewis – No Right to Love You
Avril Lavigne ft. YUNGBLUD – I'm A Mess
Bring Me the Horizon – Avalanche
Bring Me the Horizon – Happy Song
Alec Benjamin – Mind is a Prison
Anson Seabra – Trying My Best

Blackthorn Academy Campus

It's easy to lose your way at the mysterious Blackthorn Academy. But with a little luck, and this handy map, I'm sure you'll do just fine… maybe.

1

Bonds

How could I tell her she owned my heart from the moment she punched me in the face as a toddler?

Riley sat back on her bed against the wall, closing her book, and exhaled with a dreamy smile. “Emley Rison really has a way with words,” she said, rolling her head against the wall to look at Blaire.

“I can’t believe Ryan waited so long to tell Shelby the truth.” Blaire shook her head before taking the last bite of the grilled chicken wrap she’d brought for lunch to Riley’s dorm room.

“Hey! No spoilers. I’m only halfway through.”

“Alright. Alright.” Blaire held her hands up in surrender. “But you’ll see what I mean.” She wiped her mouth with a napkin and glanced at Mera, who had arrived moments earlier. “What?”

“Nothing really.” Their friend sat on the foot of the twin bed, slipped her combat boots off, and then tucked her legs beneath her to get more comfortable. “I don’t understand the draw of those types of books."

"It's romance," Riley said.

Mera's head cocked to the side as if to say, "And?"

Riley huffed and held the small hardback up as if she were a preacher about to break into a sermon at church. "So life doesn't always go the way you want it to, but in these books?" She slapped her small hand on the cover. "Things go according to plan—*usually*. Besides, it gives some of us the chance to feel what we haven't before, or what we've wanted to feel."

She climbed off the bed and crossed to the two bookshelves perpendicular to her bed in front of her closet. When she slid the hardback between others from the same author, she spun around and sighed. "You have Kai... maybe that's why you don't understand."

Mera's bond with Kai seemed so perfect. Where one moved, the other followed. They each knew what the other needed with only a look. Riley recalled Blaire expressing how eerie it felt when she first met them after joining Blackthorn Academy. She wasn't rude about it. She simply pointed out how it seemed like they could read each other's minds. Maybe they could and didn't tell anyone. Riley wanted that.

"Things don't go according to our plans, or the way we want them to, just because we're pair-bonded. It doesn't work that way."

Riley resisted the urge to protest further.

Whenever she mentioned longing to find her Korrena pair, Mera urged her to be patient, while Kai waxed poetic about how good it'd feel when it happened. Both argued that waiting would be worth it, but also warned pair-bonding wasn't as smooth as it appeared for them. They'd had years to reach where they were.

But what if it never happened? Not all Vasirian found their Korrena. The one person meant for them on a soul-deep level. A true mate in its simplest explanation.

Not having a pair at the expected awakening age of seventeen to eighteen was seen as tragic by her kin, despite the growing number of Vasirian experiencing this phenomenon.

Her brother Aiden hadn't found his Korrena, and he was twenty. Sure, her mom had been eighty-one when she found her pair, but Riley couldn't wait that long. She lacked the patience for that. Nearly three months into her eighteenth year, and she had zilch. No rumblings or awareness around other students. Absolutely nothing out of the ordinary.

Mera interrupted her thoughts. "Finding your mate can sometimes make life difficult in the beginning."

"Don't I know it," Blaire muttered under her breath.

Riley scoffed. "Well, you're human. Of course it's gonna be different for you."

Blaire rolled her eyes. "Well, Lukas isn't human, and it was hard for him. I'm not talking about the things my species affected. Basic Korrena stuff, according to his parents and Professor Velastra."

Riley put her hands on her hips. "If I didn't know you two better, I'd say you don't want me to find my pair." She pointed a finger at her friends. "But I *do* know better, so I won't argue." She pursed her lips, glancing to the side, and spoke under her breath, "Anymore."

"I want you to find your pair, but rushing in your search can bring about disappointment," Mera said.

"I'm not rushing. It's not like I can rush it, anyway. It's either there, or it isn't."

"While that's true, if you don't relax, you might miss it when it comes along."

Riley leaned down to pick up pieces of clothing from her floor, panicked at Mera's implication. "What's that supposed to mean?"

"People oftentimes miss the signs of 'the one' because they are so focused on finding love everywhere and anywhere. This can apply to Korrenas as well. They miss their pair because they aren't patient. Sometimes even settling on a compatible mate too early."

Riley's head jerked in frantic disagreement. "There's no way I'd miss it." She dropped the shirts from her hands and went to her desk, digging through her drawers and finding a bag of jellybeans.

"You haven't heard the phrase 'good things come to those who wait'?" Blaire asked.

Riley scoffed and shoved a handful of jellybeans into her mouth.

Mera studied her for a moment. "We only wish to help you avoid making a decision you'll regret."

Riley squirmed under her friend's analytical gaze. "I'm not gonna do anything. Besides, there's no one on my radar I'd consider as a compatible pair."

"What about Seth?" Blaire asked.

Riley winced. She didn't want to go there. "What about him?"

Blaire rolled her eyes. "He'd make a good compatible pair if you did go that direction."

"That's true," Mera agreed. "But again, she's only eighteen."

Riley kept nervously chewing on jellybeans.

"Don't give up on finding your Korrena yet. But dating a little might not be a bad idea."

"Yeah, you could try dating Seth."

"Nope. Nuh uh. We are oil and water." She frowned at her friends. "What? Why are y'all looking at me like I'm stupid?"

Blaire sighed. "Have you considered dating someone else?"

"Not really." Riley was thankful to shift the focus away from Seth.

It wasn't that he wasn't worthy of dating, but their fifteen-year relationship was built on her being the little sister, as her actual big brother was Seth's best friend. It would make for a lot of awkward encounters to even attempt dating each other; even if they got past all the other reasons, it was a terrible idea.

Things between them lately already felt strained, and adding dating to that when she was so inexperienced, and he was as opposite as one could get, would probably destroy their lifelong friendship. She would never risk that.

"Maybe try that? Date someone and see how you feel," Blaire said.

Maybe Mera and Blaire were right. Maybe dating without making a commitment wouldn't hurt. Having someone else to distract her from what she couldn't have might be the thing she needed to re-center herself, to set aside that frantic need to find her Korrena pair. It wouldn't stop her from wanting it, but it could relieve her desperate fixation. If someone else occupied her time, she wouldn't obsess over the idea that finding her pair would ease the pain she felt inside over something she never gave words to.

"Yeah, yeah. I hear ya." Riley grabbed a book off her desk, putting the bag of jellybeans in its place, and moved back to the bed. She handed the book to Blaire, hoping to change the subject. "Picked this up at the mall for you at the new bookstore."

Blaire flipped the book over and read the synopsis. "Reverse harem?"

"Normally not my thing, but mercy, are the boys in this one delicious."

"I'll give it a try," Blaire said. "I actually haven't read one before." She laughed when Mera couldn't hold back a faint scoff. They never could get Mera on board with their romance novel hobby.

Riley twisted and plopped her head in Blaire's lap, lying down, and stretched her feet over to touch Mera's thigh.

With Mera sitting at the foot of the bed and Blaire at the head of it, most people wouldn't try to lie down between them, but Riley could fit comfortably in places others wouldn't. A five-four, her height was average, but her petite frame made her appear smaller—a fact everyone commented on.

She was a mouse. A shrimp. Tiny, skinny, scrawny, twiggy; she'd heard it all. The subject of how little she was came up often, and she tried to take it in stride but hated her stature being everyone's focus in conversation. Just once, maybe someone could ask if she'd ever played basketball. She'd had a great layup in middle school.

Blaire gave her an indulgent smile, in good spirits as they chatted about pairs and romance novels, even though only a couple of weeks ago Riley and all their friends rescued Blaire from one of the most traumatic things Riley had ever witnessed. She wondered if she could keep her composure the same way Blaire did if the same thing had happened to her.

How did someone come back from literally dying and not end up broken psychologically?

Nothing against humans, but Riley didn't know if human minds were weaker or stronger than Vasirian minds. Perhaps Vasirian were the weaker-minded ones. Maybe the bond Blaire shared with Lukas gave her strength. Blaire impressed Riley every day with her mental fortitude.

"Hey, are you okay?"

Riley opened her eyes and looked up at Blaire. "Yeah, why?"

"You just have this pinched expression."

Riley sat up and shook her head, toying with one of the many black rubber bracelets on her wrist. "Just thinking about everything that's happened since September."

Riley had been devastated when Blaire disappeared six months ago, thinking she left Blackthorn Academy. After sharing a piece of herself not long after joining the academy, Blaire became special to her, and that cemented a friendship she wouldn't give up for anything. Seeing not only the strength in Blaire's eyes but also the broken parts of her, Riley vowed to do everything she could to protect the human girl. Not out of a sense of obligation at being the stronger species, but because Blaire had become her best friend.

"I don't know how many times I have to say it, but I'm fine. In fact, I feel stronger than I've felt in months."

"That's from the magic, right?"

"Seems so. I still can't believe magic is real. I mean, I guess it's not too far-fetched considering your species is real and not a myth. At this point, I'm willing to believe anything is possible after what I've witnessed."

When Blaire first joined Blackthorn Academy, she mistook them for vampires. None of them blamed her for the assumption. They had fangs, drank blood, healed quickly, and aged slowly. Classic vampire traits from centuries of storytelling, except they were alive. Ignoring the small grocery list of differences, they were similar to humans. Sort of.

Riley's head tilted sideways. "Has anything else happened?"

"Like what?"

"You know." Riley waved her hand around in the air. "The glowy magic stuff."

Blaire shook her head. "No. I don't know how to control it, or if it's even still there. I don't feel any different."

When they found Blaire on an altar, cut open and bleeding to death, the magic in her blood brought her back to life. If the situation hadn't been so traumatic, Riley would have been more excited by the beautiful golden glow that healed her friend.

Blaire glanced down at her arm. "All my scars are gone. Even the ones from when I was a kid, on my knees." She flexed her hand in her lap. "Did you know I didn't bruise like I usually do from the IV?"

Mera set her phone aside. "That's an interesting development. Have you told Professor Velastra?"

Blaire shook her head, a few blonde strands falling from her messy bun. "Wasn't sure if it was a fluke or not."

"You should. If what happened in the temple changed your condition, it's worth documenting."

"Yeah, but what does it mean?"

Mera looked at Riley. "By itself? It could mean nothing. But it's worth documenting any anomaly for posterity."

"Why?"

"Medically speaking, her condition is fascinating." She smiled when Blaire made a sour face. Mera focused on analyzing anything medical, which wasn't surprising considering her concentration in health science. "Human medicine doesn't have an answer. From what records we have, there isn't anything to explain it on our end. The only outlying influence is the magic in her blood. With the king's great-grandfather destroying the records relating to our ties to magic and humans, preserving new information is paramount to future education. Professor Velastra is documenting for the records what has occurred with Blaire since she joined the academy."

"She is?"

Mera nodded. "If humans and Vasirian can be mates through magical bloodlines, it's worth documenting how it's restored." She glanced at her phone when it chimed.

Riley sighed, watching Blaire pluck at the hem of her thigh-high uniform stockings. It didn't take a genius to tell the topic made Blaire uncomfortable.

Riley wondered if things between the humans and Vasirian would reach a point of restoration. Blaire had told her she was more willing to become a Vasirian than she had been before bonding with Lukas, but with the crazies coming out of the woodwork at every turn to give her a hard time, Riley couldn't blame her for hesitating. It wasn't about blood and death anymore.

Truthfully, nothing held her friend back anymore except bad timing. With the trip to Europe to meet the Blackthorn Clan looming, now wasn't the time to do something so life-altering as changing her species.

But who wouldn't be uncomfortable knowing the fate of an entire species rested on their shoulders?

Mera held up her phone. "Kai is asking if you wanted a developer this time."

"Huh?"

"He's at the beauty store with Seth, Aiden, and Lukas."

"But why is he asking?"

"Because Seth said you're not answering your phone."

Riley scrambled off the bed, tripping over the pile of pink and black fabrics and tulle on the floor next to her bed in her haste to grab her phone off the desk.

Seth:

dev too? 20vol? 30?

Seth:

hello?

Seth:

i swear to god riley

Seth had been texting for the last ten minutes. Checking her volume showed her phone was still muted from earlier in the day. Groaning in frustration with herself, she hastily tapped out a reply, ignoring the way her heart rate kicked up a notch.

Riley:

No developer. Still have some. Just need the Frosé by Arctic Fox.

Riley:

Also, your texting is terrible.

Seth:

i knw the color

Seth:

also shut up

Heat rose in her cheeks as she stared down at the texts on the screen in her hands. He knew the color she used. Of course he did. He always bought her a fresh bottle whenever she needed to retouch the fading pastel pink she liked for the longer strands on top of her head. Even though he'd been buying the dye for her since she was a young teen, it always sent a thrill through her that he knew something so trivial as the color and brand she used to color her hair.

"Riley?"

Spinning around, clutching her cell to her chest like she was hiding some kind of dirty secret, her brows shot up as she took in the two curious faces peering at her.

Blaire asked, "Didn't you hear me?" When Riley shook her head, Blaire repeated, "I asked if everything is okay." She motioned to the phone.

"Yeah, why?" Riley tried to sound casual, but the way she rushed over to her desk exhibited anything but. "Mera's right. He just wanted to know if I needed a developer for my roots. He's picking up my hair dye."

She glanced in the small mirror on her desk. Her black roots weren't too bad, and with the sides and back also black and cropped short, it didn't look like it needed lightened, anyway. But she didn't want the pink hair too faded before they went to Europe. She didn't know when they'd be back.

Mera made a sound and looked back at her phone after casting a side glance at Riley through the mirror. Riley turned and leaned against her messy desk, pushing palettes and tubes of makeup from the edge with her backside.

She frowned. "What?"

"Nothing," Mera said.

"No. What was that look about?"

"It's just nice that he goes out and gets that for you all the time."

Blaire looked between them. "He does this often?"

"Every time she needs it. When's the last time you paid for your own dye?"

Riley shrugged, feeling her face flush.

Blaire's lips parted in an O. "Really."

The unspoken implications behind that one drawled word made Riley's entire body tense.

Because there were implications.

Without a doubt.

With a huff, she threw her hands in the air. "Alright, alright. So Seth buys me bottles of hair dye. Big frickin' whoop."

Friends did that sort of thing for each other. It wasn't like he was buying her jewelry, chocolates, and flowers. Though, truthfully, she wasn't into that sort of thing. If she did have a boyfriend, Korrena, or compatible pair, she wouldn't want the traditional gestures like that. She wasn't traditional. From her soft pink, long-on-top pixie cut with natural black on the back and sides, to her alternative style and her larger-than-life personality—as Blaire so eloquently put it—she didn't fit traditional social norms for human girls in the small town of Rosebrook Valley, Georgia.

Her mama always said she had the look of a Los Angeles wild child but too sweet a heart to leave.

She stomped across the room and opened a trunk at the foot of her bed, digging through an assortment of skirts and band tees to get her comfortable pajamas out. She didn't want to go out today. All she wanted to do was touch up her hair and finish reading the second book of the *Unrequited* series by Emley Rison.

She certainly knew a thing or two about unrequited love; but like an addict, she couldn't stop indulging in something that caused her pain.

"Hey," Blaire's soft-spoken word broke through her tension. "Mera didn't mean anything by it. It's nice Seth does that."

Mera set her phone back down. "I really didn't. Kai pays every time I go to the salon. I'm envious you can do your hair on your own."

"Well, your hair is also extremely long." Riley put a hand on her hip. "Considering how deep the burgundy is, your shower would look like a crime scene to do it on your own. I still have to go get it cut."

What she didn't add was that Kai was Mera's pair; it wasn't odd for him to pay for her to get a little pampering. Pointing that out would only open up teasing about something going on with her childhood friend that she was not prepared to talk about. Nothing was going on, anyway.

Her friends meant well, but she didn't want to go there again. She barely avoided the topic earlier.

Thirty minutes later, the door opened to her dorm, and she looked up from her book as Seth strolled in like he owned the place followed by Lukas and Aiden. He never knocked when he came by. Of course, she didn't either when she barged into Aiden and Seth's shared dorm room, but that was beside the point. She left her door unlocked to allow it.

Mera had already left to go meet Kai, but Blaire still sat at Riley's feet on the bed, leaning against the wall. Riley lay on her back to read with her upper body against her pillows, already changed into fuzzy black pajama pants with white polka-dots and a black tee with a cartoon grim reaper with heart eyes and the saying "I'm coming for you" on the chest.

Blaire got up and moved to the unoccupied bed on the other side of the room to sit with Lukas. Riley's roommate for the semester had dropped out, so she had a room to herself now. Perfect for whenever everyone wanted to hang out, though they usually did that in Aiden and Seth's room.

Aiden took the seat at her desk.

Riley looked up as a shadow from the body standing over her blocked out the overhead light. Gray eyes light enough to be translucent stared back at her.

Seth Emerson.

Childhood friend.

Pain in my ass.

He smirked as his gaze fell on the design of her shirt before he set the drugstore bag on her desk and tossed a blood packet on the bed. She looked at it, sat up, bookmarked her page, and set her book aside.

"How'd you know I needed this?" She missed having one with her lunch. Blaire brought their lunch to the room, and Riley didn't bother to ask her to bring a bag of blood. Blaire might accept they weren't human, but that didn't mean Riley wanted to push her. The blood they consumed was human blood, after all—even if donated from clinics across the Southeast from Vasirian staff. Through simple acts of compulsion, manipulation of memory used for the survival of their species left humans none the wiser about the blood exchanging hands.

Riley scooted to the side to allow Seth to sit next to her as she took in what he wore. She always noticed his clothing. Majoring in fashion, of course she noticed. Light-wash jeans with a few small rips in the thigh molded to his lean muscles in a way that suited him, and the shorter sleeves of his white T-shirt showed off the vast collection of black tattoos covering both arms. Simple, but it worked for him.

"Didn't." He lowered himself down onto her bed to sit against the upper wall. Putting his back to her pillows, he crossed his feet at his ankles on her bed covers; his loosely tied black combat boots drew her attention. They'd better be clean. "Still reading that smut?"

She resisted the urge to smack the playful grin off his face with her book. "It's not smut, thank you very much. Emley Rison writes romance."

"So you're telling me there's no sex?" He looked disappointed.

Blaire laughed and Riley's face flamed.

"I'm not saying that. But not in this book. At least, not yet."

"But there will be."

"I don't know." She glared at Blaire in warning. "Don't tell me!"

Blaire made a zipping motion with her fingers on her lips as Lukas chuckled and buried his face into her neck, kissing the Korrena mark there—a small black symbol unique to the pair branded like a tattoo on the skin. Proof they were bound to one another at a soul-deep level.

When Riley sighed, Seth reached over and turned her face toward him with his fingers on her chin. "What?"

"Huh?" She pulled her face back, disconnecting his touch from her skin.

"What's wrong?"

"Nothing."

His expression told her he wasn't convinced, but he dropped

it. Sometimes he was too perceptive of her moods. They grew up together, so it didn't surprise her. But sometimes, it wasn't welcome. Sometimes, she needed space to breathe and think. It got harder every day to do that. Harder to hide what she didn't want him to see.

She didn't know if it had to do with her best friend and her other childhood friend, Lukas, becoming Korrena bonded, or the fact she was eighteen and still without a pair. She didn't know the reason, but she didn't like the lonely feeling that had settled into her heart in recent months.

Aiden knocked his knuckles on the desk "So," he hedged, looking over at Lukas. "He's got news."

"I think this is about Europe." Lukas pulled a folded sheet of paper out of the back pocket of his black jeans. "Didn't want to read it without you, even if it's addressed to both of us." He handed the letter to Blaire.

Blaire scanned the page before looking up. "They haven't booked our flights yet and won't until we get an official summons, but the Blackthorn Clan say they want us in London at the end of March. My passport will be here next week."

"Anything else?"

Blaire shook her head, looking at Aiden.

"Maybe we'll get more information closer to the date," Riley said, finally taking her first sip from the blood packet Seth brought her as he turned to face her brother. She needed to ask Professor Velastra how long they would be there. While no school sounded exciting, she worried her grades would drop if they were gone too long.

"What do you think it'll be like?"

"Europe? I dunno, man. Haven't been."

"No, not Europe. I've been. You know Kai and I went to Germany for a family thing a few times as kids. Haven't been in years, though.

I mean meeting the Blackthorn Clan."

"Well, the ones we met when we rescued Blaire seemed nice," Riley chimed in.

Lukas made a pained sound, and Riley grimaced. "Sorry."

Bringing up the recent trauma wasn't the best. The mental wounds were still fresh. Riley hoped Blaire could talk Lukas into therapy. Blaire was already back in therapy over things she went through last year. The experiments and ritual added more reason to be there.

When everything happened with Blaire, the clan stripped the Order of their school administration titles and authority over the Vasirian in this part of the world, and they now awaited trial for their crimes. Riley and her friends were being summoned to Europe as witnesses.

Seth took the empty blood packet from Riley and tossed it in the small trash bin beside her bed. "There were only three members of the Blackthorn Clan there, though. How big is it?"

"The clan is apparently very large and not all live close by." Aiden sat back in the chair and crossed his arms. "Tobias is a member, but he's not part of the main royal court, which isn't very large. I think we met almost all of them."

"How do you know all this?" Seth asked.

Aiden shrugged with one shoulder. "Asked the professor."

"I still can't believe Tobias wasn't a bad guy."

"He still didn't stop what happened to Blaire," Lukas said with disdain.

Tobias Nilsson had infiltrated the Order as a member over twenty years ago, and only now did the Blackthorn Clan put the Order's corruption to an end. It almost cost Riley her best friend to reach that point. Riley grumbled about this often. How could he stand being part of the Order for so long if he didn't agree with their methods?

Blaire sighed. "I knew something felt off. I could see it in his eyes. He didn't like what was happening."

"Again, it still didn't stop it from happening."

Blaire placed her hand on Lukas's jaw and pulled him in for a gentle kiss. "But it's over now, and I'm with you." She gazed into his eyes, and he instantly relaxed.

Riley's stomach clenched, and she looked away.

Seth rubbed a hand over his face, catching her attention. He met her gaze when he noticed her attention on him. The tiredness she thought she caught on his face was gone. She shook her head. He tilted his head in question, the sandy brown long strands on top of his head flopping to the side.

"I'm hungry," Lukas said, standing and pulling Blaire to her feet, breaking Seth's focus on Riley's face. It was a good thing too. Having his attention for too long always made her squirm.

Aiden stood. "We're going to the movies tonight, right?"

"There's this new one that just came out yesterday I want to see. We can get dinner before," Blaire said, looking at Lukas. "Up to you two, since you agreed to my movie choice." She furrowed her brows at Riley, likely over her attire. "Aren't you coming?"

"Nope," Riley said, popping the p. "I'm vegetating tonight. Hermit mode activated." She lay back on the bed and wiggled into the bedding beside Seth. "I wanna finish this book and do my hair."

Aiden slid the chair under Riley's desk and asked Seth, "You coming with?"

"Nah." Seth pulled his phone out of his pocket and frowned at the screen. "Gonna get stuff done I need to take care of."

"Stuff. Right. Lock the door at least. I don't want to walk in on your naked ass again." Aiden shuddered, as if recalling the moment, and Riley turned to face the wall on her side. She so did not want to hear this.

Seth rolled his eyes. "I'm not doing that."

"Whatever, man. I don't care. Really." He held his hands up. "No judgment. Just not wanting to see it." He chuckled when Seth tossed one of Riley's throw pillows from the floor beside the bed at him.

Aiden opened the door and left the room, Blaire and Lukas following. They shut the door behind them.

"Hey."

Riley flinched at Seth's smooth voice way too close to her ear. She turned her head, and her nose almost touched his. She snapped her gaze back to the wall, tensing when his warm hand rested on her upper arm.

"Riley."

"Hmm?"

"What's going on?"

"What do you mean?"

"I don't know. Something's off. You're more tense than usual."

"It's nothing." She traced patterns on the wall in front of her with her index finger. "Just got a lot on my mind today."

"Like?"

"Don't you have stuff to take care of?"

Before she could process the move, she found herself wide eyed on her back, a pair of firm hands holding her shoulders. He had shifted to place one leg off the bed, and his other knee braced his weight beside her so he didn't crowd her. He held her in place, keeping an entire arm's length between them.

"Talk to me."

Her eyes shifted to the book beside her on the bed, and Seth's eyes followed, creases forming between his brows.

"The book? The book has you upset?"

She couldn't understand why he seemed distressed by that fact, but she didn't want him feeling that way, so she quickly shook her head from side to side. His entire body relaxed, and his hold loosened until he let go. He sat down on the edge of the bed, still facing her, allowing her to slide up into a sitting position.

"It just reminded me of not having someone—well, not having my pair. Not necessarily someone."

He put his elbow on his knee and rubbed his eyes. She was grateful he didn't argue with her about Korrena pairs. Seth wasn't a subscriber to the process. Riley never understood why, but Seth didn't like it. He thought it took away free will, and that biology was forcing people to be with someone they otherwise wouldn't want. He'd loosened up that thought process after getting to know Blaire and seeing how things developed between her and Lukas, but by things he said, he hadn't fully come to terms with thinking it was something worth wanting.

"But you haven't read the book since we got here, and just a bit ago you…"

She frowned when he trailed off. "What?"

He shrugged. "Something seemed off."

"When?"

"When Blaire kissed Lukas."

She'd felt a pang of jealousy that Lukas's entire body gave in to Blaire when she soothed him. Their connection made it possible. Sure, someone could do that with any lover, but the bond cranked the ability up to amazing levels—at least, that's what she heard about it.

Sensing what your pair felt through an empathic link to anticipate how to help them sounded like a dream.

Riley shook her head. "It's fine."

"What is?"

Her nose wrinkled. "I meant it's nothing."

"No. You said 'It's fine.' So it must be something."

Seth and his technicalities.

"I was jealous, okay?" She threw her hands up then crossed them over her chest. "You happy? I was jealous of my best friend and her pair."

He looked momentarily stunned, and his features pinched. "You like Lukas?"

"What the—no!" Riley smacked Seth's knee. "The bond, you idiot. I envy what they have. It looks nice to have someone who can just… make things that bother me go away. Stuff like that." She cut her eyes at him. "Why am I talking about this with you?"

Seth shrugged. "Because we talk about shit."

"Not this kinda stuff."

He shrugged again.

"Shouldn't you go? I'm sure whoever you have waiting is getting impatient."

Seth's hand fisted on the black bedding beside her leg and he sighed. "No one is waiting for me tonight."

"Tonight."

"Right."

Riley shifted uncomfortably. This was why they didn't talk about this sort of thing seriously when they could talk about anything else. The closest he got to anything regarding romance or sex was little jokes and whispers in her ear in front of the others to embarrass her. Games. Never serious.

She hated how Seth had so many girls in their university wrapped around his finger. One phone call and he could have someone keeping his bed warm for the night, while Riley hadn't been with anyone. The comparison in experience, and his openness to do those things casually with others, made for awkward conversation between them.

The idea of trying her hand at casual dating like her friends suggested sounded more alluring the longer this uncomfortable conversation went on. Anything to move past her feelings.

"Then what are you doing tonight?" She hated how soft and small her words sounded.

"I planned to do homework for my Creative Writing class while I didn't have Aiden there playing video games, but if you're not feeling good, I can stay."

Riley shook her head against her pillow. "I'm fine. It was only in the moment."

"You sure?"

"I plan to touch up my hair then read some more. I doubt that's going to appeal to you."

He shrugged. "I could always bring my laptop over. I have other work I need to do too."

Riley's brows collided. Seth hung out with her a lot—with the others. They rarely hung out alone in her room anymore, only occasionally spending time together outside of school or on school grounds. As in, the last time he spent extended time in her room by himself was around the time he turned eighteen—close to over a year and a half ago. Since then, he'd avoided her room like the plague. She never understood it. Maybe the women and girls he started sleeping with didn't like it. It was a mystery she didn't bother to focus on.

"Wouldn't I disturb you just like Aiden?"

"Do you plan to play loud video games and yell at the TV?"

"No, but I play music while I do my hair."

"Whatever. I still have to go get the laptop. Plus, if you don't plan to go out for dinner, I can go grab us something while you do your hair."

"You sure?"

"If it'll keep you from being whiny tomorrow from being left to your thoughts tonight, then yes."

She smacked him on the arm, and he burst out laughing. "I don't whine."

"Sure, you don't."

That's more like it. She was starting to not know how to react. He hadn't been so open and willing with her in a long time. She'd gotten used to him keeping her at arm's length but still being the comforting presence she needed at the worst moments. She still recalled how his arms banded around her when she first got the email from Blaire after the kidnapping. The wild look in his eyes when she called him for help, and he hadn't known what happened. She shivered at the memory.

He stood and cleared his throat. "Want greasy fast food, or something of substance?"

"Nuggets and fries."

Shaking his head, he stood from the bed, stretching. Her gaze fell to the strip of skin exposed above his jeans.

No hair.

Holy shit, does he shave?

She realized too late he'd already lowered his arms when she looked up to find him staring at her in question.

"You shave your stomach," she blurted without thinking.

He started laughing, and she wanted to crawl under the bed and build a home for herself, never to be seen again. They could deliver her blood and meals. Humans had food delivery services. Blackthorn Academy could cash in on it.

At least her word slip made him laugh. He didn't do that around many people. Let go and laugh. Chuckle or smirk, sure. But a genuine laugh with real volume? Not often, and only around their small circle of friends. Mostly her and Aiden, though.

His tongue moved over his lower lip, and he gave a half smile. "I do." Amusement laced his voice.

"When did you start doing that?"

"Oh, Riley, you're interested in my grooming habits now?" He tucked his hands in his pockets, a taunt in his voice.

She was never a match for Playful Seth. The jokes were usually more than her inexperienced heart could handle, but they weren't as rare as they used to be. He wasn't trying to seduce her; he enjoyed getting a rise out of her any way he could.

She gave as good as she got typically—just not this brand of warfare.

"No! I mean, the last time we went to the beach, you hadn't." Nope. Seth had a dark brown treasure trail leading from his navel into his swim trunks then. No hair on his chest or stomach, though, which was likely natural. Why did she remember this? His voice brought her attention back to him.

"That's before."

"Before?"

"Mmhm."

"Before what?"

"Before I started working more on my build. Lifting Aiden's weights. Running with him when shit hadn't been going down around here. I don't wear a shirt when I do and thought it'd look better without the hair."

She hadn't seen him without a shirt since the beach, and that was two summers ago. The no shirt explained the light tan he developed. She didn't know he was trying to build muscle. It wasn't like he lacked it to start with, but he had filled out more since their last beach trip. His waist was still trim and his legs long and lean, but his arms held more definition and muscle. She didn't know what was beneath the shirt, but she imagined if the arms were toned, it probably carried beneath his shirt as well.

"And before you ask, because I know your curiosity kills your filter, it's mostly all gone."

"All gone?"

"Mostly."

His eyes flicked down, and her eyes followed, but before she even reached below his stomach, the meaning caught up to her. She looked up at him with wide eyes, and he laughed again.

"Seth Emerson! I do not care about what that looks like."

He shrugged.

"I really don't."

Not seducing you.

He shrugged again. The non-committal move annoyed her.

"Go get your laptop and food before a night of being a hermit turns into a night behind bars for committing murder."

"It's not that big of a deal."

Maybe not to him. With him more into sex with others, maybe it was something he openly talked about with other people, too. She was fine to talk about it with someone like Blaire—she wasn't a blushing little girl—but not with him.

Other than the occasional jokes, she wasn't used to it with him. He didn't make her feel uncomfortable; it embarrassed her that she *did* care if it went all the way down.

A little.

Maybe.

Shut up, brain.

"Don't forget to get another blood packet on your way back," she mumbled, picking at the bedspread. She couldn't look at his face. "Oh, and don't forget the milkshake!"

His low laugh followed him out of the room.

When she flopped back on the bed and rubbed her hands over her hot face, the smell of sugar cookies and vanilla he left behind on her pillow mixed with his cologne, making her squirm. With a sigh, she shut her eyes. She couldn't keep going on like this.

In the past, whenever a guy had shown interest in her, she didn't reciprocate—too hung up on what she really wanted.

She was an adult now. It was time to change herself.

Time to be more open to the idea of dating and living a life that didn't revolve around pining after something or someone she couldn't have.

2

Mistaken

Inclement weather caused the cafeteria to be more crowded than usual during lunch, and the space buzzed with life as students filled the tables. Rain ran in rivulets down the floor-to-ceiling windows that overlooked the woods behind the academy. Higher than normal humidity for the end of February created an eerie fog beyond the glass. The rain would sound peaceful against her dorm window, away from the chatter of students. The kind of weather she would normally read a book and binge junk food to, unless she made a trip to the mall outside of town.

Riley looked up as Aiden approached the table. He put his tray down and looked at the empty seats. "Where is everyone?"

"Mera is preparing for some medical convention, and Kai is with her." She moved her salad around with her fork. "Blaire finally convinced Lukas to attend a joint therapy session, but he just texted saying they're on their way."

Aiden's brows rose. "Really? Huh. About time."

With everything their friends went through and the struggles of Blaire's humanity, their friends needed additional help. Riley fully supported the decision to seek it out and would do whatever was necessary to help them find their way again.

"There's Layla." She pointed with her fork.

Riley's newest friend set her tray down and smiled brightly, her olive skin darkening on her cheekbones. In the little time they'd known each other, Riley concluded Layla blushed a lot. In fact, she appeared doll-like in many ways. Large round eyes, small nose, cute face… she looked like someone's little sister, not one of the university students. But when Mera explained Layla was her cousin, and how sheltered she was, it made sense they hadn't had contact with her over the years.

"It's really starting to come down out there. I was lucky to get inside before it started." Layla smoothed her burgundy and black paid uniform skirt beneath her and sat in the chair beside Riley.

"At least it isn't supposed to last." Riley turned to Aiden. "Where's Seth?"

"He was with me when we got in line for food…" Aiden turned back to the buffet bars that took up the back end of the cafeteria.

Multiple spreads of several types of foods made to appeal to the different students attending Blackthorn Academy graced the buffet. Foods Riley had never heard of before often made their way onto the buffet tables to accommodate different cultures. An entire bar dedicated to drinks lined the far wall of windows, with several glass refrigerators of blood bags positioned to the left of that.

That's where she caught sight of Seth.

As he turned from the fridge with a tray in one hand and a blood packet in the other, Riley resisted the urge to roll her eyes, but she couldn't contain her sigh of exasperation. "What happened now?"

Aiden made a noise of question around his bite of shredded barbecue chicken sandwich.

"His eye," she said, frowning. The darkening bruise was obvious even from where she sat on the opposite side of the cafeteria. Her grave expression grew as he got closer. Whatever happened had to be recent if his natural ability to heal hadn't started yet.

She hadn't taken her eyes off him as he made his way toward their table. He wore his white button-down shirt tucked in properly into pressed black slacks, but the top button was undone, and his plaid tie was pulled loose. He'd rolled his sleeves up his forearms, showing off the black ink on his skin. He'd ditched his uniform jacket somewhere along the way.

The school implemented a strict dress code, with uniforms and everything, despite them being college students. Her dad mentioned once it might be to avoid any cultural offense to students who came to the academy from remote areas of the world. She didn't know and never questioned it. They were allowed to accessorize how they deemed fit, but in the last two years they'd become strict about requiring things like the cardigans and jackets the school provided over personal wardrobe and keeping the uniform proper and neat.

Blaire and Lukas moved into Riley's line of sight, blocking her view of Seth as he walked toward them. They sat down in the seats across the table with their lunches.

"How'd everything go?" She wasn't going to mention therapy. Layla was new to their circle of friends, and Riley wasn't sure how Blaire felt about divulging personal things—even if Layla knew about all the shady things that occurred in the academy recently.

Lukas muttered something under his breath and drank from his blood packet, staring toward the windows with a dour expression.

Riley suppressed a giggle. "That well?"

"It actually went great." Blaire glanced at Lukas and shook her head. "I think that's the problem. I think he hoped it would go terribly and prove his point about not needing it."

"I can hear you, you know."

"Was it really that bad?"

He sighed. "No. I'll go as long as we need to." His brows knotted. "As long as that woman doesn't get it in her head to bring my parents or other people into it. Just us."

Blaire leaned toward him and put her head on his shoulder. "I don't think Professor Sinclair will do something that makes you uncomfortable, but we can tell her next time."

Seth moved around behind Riley and put his tray on the table, sitting down between her and Aiden.

Blaire's eyes widened. "What happened to you?"

Seth touched the skin around his eye. The bruising spread onto his cheekbone, but it would be gone in another couple of hours, if that. "Doesn't matter."

"I thought you stopped getting into shit, man," Aiden said. "You're too old for it now, and Lukas and I won't always be there to clean up the mess."

Seth sucked his teeth. "I don't need you two to 'clean up my mess' or anything. Besides, I didn't seek out the fight, but I sure as hell wasn't going to sit back and take it."

"So who'd you piss off this time?"

Seth glared at Riley. But like always, it was obvious to her there wasn't any actual heat behind it. "What makes you think this is my fault?" She shrugged and lifted a cherry tomato, but before she could take a bite, Seth snatched it and tossed it into his mouth. "Well?"

She resisted the urge to give him another black eye—barely. She wasn't a violent person, but Seth was a special case. "Isn't it always?"

"No. How was I supposed to know she had a pair?"

"Wait," Aiden said with a shake of his head. "Don't tell me you slept with someone's Korrena?"

Seth cringed.

"What the—"

"First of all, I didn't sleep with her," he started, putting a hand in front of Riley's face to halt any remark she might make. She swatted it away. "She invited me to her room and then tried to kiss me. He walked up when she did. I didn't know."

The rest of the conversation faded to white noise in her head. She never enjoyed listening to anything involving Seth and his conquests—or whatever he wanted to call them. She didn't want to hear about, and wasn't interested in, his sex life.

It was how they maintained the friendship they had. Sure, people questioned their closeness, but it wasn't anything more than they'd find between an obnoxious older brother and a bratty little sister. Even the crude jokes and innuendos could be explained away as siblings trying to one-up the other. Family was all they were and all they would be. She could live with that.

So why did her stomach twist every time she told herself that?

"You still want to go?"

She looked up and met Blaire's gaze, halting the tapping of her short black nails on the surface of the table. "What?"

"Tybee Island."

"Oh, yeah." She sat up, her mind latching onto the subject, when she remembered enough about their previous conversation to not seem awkward for her gap in attention. "Yeah! Who's all going?"

Lukas and Blaire had been trying to plan a trip out to Tybee Island to Lukas's parents' beach house for months for everyone as a joint birthday celebration; with spring break happening before the upcoming European trip, it seemed like the only time they could go for a while.

"All of us, Mera, Kai, and Charlotte."

"Charlotte?"

"Yeah, she quit the diner and is taking time off before she leaves for college, so she has free time."

Blaire's best friend from high school was the only other human they regularly interacted with. Unlike Blaire, she knew nothing about their world. Nothing about what they were. Normal humans didn't know about Vasirian. As far as they were concerned, Blackthorn Academy was an exclusive university for children of the rich and powerful of the nation. Vasirian had to hide their existence from humans, which made making friends or forming any type of relationship outside of their own kind harder. They always needed to tread carefully with Charlotte and her mothers.

The only reason administration even permitted Blaire on school grounds was her unique status as the first human—well, the first *modern* human—to share a Korrena bond with a Vasirian.

"Is it going to be okay to bring her?" Seth asked.

Layla looked across the table at him. "Why wouldn't it be?"

"I mean, we're going for a week or two, right?"

"A week," Lukas said, taking a drink from a water bottle. "Professor Velastra wants us back on campus for the second week of spring break in case the summons comes in."

"I thought the date was decided."

"No. Just the time frame."

"I'm so glad your parents were cool with you coming with us," Riley said, turning to Layla.

She flushed and tucked strands of long mocha hair behind her ear. "It feels so stupid to have to get their approval."

Riley understood, though. Layla aspired to be a journalist. Her parents didn't want that for her, but as long as she played their game, they wouldn't interfere with her career choice. They didn't see her as an adult until twenty years old—unless she found her Korrena first.

"No sweat. Don't let it get to you. I think we all have some hangup with our folks."

"Your mom is actually pretty great," Lukas said, tucking his hands in his slacks and leaning back in his chair.

Riley groaned. "She is, but she can be pushy."

"She's not that bad," Aiden scoffed.

Riley glared at Aiden. "That's because Mama doesn't see you as a baby like she does me."

As the youngest of four, her mother couldn't see her as anything but a child because of it. Being a high school teacher didn't help in the slightest, since adolescents constantly surrounded her. With Riley's father stationed in New York for work, her mother set her sights on babying Riley whenever they came in contact with one another. Of course, her mother did that with all Riley's friends, but it somehow felt like *more* with her. Maybe she was overthinking it.

She did that a lot.

"Well, you are little."

She turned her glare on Seth, who tilted his head.

"I'm big enough to take *you* on."

"That so?" He smirked, reaching over and taking the last strawberry out of her fruit bowl. He ate it lazily, eyes locked on hers.

Seth had a death wish. It was the only way to explain it in her mind. When he tossed the stem back into her empty bowl, she growled at him. He kept stealing her food. Cookies, fruit, vegetables… it didn't matter.

She waved her hand toward the buffet. "There's a whole bar over there full of—" Her words cut off when an upperclassman jostled her forward, bumping her chair as she moved past Riley to throw her arms over Seth's shoulders from behind.

"I'm so sorry about that," she said with an apologetic smile in Riley's direction. "It's so dang crowded in here today."

Before Riley could comment, the girl turned her attention back to Seth. "Seth," she pouted, running her fingers into the top of his hair, messing it up. "I thought you were comin' by."

"Nope."

Gone was the playful taunt in his voice when he spoke to Riley, replaced with a cold apathy that made her shift uncomfortably. In fact, the mood at the table plummeted right along with the temperature of his tone.

Riley glanced at Layla and Blaire. Layla focused on her spaghetti, not eating, just moving the noodles around. Blaire frowned, looking between Seth and Riley, who wondered what her friend was thinking. Blaire used to question the status of their relationship, but either she had convinced Blaire there was nothing there—which there wasn't, at least between them—or Blaire had finally given up on trying to wring water out of a dry rag.

In fact, other than suggesting Riley potentially date Seth the other night, Blaire had stopped bringing it up altogether.

Aiden shook his head as Seth sat unmoved by the girl clinging to his back. Her long, honey blonde hair fanned like a curtain, almost blocking Riley's view.

"Will you come by later?"

"I don't think that's a good idea."

"Why not?" She ran the tip of her finger over the side of his neck, and he pulled away, sitting up, effectively dislodging himself from her embrace. She stood upright and posted a hand on her hip, jutting it out to the side. "I thought we had fun."

"We did."

Riley wanted to feel bad for the girl, but other than freshman—whom he rarely messed with—the kind of girls Seth slept with knew his modus operandi. He never hooked up with a girl twice. Riley knew that much, at least. He rationalized this by saying his actions avoided the girls trying to form a relationship he didn't want to give. It didn't stop the more persistent ones from trying.

Even if she didn't want him acting warm to the girls, he didn't have to be cold either. She wished he would stop playing around, and then this situation wouldn't keep happening.

"Come on," the girl said, sitting down on Seth's lap sideways, looping her arms around his neck. "I've had a crappy week. Keep me company tonight. You owe me."

He raised his brow and finally met her gaze. "Owe you?"

"Yeah. Remember? You said you would make it up to me last time when you couldn't—" She stopped talking when Seth placed his hand on her bare thigh at the edge of her uniform skirt and ran the pad of his thumb across her jaw.

"I do owe you, don't I?" he said, tilting his head slightly and lowering his voice.

She giggled and looped his tie around her hand. "So does that mean you'll come?"

Riley tightened her fists on the table and calmly stood from her seat. "I'll catch y'all later."

She gathered her things, avoiding eye contact, and made her way out of the cafeteria. She didn't even know if anyone noticed her get up and leave.

Look back.

An impulse she shouldn't indulge, but she couldn't help it.

Her gaze collided with darkened steel where Seth had turned his head to stare at her while the girl, having slid into the chair Riley vacated, still yammered away, the others at the table making polite conversation with her. Which wasn't an issue. The girl did nothing wrong, outside of being pushy and gauche by airing private business in front of everyone.

Riley stood there for longer than she felt comfortable doing before she broke eye contact and left for her dorm.

Something seemed off about the way he looked at her, and with her own thoughts and feelings in the last few months in turmoil, she couldn't shake the jittery feeling under her skin.

Few things she could do helped when the uncomfortable feeling of losing control swept over her. She could indulge in retail therapy, but she didn't feel like going out alone—she also didn't want to be with anyone at the moment. She could eat junk food. But she was full, and the temporary boost wouldn't last. So that left her fallback when she wanted to be alone and needed to burn out the jitters… clean.

Getting away from the cafeteria took longer than Seth wanted, but the girl wouldn't stop talking. Even after he put her in Riley's empty seat as soon as the space opened.

He didn't want the girl in his lap. She wanted something from him he wasn't willing to give. Something he hadn't wanted to in a long time; it wasn't doing the trick anymore.

Quick sex with no strings attached lost what little appeal it had a while back when the one reason he did it in the first place stopped working. It still didn't stop girls from trying, and occasionally, he gave in to them, hoping to fill the gaping void inside and quiet the noise. It was either that or fight. He was now at an age where he'd face bigger consequences than suspension for fighting.

After he watched Riley leave with an expression he couldn't read, he wanted to follow her and see if she was okay. He hated when she got upset. It was rare, but when it happened, it could last for days. It made the noise in his head grow louder.

Others might not realize it, with the way she always exuded a bouncy, happy aura, but he could read her. They'd been together since they were in diapers. No one knew her like he did.

His gut told him something wasn't right.

By the time he made it out of the main building and across the cobblestone courtyard, his uniform shirt was plastered to his skin and his hair was soaked. He probably looked like a drowned rat, but he didn't care.

Once inside the dorm building, he pushed the longer strands of his hair back and wiped the water from his face as best he could without a towel. He regretted not bringing his uniform jacket to classes with him, especially as he made his way to Riley's dorm room via the stairwell where the heat wasn't as strong as the main halls. He should have taken the elevator, but he didn't want to wait on it.

As soon as he stepped onto her floor, the sounds of The Pretty Reckless' "You Make Me Wanna Die" greeted him.

Most of the student body was still at lunch, so the volume wasn't a problem, but Riley usually only blasted her music like that when caught up in frenzied cleaning. She did that when caught up in her own head.

He sighed and made his way down the hall to her door, pushing it open without knocking. It wasn't something they did.

His intuition had been right.

A quick scan of the room already showed a vast improvement from its usual state of what Riley so affectionately referred to as "organized chaos."

The desk, normally covered in makeup, jewelry, candy, and other scattered baubles, now looked organized, with necklaces and bracelets hanging on hooks on the wall above the desk, nail polishes lined up against the wall, and the makeup stacked neatly. He imagined half of it was in the drawers with the candy. Hidden mess.

The bed was made, with all the throw pillows—normally discarded on the floor next to it—lining the wall. In fact, most of the things that littered the floor—like most of her boot collection—were put away.

Her old roommate's desk chair still sat piled with clothes Riley had worn once and not put in the laundry. She always said unless it was underwear, there wasn't a reason to wear out the fabric with excess washing. Who was he to judge? She was the one in school for fashion.

Riley sat amid everything on the floor, sorting through a pile of clothes. Folding and stacking them. The trunk at the end of her bed was open to add the folded stacks into when finished.

He stepped farther into the room and closed the door behind him.

Sighing when she didn't so much as register his arrival, he reached over and turned off the stereo on her ex-roommate's desk. Instantly, the sound started blaring through the cell phone beside Riley on the floor when the Bluetooth dropped the connection. She startled and spun around, looking up at him before finally turning the music off.

Her smokey-blue eyes, heavily shadowed in black makeup, widened. "Did someone try to waterboard you?" She stood and held out her hands in front of her. "Don't move. You're dripping everywhere."

He waited awkwardly while she went into her ensuite and retrieved a towel, returning to him and rubbing the rough material over his arms, hands, and shirt. She held the towel up and he lowered his head for her to dry his hair, neck, and face. When she finished, she raked her small fingers through his hair, combing the strands back into place. He resisted the urge to groan in appreciation at the comforting feeling.

"You know, I could have done that myself."

"But now you owe me."

She stuck her tongue out and sauntered back to the bathroom to put the towel away as if she hadn't echoed the same sentiments the girl in the cafeteria had. Did she even realize it? Probably not.

He'd rather owe Riley.

"Why are you here?" She leaned on the door frame leading into the bathroom and crossed her arms over her midsection.

"Wanted to see if you were alright."

"Of course."

Lie.

"Why wouldn't I be?"

Seth's jaw tightened. How was he supposed to know? That was why he came to see her. "Well, you left without saying much, and you're in ultra-clean-mode…"

"Ultra-what?"

"The cleaning frenzy thing you do." He waved a hand at the room.

Riley blinked and looked around. "I wouldn't call it a cleaning frenzy, per se." She dragged the last letter out as she rolled her head to the side, avoiding eye contact. "It needed straightening up."

"Riley." He gave her a flat look. "It always looks like a mini shopping mall exploded in here. You only organize like this when something's wrong."

"Nothing's wrong."

"Don't lie to me."

"I'm not."

Her eyes widened at the growl he wasn't able to contain. "Stop.

Lying."

"I don't know, okay?" She stepped away from the bathroom, moving across the dorm room to stand in front of her desk. "I've got a lot going on up here"—she tapped her temple—"after things went down with Blaire, and ever since my birthday…"

Seth's eyes narrowed at her silence. "Ever since your birthday, what?"

"It's stupid."

He softened his tone. "Tell me."

"Just the stuff I told you last night that bothered me. It really became a problem after my birthday. This"—she waved a hand at the room—"helps."

He let it go. There were many reasons her eighteenth birthday would bring about stress and intrusive thoughts. Especially for their kind, if they were unpaired—which was a big deal to Riley. That fact ate away at the edges of the void inside of him, making it grow larger every day.

Why was it so imperative for so many of their kind to want a Korrena? It made him sick.

"That still doesn't explain why you left the cafeteria the way you did." *Or why it* felt *like you were upset.* It was crazy how well they knew one other if a weird thought like that filtered into his brain.

"Can we pretend we discussed this and you made some weird joke at my expense and skip to the part where you leave?"

"What?" His brows lowered in confusion, and he scoffed. "No."

She sighed. "Didn't think so. You're so stubborn."

"Me? I just asked a question."

"I just didn't want to sit next to you and your arm candy. Is that so wrong?"

"She isn't arm candy."

"Fine. *Lap* candy, then." She huffed an irritated breath.

"She isn't that either."

"Whatever you want to call her. I'm sure she's a nice girl, but you only have one purpose for her."

"Oh really. And that is?" He crossed his arms across his chest and cocked his head to the side, feeling defensive considering the girl didn't serve the purpose he suspected Riley thought. If this conversation had happened a few months ago, he wouldn't refute the insinuation, but things hadn't been the same for a while.

"Don't make me say it." Riley turned to her desk and unstacked and restacked the eye shadow palettes in front of her.

"No. I want to hear it. How can I understand if you don't tell me?"

"Sex!" Riley turned and glared at him. Her cheeks reddened and her fists tightened at her sides. "Love them and leave them, right?"

"Huh. Didn't think that's why you'd be upset and leave the cafeteria."

She twisted and grabbed a small octopus plushie from the desk and threw it at his head. He barely dodged it. "That isn't why I left!"

"What the hell?" He looked at the stuffed animal on the floor. "Why'd you do that?"

"I didn't leave because of your sexcapades."

His lips flattened to contain the laugh building in his throat. He'd never heard that word before. After a moment of composing himself, he met her eyes. "So tell me why."

"Just leave."

After being punched for something he didn't do and having another girl try to lure him to her room when he wasn't interested, and now being called out for something he didn't do again, his patience for the day was gone. Having Riley demand that he leave when all he wanted to do was fix whatever the hell was upsetting her grated on his last nerve. He could walk away and start again tomorrow, but it always felt wrong to leave Riley alone if she was upset. "No. You're going to tell me what's wrong, or I'm not leaving."

Before Riley could throw the Rubik's Cube she had picked up, he marched forward and placed his hands on her upper arms. Pushing aside his irritation, he bent his upper body to be eye level with her. He wasn't as tall as Lukas and Aiden, but at six feet, he stood much taller than Riley, and he didn't want her to feel crowded or intimidated by towering over her.

"Stop it." He spoke firmly, but with no bite to his tone.

When he released her and stood to his full height again, she set the toy on the desk and moved back to her clothes pile.

She sat on the floor, sorting through various pieces of clothing for several strained minutes before she finally asked, "Why are you fighting and sleeping around? You didn't used to be like this."

He stood looking down at her on the floor, debating how to answer her. The answer ranged from simple to so complicated even he wasn't sure how to process it. If he couldn't, he didn't expect someone else to.

He went with the simple answer.

"I've always fought. Aiden, Lukas, and I have always stirred up shit."

Riley paused, a shirt held up in her hands, her gaze fixed on the window near the foot of her bed where rain ran down its surface in sheets. "They stopped a long time ago. You did too until you turned eighteen. You've been a loose cannon for almost two years."

"Not that long."

"Close enough."

He made a non-committal sound but said nothing. What could he say? She wasn't lying.

"And the girls?"

“What about them?”

“Why are you sleeping around with unpaired Vasirian?”

“Why do you care?” He pitched his words low, and he half expected her not to hear him. Part of him wanted to snatch the words back because he feared the answer.

Riley lowered her arms, dropping another shirt she was folding. She turned her entire body to face him, still sitting back on her heels. “I’ll always care. You’re my family, Seth.”

He exhaled heavily and moved toward her, dropping to sit on the floor next to her and the clothes with his back to the side of the bed.

“Never imagined family could give me an ulcer.”

Riley rolled her eyes. “Dumbass. Even if that were true—which we know it’s not because I’m amazing—it’d be gone by tomorrow.” She pointed at the pile of unfolded clothes. “Make yourself useful.”

“You’re so spoiled.”

“Again, it helps that I’m amazing.”

The return of her smile and corny jokes made him relax, but he still wanted to explain things. He didn’t owe her anything, but he couldn’t shake how it made him uncomfortable not to explain. He didn’t want Riley to mistake what the interaction with the girl meant.

“If it helps, I never planned to sleep with her.”

Riley shrugged like she didn’t care, but he needed her to know the truth about things with that girl—a girl whose name he couldn’t even remember.

“I met her in one of my Creative Writing classes a year ago. We worked on a project together and some of the times it took place in her room. Her roommate told her about me. That I didn’t have hang-ups about saving myself for a Korrena or anything like some people do. The roommate told her I had… well, I slept with her roommate’s sister once.” He grimaced but Riley didn’t move, her hands resting on her thighs as she listened, her eyes focused on the window again. It was somewhat unnerving how still she sat; she normally always had to be moving or fidgeting with something. "Which was true, but it was only said to further back up her roommate's argument."

"What argument?"

"That I would be easy to get into bed." He shook his head. "Which isn't true. I know I've slept around, but I'm not just… It's not with a ton of people, despite what the rumors say, and it isn't with just anyone." He prayed she didn't ask what the criteria was. He didn't want to lie to her. When she said nothing, he continued.

"So one evening, around three months ago, I think, I was dropping off something I still had of hers since we no longer shared a class that semester." He stretched his leg out and bent one knee, crossing his arms on his stomach. "She invited me in, and we started talking about our new classes and the assigned essays. Up until this point, and the entire semester prior, she hadn't showed any interest—at least that I saw. So when she tried to kiss me, and I dodged her, she got really upset. Like super upset. Going on and on about what her roommate told her and what she heard from other girls."

He scrubbed a hand over his face. "She started talking about how something must be wrong with her. I didn't know what to do with it. I told her I don't kiss anyone—which is true—but I just wasn't in the mood for anything at the time."

"You don't kiss people?"

"No."

"Why?"

Riley finally turned her face toward him, but he couldn't hold her stare. He began looping a loose string on one of her corset tops around his fingers to distract himself from her probing gaze.

"I just don't."

Riley only nodded, allowing silence to settle between them. He needed to finish the story, because it would ultimately explain what happened in the cafeteria. Because no matter the reason why, or whether or not Riley wanted to admit it, something about what happened between him and that girl bothered her. Whatever it was felt like a poison in the air infecting their friendship with its fumes with every second that passed.

He needed to fix it.

"She took my not being in the mood to mean I gave her a rain check. I've avoided it for a few months, and even tried to tell her straight up I wasn't interested, but then she got sad, and I got stupid, and—"

"Flirted," Riley finished dryly.

"Yeah, flirted."

"She knows what she's doing."

"Probably." He closed his eyes and laid his head against the bed. Blowing out a breath, he said, "But yeah, when she said we had fun, we did." He rolled his head to the side and looked at Riley. "As classmates. Challenging each other with our assignments, good humor—all things we did with the others in our class too. It clearly meant something more to her."

Riley threw a shirt at him and shook her head with a soft laugh. "Hopeless. Just tell her like it is and be done with it if you really don't want anything with her. Otherwise, do whatever you gotta do. Either way, you gotta do something or cut her loose. It's not nice to string her along."

That wasn't his intention. He was so tired of the game it was easier to keep playing it without going all in than it was to fold his hand and face a potential fallout. He hated the fallout when girls wanted something he couldn't give them.

Seth wasn't the kind of guy who strung people along, and it bothered him that his actions gave Riley that impression. He needed to do something to change that. If that meant manning up and telling the girl point blank it wasn't going to happen between them, he would.

At least he could keep one relationship intact. When it came down to it, his connection with Riley mattered the most.

3

Crossing Lines

If there was one thing Riley knew for sure, it was that fashion was her calling. She loved the various textures and vibrant colors she could work with—even if most of her wardrobe consisted of black and some shade of pink. The ability to create without barriers or restraint always left her feeling free and fulfilled.

Fabric in shades of orange and teal lay in piles scattered on the floor around her as she tried to figure out the placement on the base of the mannequin she crouched in front of in the center of the room.

"Riley, dear. If you do a quarter fold and pinch the top like this"—her hands were guided into position by her boss Sara's soft, tanned hands accented by several silver rings—"you'll be able to secure it with a pin. This way, if you follow the same technique all around, you'll achieve the fluttery mermaid look."

Once the pleat was pinned in place, Riley sat back and looked up at the willowy Native American woman standing over her. "I think I get it. Yep, I think I see what you're saying."

"Perfect. Finish the base for this dress, and then you can go home. I'm closing a little early today so I can take the dresses we finished yesterday to meet with the bride for approval."

Sara put a large plastic bin on a shelf on the back wall where dozens of labeled bins and plastic containers with drawers were stacked. She waved goodbye before she passed through a curtain of beads hanging in the doorway separating the crafting room from the main hall leading out to the retail portion of Uniquely You, a clothing boutique that specialized in boho chic styles as well as offering custom tailoring to pad their revenue throughout the year.

When Charlotte first said that her adopted mother Sara—the owner and head seamstress of Uniquely You—was willing to take Riley on for the interning portion of her degree, allowing her to get real world experience in fashion design, she almost forgot her own strength in how she bowled over Charlotte in excitement. Even with everything happening at the academy, she managed to show up for all her scheduled lessons. It wasn't like she could tell Charlotte or Sara about the chaos happening at the academy. But in ensuring she met her intern requirements, the big project she needed to complete for her Fashion Illustration and Textile Design course suffered.

"Still here?"

The beaded curtain's tinkling, and the light and sweet sound of Charlotte's voice made Riley look up from collecting fabric from the floor and putting it into plastic bins for storage. Sara always told her not to worry about organizing everything, but Riley was so grateful for the opportunity, she aspired to be as helpful as possible.

"Mom asked me to lock up the shop, but I heard something back here."

"I'll be finished soon."

Charlotte waved a hand dismissively, pulling off her lightweight white jacket. She sat down on a chair close by, folding it in her lap, and adjusting her lavender sweater. The color made the cherry-red of her curls that she had bundled on top of her head in a claw-clip pop.

"No rush. I have nothing else better to do." She shook her head. "Now that I quit Ricky's Diner, and have all my stuff together for school, I'm kinda at a loss of what to do, you know?"

It was disappointing to know Charlotte was leaving Rosebrook Valley for Athens, but she had more opportunities at the University of Georgia than she did locally. It wasn't like she could attend Blackthorn Academy. Blaire was the only human exception. Though, maybe it was a thing, at least for now. Especially with the trip to Europe looming. Riley didn't know what to expect.

"If I didn't have this stupid project breathing down my neck, I'd say shopping, but I have to get back or I'm going to be so screwed." Riley flopped back on her back on the floor and kicked out her legs, the buckles that went up the sides of her knee-high platform boots jangling with the motion. Her head rolled to the side to look up at Charlotte. "You're still coming to Tybee Island with us, though, right?"

"Uh huh. I'm looking forward to it. It'll be my last hoorah before I leave."

"Why not wait until the fall?"

"I could get into some summer stuff with the university, and it will speed things along for me." Her shoulders lifted slightly. "Means less time away from home."

Riley watched as Charlotte looked away, but she didn't miss the shuddered breath or hard swallow that followed the word "home." She wondered if Charlotte spent any time outside the valley, or if this was her first time away from her mothers. With family scattered all over the world, Riley still didn't feel homesick. Sure, she was within spitting distance of her mom and where she was born, but people could feel homesick if their family was somewhere else.

Home was found in people, not places.

Riley's older sister and father lived in New York for work—though her father recently paid a visit to the academy. And her eldest brother lived in Seoul. But she didn't feel lonely.

Her older brother, Aiden, went to the academy with her. She also had Lukas and Seth. And in the last year, Blaire was added to her little makeshift family. She could see Charlotte fitting so well into their familial circle… if only the divide between their species wasn't a factor.

She sighed. Now wasn't the time to dwell on things that she couldn't control.

When Riley looked back at Charlotte, it was to find her smiling down at her phone.

How long had Riley spaced out?

She observed Charlotte for a while in silence, tapping her blunt, black nail against her opaque black stockings, toying with a long, splitting run on the side of her thigh. The tears were strategically placed for a fashion statement, but Riley's constant need to do something made her go through more pairs than she'd like. She kept making the holes and runs bigger.

Eventually her need to move won out, and she sat up abruptly, startling Charlotte into almost dropping her phone. Her cheeks were red, and her emerald eyes sparkled with a giddiness Riley hadn't seen before.

"Whooo's thaaat?" She resisted the urge to laugh as Charlotte's fair skin turned almost as red as her hair; freckles disappearing into the blush.

"No one." Charlotte hurriedly stuffed her cellphone into her back pocket. "Shall we go?"

"'Shall we go?' Look at you turning into a regular ole debutante."

Charlotte grumbled something under her breath and shook her head, but Riley could hear her soft laugh. When she lifted her arms to slide her jacket on, Riley couldn't resist. She grabbed the phone sticking more than halfway out of Charlotte's pocket.

"Hey!" Charlotte spun.

Riley shrugged. "It was gonna fall out. You should be thanking me it didn't break." She laughed when Charlotte rolled her eyes. "Can I look?" Riley wasn't really going to invade her privacy. They weren't that close yet, and even then, if it were something serious, she wouldn't do it.

Charlotte let out a long exhale and shrugged. "May as well." She held her hand out and Riley raised a brow. "To unlock it?"

"Oooh, duh. Sorry." She passed Charlotte her phone as she grabbed her oversized black sweater with a big white heart on the front dripping paint, pulling it on over her tank top. She'd taken it off while working because it got hot in the crafting room. It was big and baggy, but only fell to her hips, she could wear it with one of her favorite black pleated skirts.

"Here you go."

As Charlotte made her way through the beaded curtain and toward the front of the store to leave, Riley followed, looking down at the open text conversation between Charlotte and her brother Aiden. Her gaze snapped up to the back of Charlotte's head after a glance at the last couple of messages Aiden sent.

Riley hadn't read their conversation, but a brief glance to see who it was, had her seeing a couple lines. Was Aiden flirting with Charlotte?

She knew they'd been texting off and on with everything that had happened with Blaire. He was Charlotte's source for information because Lukas had been a wreck. They couldn't share what was really happening with Charlotte—at least not everything. She knew Blaire was kidnapped at the end of last year. But only that an obsessed student did it—which was true. Not all the extra details that would have her committed if she tried to tell other humans. Thankfully, when she was informed Blaire would undergo some testing afterward, she didn't question it. Riley had no idea how they would explain the experiments and ritual away.

Still, had Aiden grown closer to Charlotte than anyone knew?

"Sooo," Riley hedged. "My brother?"

"Yes."

She resisted the urge to giggle at the stilted way the word sounded. She didn't want Charlotte to be uncomfortable, so she said, "That's cool. He needs more friends."

Charlotte's shoulders lowered as she visibly relaxed.

Riley didn't have a problem with it. The problem came from Vasirian law.

Beyond a night of meaningless sex, Vasirian couldn't form a proper relationship with humans. The law didn't say they couldn't date, but it was frowned upon because the likelihood their secret would be exposed grew the longer they spent with a human in such an intimate way.

Then there was the problem with ignoring the possibility of finding their Korrena pair, or even a compatible pair. Even if they never found their Korrena, there was always the option of taking a compatible mate. Not too unlike a marriage between humans. Compatible pairs went through the same claiming ritual Korrena pairs did, with nothing locking in place.

No empathic connection.

No euphoric blood.

Just love and the pomp and circumstance of sharing blood with sex for the first time.

It wasn't what Riley wanted, but it was better than nothing.

Still, Aiden and Charlotte couldn't be more than friends, or even a fling, really. Riley didn't like the idea of the possible hurt her brother or her friend might face when Aiden had to step away. Unless Charlotte did first. She was going away to college, after all.

Maybe there was nothing there.

Maybe she was overthinking things like usual.

The early morning sun warmed Riley's skin in the flowering apricot tree grove along the drive between the main gates and the academy. The sunny day was going to be a welcome change from the winter chill of the previous month. She closed her eyes and breathed in the sun's energy and the delicate scent of the blossoms.

With March's warmth came the promise of spring, and with spring came spring break. Last year, she and her friends spent spring break hanging around the academy, completely oblivious to how their worlds would change in the weeks that followed and how life around Blackthorn Academy would never be the same again.

Given the time of year when Lukas told them all he'd found his Korrena walking the streets in town—a human, no less—it sounded like an April Fool's joke. But Lukas wasn't a joker. In fact, of all of them, Riley was the most likely suspect to make a joke like that, but she wouldn't. Korrena bonds weren't a joking matter.

The chime of a text notification cut through the electronic rock mix in her earbuds.

Seth:

where r u

Riley:

Apricot grove.

She sat up and put her phone aside. She frowned at the poster board with cutouts from magazines, fabric swatches, and sketched designs she made with notated measurements. The thing reminded her of a collage from a middle or high school elective, not a college fashion design course.

Would this be enough?

She grimaced at the naked Barbie doll mounted to a board with superglue on its feet. She'd asked Seth to bring her a few items to bring one of her collage designs to life on the doll; it would have to be enough. She was out of time. Spring break and the Europe trip would need all her focus.

Picking up the box cutter from the grass beside her, she trimmed the edges of the pattern for the doll's dress. Scissors or an X-ACTO knife would be the practical choice, but she forgot those in her dorm.

For ten minutes she got lost in her own little world, tongue peeking out of the side of her mouth as she bobbed her head to music, sketching ideas with colored pencils in her sketch pad. Her face scrunched when a large shadow blocked the sun over her paper. Huffing, she sat up.

Seth stared at her drawing, crouched in front of her, his arms draped over his thighs, hands hanging between his legs. "New design?"

She pulled the earbuds out of her ears. "Huh?" When he motioned to the rough sketch of a black and blue jumper, she nodded. "Oh, yeah." She blinked a few times in confusion. "Uh… Seth?"

"Mm?"

"Where's my stuff?"

She set the sketchbook aside and returned to cutting at the fabric in front of her. Once her focus was torn away from one task, she tended to flit to the next, get consumed by it until something broke her fixation, and then the cycle would repeat. It was a headache being in her head. She often had six things going at one time and had to force herself to see one through. To do that, she had to completely shut out everything—even basic needs—and hyper-focus, but it got the job done.

"Right there."

Her gaze panned to where Seth pointed. A cardboard box overflowing with fabric sat next to her. When did he put it there?

Digging around in the box, she set out a few items she needed, and then frowned, looking over her shoulder at him. "Where's my craft scissors?"

"What?"

"My. Craft. Scissors." She made a snipping motion with her index and middle finger. "The things I use to cut fabric with?"

"How the hell should I know?" He dropped back to sit down, draping his arms on his knees after loosening his uniform tie. "You told me to get the box." He waved a hand. "I got the box."

Riley grumbled and sat back down, glaring at the naked doll and the fabric in front of her. She didn't want to go back to the dorm and try to find where she misplaced the scissors, so she'd have to make do.

As she sliced into the fabric in front of her with the box knife, Seth said, "Why do you need it when you have a perfectly decent blade right there?"

"Because."

"*Because?*"

"Because I prefer the scissors."

She could practically feel the eye roll but stayed focused on the fabric.

"You know, you could be a little nicer considering you have me running around being your gopher."

"Nicer?"

"I mean, what's in it for me?"

"The knowledge you helped me on my journey to greatness."

Seth always joked about wanting payment for his hard work whenever he did anything for her, but whenever she *did* try to do something for him, he always refused it, so he couldn't be serious.

"Journey to greatness?"

"Yep."

"And a box of fabric and knickknacks is part of that?"

"Yep."

"I think our ideas of greatness vary dramatically."

She pinned the first cut pieces in place on the form around the hips of the doll to create a ball gown skirt. Satisfied, she cut the next pieces, never taking her eyes off her task. Her stomach rumbled at the smell of sugar cookies in the air.

"When's the last time you ate?"

"Breakfast."

"You weren't in the cafeteria."

Busted.

"Got something from the canteen."

She was likely not convincing Seth. He could read her like a book typically, but her attention remained on the fabric—maybe that would help.

"Riley."

Guess not.

"Yes?" She added as much casualness into her tone as possible.

"When'd you eat last?"

"I'm fine. Jeez." She waved a hand in his general direction before placing it down on the fabric on the ground. If she'd known she would have to cut straight lines this way, she'd have brought a self-healing cutting mat for stability. She sighed. It wasn't like she tried to be argumentative with Seth; she honestly couldn't remember the last time she ate. It wasn't the first time that had happened—not the first this week, even—and certainly wouldn't be the last. "I'll get something when I'm finished with this," she said to placate him.

The sound of him sucking his teeth let her know he was far from satisfied with that. But he had to take it a step further. "I'm not going to always be around to make sure you eat or drink blood. Aiden, either."

His attitude rankled.

"I don't *need* you to make sure of anything." He and Aiden were as bad as her mother. She was a grown woman now. Eighteen. "I can take care of myself."

"Riley," Seth said with an exasperated sigh. "I know you can. But you don't. Not like you should."

Her head swiveled as she shot him a glare intended to cut him down a peg or two, but she yelped instead, tears springing to her eyes. She looked down at her hand.

Blood ran down to her wrist from a long cut along the side of her index finger. Her gaze moved to the fabric and box cutter she dropped. Blood glistened on the sharp blade and stained the fabric. *Great.* At least she had more of that color in the box.

Before she could search for something to clean her hand and staunch the bleeding until her natural healing took over, Seth snatched up her hand with the offending cut, wrapping the fabric she had been cutting around her hand.

"This is what I'm talking about."

"Huh?"

"You don't look out for yourself."

Riley stared at him, dumbfounded. How did accidentally cutting herself—because he'd distracted her—equate to neglecting to eat because she was too focused on her project?

"You weren't paying attention."

Confused and frustrated by his words and the sting caused by the material of the fabric, she pulled away from him and sat back against the tree. She tucked her legs beneath her and threw the fabric down. Her finger still bled, but not as heavily.

"Maybe I would have been paying attention if I weren't being lectured. I'm not a child, Seth. I wish you wouldn't treat me like one."

Seth's dark laugh brought her gaze to his face. He tilted his head. "I haven't seen you as a child in a long time, Firecracker."

She wanted to argue with him about that ridiculous nickname he used occasionally, but she was hungry and tired, her brain overloaded from the project. Her finger hurt.

When he didn't say anything more, she followed his gaze to her hand resting in her lap. When she looked back at his eyes, she caught the fading traces of a white glow.

"Seth?"

Slowly, he moved to kneel in front of her on both knees. His breathing sounded labored, and again, the silvery-white glow shone at the edge of his heavy-lidded steel eyes.

Her heart raced as he lifted her hand.

Trying again, she asked, "What are you doing?" She didn't know what was going on, but her entire body hummed with nervous energy.

Frustrated with his lack of answers, she opened her mouth to speak again, but froze when he lifted her fingers to his mouth with shaking hands.

What in the…

Her brain had barely caught up when the slow drag of Seth's tongue over the cut on her finger obliterated thought.

The breath she sucked in made her lightheaded. Or maybe it was the fact that Seth-freaking-Emerson, her childhood friend who had always been like a big brother to her, was tasting her blood.

A primal groan ripped into her thoughts, bringing her back to the present before her brain could go on a tangent.

Seth remained muted, pausing after a second pass of his tongue, his eyes still closed. Shoulders shaking, he dropped his head forward, but still held her hand tightly.

His words were whispered, a strained, "What the fuck?" as he pulled in deep, calming breaths.

"Um. Seth?"

His head snapped up, glowing eyes colliding with hers, and she shrank back against the tree in surprise.

"Are you okay? What's going on? Why did you—"

Her words died at the sound of his growl, and she squealed when he reached out and pulled her toward him again, almost putting her into his lap, not allowing her to put space between them. She sat flush with his chest, their lower halves separated as they sat on folded legs. He buried his head on her shoulder, shuddering.

"Seth, you're freaking me out."

His left arm remained banded behind her lower back, but he slowly lowered his right to take hold of her nearly healed hand again. Blood remained on her skin, and he stared at it for so long Riley squirmed from the inactivity.

Inhaling deeply, he stooped and trailed his lips across her hand and up to her finger, where he proceeded to pull it into his mouth, lacing his tongue around the digit.

The moment the pull of her blood left the wound into his mouth, she gasped. No one had ever tasted her blood before, much less drunk from an open wound.

Her breathing became heavier, and her eyes fluttered closed. She bit the inside of her cheek to avoid embarrassing herself with the sound that bubbled up in her throat. She flushed warm all over, and her nipples pebbled beneath her clothing. The friction felt nice, but her mind was in a riot of confusion. Confusion over how her body responded to having someone drink her blood, but also at who elicited the reaction.

She squirmed, rubbing her thighs together against the pulse that throbbed like a heartbeat between her legs. Seth's arm tightened around her in response, and he released her finger from the prison of his mouth.

The hand that held her hand so tightly gently cradled the back of her head and pulled her against his chest. His heart pounded thunderously beneath her ear, and she could still feel him trembling against her. He held her as if he were comforting her, but she got the impression *he* was seeking comfort. Maybe he was as confused as she was. But he said nothing as he kept her head tucked beneath his chin, and she was too afraid to voice her questions aloud.

What just happened?

What was wrong with him?

Her feelings for Seth weren't those for a friend or brother entirely, but she'd never let herself venture into sexual thoughts of him. She certainly didn't consider sharing her blood—with anyone.

Any time her mind tried to tease her with more than an appreciation of Seth's looks, she shut it down at once. She wouldn't allow Seth to star in her fantasies. Only book boyfriends. But she couldn't deny the way her body had just responded to him.

At least, not to herself.

She'd deny it all day to him; he wouldn't hold that kind of power over her.

Finally getting her head together, she squirmed, needing space. With the movement, Seth came back to himself. He let go of her and scrambled to his feet as if someone had lit a fire beneath him.

Without a word, he turned and stalked out of the grove, heading straight for the dorm buildings.

Riley's now healed hand was cleaned of blood, as if she never hurt herself. The only evidence anything happened were the box cutter and stained fabric lying on the grass.

She slumped back against the tree.

This wasn't the first time she'd cut herself or bled around Seth. Skinned knees, paper cuts, knives from cooking at her parents' home… it wasn't like Seth had never witnessed her bleeding.

He didn't have issues with Vasirian blood; he only had a sensitivity to the smell of human blood.

But not only did he lick her blood to clean her hand, but he drank from her. She felt him suck at the wound.

What in the hell just happened?

4

Confusion

Riley knocked on the dorm door and bounced from foot to foot impatiently. It took her a while to calm down and refocus after what happened in the grove, but she managed to get her things sorted and bury herself in completing the project to distract herself from what happened with Seth.

When her hands shook as she packed everything away, signaling an adrenaline crash and the telltale signs of lack of blood consumption, she remembered she'd also skipped lunch. She made a quick stop at the canteen for a wrapped sandwich and a blood packet from the cafeteria after dropping her things off in her room then she beelined for Blaire's dorm.

Riley knocked again, hoping Lukas and Blaire hadn't gone out for the evening. She needed someone to soundboard this mess in her head, and Aiden was certainly not the one. While Aiden was Lukas's best friend and vice versa, Seth and Aiden were like brothers. Aiden would drive her crazy with teasing if she told him. Nope. Not going there.

Blaire was safe. She'd understand.

Riley was about to knock again when the door opened. Lukas stepped back to let her in, pulling a black T-shirt over his head. His hair was damp, and he moved with fluid grace—not his usual stiffness, like he was on edge all the time. The way Blaire perched on the edge of the bed finger-combing equally damp hair in a pair of pajama shorts and an oversized T-shirt that no doubt belonged to Lukas left no need to guess what she might have interrupted.

"I can come back," she said, and then frowned. Normally, she didn't balk at dropping in and surprising her friends like this, but with what happened earlier, she felt out of sorts.

"Stay," Blaire said. "We just got out of the shower."

Lukas sat in the desk chair, the chains on the hip of his black jeans clinking as they connected with the wood. "I'm going to meet the guys for dinner, anyway. Pizza night." He pulled on his leather boots and pushed his long hair back from his face as he stood. Walking over to the side of the bed, he leaned down and kissed Blaire deeply, cupping her jaw. "I love you," he said softly over her lips before pulling away and heading for the door.

Blaire licked her lips, a smile of pure bliss on her face.

"Oh gods, you two are gonna give me diabetes." Riley collapsed on the bed next to Blaire, already feeling better around her best friend.

"Is that even possible?"

"I don't think so." She looked at the ceiling in thought. "I mean, we can have allergies, and common human diseases aren't strong enough to override our immune defenses, but things that are a constant like, say, Type 1 diabetes, I'm not sure."

"Cancer?"

"No. I mean, we get sick for a brief period, but our body burns it out in a month or so. At least, it did for Professor Sunderland. I guess diabetes could be the same way. I've never met a Vasirian with diabetes, so it's likely."

Blaire shook her head, pulling her long, blonde hair into a ponytail. "I don't see how you don't know."

"It's not like they have to teach us things that are natural to us. I mean, do they teach humans about things like that?"

"Huh. Not really." Blaire opened a tube of lotion and squeezed a dollop into her palm and began smoothing it over her legs. "I mean, we have science classes that teach us basic stuff… so I guess we learn *something*, but no one remembers it, and it's never so in depth that we know of every disease and potential sickness or ailment there is. That's why there's medical school."

"See? It's the same for me. If they taught it, I've long since forgotten because it doesn't affect me."

Blaire finished with her lotion, the air now scented with a rose and citrus blend, and turned on the bed, sitting cross-legged. "Finish your project?"

One side of Riley's nose screwed up. "Barely," she said, not even attempting to hide her frustration.

"Alright, spill."

Causal conversation about Vasirian health versus human health wouldn't hold back the inevitable. She needed to get herself together. What happened in the apricot grove wasn't a big deal. *Keep telling yourself that. You'd have an easier time convincing Blaire demon pigs are real.*

Riley sighed. She couldn't even laugh at her own chaotic thoughts.

Glancing over at her friend, who sat waiting with her hands in her lap holding her bottle of lotion, she couldn't not say something. That's what she came here for anyway, right? So how did she go about this?

She blurted, "Seth drank my blood," then squeezed her eyes shut and winced.

Okay… to the point it is.

She cracked an eye open and peeked at Blaire to gauge her reaction.

Blaire's mouth hung open as she blinked a few times. She looked like a robot trying to reboot her brain from a system crash.

When she finally got her wits about her, she asked, "What happened? I mean, I know what happened… but the how and why, I don't understand."

Riley shrugged, but the motion wasn't super effective on the bed. "I accidentally cut myself with a box cutter when we were going back and forth about something… I can't even remember what anymore."

"Par for the course." Blaire nodded. She wasn't wrong. "So you cut yourself. And then?"

"Well, things seemed fine. Still running off at the mouth, but then something changed. His eyes glowed, and his breathing was all messed up like he just ran a mile." Riley picked at the black polish on her nails. "He grabbed my hand and licked my wound, which shocked the hell out of me." She threw her hands up before dropping them to the bed. "And because he wouldn't say anything, I freaked out."

"Rightfully so." Blaire nodded, her eyes wide in response to Riley's confession, but she was just getting started.

"So, like, at one point he…" Riley cut her gaze to Blaire and then away, mumbling, "He started sucking the blood from the wound."

Blaire's hand covered her mouth, and she leaned in, whispering as if someone could be listening in, "Did he bite you?"

"Nope. Just drank for a bit."

"What happened after that?"

Riley's face burned with embarrassment, recalling the way her body responded to the way Seth's tongue wrapped around her finger; the way his lips felt against her skin; the sensation of her blood leaving her body. She shuddered.

"He left."

Blaire narrowed her eyes, confusion crossing her face. "Left? That's it?"

"Well, no…"

"Okaaayyy. So what else?"

Riley sat up and scooted until her back met the head of the bed, her eyes tracking around the space. Other than the queen-sized bed that sat central to the room, Lukas and Blaire hadn't decorated much. A couple of desks and a bookshelf rounded out the furnishings. With everything that happened in the last several months, and moving into the new dorm right before they both spent time in the dungeons and dealt with the Order, it wasn't a wonder they hadn't gotten the opportunity to do much to personalize the space.

Riley startled when Blaire waved fingers in front of her face to get her attention before asking, "What else?" Her friend didn't push for her to explain the spacing out; she was used to it. She understood it.

It was nice to have people who accepted her, even when she didn't always like certain aspects of herself. Of course, they didn't know that. Riley was the joker, the one who smiled and brought liveliness to the group as needed.

She exhaled a heavy breath, her cheeks puffing out with the force. "It felt good," she finally said, meeting Blaire's eyes.

Whatever Blaire saw on her face made her expression soften. "Of course it did. You like him."

Riley shook her head emphatically. "Drinking blood isn't supposed to feel like that."

Blaire's brows drew together. "Okay, well, I'm confused."

"Um." Riley rubbed her hands on her overheated cheeks, probably making the blush she was trying to get rid of worse. "Like, it felt good… *there*." She groaned in frustration. She said she wasn't a child, so she needed to stop acting like one. "You know, the girly bits." *There. That wasn't so hard.*

"Oh," Blaire said, studying Riley's face for a bit before saying, "I guess my statement still stands."

"So does mine. Aside from Korrena pairs, or willing humans who get a dopamine kick from our bite—which we're not allowed to give—no one should feel horny over blood consumption." She rolled her lips together to keep from addressing the whole liking Seth situation. This reaction was confusing enough.

"Listen, maybe you're overthinking it," Blaire said.

Riley raised a brow, making her friend laugh. Blaire knew she overthought *everything*.

"Okay, you are most definitely overthinking it. Not to diminish your feelings or anything. Just considering the situation pragmatically. You haven't had sex before, and I don't know your experience outside of that."

A couple of kisses in high school.

"But if he was sucking on your skin, I'm not the least bit surprised by your response. The blood part might not have had a single thing to do with it."

Riley laughed. When put like that, it made perfect sense. The proximity in the way Seth held her, his mouth on her skin, his tongue tickling nerves in her finger… it made sense her inexperienced body would respond.

So that left the question of…

"Why did he do it, though? He's never tried my blood before."

"That one I can't tell you." Blaire shook her head. "But I don't know Seth as well as you. If you don't have a clue, I think it's best to wait and see if he says anything or chalk it up as a fluke. What do you want to do?"

That was the question of the day. What did she want to do about what happened? Ignoring the situation felt like the best choice. She could go back to living in blissful ignorance of the way Seth made her body feel. But something in her gut told her that wasn't an option.

Seth stared at the ceiling, the sound of the running shower in the ensuite lulling him in and out of the edge of consciousness. He wished he could fall asleep and forget the entire day even happened; but every time he closed his eyes, the color red overtook him, jolting his body awake with an unfamiliar ache.

He still couldn't comprehend what happened to him in the grove. Nothing about his interactions with Riley went any different than usual, and it wasn't the first time she'd hurt herself around him. But when the scent of her blood mingled with the distinct, aromatic scent of sweet tiger lilies and smacked him in the face when he moved close to inspect her hand, he lost all reason. He couldn't even begin to explain the reaction beyond what it was at the core: hunger and lust.

Like a rogue Vasirian, he latched onto Riley's wound and fed. The taste of her blood on his tongue evoked a firestorm beneath his skin and, if not for the quickly closing wound, he'd have gorged himself.

He would not bite her.

His tongue trailed over his lips, chasing the phantom taste of her lifeblood that still taunted him in his memory.

Aside from blood packets, he'd never tasted another living being's blood. It was forbidden to drink from humans—and considering his weakness over the scent, he'd likely kill them—but not to drink from other Vasirian. Most didn't do that though, saving their blood for their Korrena only; but there were others who shared freely. Who was he to kink shame? It just wasn't his thing.

He never shared his and never took another's blood when offered.

Until today.

But it wasn't offered.

He ran a hand over his face and groaned into his palm. Riley hadn't stopped him, but he didn't ask first, either. He felt like the biggest tool.

The bathroom door opening grabbed his attention. Steam billowed from the open doorway as Aiden stepped out wrapped in a towel, heading for their shared closet.

A few minutes later, he reappeared in a pair of loose athletic pants with a bright green drawstring and stripe down the side. He rubbed the remaining droplets of water from his bare chest and tossed the used towel in a small laundry basket they kept next to the closet door.

"Lukas is picking up a couple pizzas and coming over later. You haven't had dinner, have you?"

Seth sat up and tried to keep an impassive expression. "Does that mean Blaire is coming too?" Where Blaire went, Riley was likely to follow. He wasn't sure if he was ready to see her so soon. Not while his head wasn't on straight.

"Blaire?" Aiden used his fingers to brush the wayward wet strands of inky black hair back, forgoing a brush entirely. "No. I think she was going to get a canteen dinner. You know she hates pizza." His brows lowered. "Why?"

Seth eased himself up on the bed and placed his hand on his shoulder, rolling it until he heard a pop. "Nothing." He repeated the action with the other arm.

Aiden crossed his arms across his chest and planted his feet in a wider stance with a raised eyebrow. Normally, a move like that would look ridiculous—a try-hard, posturing move—but it always worked for Aiden. It helped that he stood a couple inches over six feet and had the classic build gym guys envied and women swooned for. He wasn't as big as the typical gym rat, but his arms and chest were defined. He also had a definition to his torso and abs, but not so cut that his abs looked like tide pods—as Riley liked to call it. Aiden wasn't the tallest, but he was the biggest of their friend group, and he kept up his physique with physical activity when possible.

Seth used to strive to look as built as Aiden when they were growing up, but not anymore. He admired the hard work Aiden put into keeping fit, even when it wasn't exactly necessary for their kind—though it helped. It could make the difference between getting pummeled or not. But even the weakest Vasirian could tap into preternatural strength. For the most part, it came down to an aesthetic thing for Vasirian and a slight edge over the competition in a fight if necessary. Which was why Seth wanted to keep up his own build. He liked the body he grew into, but he wanted more definition, so he joined Aiden in his workouts to make it happen.

Still, Seth never felt intimidated by his best friend. Aiden would never hurt him. Aiden wouldn't hurt anyone.

"Really? That shit doesn't work on me."

"So? You're still gonna tell me what's up."

"I am, am I?" Seth scoffed. "I think you're mistaking me for someone else."

Aiden rolled his eyes. "But seriously, something wrong with Blaire?"

Seth shook his head. "Nah." He knew to be careful when it came to talking about Blaire.

When Lukas's human Korrena showed up at the academy, Aiden

took it on himself to do what he always did—play protector. But in a move even Seth couldn't predict, Aiden started catching feelings for the girl. And with Blaire and Lukas at odds—practically dripping disdain for one another from their pores at times—Aiden took his shot. Which Seth had to admire. If someone didn't want a bond, they shouldn't be forced into it.

The entire concept that biology suddenly flipped a switch in their heads and they would become mindless slaves to desire and want for someone they might have hated before that moment made him sick. That was what he initially saw when he looked at Blaire and Lukas. He would never be one of those pair-bonded saps.

Even as emotions grew between Blaire and Lukas as more time passed, it still stood to reason that if Lukas hadn't briefly seen his Korrena mark on her skin a year ago, none of what followed would have happened. They never would have fallen in love, because humans weren't allowed in their world.

"Just figured if Blaire was coming, so was Riley."

"And?" Aiden dropped onto his bed, propping his back against the wall beside the window. "When has that ever been a problem?"

Since I fed from her like an animal.

His gums still tingled at the urging he felt from his fangs desperate to break through. He hadn't bitten her, but that tingle scared the hell out of him.

"It isn't."

When Aiden pinned him with a look, he laughed low.

"Okay, it is. Things got out of hand earlier. I don't wanna deal with her right now."

Aiden sat quietly in his usual way when he knew there was more. Not questioning immediately; waiting him out.

"I think I messed up," Seth finally said, a slight rasp to his voice with the strain of his confession. What he would tell his best friend next might get him his second black eye for the week. "Riley cut herself, and I somehow ended up drinking her blood."

Aiden squinted, tilting his head ever so slightly. "Somehow?" He broke the word in two slowly, as if he couldn't process the word.

"I mean, things just happened."

"Listen, I love you like a brother, but that's not going to cut it. Not when it comes to my baby sister."

Seth muttered, "I know." That fact was one reason he refrained from sharing his inner thoughts and the full truth about what took place in the grove.

How did he tell his best friend that tasting his little sister's blood aroused him more than anything he'd ever experienced before? In truth, it wasn't really Aiden's business, but he'd opened Pandora's box, so he had to tell him something.

Seth detailed how, like usual, they bickered about inane things that mattered little in the grand scheme of life but would leave a gaping wound in his chest if the moments were missing. Of course, he didn't *say* that last part. He wasn't stupid. Aiden knew his feelings for Riley were far from brotherly, but Seth wasn't going to start pouring his heart out either. He had other places to focus those feelings and words he refused to give an audible voice.

"Then something in me flipped. I responded to the smell of her blood in the same way I do to excess human blood." He pulled himself up higher into a fully sitting position on his bed. "My throat burned, and my skin was vibrating with the need."

"So she let you drink her blood from the cut?"

Seth's self-deprecating laugh had Aiden frowning. "I took it. I didn't ask."

"Excuse me?" Aiden slid to the edge of the bed. "Talk fast, because

I know you didn't just tell me you did something like that without her consent."

Mouth dry, Seth moved to the edge of his own bed to be on an equal footing and held up a hand. "Before you smash my face in, hear me out." He totally deserved Aiden's ire.

Aiden's eyebrows narrowed into a deep frown as he waited, his tension palpable from across the room.

"I didn't ask, no. But I didn't force her into anything. She didn't stop me. Didn't say no. Didn't try to push me away." He carded a hand into the long hair on top of his head and held onto it, resting his elbow on his knee. He held Aiden's critical gaze as he added, "When she squirmed to break whatever connection we had, I let her go." He sucked in a scant breath that made his nostrils flare. "You know I would never do *anything* to hurt her. I'd sooner cut off my own arm."

Aiden's shoulders lowered, and he ran his tongue over his teeth. "Yeah. I know, man. I just had to be sure. You're both my family, but Mom would take me down to the coastal marshlands and find an alligator or three to teach me a lesson if I let something happen to Riley." He gave an exaggerated shudder, and just like that, confirmed he wasn't angry.

Still, part of him wished Aiden had thrown the punch, a part he suppressed.

"Alright, so what do you mean about a connection? What aren't you saying?"

"Without going into details that will probably get me punched, I felt more alive than I ever have in my life the moment I tasted her blood." He clasped his hand over the side of his neck, resting his elbow on his knee. "I knew when I smelled it that something was different."

"What are you saying?"

"I don't know." He laughed, letting his hand fall. "Your guess is as good as mine."

"Maybe she's—"

Seth growled. "Don't say it. She's not. She can't be."

There were so many reasons having Riley as his Korrena would be a terrible thing. None of those reasons he wanted to think about at the moment.

"Why not? Would that be such a bad thing? Look, I've held my tongue for years, but it's gotten ridiculous." Aiden shook his head. "You can lie to yourself and her all day, but it's obvious to anyone who spends time with you two that you're in love with her."

"Nothing happened when I came of age. But now she's eighteen and there's nothing on her end." Seth sighed. "Besides, she and I feel very different things for one another."

Aiden's mouth gaped. "Are you kidding me?"

"What?"

"Riley has looked at you like you alone hang the moon and stars since you were kids, man. How do you not see that?"

"I'm like an older brother to her. She said it herself. We're just friends."

"No. *I'm* the older brother." Aiden pointed at himself. "You sure as hell don't see her letting me pull her into my lap on the regular." His facial features twisted into a grimace. "Not that I'd want to, mind you."

"We're friends. That's all we can ever be."

"Yeah, I don't understand that part."

"She wants her Korrena pair. I'm not Prince Charming with the magical mark to sweep her off her feet." Seth stood from his bed and stalked over to his desk to unplug his laptop and carry it to his bed. "And as much as it pains me, I won't deny her that dream by acting selfish." He sat back against his wall with a heavy exhale. Flipping the lid of his laptop open, he navigated to where he wanted to go. He needed to work.

The best thing he could do for Riley was what he always had. Watch from the sidelines to protect her, to be her friend, her shoulder to cry on, her punching bag, and anything else she asked of him.

Until she replaced him.

The thought of her cutting him out of her life and replacing him with someone else made his chest ache and his head throb.

"Are you ever going to tell her the truth, at least?"

"About?"

"Who you are."

Seth's fingers stilled over the keys of his laptop. "Didn't plan on it."

"You're one stubborn jackass when you want to be, man." Aiden looked at his phone, chuckling, and then stood and walked to the door.

Seth rolled his eyes. "Don't act like that's a new revelation."

"It's not," Aiden said, pulling the door open to their dorm. "Finally. I'm starving." He reached out and took the two boxes of pizza Lukas held, leaving him carrying a bag. "Did you get extra cheese?" He looked over his shoulder at Lukas.

"Hello to you too," Lukas said with an eye roll.

Aiden laughed and carried the pizzas to the bed, clearly done with the topic, much to Seth's relief.

Some secrets were best left in the dark, in a place where hearts and lives existed bound by barbed wire. Where with one wrong move, the truth of those secrets would slice through and leave nothing but ruin.

While Lukas and Aiden set up for dinner, unloading the bag of its contents of canned drinks, bottled water, napkins, and paper plates, Seth lost himself in his latest spark of inspiration, desperate to push everything that happened earlier in the day to the farthest reaches of his mind.

Whenever he needed to escape, he could open a blank page and create something from nothing. Create his own reality where the rules of the waking world didn't apply. It was why he chose the major he did.

Writing gave him release. Most of the time, it felt like his spoken words and thoughts filtered into the void. Everyone stayed too focused on their own lives, relationships, families, and whatever personal crisis they were dealing with. It didn't help that he tried to keep his interactions light, not too deep. He didn't want to get deep with anyone. He wasn't antisocial, exactly. He just didn't see the point in blind trust.

He looked up from the screen in time to catch Aiden shoving a laughing Lukas off the bed. Seth shook his head slowly, a small smile crossing his face at their antics. The people he sincerely trusted he could count on one hand: Aiden, Lukas, Blaire, and Riley. The only people he would attempt to have something deeper with.

Everyone wanted something from someone. The girls he took to bed used him for his looks and whatever pleasure he could provide—which was all he used them for. He admitted to himself their looks served a different purpose than physical attraction.

The girls he slept with provided a release. A momentary reprieve from the noise in his head. He'd taken Riley's complete opposites to bed in an effort to push her out of his mind, but even that couldn't stop Riley's face being what he saw when he closed his eyes as he came.

Always her.

Sure, the sex was good with others. The girls aroused him physically. But Riley? She set his blood on fire, and his grasp on his control was beginning to slip.

Seth dug his fingers into his eyes. Even in a crowded room, and the work he enjoyed open in front of him, he couldn't escape her. She always found her way back into his mind, and he didn't know what he was going to do about it.

5

Reprieve

The sound of seagulls, wind chimes, and the smell of the salty ocean air greeted Riley as she stepped out of the rental SUV when Aiden pulled into the driveway at Lukas's parents' beach home next to Kai and Mera's small car. There was a slight crispness in the morning air, but by midday it would be warmer. Even if the weather was too chilly to swim, she couldn't wait to dig her bare toes in the sandy beach.

Stretching her arms over her head, trying to shake off the stiffness of the drive from Rosebrook Valley to the island, she looked up at the two-story modern home painted a deep navy blue with white shutters, white railing, and stairs with a wrap-around porch. Planter baskets of dangling ferns hung by chains from the porch covering and pots of smaller flowering plants decorated the steps. Lukas mentioned his parents hired someone to come and get the place ready before spring break. The exterior touches said a lot for their attention to the upkeep.

"Wow, it's really pretty," Layla said.

This wasn't the first time Riley had visited the four-bedroom beach house. With an attic bonus room that could accommodate additional people, the house could sleep more than seven if they also used the pullout bed in the couch in the living room. The highest point of the house featured an attic with two beds and storage. The second floor had storage closets, a full bathroom, a guest room, and the master bedroom with a balcony that opened up to look out at the beach and the Atlantic with its own ensuite. The large bottom floor extended to the left of the main part of the beach house with an open concept living room and kitchen area, and two bedrooms that shared a bathroom.

But her favorite part had to be the pool area with maintained sandy paths and flower beds Lukas's mother specially placed to line the entire perimeter except for the pathway down to the beach through the dunes and beach grass.

"Is the heat on in the pool?" Aiden asked as he rounded the SUV and started unloading the back, passing bags to Seth, Lukas, and Kai.

Lukas hefted a duffel over his shoulder and lifted a suitcase. "Should be."

Charlotte brightened. "Heated pool? We'll be able to swim?"

"Yeah. It's outdoors on the other side of the house, facing the beach, but the pool is in-ground and kept heated. Besides, as long as it's the middle of the day, it won't be cold when you get out. It's the ocean water that's cold."

"That's so cool. I've only been in a heated pool in a hotel before. I'm glad I brought my suit, but I didn't think I'd get to do more than sunbathe."

Blaire picked up a tote bag and passed it to Mera, then another to Layla, and finally took one for herself. Aiden lifted the large cooler from the back of the SUV and headed for the house. "Can you shut the hatch?" Blaire called back to Charlotte as everyone headed toward the house.

"Want me to get this other cooler?"

"What cooler?"

"There's a small one. One of those padded ones. Mom has one like it at the clinic to keep the animal's medicines chilled and insulated."

The others were already inside or on the porch out of earshot, but Mera and Riley paused and looked back to where Blaire stood, turned toward Charlotte.

"I didn't think we had more than one—"

"Oh, yeah! Yeah!" Riley handed Mera the travel case she carried and rushed to Charlotte. She pulled the bag from the back of the SUV and put the strap on her shoulder. "Forgot that one. Can you get the hatch? Thanks." She smiled and turned and rushed to join the others. When she reached Blaire, she mouthed without sound, "Blood."

Blaire nodded and turned to Charlotte as she joined them. "Mera and Kai are leaving after the party tonight. That's why they drove in a different car."

"Why?" Charlotte asked.

"I don't know the details." Blaire looked at Mera. "A family thing, right?"

"Yes. My parents flew in from Australia for a medical conference in California and require my attendance. Kai will come with me. Our plane leaves from Atlanta tomorrow afternoon."

Riley rushed ahead to let them talk while she dealt with the cooler of blood. "Lukas! Where should I put these?"

The front door opened directly into the spacious kitchen with a center island surrounded by stools. She set the cooler on top of the granite counter before moving to the wall and flipping on the light switch beneath the pale wooden cabinets. The hanging pendant lights came on over the center island, adding to the natural lighting that filtered in through the window over the sink that looked out toward the sand dunes and ocean.

"What are you yelling about now?"

Riley spun around as Seth sauntered into the room with his hands tucked into his pockets. "I'm trying to figure out where to put this stuff before Charlotte comes in. She almost picked it up herself."

"What stuff?"

She pointed at the cooler behind her on the counter.

Lukas came through the doorway to their right. "There's a fridge with a lock on the patio through the sliding glass doors in the living room. Take it out there."

"Where's the keys?"

"Keypad combination 0712."

Aiden raised a brow, leaning on the open archway leading to the living room. "Your parents use your birthday?"

Seth turned. "How the hell did you make that connection?"

Aiden shrugged. "It made the most sense."

Riley grabbed the bag from the counter and squeezed around Lukas and Seth to leave the kitchen. "I'm so ready to eat lunch," she said as she made her way into the living room, through the sliding glass doors, and down the wooden steps into a screened-in patio. She had been so excited for the trip this morning that she only had a blood packet and string cheese.

To the right of the back door paddle boards, floats, and other pool accessories lined the wall, and a cozy outdoor couch with vibrant coral, navy, and white accent pillows sat against the far side of the porch near the screens looking out at the ocean. To the left, a wooden porch swing with white cushions and navy starfish throw pillows swayed in the breeze. Behind the swing sat an unassuming wooden crate with a tray of glasses and a carafe on top and a keypad on the front.

She crouched in front of it and punched in the code, opening the wooden doors. Two metal mini fridges with glass doors hid inside the crate. One sat empty, while the other was filled with cans and bottles of various alcoholic beverages. Glancing at the sliding glass doors to ensure Charlotte wasn't nearby, she unloaded the blood packets into the empty fridge.

"Here."

Riley jumped and almost dropped the last blood packet in her hands when something cold and wet grazed her cheek. She spun and looked up from her crouched position with her hand on her chest. "Jeez, Seth. Are you trying to kill me?" She shoved the packet into the fridge, closed the door, and stood.

"It's not that dramatic."

"You scared me. I'm going to die of a heart attack." She posted her hands on her hips. "I thought you were Charlotte." Her gaze settled on the bottle of water in his hand and the plate with a sandwich on it in the other. "What's this?"

"Food." He tilted his head, motioning for her to follow him. "You said you're hungry."

She shoved the cooler beside the wooden crate and locked everything away before following Seth over to the couch, taking a seat next to him.

He took half the sandwich and set the plate and water between them. "Eat up."

"Why'd you make me a sandwich?" She took a bite—turkey breast, cheddar cheese, lettuce, tomato, and spicy mayonnaise. Delicious.

"I happened to be hungry, too."

She groaned, finally having something of substance besides blood filling her belly. "Well, thank you." She patted her stomach and closed her eyes, listening to the sound of the waves in the distance and the hum of the ceiling fan overhead.

She'd almost fallen asleep when Seth said, "I'm sorry."

Opening one eye, she peeked over at him, hunched over, elbows on his knees, hands clasped together. "What for?"

"The grove."

So they weren't going to ignore what happened.

She sat up and poked his side, making him jerk upright. "Hey, look, I know you have a weird thing about blood." She immediately shifted her gaze from his stricken look to the wood beneath her feet. "Maybe it extends to our kind, too. I mean, have you ever been around a lot of Vasirian blood spilled before?"

"Other than when I've gotten into a fight?"

"Yeah, because I doubt you're focused on the blood then."

"Not really."

"There you go. Don't overthink it. That's my move." She twirled one of her many bracelets anxiously. While she wasn't sure that was the case for what happened or not, it was the easiest solution that didn't put a spotlight on it for further discussion. It kept her from having to expose her own reactions to what took place under the blossoming apricots.

"You're not angry? I figured you'd avoid me."

"Nope," she said, standing up. "You wish you could get rid of me that easily." She waved over her head as she stalked toward the sliding doors. "It ain't happening, bud. Now let's get inside and unpack before we get crappy rooms."

"Rooms are already figured out." Seth gathered the dirty plate and water bottle. "Charlotte and Layla are taking the two beds in the attic room. Blaire and Lukas are taking the master bedroom upstairs, with Aiden taking the room across the hall. So that leaves downstairs for us."

Riley stopped walking, and Seth bumped into her from behind.

"What's wrong?" he asked.

"Um. Us?" She turned around and looked at him. *Is he insane?* "We're sharing a room?"

The corner of Seth's mouth quirked. "Problem?" He stepped around her and went for the kitchen to put the plate in the dishwasher and the water back in the fridge.

"Uh, yes! Why are we the only ones sharing a room?"

"Charlotte and Layla, and Blaire and Lukas are sharing rooms."

"Why can't you share with Aiden?" She climbed up onto a barstool and put her arms on the counter. "You guys share a dorm. It makes sense."

Seth turned and leaned across the counter, mirroring her pose, leaving only a foot or two between them. "Are you that opposed to sharing a room with me?"

Riley looked toward the hallway and then back toward the living room and the stairs that led upstairs. Where was everyone?

"Riley."

"Huh?" She spun back around. "Oh. Yeah, I mean, no. No, I'm not opposed."

"So you want to share a room with me?"

She leaned away. "I didn't say that!" The high pitch of her voice made her cringe.

He smirked. "Technically, you did."

"You tricked me!" She smacked the counter.

"Actually," he said, reaching out and tugging on the string of her hoodie jacket. "I never once said we were sharing a room."

She spluttered. "What? But you said…"

"I *said*, 'that leaves the downstairs for us.'" He let go of the string.

She straightened her back; she had leaned toward him across the counter when he took hold of the string as if drawn like a magnet.

"There are two rooms down here, remember?"

Her mouth gaped open, and she wanted to smack him when his lips twitched. How could she have forgotten? She didn't have the opportunity for another retort because Charlotte and Layla opened the front door and came inside, followed by Kai and Mera.

Riley turned on the stool. "Where've y'all been?"

"Went to the grocery store to grab a few last-minute things for tonight," Layla said, smiling at Charlotte. "It's such a shame you're leaving. You're so fun."

"Aw, you're too sweet. I'm going to miss it down here."

With Charlotte leaving for the University of Georgia at the end of spring break, they decided to throw her a going away party that also doubled as the multi-birthday party for everyone who didn't get to celebrate with all the crazy things that had been happening at the academy in the previous year. They all needed a break, and Charlotte's leaving made a perfect excuse to celebrate and get a reprieve from the constant instability they found themselves part of.

No magic, secret rituals, corrupt councils of madmen, crazy kidnappings, or confusing issues surrounding human mate bonds. Just friends, good food, sand, and fun.

Riley bounded into the living room with a bowl of tortilla chips and another of cheese dip, setting them on the glass top coffee table at the center of the room covered in beer bottles, soda cans, a couple of bottles of harder liquors, and various snacks.

Earlier that night, Lukas and Aiden grilled hamburgers and hot dogs on the grill out back for one last dinner before Mera and Kai left for the airport. Now they were all in their pajamas and lounge clothes, sitting in the living room drinking and playing party games.

She plopped down on the white love seat next to Layla and rubbed her hands together. "So what's next?" She looked around the living room. Seth sat in a plush white chair that matched the sofa and love seat across from her on the other side of the coffee table, and Lukas, Blaire, Aiden, and Charlotte were all squeezed together on the couch directly in front of the table.

They'd already played a few card games and several rounds of Never Have I Ever, which resulted in both Blaire and Riley getting a pleasant buzz and Layla needing to be cut off entirely. Their bodies burned alcohol faster than humans, but they needed a reason for Layla's sobering up to be believable for Charlotte, considering how much Layla needed to drink for that game when all was said and done.

It surprised Riley how different Charlotte was from Blaire in experience, but it made sense considering how sheltered Blaire's family kept her before she came to Blackthorn Academy.

Blaire took a drink of the soda in her hand and looked at Lukas. "What about Truth or Dare?"

"Oh, I've never played that before," Layla said, grabbing a chip from the bowl and dipping it into the cheese.

Seth snorted. "That's such a child's game."

"So?" Blaire frowned. "It'll be fun. Where's your sense of fun?" Apparently, a buzzed Blaire was a pouty Blaire. Lukas shook his head and wrapped his arm around her shoulder, and she leaned into him.

Riley laughed and taunted, "Yeah. Are you afraid, Seth?"

"Me?" He put his elbow on the arm of the chair and rested his cheek against his index finger, his chin resting on his thumb as he cocked his head sideways. "Kind of like you were afraid to share a room?"

Riley spluttered the drink she had just taken.

"Wait, what?" Aiden looked between them. "What's he talking about?"

"Nothing! He's an idiot."

Charlotte leaned over toward Blaire. "What'd I miss?"

"I dunno." Blaire hiccupped. "I missed something too." She giggled.

"Just a little… misunderstanding earlier. Right, Firecracker?"

Riley stuck her tongue out at him.

"I really haven't played that since I was a kid, but it sounds like fun," Charlotte said, taking a small sip from the beer bottle Aiden opened for her.

"I'm game." He shrugged.

"Whatever. No skin off my back." Seth shifted and sat forward, grabbing a beer for himself. "Who's first?"

"Me!" Riley jumped up.

Seth shook his head and grinned, taking a drink.

"Okay, um…" She tapped her lips and looked around at everyone before pointing at Lukas. "Truth or Dare?"

Lukas put his bare feet up on the coffee table, crossing his ankles. "Truth."

"Boooring. Fine. Did you really lose that birthday gift I made you in middle school or did you throw it away?"

His mouth fell open. "What?"

"You heard me." She crossed her arms. "You said you lost it. I worked really hard on that key chain."

Lukas looked over at the others.

Aiden shrugged. "She's like an elephant. Never forgets."

"I had no idea what you were talking about until you said key chain." Lukas shook his head. "The truth is, my old roommate stole it for his girlfriend. She'd seen it on my desk when she visited the dorm and thought it was cute."

"Well, damn." Riley dropped back onto the edge of the love seat. "Ah, well. What can you do? Your turn."

"Do I have to?"

"Yep!"

Lukas glanced at Blaire, who shook her head, burying her face in his shoulder, and he chuckled. He moved his gaze to Aiden, lifting a brow.

"Dare."

"I dare you to lose the shorts and run a lap around the house."

"Dude. The neighbors are out on their deck."

Lukas laughed. "Oh, I know. This is payback for the last time we played this game."

"No way."

"What happened?" Charlotte asked, taking another sip of her drink.

Lukas looked at her. "This asshole made me do the same thing, but around campus. I ended up getting into trouble, and my parents got called in for a disciplinary meeting."

Blaire sat up and looked at Aiden. "You didn't."

"I did," Aiden said, barely containing his own laughter. He took a large drink of his beer. "Fine." He put the bottle on the table. "Payback is a bitch." He stood and whipped his T-shirt off and dropped it on the couch behind him before walking to the sliding glass doors and onto the back patio. As soon as he stuck his thumbs in the waistband of his athletic shorts, Riley looked away. She did not want to see her brother's naked ass.

Charlotte covered her mouth, her eyes widening. "Oh, wow."

Layla and Riley collapsed against each other, giggling. Apparently,

Charlotte didn't look away fast enough.

They continued to play, the dares ramping up and the truths becoming less and less frequent the more alcohol they consumed. The game went well beyond the Truth or Dare games they played in high school, and more like the college games that often got their peers into trouble. Mostly the first-year students. As the course load increased, the parties became less frequent with the upperclassmen at Blackthorn Academy. Riley and her small friend group didn't participate in most of them anyway.

"Okay, Riley," Charlotte said, sitting up on the edge of the couch and giggling before she even got the rest of her sentence out. Aiden had started watering down her drinks to keep her from getting sick, but she'd switched to water in the last ten minutes on her own, so they didn't have to cut her off.

"Um, truth?"

"Nooo, don't do that!"

"Yeah, take the dare," Blaire said, looking at Charlotte, and they both started laughing.

Riley squinted at the conspiratorial way they looked at one another. Those two were up to something, but she was too buzzed to piece it together. She glanced over at Layla for insight to find her dozing against the arm of the love seat. Aiden lifted his hands and Lukas shrugged. Seth waved a hand for her to continue. They apparently had no idea either.

"Fine, fine. But after the last dare you gave me, go easy this time." Her stomach still hurt from all the cheese dip Charlotte dared her to eat.

"I promise not to make you eat anything."

"Thank you," Riley breathed. "Okay. Dare."

"I dare you…" Charlotte glanced at Seth then back to Riley.

Oh, no.

"I dare you to kiss Seth."

No, no, no.

Riley met Seth's gaze with wide eyes. His face paled. He didn't want this either. She tore her gaze away from him. "Veto! Give me another."

"Nope. No exchanges. You used your one veto earlier."

"But he doesn't kiss people." Riley crossed her arms stubbornly. "Like, that should be against the rules to make him."

Charlotte raised her brows at Seth. "Really? I mean if it's going to bother you…"

Aiden rubbed his hand over his mouth, resting his elbow on his knee. "Well, shit." He looked at Seth. "You alright, man?"

Seth grunted then cleared his throat. "Yeah, sure. Come on, let's do this. I mean, at least we don't have to watch Lukas and Aiden kiss again." His nonchalant tone did nothing to ease the swarm of butterflies fluttering in her belly.

"It wasn't *that* bad to watch," Blaire mumbled.

Lukas pulled his shoulder-length hair back and used a hair band to secure it in a low ponytail. "Yeah, that isn't happening again."

The ripple of laughter through the others gave her a moment to stall.

At least they weren't the only two dared to kiss during this game. But Riley never thought this combination would happen. Did she want to kiss Seth? Yes, and no. It scared her. It wasn't her first kiss, but it was Seth, and he didn't look like he wanted to. Which wasn't surprising if he never kissed people, but why was he all of a sudden willing to do it? Either way, the kiss would mean something different to her than him, and that sat in her stomach like a bowling ball.

No, she simply needed to stop overthinking it and look at it objectively. This was a dare in a stupid drinking game. Nothing more. Maybe that's why he was fine with it. It wasn't anything meaningful.

She took a deep breath and stood, walking over to stand in front of Seth's chair between his spread legs. He looked up at her, his hands resting on the arms of the chair.

"Well, get on with it," he said casually, like he didn't have a care in the world.

"It's a two person dare."

"Not necessarily. She dared *you* to kiss *me*."

"Oh, for the love of…" Riley leaned forward and put her hands on his shoulders to stabilize herself. His sudden intake of air cooled the space between them before she brushed her lips across his in a quick kiss. She pulled back just as swiftly. "There, are you satisfied?" She stood and glared at Charlotte.

"Hardly. Aiden and Lukas gave more effort than that."

"What am I supposed to do when he won't participate—"

Riley yelped as Seth sat forward and grabbed her wrist, pulling her down, her knee landing between his legs, the other beside his hip so she straddled his thigh. His other hand cupped the back of her head and brought her face to his, where he captured her lips in a deep kiss, pulling back only a fraction before delving back in when she made a soft sound instinctively at the loss.

She tilted her head as he devoured her mouth. The way he advanced on her, staking a claim, had her reaching her hands to his shoulders to keep herself balanced so she didn't have to sit on his leg. She squeezed the muscle there tightly when he banded the arm that wasn't holding her head prisoner around her back.

His full lips felt like fluffy pillows the way she always imagined when she'd looked at them in the past. His upper lip was thinner and with a severe Cupid's bow, but his lower lip looked bee stung all the time; it was entirely natural.

When she moaned into the kiss, her lips parted, and he took advantage, sliding his tongue along hers, eliciting a whine that would normally embarrass her if her mind wasn't clouded with desire. His answering growl made her body shudder and get weak.

Seth slowed their kiss until it became languid and passionate, less frenzied and consuming. With the scent of sugar cookies, cologne, and his taste invading her senses, Riley lost herself.

The sound of a clearing throat behind her broke through the haze, and Seth jerked away from her, releasing her head and staring at her with wide eyes. His lips glistened, and her own tingled. She wanted to kiss him again, but he looked freaked out.

No, it wasn't just her lips that tingled. Her own eyes widened, and she gasped when she realized the reason he looked freaked out. It wasn't just the kiss. Her fangs had broken through her gums. If Charlotte spotted them, they were screwed.

As much as she wanted to get away from Seth, he was the only thing she could use as a buffer. With that thought in mind, she buried her face on his shoulder, her hands bunching the front of his T-shirt.

Why were her fangs descended? What was wrong with her?

"Jesus, I think I might be pregnant from that kiss," Charlotte said.

Lukas laughed from the kitchen, and Aiden snorted into his beer.

Blaire coughed. "That is such a cheesy thing to say, but I dunno… you do have a point."

"Well, I guess he participated that time," Aiden said, chuckling.

"I told you it's just a stupid child's game," Seth said derisively, but his voice sounded raspy and unsteady. "You're all drunk and this was stupid."

Riley tensed, tucking her head down, staring at her own lap instead of resting against him. She wanted to move. Her fangs had receded, but humiliation weighed heavily in her heart, and she didn't want to face the room.

"Alright, I think you've had too much to drink." Lukas moved around the couch and circled the chair Riley and Seth sat in, carrying Blaire in his arms toward the stairs. "Aiden, can you make sure Charlotte gets upstairs? Layla's already passed out."

"Yeah, man." Aiden helped move Layla into a more comfortable position on the love seat, and she snuggled into the throw blanket he lay over her from the back of the couch. He turned to Charlotte. "Ready for bed? Need anything?"

Charlotte fanned herself. "Some more water. It's so hot. I drank too much." She pushed her curls out of her face and slumped back on the couch.

"Come on," Aiden said. "I'll get some water after I get you to your room."

Aiden guided Charlotte up the stairs, his hand looped around her lower back guiding her wobbly steps. Riley wondered if Charlotte would have a hangover and how bad it would be.

Once the room cleared out, Seth let out a heavy breath. "Everyone's gone. You're safe to get up," he said softly. When she didn't move right away, he put his hands on her upper arms and shifted to move her from the chair, getting up himself. He pushed his hair back and sighed. "I'm going to bed." Without another word, or another glance her way, he left the living room. Moments later, his bedroom door closed down the hall.

She lowered herself to sit in the warm chair he vacated and stared at the empty bottles on the table. The kiss they shared had been the single hottest thing she'd ever experienced in her life, but all she could feel in this moment was shame and rejection. Shame for her behavior and how she fell into his kiss without reservation. Did he now know her secret?

Seth seemed to enjoy the kiss, but were his actions out of passion or experience? The insistent way his lips moved against hers. The caress of his tongue. Did he kiss those other girls the same way?

Her stomach turned sour, and she bolted for the sliding glass door, across the patio, and around the side of the house to vomit into the sand. There was no way she could use the bathroom downstairs that her bedroom shared with Seth's. He would hear it then question her. She couldn't handle the confrontation right now.

Wiping her mouth, she sat on the ground and dug the heels of her palms into her eyes, resting her elbows on her knees.

What had she expected to happen after they kissed? Seth already felt tense before it even happened. Her own taunting was the reason he even initiated anything more than the quick kiss she gave him.

Between the alcohol, the stupid game, and her own mixed-up emotions, she felt like crying. She wouldn't. But she felt like doing it. Instead, she laughed. Laughed until her stomach hurt for a different reason and she felt lighter.

This was Seth.

One stupid kiss that meant nothing to him wouldn't ruin what they had. She wasn't going to lose him over that.

Seth put a pillow over his face. The sound of the ceiling fan in his room did nothing to drown out the noise of Blaire and Lukas overhead. He thought Blaire would be too drunk for sex, but apparently after several hours of sleep, his friends decided to ignore the fact that their bedroom wasn't soundproof.

The need for both a blood packet and sleep kept him restless, but he could hear Riley moving around the hall and in the bathroom connected to his room. He had no idea what she was doing, but he couldn't face her. Not this soon.

Kissing her had been the best and worst thing he could have ever done.

To feel her give in to him and accept his kiss made his heart sing, and the sounds she made set his blood aflame. Even his wildest imagination couldn't hold a candle to what kissing her for real felt like.

How could he just forget it happened?

It took every ounce of willpower he had not to lift her small body into his arms and carry her from the drunken party to his room and show her what he really wanted, because she thought he didn't want her. But that's what he wanted her to think. It was safer that way. For both of them.

He couldn't be what she needed or wanted.

Even if by some miracle she returned his feelings beyond a fleeting crush or physical attraction as she started becoming more experienced as a woman, she wanted her Korrena. Something their own genetic makeup refused to grant him. He would forever curse the entire process of pair-bonding as a result.

A soft knock on his door ripped into his downward spiral, and his jaw clenched. He knew who stood on the other side. He couldn't ignore her.

He tossed the pillow aside and stood from the bed, crossing to his open suitcase in the room's corner to grab a T-shirt. After earlier, he didn't need to be half naked around Riley. Once properly dressed in black sweats and a Lorna Shore band T-shirt, he padded barefoot to the door and opened it. The light from the small lamp on the side table in the hallway illuminated Riley, fresh faced without makeup, ready for bed.

She peered around him into his darkened room. "Did I wake you?"

He leaned his forearm against the door frame, holding the door handle with the other. "No. I can't sleep with all that going on." His gaze moved to the ceiling then back to Riley. They both started laughing when the muffled sounds of the headboard rhythmically hitting the wall picked up, as if summoned by his words. "Want to come in?" When she nodded, he stepped back, flipping on the light switch.

Riley went to his bed and collapsed where he had been lying before, tucking his pillow beneath her head.

"Comfortable?"

"Your bed is more comfortable than mine."

His lips twisted and his brows pinched. "Why do you always say that?" This wasn't even his actual room.

"Because it's true." She yawned. "But also, it's because of the smell."

"The smell?"

"I told you before. You smell like sugar cookies. I want to know what body wash you switched to."

He crossed his arms. "And I told *you* I didn't change my body wash."

This wasn't the first time since December Riley mentioned he smelled like sugar cookies or vanilla. At first, he thought the smell came from Christmas food or other items that rubbed off on him, but as the months progressed, it didn't seem to go away. He had no idea what she referred to, but he used the same body wash, deodorant, and cologne he always had.

"Whatever." She threw the sage green starfish accent pillow used to decorate the tan and white bedding at him, nestling into the bed. "When your pillow smells like this, it's comforting and makes me sleepy." She rolled over and buried her face into the pillow, and he lay his head back, silently praying for patience. Now he would have to smell *her* scent all night long.

"Okay, nope." He approached the bed and rolled her off the pillow onto her back. "Up."

"But I don't wannaaaa," she whined. "Let me sleep here. You take my bed."

"Are you still drunk?"

That made no sense. It'd been hours since the party, so her system should have burned through the alcohol by now. Did she continue drinking after he left her in the living room alone? Was that why she kept walking down the hall?

"Nope," she said, popping the P. She sat up quickly. "Ooo, I know! Let me do your makeup!"

He burst into laughter but fell silent when she said nothing more. "You're serious?"

"Of course." She got up on her knees on the bed, holding her hands out to steady herself, and he stepped forward, taking her forearms to brace her. She studied his face. "Your pale gray eyes would look really pretty with guy liner."

"Guy liner," he said flatly.

"Mmhm." When she lowered herself to sit on her heels, he let go, stepping back. "Come on, Seth. Pleeease. I've had a bad night. Cheer me up. It'll be fun!"

"You've had a bad night? What happened?"

Riley's bright expression fell, and she shut down. He didn't like it one bit. Again, he wondered what happened after he went to bed. But he didn't push her for an answer, not when the urge to fix whatever had her upset ate away at him.

"Alright. Go get your shit."

Her crestfallen expression was enough to make him to cave like a house of cards.

Her quick movements when she pushed off the bed and threw herself into his arms barely gave him the opportunity to react. With his arms around her waist, she looped her arms around his neck and held on tightly, her feet dangling above the floor. "Thank you!" She squirmed, and he gently set her down. "Don't lock me out when I leave, or I promise you'll regret it." Climbing off the bed, she rushed out the door.

The few minutes alone gave him the opportunity to sink onto the bed and take a take a much-needed breath. Regrettable decision. Tiger lilies mingled with his cologne, and the urge to simultaneously throw his pillow across the room and bury his own face in the fabric made him restless. He sat back up and rubbed his eyes before Riley came back into the room, shutting the door behind her.

Climbing onto the bed, she handed him a blood packet and set one beside herself, scooting to sit against the wall and stretching her legs out in front of her. His gaze shifted from the thin cotton shorts with little white bats to her black painted toenails. The allure of her smooth, pale legs after the kiss earlier wasn't doing either of them any favors.

"Drink that, and we'll start," she said, oblivious to his internal struggle, already drinking from her own packet.

He cleared his throat. "Think Charlotte will be alright?"

"Hm?" She licked droplets of blood from her lip. "Yeah. Apparently, her moms aren't opposed to her drinking if she's with them, and now that she's going off to college, they told her as long as she's with someone she trusts, they are okay. They trust Blaire, and I think Sara trusts me and Aiden." She shrugged. "I haven't met Elizabeth, but Sara is cool like that. I mean, it's university. It's going to happen. Better to teach her how to handle herself and who to drink with than have her find out things the hard way. I've heard awful things about some of the human universities and their frat parties."

"How do they know Aiden?" He leaned back against the headboard.

"Well, he's come with me a few times, and he and Charlotte have sorta become friends or something." Her gaze moved off to the floor. "I hope he knows what he's doing. I like Charlotte, but she's not like us."

Seth wondered what was going through her mind. "There's something going on between them?"

That would be surprising. Other than Aiden growing temporary feelings for Blaire when she first came to the academy, he wasn't the type to date around. That situation wasn't normal, though. Something different existed between them that everyone around them saw. Aiden and Blaire held a connection even Lukas couldn't refute or match. A connection as mysterious as a human being bonded as a Korrena.

"I don't know, honestly. I think it's just harmless flirting in texts, but I don't want either of them to get hurt. There are multiple ways that can happen." She reached out and took his empty packet from him. "I'll take this with me when I leave. Lukas told me there's a locked disposal bin on the back patio with the same code to put used packets. Now come here." She grinned, shifting into a cross-legged pose facing him. "Time to get pretty."

Groaning, he sat forward and mirrored her pose, crossing his legs. "Let's get this over with so I can go to sleep." If he were honest, he wasn't ready for her to leave, but he didn't want to admit that. Things between them lately weren't as stable as they used to be.

Riley unzipped her makeup bag and pulled out a packet of makeup wipes and a kohl pencil. "Ready?" She disinfected the pencil and moved up onto her knees again, her thighs against his shins.

"As ready as I'll ever be."

"Tilt your head back and look up here," she said, pointing to her face. She leaned forward, rested her palm on his forehead, and used her thumb to lift his brow, stretching his eyelids as she leaned close to his face, bringing the pencil to his eye. He resisted the urge to flinch away from the foreign object. How did people do this to themselves every day?

The longer she continued, the more he relaxed. Either from growing used to the repetitive movements, or the song she hummed softly as she worked lulling him into releasing his tension.

With anyone else, he'd vehemently refuse to take part in something so asinine, but Riley wasn't just someone else. She might frustrate him beyond belief at times, but her genuine kindness and optimism for life made her shine brighter than any gemstone he'd ever seen. She made people feel like they mattered and did whatever it took to lift their spirits. If she was having a bad night, then he would be that person for her. She deserved that. She needed to know her feelings mattered as much as everyone else's around her, and that it was okay to let go without putting on a mask.

He felt like a hypocrite for thinking that when he wore a mask himself, but he wouldn't let her suffer the consequences of choosing that path if he could help it.

"There." Sitting back on her heels, she blinked a couple of times. "Wow," she breathed. "You look... wow." The pinkness that moved over her cheeks was obvious with her lack of makeup. His eyes fell to her parted lips. She was too close. Way too close. "Seth?"

"Huh?"

"Do you want to see?"

"What?"

"Your eyes." Her expression bunched then she shook her head. "Do you want to see the final result?"

"Oh, yeah. I guess."

Breaking eye contact, she turned to dig out a compact with a mirror from her bag and handed it to him. "I knew your eyes would look amazing lined in black." She nodded to herself. "It's hot. Like, seriously hot."

His pale gray eyes looked even paler framed in thick kohl liner. It wasn't his thing, but he could appreciate the sentiment of Riley's words and understood why guys like his brother Kai wore the liner. But Kai defined gothic.

The liner gave his own eyes greater depth and intensity. People often complimented him on his deep-set brows and piercing eyes. Blaire once said they looked like they could stare into someone's soul. He had laughed it off. He didn't know how to take compliments. With the liner, even he got the appeal. But hearing Riley say he looked hot did weird things to his insides. What was he? A prepubescent boy?

He closed the compact and handed it to her, meeting her eyes.

"So what do you think?"

"Don't tell my brother I let you do this. He'd never let me hear the end of it."

"You still didn't tell me what you think." She huffed and pushed his shoulder.

Snatching her wrist as she pulled her hand back, he froze when she gasped.

The move had been reflexive, but it was also what he did in the living room before he pulled her into his lap. He looked down at his hand wrapped around her tiny wrist that was free from all the bracelets she normally wore. He didn't often see her in her pajamas. Free from all the bracelets, stockings, boots, punk princess clothing, and glam makeup. She was beautiful with and without it, but seeing her porcelain skin bare lit something in his hindbrain, and he couldn't help but want to touch her.

His thumb brushed the soft skin at her wrist as he stared at the blue vein beneath the pale surface. The pulse that thumped with each pass of his thumb called to him.

"Seth, please," she whispered, and his gaze snapped up. Wide blue eyes stared back at him, and her quickened breathing made the large white bat on her black T-shirt move up and down.

What was she asking for?

Riley's expression shuttered as he stared dumbly at her, and she pulled her wrist from his hold. Grabbing her makeup bag and the blood packets, she rushed out of the room, slamming the door behind her.

He lifted his hand and glared down at the trembling appendage as if it offended him. Collapsing on his back, he covered his eyes, planting his feet on the bed with his knees bent. They had to get back to normal. He wouldn't lose her because he couldn't keep his heart and cock in check.

Riley meant more to him than the world, and he would endure anything to ensure she stayed part of his life.

6

Playing with Fire

The rest of their time at Tybee Island passed without incident. While they occasionally drank, they never got so far into it again that it devolved into drunken party games leading to poor decisions and awkward feelings. After she fled Seth's room to avoid telling him to stop touching her because it hurt her heart for him to do it, Riley had done her best to keep a cheerful face. Eventually, the smile became natural again when she realized he wasn't angry with her for running away.

Classes resumed for the students of Blackthorn Academy at the end of March, but Professor Velastra granted Riley and the others an extra week off while they waited for their summons to Europe for last minute preparations. Their professors had sent over assignments for them to work on in their downtime, but with the mid-term projects finished before spring break, there wasn't a lot to do the first week back.

Riley put her tray on the table, joining Aiden, Lukas, and Seth. "Where's Blaire?"

"Professor Velastra called her to her office before we left our dorm," Lukas said, opening a bottle of water. "Layla isn't with you?"

Riley smoothed her short, pleated uniform skirt beneath her and sat. She scooted her chair forward, looking at her brother. "She's with her roommate having lunch." She lifted a slice of pepperoni pizza from her tray and took a bite.

"Are you going by Charlotte's mom's shop today?" Aiden asked her, setting down his fork.

"No, why?"

"Charlotte told me her mom wanted to discuss plans for the drive to Athens next week."

"Athens?" Seth asked.

Aiden looked at him. "Yeah, I told Charlotte's moms I would go with them to help Charlotte get moved into her apartment there. I didn't want to leave two women and Charlotte, as small as she is, to deal with moving furniture."

Blaire put her tray on the table. "You're going with Charlotte? I'm so glad to hear that. She's been worried about her moms driving back alone through the Atlanta traffic; they don't travel a lot." She pulled out her cell phone from the back pocket of her jeans.

"Finally gave it to her?" Seth looked at Lukas, and Blaire smiled, sitting down next to him and tapping on the screen.

"It only took me five months," he said with a chuckle.

Lukas bought Blaire a cell phone as a birthday gift, since she'd never owned one before because of her restrictive family situation, but before he could celebrate her birthday with her in October, everything fell apart with the kidnapping and then the experiments.

"How do you like it?"

Blaire looked up from her phone at Aiden. "It's not too hard to figure out. Some stuff I've had to have Lukas help me with, like navigating the app store, and how some apps work, but I think I'm getting it. The important stuff I know now, at least."

Riley swallowed a bite of her side salad. "Do you have our numbers?"

"Yep. Lukas programmed them all in last night." She tapped on her phone for a minute or two, and one by one, everyone's phone made noises. "Now you have mine." She smiled. "I was up late Face Timing with Charlotte." She smiled at the device in her hand. "I think it's really cool I can do stuff like that. You know, see her without going into town and setting up time out of school and her helping her moms. We'll still be able to see each other when she's away at UGA."

It warmed Riley's heart to see Blaire so excited about something they all took for granted. In general, all students at Blackthorn Academy came from some degree of wealth. Not all were millionaire-level rich; but at a minimum, students of the academy were part of the upper class. Their kind didn't live for centuries without amassing wealth in reserve to pass down through the generations.

Lukas leaned over, looping his arm over the back of Blaire's chair, pointing at her phone screen and talking low. She started laughing when he whispered something in her ear, and he smiled.

Seeing the way the two of them interacted, knowing everything it took to get them to this place, brought tears to Riley's eyes. Blaire was her best friend. Lukas was her brother without blood. They deserved it.

"So what did the professor have to say?" Lukas asked when Blaire put her phone away.

She glanced around the cafeteria and leaned toward the table, lowering her voice. "Blackthorn Clan contacted her while we were at Tybee Island. She waited until our return, but next Thursday we'll catch a flight out of Atlanta nonstop to the United Kingdom."

Riley frowned. "Nonstop? So private jet?"

"No. The clan thought we might draw attention to ourselves from the wrong people."

"That doesn't make sense."

"Actually, it does," Seth said, glancing at Riley. "If word has spread in Georgia about the Order's arrest and the connection to the students of the academy, there's no telling if the Vasirian who work at the airport won't recognize us."

"Yeah, but those same Vasirian work the public terminals too."

Aiden shook his head. "I get it. The likelihood of something happening in front of the humans in the main areas of the airport, or aboard a commercial flight, is slimmer than being isolated for a private flight."

Lukas nodded, tossing his empty blood packet on his tray. "We already have to watch ourselves around the academy so others won't know our involvement in the trial. The older adults are likely to take greater issue with students being involved."

"I won't be able to fly with you guys," Aiden said, setting down his can of soda.

Riley frowned. "Why not?"

"I leave sometime next week to help with Charlotte's move, remember? I'll have to fly out separately when I get back."

Blaire's brows puckered. "Couldn't you get Sara and Elizabeth to drop you off in Atlanta on the way back?"

He shook his head. "I know it isn't that much farther, but I want to make sure they make it back. Mom already said she'll drive me to the airport if you guys leave before I get finished. I kinda already expected this to happen."

At least Aiden thought ahead. The idea of her brother not coming with them when tensions were high in the Vasirian world made her uneasy, but it wasn't like Riley wanted Charlotte and her moms to be stuck either.

"Okay, so we have a week to go before we need to leave." Riley reached over and took the small brownie off Seth's tray that he hadn't eaten yet, grinning when he batted her hand away. "What are we going to do in the meantime? Spring break is still here for us."

"I've already got everything I need." Blaire looked at Lukas. "Do you need anything?"

"I don't need anything special."

"Well, I wanna go shopping," Riley said.

Seth chuckled. "Of course you do."

She glared at him. "Yes, I do." Looking back at Blaire, she said, "It's going to be chillier in Europe than here. Do you have anything for colder weather?"

"Uh, yeah? I mean, it can't be much colder than winters around here, right?"

"Well, I Googled it last night. Their March and April highest temperatures are like our February and March lowest. You might need something a little warmer."

"You just need an excuse to shop."

Riley spun in her seat and pointed her finger at Seth. "I don't need an excuse, but I'll take one." She went to turn back around but paused. "Oh, and you're coming with."

"Excuse me?"

"You're. Coming. With. Us."

"Who decided that?"

"I did."

Seth crossed his arms over his chest. "What's in it for me?"

"The pleasure of my company."

"You're not nearly as funny as you think you are."

"Well, I think I'm a delight. Hilarious, really."

"Whatever."

"Oh, come on." She sat forward in her chair and grasped his forearm. "Please come with us. I want you to show me where you get that sugar cookie stuff you use."

"I told you I don't use anything that smells like sugar cookies." Seth glanced at the others at the table, who showed varying degrees of amusement at the exchange. "Can one of you please tell her I don't smell like a bakery?"

Aiden leaned over and took a big whiff of Seth's T-shirt sleeve. "Sorry, but I just smell his cologne. I've never smelled cookies in our dorm."

Riley gawped. "What?"

"Yeah, I don't think he smells like cookies either," Blaire said.

"But he…" Riley lifted Seth's arm and put her nose to his wrist, inhaling deeply. The scent of vanilla sweetness hit her sharply. "Here! Smell this!" Seth slapped his other hand on the table to catch himself from face planting into the surface when Riley pulled his arm across his tray toward Aiden. "His wrist smells like it really heavily."

Aiden raised a brow and leaned down, giving a sniff. He sat back in his chair and shook his head. "Nothing. I have no idea what you're talking about."

Riley released Seth's arm, and he rubbed his wrist.

"I told you. Maybe you need to go to the health wing and get your sinuses checked out."

As much as they called her crazy, Riley knew what she smelled. The sweet scent comforted her and helped her sleep the one time he'd left it on her pillow. If it was a new cologne or body wash she wanted to get her hands on it and use it in her room. Something to help relax her mind before bed because she always had difficulty shutting down her thoughts and letting herself drift away to sleep, and things like sleeping pills weren't strong enough. She'd even tried buying a few warm vanilla sugar scented candles and lotions, and a cookie scented set too, but nothing matched the unique scent Seth carried. Maybe it was the combination of his cologne and the cookies? She'd have to find out what cologne he used, too.

Blaire looked at Lukas. "Maybe I should get a new coat. Mine is pretty old."

"I don't mind going. You going to go?" Lukas asked Seth.

Seth rolled his eyes. "You know I will." His eyes cut to Riley, and he shook his head. "I'm not buying a milkshake this time."

"But!"

"No."

"Fine. I'll buy my own."

Aiden dropped the crust of his pizza on his tray. "It's a shame we couldn't spend more time at Tybee Island. It'd been a long time since I went to the beach."

"I know." Riley opened a can of soda and took a drink. "Think we can go back before the flight?"

"We'd have to rent a car and pack everything then repack and do your shopping trip before the day you guys leave." Aiden shook his head. "We'd barely get a day or two to really spend there. Besides, I still have to go to Athens first."

"Speaking of Tybee Island," Blaire said to Riley, and everyone looked at her. "I want to talk to you about the Truth or Dare game."

Riley nearly spit out her drink, coughing and choking it down. She quickly set the can down and pushed back from the table, standing up. "Nope. Goodbye."

Seth stood and reached for her, looping his arms around her waist and dropping back into his seat, taking her with him. "Easy, Firecracker."

"Hey, it's not anything bad," Blaire assured her, but Riley's mind was a riot of panic.

She didn't want to talk about the kiss, and now she was sitting in Seth's lap thinking about it. She squirmed on his lap, and he grunted as her elbow connected with his ribs.

When she tried to stand again, his hold tightened, and she froze at the real and alarming feeling of him swelling in his slacks. Her uniform skirt and fishnet stockings weren't much of a barrier for her to be mistaken in what she felt.

Seth was hard.

Impressively so.

She'd been in his lap dozens of times before—more times than she probably should have over the years considering their sibling-ish friendship status—but he always positioned her on his thighs or even in the chair between his legs. This time she'd landed differently.

In reflex, she squirmed to position herself so he wasn't pressed so firmly against her, and a drawn-out hiss entirely too close to her ear was followed by a low growl. She froze and swallowed at the invisible ball stuck in her throat, suddenly too hot all over. Her muscles hurt from the tension she held in her body.

"I just wanted to mention that I saw your fangs after you two kissed"

"Shit," Aiden said. "Did Charlotte see?"

"I don't think so. I hope not. She didn't mention it. But I wanted to mention it because I was worried if *sanguis manie* wasn't the cause. I wouldn't have mentioned around everyone else, but I still have so much to learn about Vasirian and thought having everyone's input would help." Blaire frowned.

Riley didn't think Blaire overstepped, even if the subject embarrassed her. She sometimes didn't keep up with her blood packets, so it didn't surprise her that Blaire suspected *sanguis manie.*

The cause wasn't blood mania though. During the party, despite a decent buzz from the alcohol, her mind stayed lucid, and she'd had enough blood before the kiss to know that what caused her reaction was unrelated to *sanguis manie.* Still, the very real and very insistent urge to bite Seth after the kiss they shared was weird, and she didn't know what to do with it.

"Oh, no. Not at all. I had blood that morning, but I wasn't in need or anything."

"Then what happened?" Blaire asked.

"I don't really know," she whispered. She didn't want to lie to her friend, but she supposed it wasn't a *complete* lie. She couldn't say for one hundred percent certainty that the reason her fangs descended and the urge to bite Seth were related to arousal prompted by the kiss, but it wasn't much of a stretch to assume a correlation, and it terrified her.

She needed her brain to stay far, far, far away from those thoughts. But sitting there on Seth's lap—even positioned away from the erection just inches away—the thoughts wormed their way through the cracks into her mind and set up home. It was hard to ignore the familiar tingle in her gums.

"Either way, I know Charlotte didn't see. That's why I didn't move until she left the room. Plus, I needed to cool down. I was irritated about having to kiss Seth." She snapped her fingers and pointed. "Hey! Maybe that's why my fangs descended." Her forced laugh likely fooled no one.

"If you say so," Blaire said quietly.

Yep, fooling no one.

Riley's back straightened when Seth leaned forward and whispered into her ear, "If it irritated you so much, why did you moan into my mouth?"

He likely meant it as a joke, judging by the chuckle that followed. It wasn't the first time he'd made a perverted joke just to get a rise out of her or make her blush.

Blaire, Aiden, and Lukas had already turned their attention away from them, discussing the trip to Europe, and Riley had finally had enough of Seth having the upper hand.

It was time to be bold.

Time to fight fire with fire.

If he wanted to embarrass her and tease her, she could play the game. Maybe.

Taking a deep breath through her nose, she rocked her hips back against him, meeting the hardness she'd shrunk from previously, and he hissed in response. It surprised her how much she enjoyed the feeling of not only the power of making him respond to her, but also the physical feeling of moving against him.

Seth shifted and leaned in, his lips grazing the shell of her ear as he whispered, "You're playing with fire." The sound of his voice, raspy against her skin, sent goose bumps over her legs and arms.

"What do you mean?" As much as she tried for steadiness, her voice cracked with the soft-spoken question.

His fingers dug into her hips slightly and he shifted his hips forward and up against her, allowing her to feel the entire ridge of what he was working with. She had to bite the inside of her cheek and swallow a gasp to keep anyone from hearing. She did not expect that response when she tried to match his teasing game. This didn't feel like teasing.

Settling and shifting to rest one hand against her stomach, the other on her thigh, he leaned back in to whisper, "You don't want this. This isn't what we do." He paused. "Or did that kiss change things?"

Riley found it difficult to hear him over the sound of the blood rushing in her ears. Was she hyperventilating? No. But she felt like she would pass out. She couldn't even find the fortitude to shift off of his obvious arousal, and it set up an ache low in her core she couldn't ignore.

"Hey," Blaire said, her face pinched in concern. "Are you alright?"

"W-what? Yeah, fine. What's up?"

"You're really red and breathing hard."

Aiden turned to look at Riley. "Yeah, you don't look so good. Are you sure you're okay?"

Riley waved a hand in front of her face rapidly, as if swatting mosquitoes. "Just thirsty," she said, voice pitching and cracking again. She cleared her throat. "I'm good." Picking up Seth's soda, she took a long drink, swallowing down hard when Seth slid his hand beneath the one she had been digging her nails into his thigh with.

How long had she been doing that?

He slowly ran his fingertips across her thigh to the edge of her skirt and stopped. The heat from his palm against her burned through the fishnet against her skin.

Snapping out of the haze of lust, and the whirlwind of panic her mind fell into, she jumped up from Seth's lap. "I think I'm tired. I'm gonna take a nap."

"If you're sure you'll be okay…"

Riley smiled at Blaire, grateful for her concern. "Yep. I'll call you if I need." She stepped away from Seth and didn't look back.

His words were absolutely correct. This wasn't what they did. They'd been together since diapers, and never once had they breached a line like this. Never had she felt him physically aroused—or even flaccid. It was a line never crossed. It wasn't who they were to each other.

Ever since the day he sampled her blood, and the kiss at Tybee Island, things between them shifted on a strange pendulum between uncertainty and normalcy.

But no matter how the lines blurred, and as much as what just happened felt good physically, she wouldn't be another notch on Seth's bedpost.

He'd likely not been with anyone lately and was just wound up, and he found her conveniently fun to tease, like always. Only taking it too far because for once she teased back. That had to be the reason. It was her fault it went so far. How could she do something so stupid?

He wasn't serious.

She needed to protect her heart.

7

Knowledge

Riley sat on the edge of the large marble fountain in the center of the cobblestone courtyard in front of the main building of Blackthorn Academy, tapping the heels of her knee-high boots against the side of the stone as she swayed her legs, unable to sit still. The buckles on her boots clinked and added to the melody she created with each rap of her heels as she looked around, waiting for Blaire to finish up at the library on the third floor.

The rows of red and burgundy stained-glass windows framed in ivy leaves lining the front wall of the main building reflected the bright midday sun. Even from the valley below the academy, past the main gates and down the tree-lined road, the bold, bloody mosaic caught the eye of the town's residents as they walked through Valley Center Plaza. While beautiful from the outside, in the darker halls of the interior at the right time of day, the light pouring through the windows bathed the marble floors in blood.

Students moved about the courtyard, going to their classes, the dorm buildings to the left of the fountain, and the staff buildings to the right. People watching fascinated Riley. The things people did when they thought no one was watching were especially interesting. Like the couple hiding beneath the shade of a palmetto tree at the edge of the dorm building making out and even exchanging blood. And the guy sitting on one of the stone benches between the flowering bushes in front of the hedge maze learning crochet from one of the lunch workers. Riley smiled. The same lunch worker had helped her on her last sewing project for her class.

Her gaze shifted from the hedge maze behind her at the heavy slam of the main building's large double doors. She jumped to her feet as Blaire descended the marble steps.

"Hungry?"

"Starving." Blaire motioned to the square, hard-bottom cooler tote sitting on the edge of the fountain. "That our lunch?"

"Oh no, that's the cooler from the trip the blood packets were in. Aiden left it in my room and texted me to drop it off at his dorm while he's gone with Charlotte and her moms. Do you want to go change and get Lukas while I do that? We can head into town after."

Riley had already taken the opportunity to change while waiting, opting for a fun outfit of sheer black stockings with a spiderweb design, a black pleated skirt with mini chains around the waist, and a holey sweater striped in black and lime green. By the time she finished, she didn't think there was enough time to stop by her brother and Seth's dorm room before Blaire would be ready, so she waited to drop off the cooler.

"Yeah, I don't wanna wear my uniform to the restaurant or mall. Lukas texted me saying he was waiting for me, anyway. I think he's going to have Seth meet us in the courtyard."

"Is Seth in his room?"

"It didn't sound like it from the way Lukas talked, but I don't know. I'll tell Lukas to text him."

When they reached the dorm building and went inside, Riley stopped off at the floor below Blaire and Lukas's room and headed down the hallway to Seth and Aiden's room.

Humming to herself, she twisted the doorknob, pushing the door open. Aiden said Seth would leave it unlocked for her today when he was gone, so she thought nothing of it until she stepped inside to the sound of giggling and the sight of a girl with long brown hair with blonde ends straddling a body on Seth's bed. Hands rested on her thighs, bunching up her uniform skirt, but nothing else was exposed.

The girl bent forward, but before she could kiss him, Seth moved his head to the side, causing her head to tuck into his neck. Seth's gunmetal eyes locked with Riley's, and he jolted.

"What's the matter, baby?" the girl asked, sitting up and moving her hands to the buttons of her shirt; her plaid mini tie was already undone.

Seth reached up, stilled her hands, and shook his head.

"Sorry to interrupt." Riley rolled her eyes and moved to her brother's side of the room to set the cooler on his bed. "Should probably lock the door next time."

She tried to sound nonchalant, like catching him with a girl didn't affect her; but with the things that happened between them lately, it was hard to achieve. It wasn't the first time she'd seen a girl all over him. It wouldn't be the last.

"Maybe you should knock," the girl said, twisting her upper body on Seth's, still not having the decency to get off him. "This isn't your room, you know."

"I'm delivering a cooler for my *brother*." Riley put her hands on her hips. "That a problem? I have permission to be here."

"Ugh." The girl laid her head back and made a huff of exasperation. She turned narrowed eyes to Riley. "Can you not read the room?"

"Not really," Riley said, feigning innocence. "I didn't see any words."

"Words? What are you… No, never mind. I don't care." The girl turned back to Seth and put her hands on his stomach. "You've done what you came here for. You can leave."

Riley's eyes moved from the girl, who dismissed her like she owned the place, to Seth. He still stared at her in frozen silence. Was the uncomfortable expression on his face from being caught in the act or the fact that she was in his space while another girl sat on top of him—even if they were both dressed?

When they continued staring at each other, the girl groaned in frustration and glared at Riley. "Why are you still here? Can't you see we're busy?"

Why *was she still here? Why couldn't she get her feet to move?*

"Unless you're wanting a show? I mean, that's kinda weird considering the rumors, but I always thought they were bullshit."

Don't take the bait… Don't take the bait…

"Rumors?"

Stupid, stupid.

"Everyone knows you follow Seth around like a lost puppy dog, craving whatever scraps he'll throw your way." She shook her head and laughed, taking Seth's tie in her hand and stroking the fabric. "I mean, they say you two are like siblings, so watching him fuck me would be awkward, right?"

The way she dragged the word "fuck" made Riley cringe. She didn't want to think about what they were about to do.

"But that is where the rumors come in. Where my theory comes in."

Seth shifted his eyes finally from Riley to the girl. Still, he didn't move her. "What are you talking about?"

"Mm, just a little thought a few of us girls had about your weird little puppy over there."

"Get on with it, Michelle."

The girl—Michelle—smoothed her hands over his chest and glanced over at Riley. "We think she uses the little sister act to stay close to you. That she wants you and knows she's too weird. I mean, she's not exactly the type of girl that suits you."

Riley wrapped her arms around herself, feeling awkward for her choice of clothing. She always wore her punk goth princess style with pride. Alternative fashion was something she'd loved since she first saw glam rock bands as a little girl. But Michelle was right about her not looking like the girls that suited Seth.

"I think she knows what she's doing. Staying close in hopes you'll come to the epiphany that 'the one who truly knows me and loves me has been here the whole time.'" The nasal voice Michelle used to mock the grand epiphany made Riley want to plug her ears. "It's ridiculous and childish to think like that. This isn't a movie, it's real life. You should grow up, quit pretending you know him, realize he doesn't want you, that you're just an annoying brat, and let the adults do adult things."

Riley stood frozen, listening to the girl call her out. It wasn't all a lie. But it wasn't how things were, either. Riley didn't follow Seth in hopes he'd notice her and finally love her. They shared something these girls he took to bed would never understand.

She *did* know him. Better than they ever would.

Steeling her resolve, she narrowed her eyes and waved a hand toward Seth. "Ask him to kiss you."

"What?" Michelle gaped then laughed. "You really do want to

watch us? That's weird. Kinky, but weird."

"No. I just know him well enough"—*better than you*—"to know he won't do it."

Seth's brows shot up, his lips parting.

Michelle laughed loudly. "Honey, you're delusional. If we're going to fuck, we're going to kiss."

Riley crossed her arms and raised both brows in challenge, cocking her hip. Seth wouldn't do it. He'd told her as much. Judging by his surprised expression, he didn't expect her to remember that little gem. She only wished she knew the why behind his choice.

"This is stupid," Michelle scoffed and looked down at Seth. "Fine then. Kiss me." She leaned down, and like before, right before her lips could make contact, Seth turned his head. "What the hell, Seth?"

"I don't kiss."

"Why not?" The pouty way Michelle said the words made Riley cringe. "I'm sure you've kissed plenty of girls."

"Not really."

"That doesn't make sense. You—"

"Don't have to kiss to fuck," Seth finished for her. When she seemed taken aback, he added, "Kissing is too intimate."

"What do you call sex?"

"Scratching an itch."

"What the hell?"

Riley wanted to laugh at the expression on Michelle's face. Challenging her not only burst the delusional bubble the girl was in but revealed why Seth avoided kissing. He didn't think sex was intimate? It made her sad to know he felt that way. Sex was supposed to be meaningful.

"Whatever," Michelle said with a giggle, responding to something Riley missed while in her thoughts. "I don't need to kiss you to get what we both want." She glanced at Riley. "Nice try, but it's still happening."

Seth met Riley's eyes. She couldn't tell what he was thinking, but she should leave. She just couldn't make herself go. Knowing Seth, she knew what would happen when the door closed, and it made her sick.

Her gaze moved to the small turtle plushie on the side of his desk. She'd given him it when they graduated from high school. No one else got the meaning, but they knew. Because she knew. She knew Seth well, no matter how much some random girl—Michelle—wanted to challenge otherwise.

Riley knew Seth's favorite animal. *Lion*—at least that's what he told others, but it really was tiny turtles. His favorite color. *Blue.* Knew his favorite food. *Cheeseburger with extra cheese, extra pickles, and no mustard—never mustard.* His favorite band. *Avenged Sevenfold.*

She knew him; no upperclassman could take that from her. Still, the words stung. What did superficial knowledge matter in the long run? Even if it came from a lifetime of being together.

Like Aiden, who she would never in a million-trillion years feel anything romantic for, Seth would find his pair and move on. They'd get together for holidays—maybe. Because Seth wasn't *really* their brother.

"Get out."

Riley flinched at the low, dangerous tone of Seth's voice when it tore her from her thoughts. She stepped back on instinct and motioned over her shoulder, her mouth parting to say goodbye.

Seth wanted her gone.

He was kicking her out.

He'd never spoken so harshly to her that she could recall. Not with the kind of venom that laced his tone when he demanded she leave so he could be with Michelle. So he could touch her without interruption. Have sex with her without his annoying little sister in the way.

Seth didn't care about her feelings.

Michelle was right.

All these years she chased after Seth and he put up with her, cleaning up her messes, keeping her out of trouble, protecting her and guiding her when she needed, and this was the moment he finally had enough.

Her thoughts rounded and rounded in circles, like a runaway carousel she couldn't stop.

She would *not* cry.

She would not give the girl he chose the satisfaction of seeing her heart break in half.

"About fucking time." Michelle's breathy laugh as she turned her head to the side and wiggled her fingers at Riley was the only sound in the room. "Toodles, poodle."

"No." Seth grabbed the girl by the hips and set her off him on the bed, pushing himself upright. "You. Get the fuck out of my room. Now."

"What? You can't be serious. You're kicking *me* out?"

"As a heart attack."

Riley rubbed her arms up and down in a vain attempt to self soothe. Seth wasn't happy and would let her hear it as soon as the girl left.

Michelle stood abruptly and put a hand on her hip. "You're seriously kicking me out"—she waved her hand down her body from her ample bust line to her curvy hips—"for *her*?" She pointed at Riley, curling her lip. "She's a shrimp who isn't much bigger than my little sister who's a freshman in high school." Glaring, Michelle crossed her arms. "I'd really invest in a push-up bra if I were you. You're in college. Guys like more than a handful here." The laugh that followed her insult was bitter and cold.

Without warning, Seth flew off the bed and stepped in front of Michelle, blocking Riley's view of her. He pointed at the door as he leaned in toward her; the anger in his voice was unmistakable. "Get the fuck out before I do something I'll regret."

"Whatever." Michelle grabbed her cardigan off the foot of his bed and pointed her finger right in Seth's face. "I only needed you to get back at Zach, anyway. I didn't have to sleep with you to make him believe it. Everyone knows you're a fuck boy, Seth."

Seth said nothing while Michelle spit her vitriol. He didn't have to. This was a classic response to rejection. Try to hurt them more than they hurt you. Still, the things she said pissed off Riley. Seth had slept with multiple girls, but he was more than a "fuck boy." There was so much more to him than his body and what others could get out of it.

Michelle huffed and trailed the same finger she had just pointed in his face down his chest. "It's a shame you didn't get to take a ride on this. We could have had fun."

Seth's jaw twitch in response. He finally snatched her wrist and led her to the door.

Michelle jerked her arm free. "Go to hell. You have fun with the mutt over there." The parting look she shot over her shoulder before opening the door made the hairs on Riley's arm prickle.

Once the door slammed shut, Seth exhaled heavily, turning to Riley. "Are you alright?"

Riley still held her arms around her upper body and shook her head, lifting her face to smile at him. "Yeah, yeah, I'm okay." She cleared her throat.

He stepped toward her and she tensed, ready for the admonishment for interrupting him. For making him face the wrath of a woman scorned.

But instead of scolding her or saying anything at all, he looped his arms around her shoulders and pulled her into his arms in a tight embrace, resting his cheek against the top of her head.

It took a few moments for her brain to catch up, but Riley finally relaxed and lifted her arms to wrap around his lower back, gripping his uniform shirt tightly.

Comforting her without words happened a lot. Seth wasn't completely inept and unable to use words to give reassurance, but sometimes the best comfort he provided came from his warm embrace. It wasn't like he could refute or agree with things Michelle said. Riley didn't want him to. Her hidden feelings—and worse, her petite body shape—wasn't something she delighted in discussing with anyone.

They stayed like that for several minutes before he gently released her to look down into her eyes. "I'm sorry for that."

"You didn't do anything wrong."

"I should have kicked her out sooner. She shouldn't have said those things to you. I'm sorry."

Riley shrugged and looked to the side. "What if some of it was true?"

"What?"

"I mean, not the wanting you and following you around because of that, but the getting in your way part."

"Huh?"

Sighing, she walked over to lean against Aiden's desk, clasping her hands in front of her. "She called me an annoying sister following you like a puppy. It's true." She laughed and met Seth's eyes. "If I hadn't been here, and you hadn't felt the need to once again protect me, you could be having sex right now."

"Like hell," he said with a scoff. "I wouldn't touch that if you paid me."

Riley twisted her fingers, laughing softly under her breath. "Sure looked like you were headed in that direction when I showed up."

"That was before I knew what a disgusting piece of work she is." Tugging off his plaid tie, he tossed it on the bed. "I have no interest in someone who talks to you like that."

He turned away and started unbuttoning his uniform shirt, tossing it on the bed and leaving nothing on but a white T-shirt tucked into black slacks.

"I'm still sorry."

"I'd rather know and go without sex than not know. I didn't even really want to in the first place, but it's been a while."

"Oh," she mumbled, looking at her boots. She didn't know what to do with that information, or what it meant.

"Come here."

She looked up to find him sitting on the edge of his bed, staring at her intently. "Why?"

"Because I said so."

"And I'm just supposed to do it because you said so?"

"That's right," he said lightly, his voice measured and coaxing.

She pushed off the desk and walked toward him. "Guess I really am a dog then," she said with a self-deprecating laugh.

Reaching out, he snatched her arm and pulled her to him until her knees bumped into the bed between his legs. He gripped the back of her knees and looked up at her.

"You can fuck off with that right now."

Riley sighed and stared down at him. Her eyes settled on his nose, not quite brave enough to meet his eyes.

"I'm serious. You are not a dog. If you really didn't want to do something, you wouldn't. If you really meant no, I wouldn't make you. But we both know that sometimes you need that."

"Need what?"

His grip tightened, and her eyes drifted up to his. The seriousness she found there unnerved her. "Need someone to guide you." Inhaling deeply through his nose, he dropped his head to her stomach, his hair flattening against the chains on her waist as he stared down at his lap. "Someone to tell you what to do. To take control. To get you out of your head."

He slowly lifted his head to stare into her eyes, and the intensity made her shift and want to step away from him, but his hold on her legs was firm and unrelenting.

Why did he think that?

And why did the idea of it sound like heaven?

It always confused her why when he bossed her around and took the situation into his own hands, the noise in her head wasn't so loud. In those moments, she simply acted, did as she was told, and let him lead. Because she trusted Seth. He wouldn't hurt her or allow someone else to hurt her, either. He wouldn't push her or demand from her if he knew it wasn't what she truly wanted. With him, she could let go and just be.

And apparently, he knew it.

He could see past her mask to the chaos of her mind. The internet browser with seventy different tabs open with three songs playing at once.

The reality of what that meant slammed into her with a force that made her chest tighten and her head swim.

She always felt Seth wielded the power to break her. Now she knew it to be true, like she knew they needed blood to survive.

Seth held complete power over her, and she was helpless to change it.

"Tell me what you're thinking." His soft cadence made her stomach flip.

"No," she whispered, trying to breathe around the invisible obstruction in her throat that cut her breaths short, clamping her lips tightly in defiance.

"Please."

"You know too much about me." Her voice sounded stilted to her own ears as she yielded to him. Why couldn't she sound strong?

"And that's bad?" He finally let her go, and she stepped away to allow him to stand and go to his closet. "I would think after all these years we'd know a lot about each other."

When he stepped into his closet, Riley let out a much-needed heavy breath. Was he acting obtuse on purpose? If he wanted to not get deep with it, she should be thankful.

Sinking down to sit on his bed, she waited for him to come out of the closet. Might as well hang around and go with him to meet everyone. She didn't want to chance a run in with Michelle, anyway. It wasn't like she was afraid of her; she just didn't want to deal with her.

Seth stepped out wearing a pair of medium wash jeans that hugged his thighs and hips and a black V-neck T-shirt with a plain chain necklace. He finger-combed his hair back off his forehead and approached her. He looked good with his tattoos on display down both arms. Where else he had gotten ink since he began getting work done after turning eighteen two years ago this August? He had to have gotten more. He said he wanted more.

"Stop looking at me like that." He sat down next to her, his eyes studying her intently.

"Like what?"

"Like you're giving me an invitation to take everything I've ever wanted from you and more."

She blinked, her brows creasing in the middle. "What are you talking about? I didn't look at you like anything." Her lips twisted to the side. "What do you want?"

Seth shifted to turn on the bed and face her. His gaze kept moving from her eyes to her mouth, and her heart rate kicked higher at the dark look in his eyes.

"Forget it. We don't have time." He stood. "Lukas texted me while I was in the closet. They're waiting at the fountain."

What did he even mean?

Too much happened too fast for her to wrap her head around what occurred, and now he wanted some unnamed thing from her.

How could she give him something she didn't understand?

The way he looked at her reminded her of the kiss they shared, and as much as she might regret it if it happened again, that look fanned a burning need to experience it again.

8

GIFTS

Finally, the day came for the flight to Europe. After clearing security, Professor Velastra led Riley, Seth, Blaire, and Lukas through the crowds to the boarding gate where they would fly from Hartsfield-Jackson Atlanta Airport to London Heathrow Airport on a direct eight-hour flight. Lukas complained about the long flight, but if they had booked shorter flights with layovers, the travel time would more than double.

Seth was eager to be on the other side of the Atlantic Ocean on solid ground. Aside from a much longer day, having a layover would force him to experience takeoffs and landings multiple times; he could live without that.

Despite arriving hours before sunrise, the airport bustled with people going from one destination to another. The cloying smells of various perfumes, colognes, body odor, and cleaning supplies irritated his nose. Too many bodies, not enough space. He adjusted his bag and sighed when the muscle beneath his eye twitched. At least on the plane he would sit beside one of his friends and not a random stranger—he hoped.

Baggage check in went as smoothly as he expected. When Riley showed up in the parking lot in front of the administration building back at Blackthorn Academy, Seth took one look at her overstuffed bag and knew it would be a problem. When the attendants at the airport weighed her bag, his suspicions were confirmed. This led to Blaire and Seth opening their modestly-packed suitcases to allow Riley to divide her excess between them.

"The Oracle will meet us in London," Professor Velastra said as they took their seats near the boarding gate after spending a couple of hours from check in until now.

Riley and her bag fiasco cemented in Seth's mind the reason airlines called for passengers to arrive two to three hours early. The whole ordeal there took an additional twenty minutes.

The professor handed out their boarding passes to each of them, and Seth silently questioned her choice of shoes for the march through airports and such a long flight. He'd never seen her without her sky-high stilettos until they passed through the TSA checkpoint. Seeing her without them made him understand why she wore them; she was easily a foot shorter than him. Her race wasn't the only factor for her petite stature, as he had seen taller Korean women before. Riley was five-four, and without shoes the professor was even shorter than her. Then there was her choice of wearing her typical school attire of a pencil skirt with a silken blouse. He couldn't dress up for such a long flight even if there was the chance of meeting diplomats of the Blackthorn Clan upon arrival. His choice of jeans and an old Avenged Sevenfold T-shirt would have to be enough.

Lukas leaned over and asked, "Why are you staring at the professor?"

"Huh?"

"You've been watching her since we sat down."

"Oh," he said with a shake of his head. "I don't know."

Why was he focusing so hard on her clothing and shoes?

"I want the window seat. You're gonna have to switch seats with me," Riley said, grabbing his forearm.

That's why.

The muscles in his shoulders and back tightened and bunched, his entire body going tense when he glanced toward the window at other planes out on the tarmac. A blue hue lingered in the sky at the edge of a sunrise, giving everything a dreary mien that would clear in the next hour once the sun fully broke the horizon. The weather report called for clear skies, and it hadn't wavered all week. He would know. He had kept tabs all week and checked it six times that morning alone.

The smell of the diaper belonging to the fussy baby a mother held next to him did nothing to ease his sour stomach.

"That's fine," he said, shifting his gaze away from the window. Better to not look at the planes and focus on something else. "I don't want the window seat."

"What's wrong?"

"What do you mean?"

"You're sweating."

He grunted.

Riley narrowed her smokey-blue eyes at him then stood abruptly. "Come with me."

"What?"

"Come on." She tugged on his arm, pulling him up. "I need a milkshake."

The professor looked up from where she sat in a chair across from them, studying papers. "Make sure you're back in the next thirty minutes, or you'll miss pre-boarding."

Blaire looked up from her phone. "There's milkshakes at the airport?"

Riley looked at her and nodded. "I looked it up online before we came. There's this burger place in Concourse B." She looked at Seth. "Want a burger?"

That Riley picked up on what was happening to him and used his favorite food to distract him from his fear made his chest ache. He licked his lips and smirked. "Yeah, that sounds alright. You two coming?"

"Why not?" Lukas said, standing. "I know she won't refuse."

"Excuse me for appreciating good food," Blaire said, swatting Lukas's arm

He wrapped it around her lower back, pulling her to his side and kissing the top of her head. "Nothing wrong with that."

Seth lifted his carry-on laptop bag to bring with him. Even with the professor there to watch their stuff, he didn't trust leaving his laptop, or the other precious item inside, out of his sight. Besides, he didn't have much time before they boarded.

Riley led them to a packed burger place with large, round ball lighting hanging from the ceiling at various heights among the track lighting. A large, wavy ceiling light spanned the entryway to the restaurant over wooden slat-encased booths with lime green upholstery. Long wooden tables with four lime green stools on each side spanned the middle of the room.

Though the eatery was crowded, people remained seated, so he didn't feel the bottleneck effect walking through the airport gave him. With the smell of hamburger meat and fresh fries in the air instead of the stifling smells of travel chaos, he finally started to relax.

They took their seats at a table. While the others opened their menus, Seth looked at his bag on the stool next to him. He didn't know why he was stressed. It wasn't uncommon to give a random gift between them, but this felt deeper. Maybe it was because of the strange electricity between them lately, or something worse, but it fried his nerves.

"Earth to Seth. Come in Seth."

His head snapped up, and he met Riley's gaze. She pointed to her right, and he turned to see a server standing there waiting for his order.

They placed their orders, and while they waited for their custom burgers, Blaire turned to Lukas. "Why isn't the Oracle flying with us? Professor Velastra said she would meet us in London. How is she getting there?"

"She's such a prominent figurehead in the Vasirian world, there would be no way our movements would stay under the radar if she traveled with us. She'll probably take a private jet, and that will seem normal. As far as I understand it, she often moves between each Blackthorn school in the system and the clan's manor."

Seth nodded. "Also, think about it. It's normal for a group of college-aged students to travel to London. Even Professor Velastra can be explained away as our chaperone, considering she's now the de facto headmistress for Blackthorn Academy while the clan sorts this mess out."

"That's true," Riley said, nodding. "It wouldn't be unreasonable for her to travel to Blackthorn Institute or even have a meeting with the clan."

"Right. But there's no easy way to explain why the new headmistress, four academy students, and a political figure like the Oracle would be traveling together, so this is likely the path of least resistance."

Lukas stopped speaking as the server approached with their food. The woman wasn't human, so their conversation would make sense to her, and Professor Velastra explicitly told them not to trust anyone outside their circle.

Blaire once asked how they could tell the difference between a Vasirian and a human when she couldn't, and they had to explain it was an instinctual thing. Seth didn't know how to explain it beyond simplifying it to "like recognizes like." That she thought they would recognize humans by blood amused him. Maybe if they were cut, sure. But contained inside the body? It wasn't any different from theirs.

Once the server left, they dug into their meal, occasionally commenting on flavors. More than once, Riley stole fries from Seth's container.

They didn't speak about travel plans any further to avoid attention; their server kept looking at them oddly as it was.

Seth wagered the strange looks and whispered conversation between her and another Vasirian staff member behind the bar along the back wall of the restaurant had to do with the human sitting with them. They kept staring at Blaire, and the server had pointed her out to the one behind the bar originally.

Considering their kind didn't associate much with humans unless absolutely necessary, it made sense for them to be curious. It wasn't against their laws to interact with humans, but a large majority of the population avoided having interpersonal relationships with humans to protect their secret. Exposing their species would lead to mass hysteria about vampires on the loose, and the fallout would be disastrous.

They weren't anything like vampires, much to Seth's comfort. He couldn't imagine having to sleep in total darkness—never mind a coffin—avoid sunlight, have no reflection, not be able to have sex because of a lack of blood flow to his cock. He shuddered. No, they were alive and well. Nothing like the undead creatures of myth except the need for blood, having fangs, and a few other abilities that made life easier for them.

After finishing their meal and disposing of their trash, there wasn't much time remaining before they had to board, so they headed back toward the gate.

Blaire and Lukas held hands, taking the lead with Riley behind them, talking energetically about this, that, and everything in between.

It's now or never.

"Riley."

The noise of the airport amplified as they approached the boarding area, and with Riley engrossed in her conversation, Seth's voice didn't reach her. With a sigh, he quickened his pace and grabbed onto her wrist, bringing her to an abrupt stop.

"Whoa. What are you doing?"

"Trying to get your attention." He adjusted his bag and carded his fingers through his hair nervously. "It's too loud in here."

"It's an airport," she deadpanned.

Blaire and Lukas had already joined the professor a few feet away, gathering their things as people lined up at the counter to enter the hall leading to the plane.

He was running out of time.

"I have something for you."

Black eyebrows rose high and blue eyes twinkled with excitement. He hoped he didn't disappoint.

"A present? What is it? Gimmie, gimmie!"

Watching her bounce on her feet as she hopped like a bunny, all the little chains and straps attached to her cropped plaid pants jangling, made him smile. Her child-like enthusiasm never failed to warm parts that usually remained cold deep within him.

Reaching into his bag, he took a breath and pulled out a hardback book, extending it in front of him and waiting patiently.

"What's this?"

He nudged the book forward to encourage her to take it, his gut churning anxiously. "See for yourself."

Taking the proffered hardback, Riley looked down at the cover and a faint gasp passed through her pink lips. If he hadn't paid such close attention to her, he'd have missed the sound completely.

Confused, wide eyes stared up at him, the bluish-gray appearing periwinkle under the bright lights of the airport.

"How did you…" Her brows crushed together. "Is this a joke?"

"No. I figured you could start reading it during the long flight. You finished the last one, right?"

She flipped the book then opened it, scanning the pages near the front where copyright and special messages were usually located. Mouth parting, she looked back up at him. Between the book contents and whatever she found on his face, it must have appeased her because the smile that spread across her face hit him like a gunshot to the chest.

"How did you get this?"

A light shrug was his only answer.

"Seriously. How did you manage to get an Emley Rison book that isn't set to release for another two months?"

"It was easier to get with the connections through my creative writing course."

If his nerves weren't lit up with anxiety waiting to see if she liked the gift, he would find her surprise humorous. It wasn't like he never gifted her anything—and vice versa—but this gift held greater meaning. An early print before release in the marketplace. Didn't readers like that sort of thing? He hoped a gift like that would make her happy. Not only to see her smile, but to try to shift the weird tension between them that had built for weeks.

She scoffed a breath and shook her head, her voice turning serious. "Seth. No one has ever seen Emley Rison in person, and you're telling me Blackthorn Academy has connections to her?" Her mouth gaped and her eyes widened farther. "Oh, my gods, is she Vasirian?"

"I didn't meet her."

Riley stared at the book in awe. "This is so crazy." She stared at the cover, where a watermark stated ADVANCED READER COPY—NOT FOR SALE. "Even an ARC copy isn't easy to get. There's a whole application process. I didn't get approved. These copies are golden. Sometimes Rison changes little things before release after getting feedback from readers of her ARC copies." The awe in Riley's voice warmed his heart.

"Look in the back. Last page."

Her brows furrowed, but she opened the book. Eyes scanning the page, her mouth dropped open as Blaire approached.

"Hey, we need to—"

Blaire's words were cut off when Riley handed her the book and rushed Seth, jumping at him and wrapping her arms around his neck and legs around his waist when he caught her on reflex, securing his one arm around her back and the other beneath her thigh.

"Oh my gods, I love you!" Her hands framed his face as she peppered his cheeks with kisses before pulling back. "This is the coolest frickin' thing you've ever given me!" She squeezed his neck tightly in a hug that almost cut his oxygen, burying her face against his neck. "Thank you, thank you, thank you!"

The loud shouting and display of excitement had several people looking and whispering, but Seth couldn't move or respond. He froze the minute the words left her lips, and it took everything in him to bring himself back from the free fall her words and actions sent him into.

"I love you." echoed on repeat in his head as Riley continued to prattle on, clinging to him, oblivious to his shock.

How easy it was for this girl to shake his foundation.

"What the hell is going on?" Lukas asked, approaching them.

Riley's head popped up, and she looked over to see Blaire and Lukas staring in bewilderment. "That book is an advanced copy of Emley Rison's final book of the *Unrequited* series! I don't know how he did it, but Seth got it for me."

Blaire's mouth parted in surprise. "Oh, wow. That's not coming out for another couple months."

"I know!"

"Yeah, but it's just a book… Why are you attacking him in the middle of an airport while we're trying not to draw attention to ourselves?" Lukas's words weren't harsh or angry, just confused.

"Oh crap, my bad." Riley looked at Seth, who'd finally managed to control his breathing. Smiling sheepishly, she slid down the front of his body until her feet met the floor then straightened out her clothes and rushed over to Blaire. "Look at the back page. He got her to sign it for me. She even left a personalized message and everything!"

Lukas walked over to where Seth stood stock still where Riley left him and shook his head. "Did good with that one. Don't know how you managed to get that, but it certainly made her happy."

Seth made a noise of acknowledgment and shrugged. His secrets were his own. As long as he could make her happy, that was all that mattered in the end.

Riley kicked back on the hotel bed, having changed into a pair of black cotton pajama pants with tiny white skulls with pink bows on their heads all over and one of Seth's plain black T-shirts she'd stolen from him before the trip that hung long on her thighs with short sleeves to her elbows. If he wouldn't show her where he got the sugar cookie product, she would take his shirt to get the scent. The yummy, buttery vanilla scent mingled with his cologne and settled her in ways she couldn't explain.

It was mid-morning, around ten, but her internal clock felt messed up. It took them around three hours to get through customs, gather their luggage, take a car service to the nearest express grocery store that was open early, and make it to The Waldorf Hilton to check in and get settled. The sleep she had on the thirteen-hour flight did nothing to ease the exhaustion she felt, so pajamas and junk food were necessary.

After opening a soda from the haul of snacks, Riley tore into a bag of soft and chewy candy supposedly unique to the British. They had a varicty of flavors, so she'd grabbed several little bags of the drumstick candy.

Blaire came out of the bathroom with eyes wide and bright, shaking her head. "This place is beautiful."

Muting the TV, Riley swallowed the candy in her mouth. "Just a hotel."

"Nicer than ones I've ever seen."

"You forget not all of us travel all over the place and have siblings in big cities to chase down," Lukas said, pilfering a bottle of water from the mini-fridge before sitting down in a chair near the bed.

Blaire stretched and yawned. "I'm so tired."

"Jet lag." Riley stuffed another candy in her mouth, chasing it with a swig of Coke.

"But I slept on the plane."

"Imagine how much worse it could be."

Blaire draped herself across the foot of the bed and groaned. "So comfy. When can we go to our room?" Her eyes sought Lukas, and he shrugged.

"Professor Velastra said to meet here for a briefing once we settled in. She's also bringing us blood."

"Bless her," Riley said with an exaggerated sigh. "I had to hide in the bathroom on the plane to make sure I had one mid-flight."

"Yeah, me too," Lukas said. "I'm starting to feel drained. It's been a while."

Blaire lifted her head from where she had rested it on her arms. "Need me?"

"It'll be alright."

She pushed herself from the bed and walked over to him, perching sideways on one of his thighs. "Don't be ridiculous. If you need it, you need it." She glanced over at Riley in question.

Riley waved her hand in the air. "Don't worry about me. I've got all I need right here." She motioned to the pile of junk on the bed, her phone with ear buds, and the new book Seth had given her at the airport.

Before Lukas could protest, she stuck the ear buds in her ears and, as she pressed play on her music app, the sound of Blaire's moan filtered through. *That didn't take long.*

Her friends wouldn't have sex or anything with her right there, but blood sharing between pairs aroused them, so it wasn't like they were acting lewd and disrespectful in her presence.

Popping more candy into her mouth, she opened the book and began reading.

When her phone vibrated against her leg, she looked at the

screen. A full twenty minutes had passed without her realizing it. A text notification from Seth said to come to the door.

Riley popped out her ear buds and looked over to find Blaire asleep in Lukas's arms and Lukas out cold with his head resting against the wall. With Blaire's jet lag, and Lukas likely getting his fill of blood, Riley wondered how quickly they passed out. She didn't have time to think much of it, or try to wake them, with the insistent knock on her door.

Rushing over to the door, she threw it open to find a grouchy-looking Seth. She hurriedly stepped out of the way as he entered the room.

"Where have you been?"

"Huh? Right here. Waiting on you and the professor."

Seth looked at the bed covered in snacks and her book, and then at the two sleeping in the chair, before turning back to her. "I've been texting you for ten minutes and knocking for five."

"Oh."

"Yeah, *oh*. The professor was with me but said she would be back."

"I had my headphones in. Lukas needed blood, and I didn't want to listen or interrupt their moment."

"Listen to what?" Seth's brows bunched as confusion swept across his features.

"Uh… you know. The sucking and wet sounds." She swallowed. "The moaning."

His eyes flashed with an unnamed emotion, and he shook his head, his lips tilting into a half grin. "Does it embarrass you?"

"No. But it might embarrass them to have someone listening in." That was only partially true. It didn't embarrass her to see others share blood, but the moaning would eventually get to her.

"Have you had blood since the plane?"

She looked up at him, pushing the sleeves of her shirt up as she rubbed her arms absentmindedly. "No."

His eyes fell to the movement, and then he paused, scanning her form with his penetrating steel gaze. "Whose shirt is that?"

"What?"

"That's not your shirt."

She shrugged.

"Whose is it, Riley? Because I know it isn't yours."

"What makes you think that?" She turned from him and went into the bathroom, keeping her back to him as she dug through her travel bag of makeup and accessories, looking for her lotion. She flinched when his large hands cupped her shoulders, and her eyes snapped up to meet his in the mirror. He didn't look happy.

"Because it's clearly too big for you. It's obviously a man's shirt."

Her eyes shifted to the side. He was going to be so mad at her for stealing his clothes.

"Now tell me. Whose shirt is it?"

"Yours," she whispered.

"What was that?" He leaned down to hear her better, and she cleared her throat.

"Yours," she repeated louder, bracing for the scolding. Seth hated people messing with his belongings. What was she thinking?

His hands flexed on her shoulders, and then loosened as he slowly released her. "What?"

She looked up at him in the mirror.

"Mine? But why?" The genuine confusion on his face eased her nerves. Better confusion than anger.

"Sugar cookies."

Dark brown brows crumpled in confusion until she lifted the collar of the shirt to her nose and inhaled. Face slack, he stared at her, swallowing.

"My shirt smells like sugar cookies?" He leaned down hesitantly and touched his nose to the place where her shoulder met her neck, right at the edge of the collar of the shirt, and inhaled deeply, making goose bumps spread over her skin. "I only smell tiger lilies," he finally said, voice breathier than before.

"Tiger lilies?"

His eyes met hers in the mirror over her shoulder. "That's what you smell like." He moved to his full height.

That was strange. She never wore anything with that scent. Her lotion changed with her mood, and on the rare occasion she wore perfume, it wasn't the same every time either.

Uncertain, she finally answered his earlier question. "It doesn't smell like it as strongly as before, no."

"Huh?"

"The shirt," she mumbled, grasping the shirt she wore at her stomach. "The smell has faded. Probably because it's been in my suitcase since the day before yesterday."

She was immensely grateful he didn't question why she stole his shirt. How could she explain to him that curling up with the scent of sugar cookies and his cologne made sleeping easier? She slept with it last night. The night he came to her dorm and rested on her pillows leaving his scent behind she realized how potently it affected her. That night was the best sleep she'd had in as long as she could remember.

Without warning, Seth reached behind his head and pulled his black T-shirt off in one swift movement. She spun around to ask him what the hell he was doing, but instead covered her mouth with her hand as he held the shirt bunched in both hands in front of his waist.

Seth told her he'd started working out more, but she hadn't seen him without a shirt since he was sixteen or seventeen. At this point she couldn't remember, and she didn't care to, because the almost twenty-year-old standing in front of her now was six feet of lean muscle that made her heart trip over itself. Whatever workout regime he did worked because his body was impressive. Her hand fisted as she resisted the urge to move aside the shirt blocking the full view of his torso and touch the definition of his stomach.

She wanted to see it all.

No. Bad Riley. Not for you.

She couldn't even laugh at her own internal jokes because they were true. He wasn't hers to touch. But damned if she wouldn't appreciate the view at least.

Having his shirt off exposed the tattoos he'd accumulated over the last two years. One full sleeve in shades of black and gray she already knew of, but it capped his shoulders entirely. His other arm had a half sleeve, but he intended to extend it to his wrist. She had never seen the script on his ribs that she couldn't make out and the two flying crows in a messy ink style on his pectoral muscle with long trails of running ink down his ribs.

"Riley." Seth's fingers snapped in front of her face, tearing her away from her perusal. "You in there?"

"Huh? What?"

A cocky grin curled his lips. "Like what you see?"

"Don't be stupid."

"Hey, I'm not the one staring." He lifted his hand and swiped her chin. "Got a little drool there."

She swatted his hand. There was absolutely no drool there. "Why are you shirtless in my bathroom?"

"Swap with me."

"What? Why?"

Holding out the shirt, he said, "Smell it."

"I'm not going to smell your shirt, Seth. It's probably sweaty from the flight."

"Just do it."

Taking his shirt in her hands, she looked at him warily, slowly bringing the fabric to her nose as he rolled his eyes in response. She couldn't control the way her eyelids fluttered closed or the slight whimper if she tried.

The sting of humiliation prickled across her skin as she held the fabric to her face, afraid to move it away and face the guy who had yet to say a word after her embarrassing slip about the potent scent of sugar cookies, cologne, and sweat .

Eventually, the silence became too much to handle, and she risked peering up at him.

He stood staring at her like he wanted to say something but couldn't get his mouth to work. Finally, he cleared his throat. "I take it it smells like cookies?" His voice sounded strained.

Why wasn't he arguing with her about the cookie smell anymore?

She nodded.

"Not sweaty?"

She nodded again.

"It is, or it isn't?"

"It is." She paused. "And cologne."

"Is it bad?"

"No," she whispered.

"Do you… want it?"

"Huh?"

"Trade with me."

She tried not to react. Tried not to lose herself in those gunmetal eyes turned silvery white in the bright vanity lighting of the hotel bathroom. But she failed. She buried her face in the shirt and squeezed her eyes shut to hide her unsteady breathing.

The tension from her physical reaction to him, the overwhelming scent, the proximity, all while feeling tired from the flight, drove her anxiety through the roof. In breathing down gulps of his scent, her shoulders eased. She could get through it. She needed to before he realized what was happening and saw behind the cracks in her armor.

Strong arms looped around her shoulders and pulled her in, and she sagged against him, keeping her face buried in the shirt.

"Talk to me."

She shook her head, forehead rubbing against the shirt acting as a buffer between her and his skin.

"Why not?"

Another shake of the head.

"Did I do something to upset you?"

She shook her head quickly.

"You're upset though."

It wasn't a question, but she still tensed in response; he wanted an answer.

"Talk to me about it."

When she pulled from his hold, he let her go. She dropped her arms in front of her, still holding the shirt tightly. "Just a mini panic attack. I don't know why."

He hummed. He'd witnessed them before, but usually the reason was obvious. This time even she didn't have an answer for why her brain revolted against her. There wasn't always a reason for why it did. Sometimes it just happened.

"It's chilly in here. Swap shirts so I can put one back on." He turned his back, leaning on the door frame and looking out into the main area of the hotel room.

Grateful for his grace, Riley pulled his old shirt off over her head then tugged on the new one he gave her. Immediately, his warmth hugged her and his scent enveloped her in a way that instantly relaxed her. Exactly what her anxiety-riddled mind needed. A second gift since they started their trip.

"Here."

Seth turned and took the shirt she held, eyeing her in the shirt he'd taken off. A strange look of appreciation and satisfaction crossed his features and disappeared so quickly she couldn't be sure she'd seen it.

Pulling the shirt over his head, he took a deep breath and shuddered.

"You okay?"

"Yeah. Just cold." His eyes raked over her. "You are so tiny."

"No way." She spun to look in the mirror in mock horror. "When did that happen?" She smiled at his chuckle and turned to face him. "Yeah, I think the growing ship has sailed for me."

Like her mother, she was destined to remain small. At least her mother was blessed with assets. She sighed. After she stopped growing in height around thirteen, the rest of her body didn't do much more either. She wasn't an ugly duckling; she knew that much about herself, but she wasn't a curvy bombshell like Seth favored either.

Her breasts were a small handful, and her waist was tiny, with barely the slightest flare to her hips. Her backside wasn't flat, but it wasn't a peach worthy of the classic apple-bottom jeans her older sister wore when she was eighteen either. Her sister always tried to tell her she was beautiful, but not fitting the typical Western beauty standard seen on the cover of magazines and Hollywood in both style and physicality left her insecure.

"She's a shrimp who isn't much bigger than my little sister, who's a freshman in high school." Michelle's cruel words weaseled into her

thoughts.

"I think you're the perfect height," Seth said, placing his larger palm on her head. "Compact and easy to carry around."

She swatted him away. "Yep, that's me. Compact, tiny, girlish."

"She's not exactly the type of girl that suits you."

Shut up.

Using her fingers to spike up her pink hair that he mushed down on top of her head, she glanced at him over her shoulder to find him watching her with drawn brows.

"What's that supposed to mean?"

"Hm?" She finished fixing her hair and turned to face him. "What's what mean?"

"Girlish. You *are* female, but you said it all irritable."

"Oh." She crossed her arms over her stomach. "It's nothing. Sorry."

"Riley," he said, his admonishing tone showing he wasn't buying what she was selling.

"Seth."

"We're not playing this game."

"What game? There's no game."

Seth's biceps flexed as he crossed his arms, and she couldn't help but stare. "The one where you lie then act coy to get out of it."

"Is it working?"

"Not this time."

Hanging her head and sagging forward, she shook her head. "You know what?" She lifted her head then threw her arms up animatedly. "I don't care! I said girlish. Like, you know, smaller boobs, no hips. I'd fit right in with high school freshmen, just like that girl said. That what you wanted to hear? Me lamenting about my lack of womanhood?"

He frowned at her disparaging laugh. "You do not look that little."

"Doesn't matter." She placed her hand on her hip. "Why are we talking about this, anyway? We don't talk about stuff like this." Her other hand gestured up and down in front of him. "You don't hear me talking about your body."

He cocked his head. "Would it make you feel better?"

"Absolutely not." She snorted derisively. "Your body isn't my business as much as mine isn't yours."

The severe frown that marred his lips made her hesitate to say anything else, and when a knock on the hotel door echoed into the bathroom, she was grateful for the opportunity to get out of the confined space. Being alone with him kept pushing them into conversations that bordered on discomfort. She didn't want to face what those subjects made her feel.

Pushing past him into the main room, she headed for the door out to the hall. Blaire and Lukas were awake, watching her. By the look on Blaire's face, they'd heard at least some of the conversation. Riley didn't like the pitying look she found there. Swiftly breaking eye contact, she went to the door and opened it to find Professor Velastra standing there carrying a small cooler.

"Come on in," Riley said, stepping back.

The professor stepped into the room and set the cooler on the dresser at the front of the room. She opened it to pull out blood packets to pass to each of them. "Thank you all for coming. I'll try to make this quick. I know you're likely all tired from the flight." Her gaze moved to Blaire. "Especially you."

Blaire snuggled against Lukas's chest as he took a blood packet from Seth. She still looked sleepy even after the nap. Riley felt tired herself, but she couldn't imagine what jet lag was like for a human with less stamina.

Seth sat on the foot of the bed and inserted a straw into the blood packet, watching Riley move to the place on the bed piled with sugary treats and soda.

The professor leaned on the dresser and clasped her hands in front of her, looking at each of them. "I wanted to give you a summary of how everything will happen now that we're here. I've received notification that the Oracle has already arrived and will meet us at Blackthorn Manor two days from now. Until that point, the Blackthorn Clan will review the recorded depositions made by each of you before we left. After the Oracle arrives, we will stand before King Adrian and the other clan members to answer any follow-up questions they may have regarding your testimonies. You are to be as concise and truthful as possible. This is not the time to be wary of those in power. You have also been given permission to speak candidly. While the situation is serious, they recognize they are dealing with students and have acknowledged this isn't a formal trial."

"Then what about the trial?" Seth asked.

Professor Velastra looked at him. "They have informed me that with the danger posed to Blaire by several of the members of the Order, you are not to bear witness to the proceedings."

"What? Why can't we go?" Riley looked at Blaire in confusion. "What danger?"

"Four of the seven members of the Order have the power of compulsion. While that might not seem threatening with the clan's guard around, it isn't advisable to take any risks. It's simply preventative measures. Add to this the volatile emotions their arrest has stirred, and it is in everyone's best interest to keep you all at a safe distance."

Lukas finished his blood packet and set it on the side table beside his chair. "So why are we even here if we're not taking part in the trial?"

"To provide additional testimony to the Blackthorn Clan if they want it. Further, they want to meet Blaire."

Blaire shifted, giving Lukas a look that spoke of worry as she gnawed at her lip. He pulled it free gently with his thumb on her bottom lip and said quietly, "They won't hurt you."

"He's correct. The Blackthorn Clan isn't corrupt like what you've found to be true with the Order."

Seth said, "According to the Oracle, that wasn't always the case, though. Who's to say it isn't still like that?"

Professor Velastra pressed her lips into a fine line.

The question was valid. With the current king's great-grandfather committing genocide to a portion of his kind and humans, it wasn't unreasonable to be wary, despite the king's fair and just reputation.

"We will remain alert, but I believe things will go smoothly."

Blaire's phone chimed, and she pulled it from her pocket. "It's Charlotte." She showed Lukas the screen. "Aiden left with her moms at around midnight."

He leaned over to look at the screen. "What time is it there?"

She squinted, doing the time math that confused Riley. "Five in the morning. I'm surprised Charlotte is even awake." Blaire looked down at her phone. "She says she couldn't sleep—which I guess isn't surprising for her first night away from home like this."

"Why did Aiden leave so late with them?" Riley asked.

Blaire tapped on her phone screen, and moments later, her phone pinged. "Traffic." She looked up. "He wanted to avoid Atlanta traffic if they waited until the morning rush hour. He also wanted to get here quicker."

Lukas shifted to pull his phone from his pocket. "Yeah, I missed a text from him. His flight lands here first thing in the morning the day after tomorrow. He'll be here in time for the meeting with the clan."

"Excellent." Professor Velastra clapped her hands. "You all are free until they summon us in two days. Enjoy the hotel's amenities, and if you leave the premises, do let me know. You are all adults, but keeping a suitable record of where everyone is while visiting a foreign country under the banner of Blackthorn Academy is important."

9

Beneath the Surface

The sun had barely kissed the visible sky through Riley's hotel window when Professor Velastra summoned the four of them down to the lobby of the hotel. She wanted them to all breakfast together before they met with the liaison for the Blackthorn Clan, who would give them the itinerary for their audience with the court later today.

Why this all couldn't be done later—like after lunch—Riley had no clue.

All she knew was she wanted more sleep, her stomach wanted food and blood, and the copious amounts of sugar she consumed the night before did nothing to perk her up this morning.

What was worse, if she wasn't so in need of her usual routine, or could stand to show her face in public without making sure her makeup and hair were done just so, she could have grabbed another hour of shuteye.

The only time that ever happened was when Blaire left—*was*

kidnapped; she didn't leave—and Riley couldn't bring herself to function much for a brief period. But even then, her impulses and deep-rooted need for some semblance of control over herself when she couldn't control her mind forced her to paint her mask back on.

Blinking bleary eyes, resisting the urge to rub and smudge her makeup, she shuffled past the long, dark check-in desk to meet her group near the short stairs by the front doors. At least the large ringed lights on the pale ceiling cast the lobby in soft lighting, which made it easier to appreciate the beautiful golden filigree designs.

A yawn slipped free when she reached Blaire. She covered her mouth, mumbling, "It's entirely too early for this."

Blaire offered a wan smile, looking not much better herself. "I know. Lukas had to carry me to the shower this morning. Is jet lag supposed to last this long?"

Riley snorted. "Carry you?" She shook her head. "He's spoiling you." Not that Blaire didn't deserve it after everything. "But seriously, why did we have to do this so early?"

"Really? That's the welcome I get?"

Riley peered around Lukas and Blaire to see Aiden climbing the stairs with a goofy smile on his face. Seth walked with him, picking up his rolling suitcase to carry up the stairs as Aiden came forward and wrapped his arms around her, squeezing. She grinned at the familiar comfort.

They hadn't seen one another in days, and she missed him. In fact, she probably hadn't spent more than a day or two away from him since childhood. She'd never acknowledge it to him out loud, but she used to cry for him whenever she went to a sleepover as a little girl, and her mother always had to come get her and bring her home. He knew she did, but she wouldn't admit it to him. It made her look like a crybaby little sister. Still, the sleepover always ended with her in his room, curled up in his bed while he talked to her about video games. She didn't understand any of what he described, but she didn't care. He did it to make her feel better until she fell asleep, and her dad carried her to her room to sleep. As she got older, she slept in his room in the school dorms if she had a nightmare, as long as he didn't have a roommate. Taking the extra bed, she could be near him and let him chase away the bad things without it being creepy.

Everyone should have a big brother to chase the monsters away.

Did all that make her a needy little sister? She didn't think so anymore—maybe when they were little kids, sure, but he was all she had. Their other siblings were much older, but she and Aiden only had two years between them. Aiden was the only sibling who stayed in Georgia. The others left them behind for their careers as soon as they were old enough. Not that there was anything wrong with it; it made her and Aiden hold on to one another tighter.

She batted his arm with her hand, wiggling away and pushing him back. "Okay, okay. I get you missed me, but you smell." She laughed and pushed away her errant thoughts.

His chuckle and knowing look let her know she wasn't fooling him. He knew she missed him.

Seth grumbled, "Don't mind me. Just carrying your bag like a servant boy. It's only been a few days. You two are ridiculous." He set the suitcase down with a shake of his head.

He wasn't serious. He always picked at how close Aiden and Riley were. Probably because he wasn't close to his older brother in the same way. Their personalities differed so much, but Kai always stayed around. Many siblings who were close in age fought. It just never worked out like that for her and Aiden. It helped that Aiden recognized her inner struggles when no one else did—except Seth. Neither knew how deep it really went, but she suspected Seth knew more than he let on, and that capacity scared her.

Aiden turned and flashed his teeth in a big smile at Seth. "Jealousy doesn't look good on you, man."

"Jealousy?" Seth asked incredulously. "What are you on about?"

"If you want to hug her, hug her." Aiden moved around them and walked up to Lukas, clapping a hand on his shoulder. They both fell into easy conversation with Blaire while Seth and Riley stared helplessly at one another.

"Don't even think about it," Riley grumbled.

"Wasn't gonna."

"Good. I'm too sleepy for whatever is going on with you."

"What?"

Riley froze, her gaze flying up to meet Seth's. She did *not* mean to say that. "Nothing. Ignore me."

"Not likely. What are you talking about? Nothing's going on with me."

Her shoulders fell, and she leaned on the railing of the stairs, scuffing the heel of her boot on the floor. "That's why I said it's nothing." She rolled her head from side to side. "I'm tired. Not thinking."

"Not buying what you're selling."

Her hands tightened on the railing on each side of her hip when he took a step forward, but she rolled her eyes as if unaffected.

"So just tell me."

She laughed. "You're like a dog with a bone."

He tilted his head slightly. "You're deflecting again."

"I don't even remember what we're arguing about," she finally said with a sigh, which morphed into a big yawn she didn't hide.

"We're not arguing."

"Yes we are."

"No we're not."

"Yes, we are."

He crossed his arms over his chest; the move made his white T-shirt strain across his shoulders and biceps. "No, we're not."

"Yes." She glared at him. "We are."

"At this point, maybe so, but we weren't, so calm down."

Her hands dropped from the railing, and she deflated. The others had moved to the desk to get Aiden checked in, leaving them alone. "Seth, I'm tired. I don't remember. I don't know what you want me to say. Just…" She pleaded with her eyes for him to understand. "Tell me what you want from me."

While their little back and forth started innocently, when her focus slipped and she forgot what he wanted it turned serious for her. It made her so mad with herself. It was so difficult to mask when she lacked sleep. She stayed in her room reading on days like that, outside of going to classes. No one noticed at school when she took the day to herself.

Awareness—of *what* she couldn't place—lit his features, and he closed the distance between them, stepping onto the step she stood on and leaving little space between them. He gently took her hand, and her fingers twitched.

He whispered softly, "Look at me."

His penetrating gaze reminded her of his words in his dorm after he kicked Michelle out.

"We both know that sometimes you need that."

"Need what?"

"Need someone to guide you. Someone to tell you what to do. To take control. To get you out of your head."

Had she asked him for that assistance now?

"Riley." His firm tone pulled her from her thoughts. "You said you were too tired for whatever is going on with me." Softening his tone, he asked, "Do you remember?"

She nodded slowly.

"Good. Now tell me what you meant by that." He took her other hand. "Can you do that for me?"

Riley's eyes slipped close, and she exhaled slowly. His gentle coaxing helped her focus. "Everything that has been happening between us lately. It's…" She opened her eyes and glanced toward the doors leading outside.

"It's what?"

"Nothing."

"No." Again, his voice slipped into that authoritative tone that washed over her skin and settled her in ways she didn't understand. "Tell me."

Her breath shuddered out of her. "I don't understand it. It's messing with my head. I can't sleep. I don't know what you want from me."

Seth released her hands and pulled her head toward him until her face met his chest. He looped his other arm around her shoulders and held her close. He said nothing until she sagged against him, finally releasing the last strings of tension that held her muscles taut. "Everything is as it's always been. I don't expect anything from you but what you've always given me." He swallowed so hard his throat clicked. With a sigh, he whispered, "I just need you to be you, Riley."

Lifting her head, she stared at him, searching for the truth in those last words in his features and eyes. She *needed* that to be true. Needed to know someone accepted her beyond the face she presented to the world. If she didn't have to be "on" all the time and could let go with one person… If it could be him…

Her thoughts came to a grinding halt. If she let him in that deeply, she couldn't walk away without falling apart when he found his Korrena, or when she found hers.

She couldn't even take her mask off around Blaire, afraid of saying the wrong thing or doing the wrong thing—again. She shook her head to push away the memory of overstepping Blaire's boundaries by revealing her secrets. Riley knew Blaire didn't hate or resent her for it, but it didn't ease the hesitation she now felt.

Smiling at him, she shoved everything down so deep it would take centuries to unearth. She'd been doing this for thirteen years, ever since discovering as a little girl that she liked him. At the time, he thought girls were gross. But when they were older, and girls weren't gross anymore, he never showed any interest in her. His series of conquests in the past year or so made it obvious his type was the polar opposite to her.

"I can do that," she said, nodding.

"Hey, you two," Aiden said, approaching them. "I'm going to my room to shower, and then Professor Velastra wants to do breakfast before we meet the clan's liaison."

Riley took the distraction Aiden supplied her to break away from the intense conversation and make a beeline for Blaire. "Aiden said something about breakfast."

Professor Velastra turned to her and nodded, twirling the pearl at the end of the chain hanging from her neck between her fingers. "I've had what you need prior to breakfast delivered discreetly to your rooms. If you haven't already taken care of that, I want you to return to your room and handle that necessity before we indulge in what the hotel offers. This will give Aiden the opportunity to settle in and clean up."

"I had mine already. Do we have time to nap?"

"No. I want you all to meet down here again in an hour."

"An hour? I thought we were down here for breakfast now," Lukas said.

"I assumed with Aiden's absence you would wish to see him sooner rather than later."

Groaning, Riley stuck out her lower lip in an exaggerated pout. "Sure, absolutely, but I think two hours sounds much better. Don't you, Professor?" She wanted to see her brother, but her sleep was important.

Professor Velastra shook her head slowly; she wasn't going to get anywhere. "Not if you want breakfast. You can skip food if you want, but I don't advise it. We will likely be at Blackthorn Manor for a while."

"Well, I'm not missing breakfast," Blaire said.

Lukas laughed. "We know. Don't worry, I'll make sure you get fed." Seth walked up behind them and chuckled.

"There better be biscuits and gravy," Riley grumbled, yawning.

"This isn't the South."

She spun around and whatever look on her face had Seth and Aiden both laughing. "Both of you shut it. You're telling me they don't have 'em?"

When Aiden stopped laughing, he said, "I think you'll mostly only find that in the States. Closest you'll get here is bangers and mash, I think." He shrugged. "Kai said it's sausages and mashed potatoes in onion gravy."

Riley wrinkled her nose. "What else do they have?"

"There's this traditional breakfast. I think they call it a Fry Up? Sausage, eggs, fried tomato, mushrooms, baked beans, black pudding—"

Riley lifted her hand, halting Aiden. "Beans?" Her lip curled. "And they serve chocolate pudding with that kind of breakfast?"

Seth shook his head. "Black pudding is blood sausage."

"Oh, there are so many things I have to say to that."

"Of course you do." He rolled his eyes but gave her an indulgent smile. No matter how much she went on tangents, he never stopped her.

"Like, what is blood sausage?" Her eyes moved about to make sure no one was too close to their group before she said in a lower voice, "Humans eat it?"

"Apparently, it's a regional thing. Kai told me about that too. It has animal fat, grains, and seasonings. It's rare they use real animal blood anymore, opting for blood powder instead."

"Powder?"

He shrugged. "That's all I know about it."

"I can't," she said, shaking her head in sharp refusal. "No way."

"Wait," Blaire interjected. "You're fine with human blood, but you draw the line with animal blood? Gee, thanks."

Riley whipped around. "Hey, no. I mean—"

"I'm kidding. It sounds really gross to me, too."

"Yeah, but you also don't typically drink blood—outside of Lukas's, that is," Aiden said.

"Still. I've seen photos. It's just off-putting."

"Exactly!" Riley waved a hand toward Blaire. "I have no idea what it looks like, but there's a difference in blood in liquid form and something made into a sausage with fat and other additives."

"So picky."

Riley pursed her lips, squinting at Seth. "You gonna eat it?"

"Not a chance."

"Then shut it."

Hopefully, they could keep the easy-going vibes now that Seth knew how much the weirdness had affected her lately. But something told her any peace would be hard won. Something shifted, leading to a weird tug inside her in the last week she couldn't explain. As if her feelings were even more tumultuous than usual. It was a huge reason she couldn't sleep well—except when she stole Seth's shirt and slept in it. His scent lulled her to sleep like a baby and kept her there without vivid dreams or nightmares.

She wondered if she could get away with swapping out and stealing shirts from his hamper without him noticing.

Way to be a creepy stalker...

"You know," Seth said with a grin. "You probably could have gotten some kind of nap instead of talking about blood sausage."

Professor Velastra looked at the dainty gold wristwatch she wore and sighed. "At this rate, there will be no breakfast for anyone, because making sure you have your other nourishment before we leave is more important. Now,"—she clapped her hands together—"to your rooms. I will reach out via group text when I want you back in the lobby."

Riley wanted to crawl into bed with the book Seth gave her. It practically called her name, whispering sweet temptation. *We'll be together soon, my precious.*

She yawning again. It was going to be a long day.

10

Blackthorn Clan

Waking up to the sound of a car door slamming, Riley blinked the last remnants of sleep away in time to see Seth climbing out of the backseat beside her and looking back into the open door of the car.

"We're here." He looked over the roof of the car and then back at her. "Blaire and Lukas are already following Professor Velastra and the liaison inside. Aiden's waiting on us."

The hour long ride from London to Blackthorn Manor somewhere out in the countryside seemed longer than she expected, because she felt completely rested from a much-needed nap.

Aiden, Seth, and Professor Velastra rode with her in one car, while the others rode with the liaison in the other. They were supposed to keep a low profile, but the sleek black luxury town cars reminded her of a presidential motorcade. The ostentatious cars attracted attention. Though, it likely didn't matter as much outside of downtown London.

Stepping out of the car, she stretched her arms over her head and tilted from side to side to work out her stiff muscles as she took in her surroundings.

The drive where they stood was paved with flattened cobblestone worn from decades of use, flanked by large trees to hide the manor from the main road. At the end of the tree line, the driveway split to wrap around an immaculate lawn and flower garden filled with yellow daffodils, tulips, and other flowers Riley couldn't name, allowing cars to circle around and leave without turning around. Small stone footpaths led to a large fountain at the garden's center.

Several stone statues stood amongst the flowers, winged statues similar to the black ones seen in the hedge maze back at Blackthorn Academy. A beautiful dragon statue at the corner of the flower garden caught Riley's eye with its ruby eyes shimmering in the sunlight.

Turning, she caught her breath in a surprised hitch. Towering over the drive stood an impressive Gothic-style mansion—though it didn't follow Gothic Revival architecture; much of the Blackthorn Manor had been built in the actual Gothic years the Revival style imitated. In fact, beyond its steep gables, pointed spires on some areas of the manor drew from the Victorian era.

In front of them, the stone manor walls rounded on their corners with several long, vertical windows stacked high, creating a bay window for whatever room was behind the glass; the lack of lighting in the room didn't allow her to see inside. Above the bay window, the recessed wall made a balcony with decorative bulbous finials around the top of the railing. A set of glass double doors with long windows on each side led to the interior from the balcony. Burgundy fabric draped over the glass, blocking the view of the inside.

Hood molding dripped ivy leaves over small windows near the top of the manor walls. The same ivy covered many areas of the exterior between larger windows on the middle stories, taking over the surface much like Japanese kudzu did back in Georgia. But unlike the kudzu from home, someone obviously maintained the ivy, an aesthetic choice rather than an issue of an old, abandoned castle left to time.

They all moved toward tiered sets of stone stairs leading from the garden up to the house, the handrails carved with the same bulbous finials as the balcony. Elaborate stone planters on each stair landing overflowed with leafy vegetation and camellia flowers. Riley thought the mansion looked straight out of a fairy tale.

Four larger lancet window panels in the center of the manor overlooked the main garden. Made of stained glass, they depicted scenes straight out of high fantasy novels and movies. A dragon soaring through the air, wolves lying with humans at the edge of streams, humans with horns and tails like demons holding another human's head with magic emanating from the contact, and a last window depicting a Vasirian wielding magic. The other stained-glass windows around the manor were similar to those back at Blackthorn Academy—burgundy, black, crimson—but these four were different, aligned with each other within a large arching molding to group them together, signifying importance.

"Are you coming?"

Riley startled and whipped her head away from the captivating imagery to look at Seth, who looked at her with concern etched in his brows.

"Everything okay?"

"Huh? Oh yeah. I was just looking at those." She pointed at the four windows.

Seth nodded. "We need to get going, or they'll leave us behind. I don't want to get on the Blackthorn Clan's bad side by getting lost around here."

Taking one last appreciative look at the beautiful architecture, Riley followed Seth the rest of the way up the stairs to catch up with the others, who had passed through the entrance hall and outside again into a central courtyard surrounded by windows and stone walls. Heavy wooden doors on several of the walls led into different parts of the manor.

The same stone footpaths leading through the flower gardens down below guided them through the central area of the manor and circled a medium-sized fountain depicting a woman held in the embrace of her lover, his head buried in her neck as water flowed from the vase she held back into the fountain.

"This place is insane," Riley murmured, but everyone ahead of her was either too engrossed in conversation or too far away to hear her. Her gaze moved from the fountain statue to the courtyard.

Around the fountain, and along the walls of the manor, small bushes, grass, shrubbery without blooms, and tiny clusters of flowers in white, purple, and red filled the central stone garden with life and color. In the corners of the courtyard, tall trees butted the corners, casting shade over stone benches.

As the liaison led them through one of the heavy wooden doors across the courtyard, Riley glanced back at the fountain, at the lovers forever encased in stone. Were they Korrena pairs? Compatible pairs? Simply lovers who couldn't help themselves?

Shaking her thoughts, she passed through the door into a corridor lined with beautiful sconces holding large pillar candles.

In front of them, a side table hosted a large centerpiece bouquet with a round paperweight covered in emeralds to one side and a knick-knack box with filigree to the other. Above this hung a large portrait painting with an ornate golden frame, depicting a man in aristocratic dress clothes posed next to a woman in a vibrant red dress with gold detailing along the bodice. Both looked no older than their forties, but it was anyone's guess how old they actually were.

"We will continue this way," the liaison said, extending her hand to the left. "King Adrian is expecting your arrival."

Turning from the group, she started down the hall, her black stilettos tapping on the marble floor, golden hair swaying against her back with each step, standing out in stark contrast to the black silk blouse that matched her designer slacks.

Everyone kept mostly silent through the unofficial tour through a portion of the manor. Who knew the reasons the others didn't break the silence, but Riley didn't want to break the spell the opulence placed on her. If she started talking about what she thought about the beauty here, refraining from driving everyone up the wall would be hard to do. Something about the candlelight dancing on the neutral walls with windows spaced every couple of feet, effectively allowing the marble floor to be cast in streams of light, spoke to her. This place had known more years that all of them combined. This place deserved more respect than her chaotic chatter.

After what felt like forever, they approached a large set of heavy oak doors. A burgundy rug beneath their feet led to the door, and on each side sat large vases overflowing with flora.

As the liaison waited next to the door, Professor Velastra turned to them. The lights of the enormous chandeliers overhead revealed the slightest bit of apprehension in her eyes.

"Ms. Lindberg informed me that all present members of the central clan have read and listened to your recorded depositions after combing through the provided physical evidence."

"Physical evidence?" Aiden questioned at the same time Blaire asked, "Central clan?"

"As stated before, the clan is larger than the main royal court.

Advisors also make up a part of the clan. Using the umbrella term Blackthorn Clan for the branching members connected to the manor may have been a faux pas, as these extended parties aren't related to the central court. The central court, the heart of the Blackthorn Clan, comprise the leaders of our kind. The king, his siblings, and the cousins make the central royal family. Their power is also in that order, followed by advisors spread throughout the world. Vasirian label those advisors as clan, but only the royal family truly can claim the title."

Professor Velastra turned to Blaire. "Along with the recorded testimony each of you provided, we provided the photographs we took of Blaire's injuries—"

"But she healed!" Riley said.

Professor Velastra's eyes cut over her shoulder to where the liaison stood waiting, oblivious to Riley's outburst. "The injuries she suffered at Vincent's hands were documented."

Lukas growled low in his throat, and Blaire put her hand on his chest to soothe him.

"The other physical evidence comes from photos of the room Blaire was kept in. The temple. The copious amounts of blood—both collected in vials and on the altar and in the gutters of the ritual site."

Riley shuddered at the memory of her friend dead on the altar. Glancing over at Blaire and seeing the pink undertone in her fair skin signaling life and health made it hard to believe the Order had nearly bled her dry only a few weeks ago.

Getting back on task, Professor Velastra said, "The purpose of this meeting isn't completely known to me. I know King Adrian wishes to meet you." She looked at Blaire, who frowned. "But he may also have questions about what happened if he felt them unanswered in the documentation." She turned toward the doors. "Prepare yourselves quickly. The royal family has waited long enough."

Riley didn't know whether to be disappointed or elated by what lay behind the doors they passed through. Part of her was eager to see the grandeur of the throne room, but the disappointment came in it being exactly what she expected of one.

The spacious room was decorated in every corner with large, wrought-iron, tiered candelabras lit to cast the space in a soft amber glow. Large braziers remained unlit, allowing the sparkling chandeliers of fine crystal overhead to supply the rest of the lighting.

The room had no windows except the stained-glass panes behind the thrones, the same glass panes depicting different beings she admired from outside. They'd circled back to the front of the manor. Without windows, the candlelight only allowed her to catch minute details of paintings on the walls around the room.

The burgundy carpet running beneath their feet followed a path through the center of the room, stopping at a set of marble stairs matching the rest of the flooring.

Riley straightened her spine as her gaze moved up the dais to a large black throne with burgundy upholstery. The magnificent piece of furniture—she had no clue what material it was made of—was detailed with elegant scrolling designs along the arms, legs, and back, with peaks at the back giving the imposing throne a sharper edge.

But it wasn't just the beautiful throne that had her body at attention, it was the man with shoulder-length midnight black hair sitting casually in the chair with his elbow on the armrest, his index and middle fingers supporting his cheek, studying the newcomers in his domain with a penetrating scrutiny in his dark eyes. His tanned complexion gave away his Mediterranean heritage. The way he watched their approach spoke of someone who knew he had all the power, despite his casual pose.

The man before her was none other than King Adrian Blackthorn.

A presence so powerful it froze her to the spot and claimed the air in her lungs when his gaze finally passed over her. The moment their eyes connected, and she saw the tempest swirling in his dark depths, she wanted to flee.

Seth stepped forward until his front met her back, highlighting that she trembled with unease. How did he know? Had he seen it? She didn't question him further but leaned into him for support when they came to a stop at the base of the dais.

"My Lord, may I introduce Professor Soomin Velastra, the de facto headmistress over Blackthorn Academy in the United States, and her students," the liaison said with a flourish of her hands, motioning to the group as if presenting a potential prize on a game show.

When he sat upright, lowering his hand, he nodded to the liaison. "You may go. I will call you if I need." His voice wasn't demanding, but the order in his deep timbre had a faint Spanish accent mingling with something Riley expected to find in the States. It wasn't the voice she expected from someone who exuded such power.

Was that what happened when they lived long enough and traveled? Did they develop their own accents or lose them altogether?

Heavy doors fell shut behind them, making Riley flinch, startling her from her thoughts. A smaller door to the left of the room opened, and both familiar and unfamiliar faces filtered into the room.

The king's older sister, Mariana Blackthorn, a tall woman with an olive complexion a few shades lighter than the king's and an exquisite eye for fashion, led the group into the room. They had all met her when she joined them in rescuing Blaire from the temple.

Today she wore a sienna chiffon blouse with cuffs that buttoned up the majority of her forearm and high-waisted fawn slacks creased perfectly down the front, accented with a gold chain belt that matched the long chain around her neck. She tossed her long, shiny curls back from her shoulder as she took a seat on a smaller high-back chair next to the opulent throne. It was a throne in its own right, but Riley didn't feel right calling it that when comparing it to the king's seat.

A man with light blond hair and extremely pale skin by comparison—Felix, Mariana's husband, if Riley remembered correctly—followed close behind, standing at her side. He wore dark brown slacks and a crisp button-down in the same fawn color as Mariana's slacks. A matching overcoat in the same color as his slacks completed the look.

The only other face Riley recognized was Gabriel Blackthorn, the king's cousin. The dark-haired man walked into the room with a confident swagger to his steps, not at all formal like his sister and her husband. What he lacked in height and build, he made up for in confidence. He even flashed their group a smile, his white teeth bright against his tanned skin, which made him appear younger. Climbing the stairs, he unbuttoned the button on his black suit jacket, revealing a purple dress shirt, and sat back in the chair on the far end beside Mariana, leaving two empty seats on the opposite side of the king. He crossed his ankle over his knee, his polished shoes reflecting the amber lighting of the room.

Finally, the last person entered the room, the door closing behind him. The moment the young guy stepped into the room, his eyes took in his surroundings, studying every face as if searching for a threat. His dark brows lowered over icy blue eyes that stood out so vividly against a lighter version of the same skin tone as the king. His heavy boots echoed on the marble as he crossed the room, pushing his dark brown hair back.

While he wore a black dress shirt with fine silver stripes, he didn't dress up in slacks. Instead, he wore a pair of comfortable-looking black jeans. Maybe he was an advisor, based on his clothing and the scruff on his face. It looked nice on his sharp jawline, but... *Don't important people like royalty have to be prim and proper—clean shaven?* He took the seat directly beside King Adrian, squashing that idea. He sat back, legs spread wide in a relaxed position, and resumed studying their group in silence.

Once everyone was seated, the king stood, and Riley almost whistled, forgetting her earlier unease. It helped that Seth gave her support by standing closely behind her, giving her the feeling of safety. Tall, like Lukas and her brother, the king wore black slacks that molded to his thigh muscles in a perfectly tailored way, and a button-down black dress shirt that likely cost more than her entire collection of boots that hugged his broad chest and muscular arms fantastically.

The ruler of the Vasirian looked like the kind of man you paid to model with as minimal clothes as possible. Of course he did. He had all the time in the world and money at his disposal to workout at his leisure. Too bad he had long hair. Riley glanced over at Blaire, wondering what she thought. She liked long hair.

Other than a fleeting appreciation for his appearance, Riley doubted Blaire would think much else. Humans tended to think negatively about large age gaps, and despite appearing to be in his mid-twenties, King Adrian was fifty years old. It wasn't uncommon for Vasirian in their twenties who hadn't found a Korrena to take a compatible mate much older. Some even found their Korrenas with large gaps in age, like her parents. Never those in the prime age for awakening as Korrena, and certainly not minors. Their kind agreed with the humans on that one.

"While you have been informally introduced to a few members of my court before, allow me to introduce you to my inner sanctum." He motioned to his right. "My older sister, Mariana." She nodded, and the king acknowledged the man standing at her side. "Her husband Felix." The king motioned to the man on the end. "Gabriel, my cousin."

"Pleasure," Gabriel said in a smooth British accent.

Adrian pivoted, motioning to the man who stood out like a sore thumb on the dais. "And this is my younger half-brother, Dimitri."

Dimitri barely cut his eyes to the king before turning his attention fully on Blaire. "And do we get the same courtesy of introductions?" He slowly cocked his head to the side. "The papers give names, but what name belongs to whom?"

"Dimitri," Mariana admonished in a blend of British and Spanish accents.

"What? Is it not to be expected?"

Gabriel released a long-suffering sigh.

No one missed Dimitri's animosity. It bled off him in waves. *But why?*

"Enough." King Adrian's command echoed throughout the throne room. "You lack patience, brother."

Dimitri sucked his teeth.

His stand-offish behavior made Riley question Dimitri's age. King Adrian said he was younger. They all appeared in their early to mid-twenties except Mariana, who appeared closer to thirty—which could easily be a decade or so older than the king, and Dimitri, who looked as young as they did—which meant he likely was just into his twenties if he wasn't still in his late teens. Surprising for a member of the court.

The king lowered himself into his seat and cleared his throat. Once Dimitri settled, he nodded to Professor Velastra.

She stepped forward and introduced Riley, Aiden, Seth, Blaire, and Lukas to the members on the dais before stepping back and resuming her quiet position at Blaire's side, hands clasped in front of her.

Satisfied, the king nodded and inhaled through his nose before speaking. "Before we get into the unpleasantness that brought you all here today, I would like to extend my thanks to you for rescuing my cousin." His eyes, so brown they appeared black, settled on Blaire as he spoke.

Cousin?

All eyes went to Gabriel as Blaire mumbled, "But I've never met him before."

Gabriel guffawed, slapping his leg. "Oh, love. He isn't speaking of me."

Chewing the edge of her lip, Blaire looked to the professor then to the king in confusion.

"Mind if I handle this one, cousin?"

Riley's mouth parted in surprise as a young guy bearing a startling resemblance to Seth stepped from the other side of the room where another door was. Similar build, same haircut—except where Seth had sandy brown hair, this guy had dyed, icy-silver hair with dark roots and black cropped sides and back. From where she stood, his eyes looked darker, maybe brown? It was as if Seth and he had swapped their hair and eye colors. *Freaky.* Seth might be slightly shorter, but it was hard to tell. His eyebrow piercing caught her eye, along with the piercings in his ears. Paired with the designer slacks and teal button-down shirt, it was hard not to stare.

"Dom!"

Riley spun with wide eyes as Blaire ran across the room and threw herself at the stranger, wrapping her arms around his neck as his arms banded around her lower back, pulling her against his body in a tight embrace. Riley immediately looked at Lukas for a reaction but was surprised to see a subtle smile on his face.

What in the world is happening here?

"I'm so glad you made it. I'm so sorry I didn't get back to the hotel in time," the stranger—*Dom?*—said as he stroked a thumb over Blaire's cheek then stepped back, looking over her head at Lukas. "Your pair is so strong, if not a little crazy."

"Crazy?" Aiden asked.

Dom looked at Aiden. "Called me a coward when I was losing myself." He shook his head. "It's the past."

Blaire moved back to Lukas as Dom took his place beside Dimitri. Lukas banded his arm around her waist in a proprietary way, but without any heat in his eyes. As if he were claiming Blaire but didn't feel threatened. That didn't fit his MO when another man approached Blaire in the past. *Why is he not ripping this guy's head off for touching her?*

"Well, I see your memory is sharp," King Adrian said, glancing at Blaire. "Clearly you remember Dominic."

Blaire nodded. "I'll never forget him. He saved me."

"And you saved him."

Dominic chuckled. "Nice to know I leave that kind of impression. Never forgotten. I like it." He tilted his head and grinned. "It was the Canada geese story, wasn't it?"

Mariana tapped her manicured nails on the arm of her chair. "Dominic, don't be such a child."

"Maria, you wound me. I've been through a terrible time." He started tapping his fingers, listing items. "Locked in dungeons. Flying economy. And a whole heap of things you couldn't imagine." He pressed his fingers to his temple as he leaned on his elbow, staring down the aisle of thrones at her. "Cut your little cousin some slack."

"So he's the stranger from the dungeons?" Riley piped up.

Eyes turned on her. Dominic's brows furrowed when their gaze connected, but she couldn't hold his stare.

Blaire nodded. "He was the one who kept me going. Was with me when I escaped."

Then Lukas's not acting out in jealousy made sense. When the Order locked Blaire away where they couldn't reach her, Dominic kept her going. From the way Riley understood it, if not for him, Blaire would have succumbed to despair and given up. There wasn't a reason for jealousy, and Lukas was finally in a place of security in their relationship to realize that.

Aiden cleared his throat. "Apologies if I'm speaking out of turn, but you're the king's cousin?" It was odd hearing her brother try to speak in a proper manner.

Before Dominic could answer, King Adrian shook his head at Aiden. "As you can see, no one here is taking formal etiquette into consideration, and I don't expect such, as this isn't a formal trial. You may speak freely. Though your respect is noted and appreciated."

Dimitri rolled his eyes.

The faintest shift of color bloomed on Aiden's ears; Riley resisted the urge to laugh. Professor Velastra had told them at the hotel they were free to speak candidly, but Aiden hadn't joined them yet.

"Yes, I'm Adrian's cousin. I had come to the States on a diplomatic trip with additional things I wanted to unearth." He gave Blaire a look. "In my side quest, so to speak, I was caught and tossed away in the dungeons. They didn't know who I was from Adam's house cat, but being caught in the archives didn't speak highly of what I was there for." He chuckled, his eyes shifting to Riley again, and she looked away, embarrassed to be caught staring. "Needless to say, once I was in the dungeons and learned of the things the Order had done surrounding Blaire during her time at Blackthorn Academy, and what they were doing to her while she was locked away, I needed to report it immediately. If I didn't get shipped off to Cresbel Asylum, that is."

"I'm still trying to understand why you sit here unaffected by taking Blaire's blood," Professor Velastra said.

"You drank from a human?" Gabriel leaned forward and stared at Dominic in surprise.

Professor Velastra looked at the royal family and then at Dominic. "I assumed you told them of what happened when you made your own report."

Felix *tsked*, ignoring the professor's apologies for her faux pas. "Going against our very laws. And you were trying so hard to keep out of Cresbel."

"*Felix*," Mariana snapped softly.

King Adrian's knuckles blanched as he tightened his fists on the arms of the throne. "Explain yourself, Dominic. Quickly." The sharpness of his tone made Riley shiver and Seth brush his arm against hers. She'd heard His Majesty was capable of a nasty temper, but that he was also a caring and fair king.

"I was weak, Adrian. Dying. If I hadn't, I would be dead instead of sitting here speaking of the events that unfolded. She freely offered."

Something about the desperation in his voice relaxed the king's posture, and he exhaled heavily. Apparently, freely given changed things.

"What has you confused?" Mariana questioned, diverting the tension.

"The student Vincent, who is in the depositions listed as Blaire's kidnapper, went nearly mad from taking Blaire's blood, yet Dominic sits here unaffected," Professor Velastra explained. "I'm perplexed."

The king sat forward. "Why would a mere human's blood drive a

Vasirian to madness?"

"It would seem during the experimentation the Order conducted, it was discovered that Blaire's blood contains magical properties. It is likely the reason for her awakening as a Korrena, and further, the reason for the volatile reaction Vincent had."

"Magic?" Gabriel cocked his head to the side.

Professor Velastra nodded. "Yes. In the reports I provided, we obtained all the documented experiments they performed to discover why she was a Korrena. Her blood had visceral reactions to runes, causing a variety of reactions to the environment around the samples."

King Adrian narrowed his eyes at Gabriel. "Did you not read anything?"

"Might have skimmed that part."

"What does this mean?" Mariana asked.

The side door opened, and the liaison from before entered, making her way over to the edge of the row of thrones. She whispered into Gabriel's ear, not daring to approach the main dais.

"We didn't know at first until we had the help from the Oracle—who was supposed to join us."

"She will be here at a later time," the king added simply. "That being said, I seem to recall my father sharing long ago an old legend about our kind and a connection to magic." He slowly shook his head. "I did not know it could possibly be based in reality."

"Adrian," Gabriel said, turning his gaze from the liaison to the king. "You're needed."

Rising to his feet, the king brought his hands together. "You may return to your hotel or check out the tourist attractions London has to offer. We will be in touch to continue our discussions as soon as possible."

Gabriel stood. "I apologize for the abrupt cut in our meeting. It was a pleasure to meet you all, and we'll certainly be in touch."

Each member of the Blackthorn Clan filed out of the room through the side door except Dominic. He stepped down the marble steps to stop in front of the group.

"I want to catch up and finally get the opportunity to meet your pair and the friends you spoke so fondly of during our little stint in hell. Won't you all join me for dinner?" Chocolate eyes pleaded with Blaire. Now that the clan had dispersed, Dominic spoke more causally.

Professor Velastra clasped her hands in front of her. "As lovely as that sounds, I am going to have to retire for the evening. The rest of you are free to stay out as long as you return before too late."

"Yes, Mom," Riley quipped. Dominic glanced at her with a half grin that made her stomach tingle.

"Great! I believe it'll be easier if we head back to the city for food, so you're near your hotel. I know a great place we can eat."

11

COMPETITION

"I'm telling you," Dominic said, chuckling. "hands down the wildest thing I've ever seen."

Riley laughed, shaking her head. "That didn't happen. No way."

"Way."

Blaire set her fork down, wiping her mouth with a napkin. "You have to be careful with him. I'm starting to wonder if the goose was real."

Dominic had just finished telling them about the time he was camping in Algonquin Park in Ontario, Canada, and woke to a mother bear and her cubs ransacking his campsite.

"It was real, and so were the bears. Worse yet, my buddies left me in the tent to make their escape. I had to hide in that tent for hours. I'm still shocked they didn't smell me."

"Hours?" Blaire's eyes widened.

"Yeah. I was too afraid to come out, even though I knew they were gone."

A Vasirian's preternatural strength would make handling a bear easier, but not without injury or possibly fatal wounds if not allowed ample time to heal. No wonder he didn't try his luck.

"Huh. Is that why you don't have a British accent or a neutral accent like the others in the clan? You're Canadian?" Aiden stabbed his fork into his lobster mac and cheese.

"Yes, but I travel often for Adrian, so I don't really have a permanent place I settle. I have an apartment here in London for extended stays when I can take a few classes at the Blackthorn Institute."

"I figured you were young like us," Riley said.

"What gave that away?"

"Well, I dunno."

His brow arched as Lukas said, "Maybe the piercings and hair color?"

Riley shook her head. "No. Age doesn't dictate that. I'll still rock this pink when I'm well past two hundred."

"Good thing too. It's cute."

Riley's face flamed.

Blaire laughed. "Don't mind him. He's a shameless flirt."

"Guilty, but I only speak the truth. That said, I'm twenty. Most of my extended education has been online when I have time to seek it out, but otherwise I went straight to work for Adrian out of high school."

Seth dropped his elbow on the table too hard, the thunk rattling the silverware. Riley looked at him briefly, raising her brow, before looking back at Dominic, who'd turned his attention to Seth.

"Hmm. I suppose I can see it. A little," Dominic said.

Seth narrowed his eyes. "Excuse me?"

"Blaire mentioned during our time in the dungeon when she first met me that she thought you and I could be brothers. That we look alike."

Riley practically bounced in her seat. "Holy crap, you thought so too?"

Seth frowned at Blaire.

"Hey now, I thought that in the low lighting. When I got a closer look, sure there were similarities, but there's clearly a difference. Especially in the eyes."

"Well yeah, Seth's are gray and Dominic's are brown," Aiden supplied.

"Men," Blaire muttered.

Aiden stopped with a fork halfway to his mouth. "What?"

"It's about the vibe. The *vibe*."

"I get it, for sure." Riley crossed her arms under her chest and nodded.

"Well please, enlighten me." Dominic turned to Riley with a lazy smile that again made her stomach tingle. Not nearly how Seth made her feel, but something sparked there. An attraction, at least.

That was new.

Fidgeting with the napkin on the table, she stared at the condensation running down the side of her water glass. "Your eyes are warm and welcoming. Open to those who approach." She licked her lips. "But Seth… Seth's eyes see more than he'll let you know he sees. He sees through you but won't let you approach. His eyes warn you away."

When she finished speaking, the table had fallen silent, only broken by Dominic's low whistle. "That's deep," he said with a smile.

"And crazy accurate," Blaire added.

Riley didn't look at Seth, but his gaze was burning a hole in her temple.

"So not only cute, but good at reading others, eh?"

Seth pushed back from the table and stood. "I'm going back to the hotel," he told Aiden, who nodded. He didn't say anything else, just pushed in his chair and left the restaurant.

Riley sighed. "But maybe not so good at knowing when to keep my thoughts to myself."

Blaire glared in the direction Seth left. "That's not on you. It's not like what you said is a bad thing." She shook her head and sipped her drink. "Don't stress it."

Aiden looked toward the door and sighed. "Maybe I should go after him. If he gets into it with someone while we're out of the country…"

"I doubt he'll be that reckless," Blaire said, frowning.

"If you're worried about your friend, don't stay on my account." Dominic set down his water glass. "There's always other days we can chat."

"Thanks, man," Aiden said, putting his napkin on his empty bowl and standing. "It was nice to meet the guy responsible for helping Blaire when she needed it and we couldn't be there."

When Aiden went to pull his wallet from his back pocket, Dominic shook his head. "Already covered."

"Really? I appreciate that."

"Oh, don't tell me. It's Adrian paying for this." Dominic laughed at the look of horror on Aiden's face.

"He won't be mad?" Riley asked, tearing off a piece of garlic bread.

"Don't know. Don't care." He winked.

"I probably should go with him, but I don't want to leave you," Lukas looked at Blaire, his pale green eyes conflicted.

She glanced at Riley. The only one at the table who hadn't finished their dinner was Riley; she had been too focused on Dominic's playfulness. She enjoyed his company.

"I can have a car take her to the hotel to ensure she makes it back safely," Dominic said, meeting Riley's eyes. "That is, if you would like to stay and chat some more? I'd hate for you to not finish your meal."

"I'd like that." Riley toyed with the napkin she moved to her lap earlier. She wasn't a demure, blushing girl—but in this moment, she sure felt like one. What had gotten into her, she hadn't a clue.

Dominic looked up at Blaire when she stood. "I know your pair wants you to go with him, but hopefully we can catch up before you all leave the country. Now that we're not running for our lives and all." He chuckled.

"Absolutely. I've been so worried about you," she said.

Dominic's warm smile in response to Blaire's words contrasted his playful demeanor from earlier. He took her hand and squeezed it before Blaire finally followed Lukas and Aiden from the restaurant in search of Seth, leaving Riley with Dominic at the table alone.

She tried to focus on her meal, but her attention kept latching onto her surroundings. The scent of pasta, grilled meat, fresh breads, and spices in the air. The beautiful paintings along the walls. The people walking along the street outside in the twilight. Everything but the things she should focus on filtered in and out of her brain in such quick succession it made her dizzy.

"Loonie for your thoughts?"

Riley whipped her head to the side to find Dominic with his elbow propped on the table, his palm cradling his cheek as he studied her.

"Loonie?" she asked.

"Canadian dollar." He reached into his pocket and pulled out a bronze coin larger than a quarter.

"Why isn't it called a dollar?"

He held out his hand, the coin resting on his palm. "Look."

Gingerly, she took the coin from his hand and studied it.

"The bird there? That's a common loon. It's where the coin gets its name."

Her eyebrows lowered as she studied the coin. "That's weird." She handed him the coin again.

"Is it?"

"Well, yeah." She stabbed a piece of chicken in her pasta. "It's not like we call our coins 'dead president head one, two, three…'"

"Touché." Tucking the coin back in his pocket he tapped the table with his index finger to a beat she didn't recognize for a few moments while she ate before he asked, "So tell me, what is the deal between you and my doppelgänger?"

Riley shot him a quick look then shook her head with a smile. "You two do not look *that* much alike."

"I'm not sure if I should be offended or not."

"Why?"

"Do you think he's attractive?"

A wide grin spread across his face as the heat in her cheeks took on physical form, glowing even through her makeup, giving him an answer without words.

"Well, if you say we don't really look alike, and you find him attractive, I must ask…" He leaned forward slightly and lowered his voice as if sharing a secret. "Do you find me attractive?"

Riley's eyes widened.

Dominic chuckled, sitting back in his chair. "If it helps, I certainly find you attractive."

"I, um." Her grip on the napkin in her lap was so hard it tore. She wasn't equipped for this. Flirting wasn't in her wheelhouse. No matter how much Blaire insisted that was what she did with Seth. Her eyes snapped up to Dominic. "You're… not bad?" She winced. "That wasn't supposed to be a question."

"Not bad? Hmm." He tapped his lips and nodded. "I can work with that. For now."

"Huh?"

"Before I explain, I want you to tell me more about what is with that surly guy and you."

"Seth?"

"Mm."

"He's like a brother to me. We've been together since childhood."

Dominic placed a hand over hers. "That's all? I get the distinct impression there's more."

Her gaze dropped to his warm palm over her hand and then back to his face. "What? Why?"

"The way you two orbit around one another. Find each other's eyes. I kept noticing how one of you is always finding ways to touch the other. It reminded me of a Korrena pair, but that isn't the case, it seems."

"No," Riley whispered.

How had Dominic noticed those things in the short time he'd been around them?

Either way, those things didn't equal a romantic connection. Sometimes—and in their case—it simply came from familiarity with one another. It was as easy as breathing to connect and be what the other needed. It was how they stayed bonded like a family for so long.

"He's always been family to me."

"But?"

Riley sighed. *Was she really going to reveal her hand to a stranger?*

"But I have always wanted more."

Yep, just laying it all out there. Years of pent-up frustration. You won't even talk to your best friend about it, but you tell this guy you barely know. Good job.

Riley winced at her self-deprecating thoughts.

Dominic stroked his thumb over the back of her hand. "I can't say I know what that feels like, but do you know if he feels the same for you?"

She shook her head. "He doesn't. He always has a girl who looks nothing like me. I'm not even a little bit his type."

"His loss," Dominic murmured.

"Dominic, I don't know how to do this sort of thing."

"Call me Dom. What sort of thing?"

"Whatever this is." She waved a hand between them and to where he held her hand after moving his chair closer. "My dating experience is limited to a kiss in high school in detention."

Dominic released her hand and sat back, giving her space. "If I'm making you uncomfortable..."

She snapped her eyes up to meet his. "No!" Shaking her head slowly, she repeated in a softer voice, "No. You're not making me uncomfortable. I'm just saying I don't understand why you're asking about Seth but acting like you're interested."

"Ahh." He nodded. "I simply wanted to know if he was my competition or not."

"Competition?"

"Yes. Because while I don't feel the pull of the Korrena bond, I feel drawn to you in a way I've never felt before. Tell me you feel the same."

"I don't know."

She thought back on the last several hours since they met. The strangeness in the throne room leaving tingles in her stomach, and the way her eyes kept being drawn to him as they ate. What did it mean?

"I haven't dated in a while. It isn't something I have much time for, but would you consider seeing what this is with me?"

Riley's hands shook as she held onto the napkin in her lap like a lifeline. One day she would be forced to face the truth that she couldn't pine for her childhood friend forever. One day, she would have to give up Seth. Maybe if she settled with a compatible mate instead of waiting for her true Korrena pair, then her heart wouldn't shatter as much when he found his.

An old conversation between Blaire, Mera, and her came to mind. They had recommended she try dating, and she resolved to change herself.

Taking a breath, she said, "I haven't dated before, but we can talk and see from there."

"I'll take that. Don't stress it. I have no expectations. I just don't want to let a possible opportunity pass."

"Okay," she whispered.

12

Fight or Flight

The ride back to the hotel was nothing short of a ride filled with misery. An entire city she had never seen before, and Riley couldn't stop crying long enough to appreciate the view. She wanted to observe the fashion of Londoners and the way the city looked at night, but she couldn't get out of her head. Tears tracked down her face as she recalled her last moments with Dominic in front of the restaurant before getting into the town car he summoned for her. Surely, the driver thought her crazy for crying in the backseat. She probably had snot on her face, but she was too frustrated with herself to care.

Before she got into the car, Dominic took her by the arm gently and told her he was fine to go at whatever pace suited her. He understood she had feelings for Seth that wouldn't disappear overnight, but he was patient and wanted to see where things went with no pressure.

She respected him for that. Respected that he respected her

feelings and didn't minimize them because he wanted to date her. So she said she would consider it but made no promises. He wasn't asking for marriage, to be compatible mates, to even put a label on anything, because really, they had just met. They were physically attracted to one another, and the company was pleasant, but that didn't mean it would grow into anything more than that. He knew that. She knew that. It wasn't the time to make rash decisions.

So why did it hurt so much to even consider entertaining dating him? Enough to reduce her to tears, even.

The car door opening startled her, and she swiftly wiped her cheeks and nose with her sleeve to rid herself of the makeup running down her face that probably made her look like something straight out of a horror film.

Stepping out of the car into the crisp night air, she wrapped her arms tightly around herself. "Thank you," she mumbled to the driver, who held her door open. When he nodded, she bolted for the doors of the hotel, her head tucked down.

The first thing she wanted to do was stop in her room to freshen up, and then she needed to see Seth. She didn't want to leave things like they were. Clearly, the words she said about his eyes upset him. She didn't want him to feel she didn't care about his feelings, and she might have hurt him. So she would put aside her own feelings to make sure he was okay. She could do that.

The soft piano music playing over the speaker in the elevator did nothing to soothe Riley's nerves as it climbed to their floor. All she wanted to do was go to bed and hope for a better tomorrow. Maybe lose herself in the book Seth gifted her before this journey began; but first, Seth deserved an apology. Even if Blaire was right and she hadn't technically said anything wrong, the fact that it upset Seth enough for him to leave meant she needed to acknowledge those feelings.

After removing her messy makeup and cleaning up in her room the best she could without showering, she changed into a pair of pink and black plaid pajama pants and the T-shirt Seth gave her to sleep in. Steeling her nerves, she made her way down the hall to Seth's room. The Blackthorn Clan went all out by reserving each of them their own rooms instead of pairing them together like roommates back in the dorms. Of course, Blaire and Lukas still shared a room.

Reaching his door, she lifted her hand to knock three times before stepping back and tugging on the hem of the oversized T-shirt, twisting it around her hands as she waited. Hopefully, he was still awake.

It took a few moments, but the door eventually opened. Seth's brows pinched as he looked down at her. He had changed into a pair of dark gray sweats and a white T-shirt, and his hair was damp from the shower. He must have come straight back to the room. For some reason, that settled Riley. If he wandered around London and got into a fight because he was upset, she would without a doubt have blamed herself for it.

"What happened?"

"Huh?"

"Your eyes. You've been crying." He stepped forward and put his hands on her shoulder. "Did that son of a bitch do something to you?"

Riley flinched and stepped back at the guttural tone of Seth's voice. He was barely suppressing an inhuman growl. She flinched when he touched her, prompting him to inspect her all over as if he could see through her clothes and find the source of her upset.

"Riley." His voice was sharp—commanding. "You need to tell me what happened. Now."

"Nothing happened."

"I swear to you I will go back to that manor and—"

"Stop." Riley lifted her hands and placed them on his chest like Blaire had done for Lukas. She might not be his Korrena, but she could try to soothe his distress. His heart pounded beneath her palm, and her arms moved when his chest rose and fell with his heavy breaths. "He didn't do anything to me. Don't call him that."

"Then who did?" he asked with barely controlled fury.

She dropped her arms and sighed heavily. "*I* did."

The confusion on his face replacing his anger so fast would be comical if it weren't for the fact they were standing in the hall, drawing attention from the room two doors down. A woman holding a robe tight around her body stared at them, and as Riley met her eyes, she raised her brows in question.

Shaking her head at the woman to let her know things were fine, Riley backed Seth into his room, away from prying eyes.

"What are you talking about?" Seth asked, sitting down on the foot of his bed. He looked as tired as she felt.

"I just felt bad for what happened at the restaurant." She sat next to him. "I didn't think what I said would upset you as much as it did."

The wrinkle on his forehead deepened. "What do you mean? What did you say? You didn't upset me."

"The eyes thing. When I was comparing you and Dom."

"Dom? You call him Dom too?"

Her shoulders lifted in a small shrug. "He wanted me to."

"I see," he said simply.

His words sounded accepting and calm, but something skittered across Riley's skin and made the fine hair on her arms stand on end. It was like his agitation was a living, breathing thing wrapping around her. It made no sense. Nothing about his body language spoke of his irritation, but she knew it was there.

"But no, what you said didn't bother me." He stood and moved to the head of the bed, sitting down and settling back against the headboard. "You were that upset over it?"

"Well, yeah." She turned on the bed, bringing her knee up to pivot to face him. "I felt bad. You left dinner early."

"I finished eating." He pulled his open laptop into his lap from the bed.

"But we were still hanging out." Riley toyed with the ends of her shirt. "I was still eating," she said softly. He never left while she was still eating. From being distracted, or going into long tangents when she talked with her friends, she tended to eat slower than the others. Seth always seemed fine to wait for her.

His jaw ticked as he typed away for a few moments. "I just didn't like the vibes the guy gave off."

"Vibes?"

He made a sound of confirmation.

"I think he's a nice guy. Funny." She frowned. "He helped save Blaire."

"And he spent the entire dinner leering at you."

Riley's brows rose to her hairline. "What? No, he didn't. He was a gentleman."

"Calling you cute, staring…"

"Seth. That isn't leering. He wasn't being rude." She stood and moved to sit beside his leg on the edge of the bed. "What's this really about?"

"Nothing." Dragging a hand over his face, he exhaled heavily and looked at her. "I think this whole thing with meeting the clan and the trip has been more stressful than I thought it'd be."

That made sense to her because she felt the same. Lately, her stress and anxiety were at peak levels and very few things calmed them. The shirt she wore was one of them.

Deciding they both needed a break from the heavy in their lives, she crawled over his legs and dropped down beside him, the weight of his body causing her to lean in toward him. She peeked at his laptop screen. "What are you writing?"

He turned the screen away from her. "Ideas for my creative writing."

"Can I see?"

"No."

"Boo. You're no fun."

He shut the laptop and set it aside on the bedside table. "And you're still not seeing it."

Riley poked him, and when he jumped and gave her a mock glare, she sighed and twisted the shirt in her hands again, wiggling her toes, the green sparkles in her black polish catching in the dim lamplight from the beside table.

He said what she said at the restaurant didn't bother him, but she remained unconvinced, and when she got something in her head she felt to be true, not much could sway her from that.

"What's the matter?"

"Wondering if you're really okay," she said.

"Of course I am."

"No, I mean… about earlier." Sniffing, she pressed her lips flat and shut her eyes against the burning sensation there. She thunked her head back against the headboard. "I don't like the idea of hurting you."

"I promise you didn't."

A hot tear rolled down her cheek against her will.

"Hey, come on. Don't."

Before she could open her eyes and ask him what he meant, his weight shifted, and then she was pulled down to the bed and pulled closer, flush with her back to his chest. She curled up tightly, absorbing his warmth. When she shivered from either his scent or proximity—she wasn't sure which—he pulled the cover over them. He must have thought she was cold.

"I don't want you to cry over something that really isn't a problem." Draping an arm over her waist, he pulled her petite body closer to his. He tucked his knees beneath hers as her backside nestled into the cradle of his hips. The difference in their size made it feel as if he were all around her, and the sensation comforted her. He laid his arm on the pillow over their head. His breath puffed on the back of her neck where his head angled down, resting on the pillow behind her. "I don't want you to cry at all."

Those whispered words were the last thing she remembered.

Groaning, Seth blinked, focusing on the ceiling, attempting to push away the remnants of sleep at the edge of his mind trying to pull him back down. He felt hot and thirsty, and oddly trapped.

What in the hell is that sound?

Finally rousing enough to take in his surroundings, he found Riley asleep, clinging to him like a koala with her arm thrown over his chest and her leg haphazardly slung over his hips. The sound that floated in the back of his mind became clearer to him. Riley was softly snoring.

When did that happen? They never slept together, even as kids.

As much as he wanted to lie there and enjoy the moment, resisting the urge to even touch her because it might wake her, he needed to get up before she woke and freaked out on him. Riley was skittish, and waking up wrapped around him would end in one of three ways.

One: she would choose flight and run from the room like her

ass was on fire. Two: she would choose fight, freak out on him, and slip into the mask where she tossed barbs and jokes to cover her embarrassment. Or three, the one he hated most: she would tuck in on herself, apologize like she'd done something wrong, and endlessly berate herself as though it was her fault.

Slowly, he slid toward the edge of the bed but didn't get far. Riley's hold on his upper body tightened with surprising strength, as if she was also channeling a touch of her preternatural strength to hold onto him until he stopped moving.

He lay there contemplating how to handle the situation in a way that would prevent the most fallout when Riley surprised him for the second time in as many minutes.

Burying her face into his neck, she inhaled deeply, and the soft whimpering sound that followed went straight to his cock. He really didn't need her waking to find him pitching a tent in his sweats—even if he could explain it away as the usual morning wood.

He didn't have time to dwell on that though, because Riley shifted her lower half against him, bringing her core flush with his hip. When she breathed in again, her hips rocked against him reflexively.

Holy fucking shit.

He was not mentally prepared for a Riley who not only smelled him, but ground herself against him. Her breaths became heavier, and the small sounds morphed into actual moans. Something he'd never heard from her. Something he doubted any other man or boy had ever heard from her, and it did things to his head. It wasn't even like *he* was causing it. Couple that with the overwhelming scent of tiger lilies perfuming the room, and he wasn't doing so well.

Seth never cared about virginity before. Never cared about how many partners someone had. He always thought the whole "save yourself" thing was stupid. He was never one of those men who subscribed to the concept of controlling a woman through her virginity. Of staking some sort of claim by being the first one to fuck her, like a dog pissing on his favorite toy. But he couldn't stop focusing on Riley's virginity. Hadn't since the day he heard her say the words out loud. It bothered him that his thoughts about it contradicted everything he always felt about virgins and their precious virginity.

The idea of another man sharing that moment with Riley. Laying claim to what belonged to—

Seth shook his head. He needed to end that line of thinking at once.

Get a grip.

Preferably not the one that would bring the most relief. That would sure go over well.

Riley had stopped moving and relaxed against him, so he tried again to move away, only to have her shift her leg and hook it around his thigh, tucking her tiny foot beneath him. She mumbled what sounded like, "Don't go," before succumbing to slumber again.

He was so screwed.

When her hand moved down to the hemline of his shirt, barely grazing his erection through his sweats, a jolt of raw electricity ignited every nerve in his body.

She fumbled blindly, grumbling in her sleep, until her small hand slipped beneath the cotton T-shirt he wore. Apparently satisfied at getting where she intended, the frustrated scowl on her face eased.

He lay there in shock as her warm hand glided over his abs. Little hums slipped past her lips as she explored, and he didn't deny her. Couldn't deny her.

He should wake her.

He didn't.

Riley tucked her head close to his armpit and smelled him. The moan that followed tested all his restraint. Especially when her hand roamed across his obliques, ribs, and then brushed across his nipple before settling on his sternum.

Too much for him. His fangs descended. The urge to taste her blood again like he did in the grove back at the academy plucked at the strings of his sanity, and those strings frayed further with every passing minute.

It made no sense to him.

The desire for another Vasirian's blood never existed for him. Until now.

Why her? Why only now?

Cursing under his breath, he managed to pull her arm from beneath his shirt. He wouldn't have her wake up in a compromising position. She didn't know what she was doing. Sometimes a warm body made you do stupid things. He would know.

He tried to extract himself with a gentle touch instead of trying to pull away with force. He turned on his side to maneuver her into a comfortable position.

Riley settled, but before he could breathe a sigh of relief and get up to go to the bathroom to take care of the situation down south, she wiggled back against him.

"Seth," she breathed, her body melting against him, giving in to a deeper sleep.

The world tilted on its axis at the idea that Riley's behavior wasn't just because he was warm and *someone*. In her subconscious, she knew it was him she snuggled against.

Never had Riley acknowledged him beyond their friendship, aside from recently, when things went too far in the cafeteria.

Things he normally saw as appreciation or lust in other girls or women he slept with or flirted with didn't register the same in his brain when it came to Riley.

She was too naïve.

There was no way she wanted him too.

Seth took a deep breath, trying to calm his rapidly beating heart. But as he looked down on her sleeping form, a pit in his stomach opened and made him feel sick.

There had always been a niggling in the deepest recesses of his mind that he refused to acknowledge.

It can't be.

If this response to him was because of *that*, he didn't want it.

It wasn't real.

At the sound of the door lock mechanism beeping, his gaze flew to the door, but he relaxed a fraction when Aiden stepped inside and shut the door behind him. Seth had almost forgotten he gave Aiden his secondary key card to come hang out while they were here. They were roommates back in the States; it made sense to him.

Aiden's heavy black brows rose when he turned back to the room. "Did not expect to see that." A slow smile spread across his face as he took in Riley on her side with Seth at her back, the covers pulled to their shoulders. If Aiden figured out how not-innocent everything had been moments earlier, and the physical state Seth's body was in currently, he would kick his ass.

Seth cleared his throat. "She was over last night and ended up falling asleep. It wasn't intentional."

Aiden lifted his hands. "You don't have to explain it to me." He sat in the chair against the wall, leaning back and propping his forearm on the table beside him. "It was bound to happen sooner or later."

Seth groaned and turned on his back, putting a hand over his face. Riley didn't move, finally settled into a deep sleep.

"It's not like that. Nothing happened. She was upset."

"Upset?" Aiden sat forward, alert now. He schooled his voice to a lower volume again to not wake his sister. "Did something happen after we left the restaurant?"

"She said nothing happened. Apparently, it was her concern for *me* that brought it on." He laughed, but his face fell far too quickly for it to even remotely resemble real amusement. The sound made Riley turn and snuggle into his side. He glanced at her and sighed, lowering his voice. "Can you believe that? She was crying because she thought her all-too-true comment about my eyes of all things was hurtful."

Aiden relaxed back into the chair again. "Yeah, I can." He rubbed his jaw as he studied Seth. "You can too, if you look past thinking you don't deserve her concern."

"What do you mean?"

"Riley cares about everyone around her, and when she feels she's wronged someone, it hurts her most. You know that."

Seth was glad Aiden chose not to address the deeper look into his psyche about what he deserved or didn't. He knew when not to push.

But he kept talking. "You saw how upset Riley was when she told us Blaire's stepbrother abused her before she escaped to the academy. Riley never asked if it was okay to share that. When Blaire pointed out how much that harmed the trust they had established in such a short time, Riley took it hard."

Seth hadn't witnessed it, but Riley's heart had been in the right place. The girls' friendship undoubtedly recovered because Riley and Blaire stuck together like glue. They'd become best friends in between Blaire being caught in the maelstrom of Vasirian politics, fighting for her life.

Riley snorted and wiggled against him, snoring with her mouth parted.

Aiden laughed. "Oh, the snoring started. You're stuck with her now."

"Shut up."

"I doubt you're complaining, so you can chill with the disgruntled grump act. It's me you're talking to."

"Whatever."

Aiden knew him better than most, and he hated when his best friend called him out on his genuine feelings versus what he showed the world. He looked down at Riley's sleeping face. Snoring or not, he would take Riley in whatever way he could have her.

Riley grumbled. "Why is everyone so loud?" She rubbed her face back and forth against Seth's ribs as if attempting to wake herself up or maybe burrow deeper and escape the sounds to sleep.

"Because that's what people do when they're awake and hungry for breakfast, little sister."

Riley's movements paused, and she mumbled, "Aiden? What are you doing in my room?" At Seth's low chuckle, her entire body froze—she stopped breathing entirely. Seth braced himself for the reaction.

He suspected either flight or apologies.

Slowly, with an air of fear Seth couldn't understand how he detected, Riley lifted her upper body until she was braced on her arms, the covers falling to her waist, and stared down at him where he lay on his back.

"What are you doing in my bed?"

Seth scoffed. "This is my bed. You're the one who fell asleep here last night."

"Why didn't you wake me up?"

He gave a careless shrug against the sheets. "You looked too comfortable. The bed is big enough for two."

"That's not… That's not the problem."

"What is?" His dark brow lifted in question.

Shaking her head, she turned and rubbed her face to banish the remaining dredges of sleep. The countdown to reality hitting her ticked down in Seth's head.

"I thought it was your shirt," she whispered. If he hadn't been so focused on her, he'd have missed the words.

So that's what it was.

The way she kept smelling him and burrowing into his side wasn't necessarily a desire to be with him, she just liked his scent. A scent he didn't realize he had until it became something he couldn't dismiss when she was so adamant it existed. The shirt she wore to bed was where she thought the scent came from.

Was that why she had it on when she came to his room?

Did she sleep in it every night?

Something about that possibility stroked the embers waiting to ignite inside him. Soothed a possessiveness he tried to ignore.

The truth that his scent brought forth such a carnal reaction from her body lit a fire in his veins and prompted him to bend his knee to keep from embarrassing himself if she—or Aiden—were to look at the bedding across his lap. He wasn't ashamed of his body, but he didn't want to deal with the uproar of such a compromising position with his best friend's little sister while his best friend sat not a few feet away. Aiden would know it wasn't morning wood. He'd been awake long enough for something like that to settle.

Riley's head snapped up to face her brother, as if just realizing he was in the room despite him speaking earlier. She twisted to look at Seth next, her big blue eyes wide in horror.

There it is.

"I—I gotta go," she stammered, scrambling off the bed. She'd have taken the blankets with her if it weren't for his grip on the covers at his waist.

Neither Aiden nor Seth had the chance to stop her, or say anything, before the door slammed shut behind her.

Flight it is, then.

13

The Mark

No updates had come from Blackthorn Manor for the past two days about when the clan had time for a meeting again. So after a short sightseeing trip around the city, everyone took the opportunity away from formal business to enjoy the amenities of the hotel.

Like the indoor pool.

The smell of chlorine in the air did nothing to take away from the relaxing feeling of lying by a pool, listening to the sounds of her friends splashing in the water while Riley read the book Seth had given her. Though, as she made her way through the last installment of *Unrequited*, it became harder for her to read it. Some scenes hit too close to home, reminding her of her own friend she would never get to call her own.

Looking up from her book, she laughed as Lukas lifted Blaire off the edge of the pool and tossed her into the water near Aiden. He laughed and lifted his arms to shield himself from the water splashing his way, moving toward the shallower end of the pool by Seth. Blaire wrapped her arms around Lukas's neck and started kissing him.

Arms stretched along the walls, Seth had lowered himself enough to be submerged up to his armpits. Riley couldn't see much of his body beneath the water, especially with how much Aiden stirred up the water when he moved next to him. They probably had to sit to get any depth in the shallow end.

Everyone was having a good time, and Riley even felt a sense of mental peace after having a couple mimosas at breakfast before they came to the pool. A definite perk about the city they stayed in: the drinking age was eighteen instead of twenty-one like back home.

When water hit her legs, she yelped and jerked back, frowning.

Blaire hung over the wall of the pool, resting on the ochre marbled floor to look up at Riley in the lounge chair. "Are you not getting in?"

"Not today."

"Aw, come on. It feels fantastic. It's heated and everything!"

Riley smiled. Blaire wasn't used to the finer things they took for granted.

"Maybe later. I didn't put on a swimsuit."

Blaire untied her messy bun that had become a sopping wet mess after she'd been thrown in the pool and tied it back in a ponytail. "No? Why not? Don't tell me you only wanted to read the whole time."

Riley closed her book and slid it into the small bag she brought down with her to protect her phone and book from getting wet. It held all their phones.

"This time, yeah."

Instead, she wore a baggy, black and purple The Birthday Massacre band T-shirt on the front and a pair of black cotton shorts in case she wanted to dip her legs in the pool while sitting on the side.

Lukas swam up to the side of the pool, brushed his hair from his face, and smiled at Blaire. He looked so different from the last several months. The stress finally fell away in favor of happiness. Riley's gut clenched again at the ugly emotion she hated experiencing around her best friend and the guy who was basically another brother. The jealousy over the bond they shared coiled inside her and emitted a noxious poison into her system that spread through her veins like poison threatening to destroy her.

"What do you want to do for dinner tonight?" Lukas asked Blaire.

"I don't have a preference."

"Riley?"

Riley shook her head and blinked away the haze over her vision. "Huh?"

Lukas chuckled. "Dinner." He leaned on the marble flooring, bracing his upper body and kicking his legs out behind him in the shallow water as Aiden swam up next to him. "Got any ideas?"

"I kinda like the idea of just doing takeout in the rooms. Have you seen the size of those plasma TVs in there? Insane."

"Is there any good takeout in London?" Seth asked, walking up between those still in the pool and Riley in the lounger.

"Why not go classic fish and chips?" Lukas asked.

Riley's nose screwed up. "I don't think those places have milkshakes."

"You don't always need a milkshake," Seth said with an eye roll.

She glared at him. "I'll have you know—" Her words died on her lips as her eyes fell on the dip of his Adonis belt, just above the hem of his swim trunks. "What the hell, Seth?"

"What?"

"Another tattoo? Seriously?"

"What are you talking about?"

When they went to Tybee Island, she didn't see him without a shirt, but when he had lifted his arms before their beach trip, exposing his lower stomach and hips, he didn't have the small black tattoo now present. It covered about three square inches, with a peaked arch at the center of a curving line, like an S turned sideways with sharp edges. Solid black dots balanced the design in each concave section of the sideways S, and a line split the center of the design and came to a sharp point like a fine needle. It differed completely from any of his other tattoos.

The longer she stared at the mark on his skin and the water rivulets sliding over it into the curve of his muscles, the more her skin tingled, and her nerves flared to life. Something wasn't right with her body. Her breath felt hard won as she stared at the tattoo. Why did it bother her? She tore her eyes away from the tattoo and let her gaze roam up the wet muscles of Seth's torso. He wasn't lying about working on his physique. He really *really* wasn't. The blood rushing through her ears as she resisted the urge to throw herself at him was so loud it made her uncomfortable.

What the hell was wrong with her?

Would it be so wrong to—*no*. She did not seriously entertain biting him.

Strong hands gripped her upper arms and shook her, and she blinked, swaying in response to the fogginess in her head. Gray eyes peered down at her in concern as Seth knelt in front of her. When his hand moved to cup the side of her face, she leaned into his hand, groaning softly.

"Is she alright?"

Riley turned her head toward Aiden's voice, and Seth dropped his hand back to her arm. For the first time in a while, she could hear the sounds of the room clearly. What happened to her?

Blaire gasped. "Her eyes."

"Shit. The humans," Aiden said, climbing out of the pool.

Lukas pushed himself up with his arms and climbed over the wall of the pool while Aiden took the stairs close to him. Both moved to stand in front of her, blocking her view of the family that had entered the pool area and were splashing about in the deep end away from them.

"Riley." Seth squeezed her arm. "Look at me."

"Huh?" When their eyes connected, his jaw ticked. "What's going on?"

"Your eyes are glowing," Blaire said as quietly as she could. Sound carried louder over water, so they had to be careful.

Why were her eyes glowing? Was it because she wanted to bite Seth again?

Riley looked back at Seth, but he wasn't looking at her face anymore. He was looking down at her stomach as if he could burn a hole through the fabric of her T-shirt, and by the movement of his jaw he was grinding his teeth.

"We need to get her out of here," Aiden said. "The glow is fading, but we still don't know what caused it. We can't risk it."

All the attention on her made her uncomfortable after such a confusing reaction to Seth's body. Seth's hands on her arms burned like fiery brands on her skin, and she needed to get away from everyone. She felt hot and overstimulated. She needed a shower, junk food, and solitude.

Riley squirmed out of Seth's grip, but he stayed squatted on the floor so she couldn't see his tattoo anymore. She remained curious about it, but not at the expense of her own health. Something triggered her to feel unwell, and she didn't know what.

"I think I just had too much to drink with breakfast," she said.

Vasirian metabolized alcohol too fast for the excuse to be

world.

Riley had never shown him any inkling that she wanted to be with him—that she even saw him as anything more than an obnoxious big brother. His jokes and actions confused her recently. If suddenly the fates decided she was meant to be his Korrena, she would respond to that biological pull, and he wouldn't be able to trust any of it to be real.

He wouldn't believe or accept it.

Pushing himself up from the floor, he picked up the bag of phones and handed it to Lukas. He asked Blaire. "Can you go check on her?"

"Sure, but where are you going?"

"To find a damn milkshake."

14

Trust

After the events by the pool, Riley made a point of avoiding Seth, and he didn't seem to have too much of a problem with it. The night of the pool incident, everyone but Seth gathered in Riley's room, concerned about her health if she truly felt ill. They told her Seth wasn't feeling well either, but she couldn't help but feel a twinge of disappointment he hadn't joined them.

She knew why she was avoiding him, but why was *he* avoiding *her*? It wasn't like he knew what she felt.

When Aiden gave her a strawberry milkshake that she knew didn't come from the fish and chips restaurant they got takeout from, that twinge became an all-out ache. No one in their friend group would go out of their way like that but one person. Even if they were mad at one another, Seth always made sure her needs and wants were met. She'd be a liar to say she didn't notice it. He took care of her.

Three days of avoiding one another felt like she lost a limb.

Even at the dinner earlier with Dominic, Blaire, Lukas, and

Aiden, she couldn't pay attention to half of what was said. Dominic had showed up at their hotel and informed them the king wished to have a thank you dinner to formally thank Blaire for what she did to free him from the dungeons, but then asked if they would join him for an impromptu dinner among friends.

Riley wasn't as sure of going as the others because Dominic was clearly interested in her, and with her feelings for Seth so volatile, especially after lusting for him in front of her friends at the pool and then getting physically ill, she didn't think she could give him the proper attention he deserved.

In spite of those feelings, she went anyway.

She already managed to fall short when it came to contact; not responding to text messages right away, and then forgetting about them. By the time she remembered or saw a new one, guilt made her put her phone away, resolving to call him to apologize for it. Somewhere in the back of her mind she wondered if this was more than her usual absentmindedness or if she was avoiding the change she told herself she needed.

He casually flirted with her, and she laughed and joked with him. He was a good guy. He would make a wonderful boyfriend for a girl with a calmer mind than hers. He had loads of energy and was talkative. For most people that would be great in a relationship, but it didn't balance her. Two chaotic forces without a grounded personality to keep them from going off the rails.

Sighing, she shook her head. That wasn't it. She kept trying to find reasons not to give the guy a chance. True, he had energy to match hers, but was that necessarily a bad thing?

"Riley, are you listening to a word I'm saying?"

"Huh?" Riley dropped her phone when her brother's words startled her. She had taken to doom scrolling through memes while

Lukas and Blaire sat on her bed and Aiden sat across from them in the chair at the table against her wall chatting about this, that, and the other.

"Where is your head tonight?"

"Sorry, sorry." She stooped to pick up her phone. "What did you say?"

"I wanted to know if you're interested in Dominic."

Gripping her phone, she shook her head. "I am not having this conversation with you."

"Come on. I'm worried about you." Aiden looked at the others. "We all are. We didn't know he was interested in dating you until tonight. Before you got up and went to the bathroom, he said he hoped you would consider him."

"I asked him what he meant by that after you left," Blaire said softly, pressing her palms together between her knees. "He told me he likes you."

Aiden scoffed. "He doesn't even know her."

"You know that's what I told him." Blaire glanced at Aiden then back at Riley. "But he said he just felt this weird tug in his gut. And Dom follows his gut."

"Well, I think it isn't a good idea," Aiden said, sitting back in his chair, crossing his arms over his chest. "What do you think, Lukas?"

"I think it's Riley's choice to make, not ours."

Aiden's lips parted, but Riley pointed her finger at him, which made him close his mouth.

"He's right," she said. "I'm an adult and can handle myself."

Aiden rubbed his neck. "I just want you to be careful *if* you choose to pursue something with him because he's connected to the royal line. It can be dangerous, especially if there is anyone who wants to be connected with him to get an in with the monarchy."

Riley moved to sit on the bed beside Blaire and leaned on her shoulder, mumbling, "I don't have any intentions of anything right now. We've only had dinner twice. He does make me feel nice, though."

"Nice? Riley, that's not how you—"

"Okay, okay. Hang on. Let's not get upset," Blaire said, looking at Aiden. "She's your little sister, I get it. But this isn't the way to go about things. Look, why don't we all go for a swim?"

"The pool's closed," Lukas said.

Aiden sat up, grinning. "Yeah, about that..." He winked at Blaire, and she laughed. "A few Vasirian on staff pulled some strings. As long as we're quiet coming and going, we're fine to do night swimming."

"As long as the human is looked after," Blaire said with a roll of her eyes. "Apparently, they are fine as long as they don't have to deal with my drowning. I get it. I'm not as durable as y'all." She shook her head as Lukas chuckled.

"So, pool?" Aiden looked between Lukas and Riley.

"Sounds good to me," Lukas said.

Riley sighed. "Why not?"

"Awesome. I'll stop by Seth's room on my way to change and get him to come, too."

Riley bristled at that but made no move to object. She missed Seth. The sooner she faced him, the sooner they would return to normal.

Three days.

Three days was all he could manage before breaking.

When Aiden came by his room, Seth jumped at the chance to have a reason to be around Riley. His skin itched with the need to be near her, and he didn't understand it.

Now, he sat on the edge of the pool with his feet dangling in the water, watching her leap from the marble flooring into the deep end as carefree as could be. Did the separation even bother her? It didn't seem like it.

Because she doesn't obsess about you like you do her.

He gripped the side of the pool and exhaled heavily through his nose. The itch to go fight something—even a wall—rankled beneath his skin.

As Riley climbed out of the pool and circled the edge, laughing as Blaire splashed her from the deep end, he took another look at the shallow dip near her hip bone above her bikini bottoms. Nothing. She didn't have the mark she claimed to see on him.

Not seeing the mark didn't rule out the possibility it existed. The mark didn't make a permanent appearance until Korrena pairs completed their claim on one another.

She wasn't saying anything about it now, so maybe she really had been ill and overstimulated from the alcohol.

He was foolish to even consider the alternative.

She's not your Korrena.

He raked both hands through his hair in frustration. Lately his mind had warred with him. A voice in his head echoing back the worst things he'd told himself over the years. Nothing soothed the discontent.

"What's up with you?" Lukas sat next to him on the side of the pool.

"Don't know what you're talking about."

"Can't bullshit a bullshitter, Seth. You're spiraling. And maybe everyone else can't see it, but I recognize it. I've been there. Denial got me nowhere."

"What am I denying?"

"I don't know. What's on your mind?"

Seth leaned forward with his elbows on his thighs, watching Blaire, Riley, and Aiden play in the water. Aiden picked up his little sister and tossed her like she weighed nothing. She squealed as she sailed through the air.

"Things have been difficult for me lately. No, not lately. For two years, but it's been so much worse in the last few months."

"Why is that? What's been difficult?"

"I don't know, and my emotions."

Lukas moved his feet through the water. "What kind of emotions?"

"Anger? I don't know. Just a lot of stuff." He twisted to look at Lukas. "Why does it matter? Since when do you delve into this emotional stuff?"

Aiden and Lukas did the heart-to-heart bonding. Best friends. Even then, at times Aiden had difficulty coaxing emotions from Lukas. Seth and Lukas, however, made a few quips about the situation and how the other handled it, told each other to piss off, and back in the day, even threw a few punches to stress their point—or save their own embarrassment. Didn't stop either of them from defending and standing by the other when it mattered most. They cared, but kept it surface level.

Lukas gave him a pointed look. "Since I discovered closing myself off and fighting everyone who gave a shit about me was destroying me from the inside out."

Seth couldn't argue with that. Not when he watched Lukas shut everyone out and even try to drive Blaire away to avoid their bond. They were the only pair who made him even remotely believe there was a chance of having a pair-bond that wasn't completely forced on them. They both resisted it for a long time, which allowed an organic love to grow. Lukas couldn't let go and stop acting so angry and resisting things out of fear. Fear of loss and rejection. Who knew what else. Seth wasn't the type to deep dive into emotions with others.

"Fighting it doesn't help. It will only hurt you in the end."

"Fighting what?"

Lukas nodded across the pool at Riley climbing the ladder.

"I don't know what you think, but I'm not fighting with her."

"No. You're fighting what you could have with her."

Was he that transparent?

Sighing, Seth shook his head. "There's nothing to have there. She deserves more than I have to give. She wants her pair. Wants that fairy tale love like you and Blaire have. Like the kind of fluffy shit she reads in those damn books." He put his head in his hands, elbows on his thighs again. "I can't give her that. I literally can't give her that because fucking fate said no."

Even as the words left his lips, he knew if fate did slap them with the ability to pair-bond, he would fight it. He didn't want to be forced into it. His entire argument was a contradiction that stood as flimsy as a pillow fort in a hailstorm. He wanted her, and to have her he needed to be her Korrena to feel worthy of her. To be her Korrena meant it was biology and not real love, so he would reject it and not have her. But if she wanted him without it, and they weren't Korrena bound, then he didn't feel worthy of her because she needed more. It made his stomach upset to even try to decipher the paradox.

"You want to be her pair?"

"No," he said emphatically, sitting up straight.

"Why are you so against it?"

"You know why. It's not real."

"Oh, come off that. You said yourself you started to understand it with Blaire and me. If one day you wake up and realize you two are Korrena pairs, then it doesn't change what we all know is between the two of you."

"There's nothing—"

"Don't even start. Just listen. You don't have to just go with the flow of the bond. It takes more than just the link. You have to nurture it. My mom has told me a lot of stuff about it. It requires a lot of work to have it snap into place beyond the claiming ritual."

"What do you mean?"

Lukas leaned back on his hands. "Well, there's a lot of communication. I've never talked so much in my life it feels like. Which is why I can talk with you about it like I am now."

Seth shook his head, turning to put a knee up on the marble floor, leaving one leg still in the water. He kind of liked the new vibe between them. "Domestic bliss suits you. I'll give you that."

"Oh, fuck off."

Seth laughed.

"But yeah. Apparently, there's this whole thing about overcoming the most primal part of yourself to stabilize the bond once you've locked it in with the claiming ritual."

"So there's more than blood sharing and sex?"

"Apparently."

"So why in the hell don't they teach us that?"

Lukas shrugged.

Blackthorn's branch schools taught about the Korrena bond from a young age through high school to prepare them for when they might find their pair in their late teens. The classes were like sex education humans went through in their schools, but Vasirian classes focused on what the Korrena bond was, when it would happen, how to complete it, and things of that nature. It left many unknowns when they entered adulthood.

"Look, I'm not trying to pry into your life. But you were there for me when I needed you. You helped save Blaire. So if I can do anything to help you with dealing with whatever is going on in your head…"

Seth nodded. "Yeah, sure."

"Alright then." Lukas pushed himself up to stand. "I think I'm going to head up to bed if Blaire's ready."

Lukas walked away to go to the deep end and talk to the others. Seth appreciated that his friend wanted to help him. It didn't mean he would take him up on it, but it was nice to know the option was there.

Aiden walked up. "Hey, Riley isn't wanting to go back to the room yet, but we're all gonna head up. You coming?"

Seth looked over to Riley, who watched him from the corner at the deep end of the pool, then shrugged. "Want me to leave, or want company?" he called to her.

"You haven't even swam," she called out, swimming in their direction.

"I guess there's your answer," he said, chuckling. He told Aiden, Lukas, and Blaire, "I'll see you three tomorrow at breakfast."

"Make sure you lock up when you're done, or they won't let us sneak in here again," Aiden said.

"Sure."

When they left the pool area, Seth turned his attention back to Riley, who lapped back and forth across the deep end. Grinning, he slipped into the water and swam in her direction as smoothly as he could, submerging as he approached, coming up beneath her. The squeal she made as he came from beneath her, arms banded around her waist, made him laugh until her foot connected with his thigh.

He cursed, releasing her. "Holy shit, that hurt."

"That'll teach you to scare me."

Laughing, he pushed his wet hair from his forehead. "Oh, come on, it wasn't that bad, was it?"

"Yes." She crossed her arms beneath her chest and gave an exaggerated pout. At his imploring look, she groaned. "Fine, no. You're such an ass."

"Yeah, but it's such a fine ass."

"You did not just say that."

"What? It's true."

"Whatever helps you sleep at night."

"You're telling me I'm not fine?"

"No one says 'fine' anymore."

"And you're not answering me." He swam closer. "Are you trying to imply I'm ugly?"

"Ugh, you're so full of yourself." She splashed him as he neared, and then swam to the center of the pool.

Following her, he laughed. "I'm not full of myself for asking a question. It's not that hard to say 'Yes, Seth, I find you ugly.'"

Riley rolled her eyes. "You know I wouldn't say that."

"Oh, so you *do* think I'm fine?"

Riley giggled, the sound warming something that had lain cold inside him for the last three days. He wanted things between them to be normal again. This was a start.

"I try not to think about stuff like that," she said, breaking him from his thoughts.

What does that mean?

"What?"

"Nothing really."

As much as he didn't want to, he let it go. Pushing when he had put distance between them recently wouldn't be good. He couldn't imagine what reason she invented for him not coming around while she felt ill. He tended to be nearer when she was out of sorts. It killed him not to be.

Swimming backwards, Riley said above a whisper, "You aren't ugly."

His brows rose, her words catching him off guard. Licking his lips, he asked, "What am I then?" He hoped he wasn't pushing her by asking. Girls told him all the time he was attractive, but only her opinion mattered.

A pink blush stained Riley's cheeks as she shook her head.

"Come on. It's just you and me here. I'll answer your questions if you answer mine."

"Like Twenty Questions?"

"Something like that, yeah." He resisted the urge to laugh. She loved playing childish games, and he would indulge her this time to get the answers he sought.

Riley glanced around the dimly lit, empty room. The lights beneath the water cast glowing ripples across her pale skin. She looked beautiful. "Okay," she whispered softly.

"Okay," he echoed. "So tell me."

"You're the nicest-looking guy I know at the academy."

His head tipped to the side. "Nicest?"

"Hottest," she mumbled.

Swallowing hard, he nodded. He didn't think she ever looked at him that way.

"Do you make a habit out of checking out other guys at the academy?"

"Nuh uh. You already asked a question. My turn."

His lips twisted. "Fine, sure. But we're coming back to that."

Riley waved a hand. "Okay, so…" She tapped her lips before using her arms to tread water again. "Why have you avoided me for the past three days?"

Straight to the hard questions.

Choosing the truth, he said, "I didn't hang out with anyone the past three days." He avoided everyone in an effort to get his head on straight.

"Why?"

"That's another question, so I get two."

"Whatever."

"I had a lot on my mind and wasn't feeling like being social."

"Was everything okay?"

"Three." He grinned.

"Ugh, seriously? Fine, whatever. Answer."

She sounded irritated, but he knew she wasn't. How, he wasn't sure. He just knew.

"Everything was fine. Just needed space to clear my head. This trip has been a lot, you know?" At her nod, he relaxed. At least she seemed satisfied with his answers. "Now, back to my question."

"What question was that?"

Smirking, he said, "Do you make a habit out of checking out other guys at the academy?"

"No, but I'm not immune to recognizing when a guy is attractive or not."

Seth smiled at the affronted look on her face. She wasn't mad, and at her age of course she would notice other guys, but he didn't have to like it. He hated it, but that was the reality of things.

"I've never seen you hanging out with any of these 'attractive' guys." His head dipped to the other side, his tone playful. "So have any of them made it to boyfriend status?"

"Boyfriend?" Smokey-blue eyes widened. "No. But that doesn't matter. You haven't had a girlfriend either!"

"Never wanted one." He shrugged, trying to keep an air of indifference when he was hanging on to every answer she gave. "Have you?"

"Maybe I haven't wanted to make one official either."

The way she worded that rankled him, the skin around his eyes tightening as he narrowed them. Did that mean she had someone in her life before? He didn't remember anyone. Had things happened? He couldn't fully mask the agitation in his voice when he asked, "So you've done other things without making it official?"

"Nope, can't ask a fourth question."

"I only asked two."

"No. You asked me about attractive guys, then boyfriends, and then if I wanted one."

Cursing under his breath, he shook his head. "Tell me, Riley. I know you're a virgin, so it can't be that serious."

"What?" she asked incredulously. "I may be a virgin, but I'm not naïve to things, Seth."

"What have you done?"

The surprised look on her face let him know his possessiveness and jealousy weren't masked as well as he thought. But the idea she'd done anything with any of the guys at the academy raked through his insides, burning a path of destruction, and left him feeling raw.

Riley looked away. Before she could attempt to escape to avoid the conversation, he moved toward her. Like he predicted, she squeaked and swam toward the shallow end, making it to most of the way before he backed her to the side wall. The water there came to just below her sternum, and her feet touched the bottom.

His hands settled alongside her shoulders on the side of the pool, caging her in, keeping himself at arm's length from her. "Tell me."

Confused eyes met his. "There's nothing worth telling."

"Nothing worth telling doesn't mean there isn't anything to tell, so just say it."

Why was he doing this? In normal circumstances, he could let things go and move on, but when it came to the idea of another guy touching her, he wanted to burn things down.

When she looked to the side, blushing in response, he knew for sure he was right in assuming something happened. He couldn't handle it.

Without thinking his next action through, he lifted his hand from the water and cuffed the front of her throat delicately.

Riley's eyes widened in panic for the briefest moment before her pupils dilated right before his eyes and her entire body relaxed, the tension coming off her in waves before dissipating like powder dissolving in water.

Interesting.

That such a proprietary act coming from him elicited such a response from her made his blood burn.

He did that.

She didn't fear him.

Quite the opposite.

The way her muscles gave in to him so easily spoke of her trust and called to something inside him. Something he didn't know existed. Was it a need to control? To own? That sounded right when he let the thoughts roll around in his head, but possessing her as his wasn't enough to explain the feeling.

Riley needed someone to take control when her mind ran rampant; he learned that long ago. Maybe that's all it was. She needed him. Her responding in the same way she did when he used his voice and words to ground her made him want to give her what she needed. He *needed* to be needed by her. It was the only time he felt worthy of her.

Gently, he stroked his thumb along the side of her throat, and her breath hitched.

He wouldn't squeeze.

He just wanted her attention.

Seth's head dipped as he leaned in, one hand still braced on the side of the pool, keeping his body away from her, still holding her throat with the other. Stopping with his cheek alongside hers, he whispered, "Be a good girl for me and tell me."

Her answering whimper went straight to his cock, and he squeezed the side of the pool to restrain himself, biting the inside of his cheek to control the sound that almost left his own throat. This was a side of her he never experienced before.

"Tell me, Riley," he whispered, the command clear in his voice. He grazed the shell of her ear with his teeth before pulling away, letting go of the front of her throat and releasing the side of the pool until he stared down at her, leaving a couple of feet between them.

He sought a balance between pushing the line of control and the amount of space between them in order to find comfort in a situation that might become too overstimulating.

Riley flushed from her cheeks to her chest that moved faster with her panted breaths.

With the long silence, he thought she wouldn't answer, despite how she normally submitted to the way he spoke, but she murmured, "I've kissed before. Nothing else, really."

His brow lifted. No experience at all surprised him, but didn't at the same time. The knowledge settled the jealousy swirling in his chest.

"You really have no experience with other guys outside of kissing?"

She looked away.

"What aren't you saying?"

"This is so stupid."

There was the firecracker energy coming back to balance things out.

"It's not. I want to know."

"Why?"

"Because I'm curious," he said matter-of-factly.

"Is it your business?"

"Yes."

Riley blinked. "Why? Since when?"

"Because I know everything about you. Or at least I thought I did."

Her expression shifted as she studied his face, and he wondered if the hurt that flickered through him at his last words showed on his face, because she let out a long breath and met his eyes.

"I don't have experience *period*. Beyond kissing a boy in high school, there's nothing outside of the joking around we've done in the last month. And the dare." Her face flamed pink.

Wait a minute…

"I don't understand. Not even to yourself?"

Seth didn't think the blush on her skin could get any deeper, but it did. "There is no way. Everyone gets off, Riley."

"It's not like that." She crossed her arms, and he recognized it for the defensive posturing it was.

Tempering his tone with genuine curiosity, he said, "Hey, I didn't mean that in a bad way. I'm only confused. Most people our age have done that sort of thing. Some multiple times a day." He shrugged. "Can I ask why?"

Her eyes focused on the water between them.

"You don't have to answer," he finally said after a minute or two of silence. He would never push her to the point of genuine distress. "I'm sorry if I crossed a line. Do you want to get out?"

"I can't do it," she blurted, still not looking at him.

"What?"

"I've tried. I just can't get there, you know?"

The reality of what her words meant staggered him.

Licking his lips, trying to stimulate saliva to help his sudden dry mouth, he shook his head. "Why not?" He hoped she felt comfortable enough to answer him. They were in dangerous territory. They never confided in one another about things this raw. But if she had a genuine problem, he wanted to help her or point her in the right direction.

Inhaling long through her nose and sharply back out, she met his eyes. "I can't get out of my head." Her lips twisted before she continued. "Sometimes everything is going fine. I feel good—I mean, *really* good—and then, the sound of the bed squeaking, or someone in the hall, or even just the random thought of what I have to do that day trickles in and I go from ninety to zero in an instant. I eventually gave up trying to reach the big finish. Especially when the other thoughts started becoming a problem."

It wasn't a matter of never having masturbated, but an inability to reach climax. He felt bad for her. The big O was the best part when it came to self-love. But something she said caught his attention more than a lack of orgasms.

"What other thoughts are you talking about?"

"It's stupid."

"Stop saying that."

"Saying what?"

"That everything is stupid. Your thoughts and feelings aren't stupid."

She huffed and sucked in her cheek. "Fine." She leaned against the wall of the pool, lowering herself until her chin brushed the surface of the water. "Sometimes it's hard not to look at my body in that moment and be disgusted with myself."

"What could you ever have to be disgusted about?"

"What? You didn't hear? I have the body of a kid. What eighteen-year-old wants to have that?"

He closed the distance between them, lifting her chin with the side of his index finger. "Your body is perfect."

She scoffed and pulled away from his touch. "Says the guy who exclusively takes girls with big breasts and full curves to his bed."

"I have my reasons." He lowered his hand into the water again and sighed. "But you're beautiful, Riley. You have no reason to be disgusted with yourself. Not everyone is suited to certain features. I wouldn't look right with the kind of muscles your brother has. It doesn't work for my frame. If I had his height with my body, I'd be almost as lean as Kai. So when I say your body is perfect, it is. Besides, anything more than a handful isn't necessary."

She sank into the water more and mumbled, making bubbles. "It's what you like, though."

"What I like and don't like doesn't matter. You don't know what I like. It just happens to be what's convenient."

Why she worried about what he liked, he didn't know, but he wasn't lying about convenience. Yes, he sought that type, but it was easy to find them. *That* was the convenient part.

"Yeah, okay." She straightened and looked up at him. "So now you know my experience and my stupid problem. We done?"

Her unexpected defensive tone made his brows lift.

"We can be." He glanced toward the exit, blatantly ignoring the warning signs of the cliff edge ahead, and spoke his next words with quiet caution. "Or I can help you."

"Huh?"

Seth turned his attention back to her face. Between his real desire to help her with something he knew caused her upset and the inferno his libido stirred, he might make the biggest mistake of their lives in this moment, but he walked right off the cliff and hoped she didn't let him meet the rocks below.

Riley gasped as his fingers trailed down the soft expanse of skin between her ribs to her navel beneath the water, and then stopped.

"I can help you," he whispered. "I've done it before, right? Gotten you out of your head?"

She swallowed audibly and shivered beneath his fingertips that barely grazed her skin. He wished they were out of the water so he could feel its softness.

"I don't think talking to me and giving… orders helps with this kind of thing." Her embarrassment showed on her face and in the way she couldn't meet his eyes. She never acknowledged out loud that what he assumed helped did help. She never needed to. He knew.

Just like he knew this would help if she surrendered to him.

"What harm is there in trying? I can tell when your mind wanders, Riley. I can bring you back." He took the chance to move closer, caging her again with his hands on the side of the pool. Leaning down, he whispered in her ear, "Nothing else has to happen. Just let me show you how good it can feel."

Riley's teeth sank into her lip. He wanted to remove them and replace them with his teeth, but he told her nothing else would happen.

"Nothing else?"

"Nothing else."

A flicker of something moved through his senses. A feeling of disappointment washed over him and faded. Sure, he felt disappointment, but something about the sensation felt alien. Not his. Shaking his head, he focused his attention back on Riley. He didn't have time to let his own mind wander.

She nodded her consent, whispering the words, "Show me."

He wanted to throw his fist into the air and thank whatever star in the sky believed him worthy of that moment with her.

"Just… don't be weird about it after like the dare. I don't want that."

His chest tightened. "We don't have to talk about it again. We go back to normal, so don't let your mind focus on consequences or discomfort. It won't be that way."

Seth didn't want her to feel unstable for something like this, so he led her out of the pool and over to the lounger, illuminated only with ambient lighting, which he hoped would make her feel secure in the moment. Less exposed.

While he wanted to take her back to the room for the most comfort, he knew how her mind worked. They wouldn't make it there before she backed out and ran away. He didn't want her to retreat in on herself, or from this.

There were so many things he could do to help her reach that pinnacle of pleasure, but he would keep it simple. He didn't want to overwhelm and scare her. Since she'd only ever kissed someone, he didn't think she would be ready for the things he wanted to do.

He guided her back onto the lounger, and she looked up at him with wary eyes. The apprehension hung thick in the air. It started making him nervous, so before she could pick up on that, he knelt at her side and placed his palm on the flat plane of her belly. Her breath hitched.

"Easy," he whispered.

She released a stuttered breath and closed her eyes for a moment.

"Any time you want to stop, it's done. No questions asked. No need to explain yourself. It'll end, and we go back to normal. Okay?"

Opening her eyes, she looked up at him with a curt nod, and the trust he saw in her eyes nearly bowled him over. She would be the death of him.

"Is there anything I can do to make you less nervous?" He kept his eyes on her face and his hand still, patiently waiting for her to call the shots. It wasn't time for him to take the reins yet.

Riley turned her head away from him, staring off toward the marble columns that lined the pool, and he pressed his lips into a tight line. Something wasn't being said, but he didn't know what.

Still, he waited.

They sat there for a good five minutes before she turned to look at him. "Can you…" She brought her hands up to cover her face, but he pulled them down, holding them in his hands, giving her a squeeze of encouragement. "This is harder than I thought," she mumbled.

"It's okay. It's just me here. You know I would never judge you."

"I don't want to make you do something you don't want to do."

That surprised him. What in the world was she thinking about that worried her enough to think she would be forcing him into something he didn't want to do?

He shook his head. "Riley, if it's something I don't want to do, I'll tell you. Just like I expect you to do for me. I trust you in the same way I want you to trust me. I trust you won't do anything I don't want, and that it won't hurt what we have."

Her lips rolled inward as she contemplated his words. She nodded as if confirming something with herself and met his eyes once again. "Can you kiss me? I mean… during? You know, to distract me—ow!" She jerked her hands from his.

Shit.

He hadn't realized he started gripping her hands tightly when she asked for him to kiss her until it was too late. "Sorry, sorry. You took me off guard." The excuse was lame. True, but lame, because there was more to it. That she wanted him to kiss her again, even if only to distract her from her nerves… he was glad he was kneeling and not standing.

"It's okay. Does that mean you don't want to? I totally get it. Like, it's weird, right? This whole thing is already weird enough. You're offering to help me masturbate just to have an orgasm because I can't think straight, and I go and ask you to kiss me when we're friends. We don't do that. Kiss, I mean. That's something boyfriend and girlfriends do, or like, lovers. And we're certainly none of those things. So, like, of course you're going to be uncomfortable with it, right? I'm sorry. We can just forget this whole—"

Seth leaned in and crushed his lips to hers, bracing one hand beside her head on the lounger. With her gasp of surprise, he licked into her mouth, not giving her the opportunity to take this as anything but him wanting to kiss her. It wasn't the time to use his words to reassure her. Not anymore.

Their tongues tangled together, the sounds of their moans echoing in the empty space, amplified by the still water beyond them.

Breaking the kiss, keeping his forehead against hers, panting against her swollen lips, he ran his other hand down her belly to her swimsuit bottom. When he she tensed, he returned to focusing on languid kisses against her soft lips until she relaxed into the chair, providing the distraction she requested and loving every second.

His heart kicked at how hot and saturated the fabric felt beneath his fingers versus the rest of her swimsuit bottoms damp from the pool water. She moaned against his mouth at the featherlight touch. He pushed aside the fabric, exposing everything to the open air of the room, but he didn't look. Didn't want to risk her withdrawing from him. There was so much he wanted to do, but she wanted only one thing in this moment, and that was what he would give her. Even though he wanted to touch every inch of exposed skin before him.

Teaching Riley and helping her discover something that only he got to show her for the first time brought him a pleasure he never experienced before. Pleasure beyond the physical. Beyond surface level. A soul-deep satisfaction he would remember for the rest of his life.

When he finally dragged two fingers through her center, her level of wetness surprised him. Wound up before he ever started. His fingers were coated, enough to make him break the kiss and stare at them in wonder. It wasn't his first time seeing a woman's arousal on his fingers, but never that level of excitement so early in the game.

Seth's attention snapped to Riley's face when her knees closed.

"Are you okay? Should I stop?"

Her hands gripped the chair, and she bit the edge of her lip. "Don't look at it."

"Why not?"

"It's embarrassing." The blush spreading across her skin, coupled with the vulnerability on her face, made his heart stutter. She was so cute.

This girl is going to be the death of me.

"It's sexy," he said. He couldn't keep the rasp out of the sound as he tried to keep his composure. If he gave in to the temptation to taste the silkiness coating his fingers like he wanted to, he'd lose her. She wasn't ready for that level of heat. "Now, do you want me to stop?"

"No," she whispered.

"Good." He slowly pried her knees apart. "Because I didn't want to."

This time, when he touched her again, she sank into the chair, releasing the death grip on the sides. Her legs fell open, one leg hanging off the lounger next to him so he could lean over her, and the other bent to leave her open to him, finally allowing him to look down at everything he touched.

So damn beautiful.

But he couldn't tell her. This was supposed to be helping her. Not baring his heart.

Fucking idiot.

Shaking his head, he looked down at her.

For not having experience, she kept herself well groomed, and the sight of the glistening arousal against the pinkness he slid his fingers over as he teased her inner folds made a groan fall from his lips unbidden.

Riley's eyes opened to look at him in surprise, but he didn't explain, just kept his eyes down and pretended he didn't notice her watching him. At this point, he didn't care if she knew how she affected him. It was ridiculous to worry about right now.

When his fingers passed over her clit, her hips jerked. Grinning, he did it again, but this time, he didn't stop. Her head went back on a loud moan, her upper body arching. He turned his attention to her face as he worked her clit with his thumb, running his fingers through her slippery folds.

It happened the way he expected.

He watched it happen in slow motion.

The squirming in her hips slowly ceased, and her upper body dropped as she panted, and a furrow drew her brows together.

He would not lose her.

"Riley," he said firmly, and her eyes snapped to his. The disappointment in them was so strong it hurt his heart. "Stay with me, baby." Her breath hitched at the endearment he didn't mean to say. "Do you trust me?"

"Yes."

Seth's fingers slipped lower, circling her entrance, and she wiggled.

"How much do you trust me?"

"Always."

His eyes rolled, his head falling back on a groan. Having her ultimate trust was the biggest aphrodisiac someone could give him.

Leaning over her, he brought his face to her ear and whispered the endearment she had responded to before. "You're such a good girl. Thank you for trusting me." He slipped a single finger inside the warmth of her body. The tightness made him shudder.

She squirmed at the intrusion, and he wondered if she ever put her fingers inside like this. To think he might have been the only one… He would never recover from this night.

"More," she said on a whimper.

As he slipped a second finger inside her body, she surprised him by reaching out to the back of his head and bringing his face to hers. He waited, and she delivered. She closed the distance and kissed him deeply.

His tongue ran over the seam of her lips, and she opened to him, inviting his passion into the kiss she initiated.

The longer he moved his fingers inside her warmth, curling them to graze that secret spot inside of her, the more she gave in to him. Before long, she had her arm wrapped around his shoulders, panting against his lips, not kissing him anymore as she rode his fingers.

He was so hard it hurt. As much as he wanted to free himself and ease the pressure, he wouldn't scare her that way.

When her arm slackened, he didn't let her mind take her away from what they were sharing.

"Stay with me," he whispered against her lips, biting at them and licking the swollen aftermath. "You're almost there. Give it to me, Firecracker."

"Seth," she mewled.

Fuck.

Hearing his name called like that nearly made him come in his swim trunks. Riley lost to lust, surrendering to him, was so different from the everyday Riley. This sweet, pliable, trusting woman before him was someone no one else ever saw. Only him.

His gums didn't merely tingle—they *ached*.

He trailed his lips along her jaw and down her neck, and when his teeth brushed the side of her throat, not biting because he promised he wouldn't unless she wanted him to, she jerked in his arms. Her head fell back on a cry as her insides squeezed his fingers, fluttering.

There we go.

Seth continued trailing soft kisses along her throat and shoulder as she came down, clinging to him tightly, her head buried on his shoulder. He whispered reassurances against her sweat-slick skin.

"You did so good, baby. So, so good."

Her answering whimper was all he got before she relaxed into his body.

She'd fallen asleep.

Not only had she given him her first orgasm, but she'd also felt safe enough to give into the exhaustion the physical, and likely mental, experience brought her.

Things would return to normal tomorrow. He made it clear he only wanted to help her. He didn't expect the experience to rattle him to the core so much. Expected nothing more than touching her externally. Not discovering the warmth of the inside of her body. Not kissing.

He didn't know if his heart could handle it.

15

CONVENIENT

Shelby told me today she wanted to find someone, get married, and have an army of kids. She grew up in a large family, so I wasn't surprised. What surprised me was the certainty I felt in my gut that if I knew she would say yes, I'd ask her. I would give that to her, even though we were so young. I wanted everything with her. The house. The kids. The rocking chairs while we grew senile beside one another. All of it. Societal constructs of "appropriate" timelines be damned.

"I wanted to talk to you about something," Blaire said, finishing painting Riley's big toe with a sparkly violet polish.

Riley closed her book after placing a bookmark inside. "Go for it."

"I know you didn't like Aiden bringing him up the other day, and I can understand why, considering he's your brother, but I have to ask… Are you really sure about things with Dom? I mean, I don't understand the whole monarchy thing and positions of power causing problems the way he explained it, so this is more of a…" The extended pause made Riley's brow quirk. "What about Seth?" Blaire finally said with a grimace, as if preparing for Riley to attack her.

Riley ensured her face was the picture of calm serenity as she asked, "What about him?"

The last week tested her ability to sort her thoughts, emotions, and physical desires more than any time in her short life.

The night before last, she shared something with Seth she would never forget. Admitting things she never in a million years believed he would find out about her. Agreeing to let him help her experience something she had trouble finding. She became someone else in his hands. Someone free.

The things he said to her were indeed words spoken in the hazy bubble of lust they created in that small corner of the poolroom. He probably called all the girls he slept with by the same names. It surprised her how much not only her body reacted to his touch and words, but also her mind and heart.

Submitting to him and being his "good girl" woke something inside her she didn't know existed. It freed her mind. She didn't have to think about what to do next. When she realized that, and he kept her from slipping, the climax she desperately sought came as natural to her as breathing.

She still didn't understand what happened afterward. Her mind slipped into a daze, like she floated somewhere else. The feeling alarmed her until the warmth of his arms soothed her and darkness pulled her under.

"I thought you wanted to be with Seth," Blaire said, stealing Riley's attention back to the present.

"Wanting and having are two entirely different things."

There. She finally admitted to her best friend what said best friend already knew.

"Listen, it really isn't my business, but I care about Dom. The things we went through… there's a bond there through that shared experience. I don't want to see him hurt. I mean, I don't think you'd hurt him on purpose, but collateral damage, you know?"

Riley wondered if Blaire had provided all the details of what took place in her time in the dungeons when the Order locked her away and on the run with Dominic. Lukas was aware of all the details, but it still didn't mean everything had been shared with the group. It still made her wonder how bad the experiences Blaire shared were.

"Okay, look. Dom is a nice guy. I do like him. And he wants to see if there's anything there between us beyond physical attraction."

"Well, he is easy on the eyes," Blaire said, lifting a shoulder. "Bonus for you, he favors Seth somewhat." She smiled.

"Yeah, well, I wonder what harm it would do to see. He knows how I feel about Seth."

Blaire sobered. The quick change from casual to serious caught Riley off guard. She leaned forward and lowered her voice, whisper-yelling like someone else was in the room. "He *knows*?"

Riley nodded.

"So not only did you tell him before me, but he's okay with dating you while you're in love with another man?" Blaire's voice had become excitable and loud by the end of her rant.

Riley sat up with wide eyes. "Whoa, whoa, whoa. No one said anything about love."

Blaire's eye roll made it clear she wasn't swayed.

"And you already knew how I felt about Seth," she said, pointing and refusing to acknowledge the big L-word. A word she hadn't spoken to herself either.

"Knowing and having your friend *tell* you is different. You still haven't."

"I have so!"

"Not really."

Riley flopped back dramatically and put her hands on her face, groaning loud into her hands. "You're splitting hairs. Tomato, tomahto."

Blaire giggled. "Sucks, doesn't it?"

Riley dropped her hands. "Huh?" The amused look on Blaire's face confused her.

"You give me and Lukas hell sometimes for avoiding our feelings. Turnabout is fair play."

"Oh, you're evil. Besides, how many times do I have to tell you there's nothing going on between us?"

Nothing she understood, anyway.

"Once more than your face turning pink every time I mention it." Blaire patted the top of Riley's foot. "But back to real talk. I think Seth cares for you more than you realize."

"I know he cares about me," Riley said, trying the oblivious card because she didn't like the direction the conversation was headed.

"No, Riley." Blaire repositioned herself on the bed, drawing her leg beneath her. "Everyone has kept quiet about it, but I can't when I see you possibly making a mistake and missing out on something special." The words that followed her exhale made Riley's eyes burn. "I think he loves you, and more than the familial type."

Riley laughed. "Not likely. I think maybe you're looking for something you want to be there."

"Uh, no. I don't think you see the way he looks at you."

Ignoring Blaire's skeptical expression with the ease only someone spent avoiding awkward things could do, she chose to focus on the words Blaire said before. Words Riley once spoke to her about Lukas.

"The way he looks at me?"

"Mmhm. Those looks are rare and sometimes once in a lifetime."

Blaire's eyes softened, and Riley wasn't sure she liked what was coming next. "And y'know what? You look at him the same way. Like someone desperately in love but afraid of taking the plunge."

Riley bristled, a wave of panic hitting her with the force of a truck. If Seth saw something similar from her, he would run for the hills. She wouldn't entertain the idea he looked at her that way. Hope was a dangerous thing.

"And the way he acts like he would burn the world to give you anything you wanted? Gotta admit, little jealous of that."

That shocked her. Even if joking, a paired Korrena having any jealousy toward another person's relationship—or in this case, a non-relationship—seemed silly.

Snorting, she shook her head. "You're being dramatic."

"I only want you to think hard on things before you make the decision to pursue things with Dom and walk away from anything not explored elsewhere."

Riley could agree to giving things more thought, but not because of Seth. Sure, they shared intimate moments lately. Really amazing, intimate moments. Their first kiss was insane, but only a dare. He'd run from her after. The cafeteria. She couldn't explain the arousal other than lack of sex with an extremely sexual person, and she ended up landing awkwardly.

Somehow, she could even rationalize with herself what occurred the other night. She'd done so for days. Each time she thought on it, her mind twisted the memories and painted the feelings they spawned with strokes of black, slowly blotting out any positive takeaway, leaving her thinking one depressing truth:

She was just convenient while in a foreign country, nothing more.

Seth would never love her the way she loved him.

16

Balance

Waiting for the summons back to Blackthorn Manor took longer than Riley expected. Another week passed where they did nothing more than sit around the hotel, check out the beautiful sights of historic London, and, for Blaire's sake, try all the new cuisine. The vacation normally wouldn't bother Riley, but she couldn't stop thinking about what happened between Seth and her at the pool. Chaotic thoughts intensified by the strangest feelings of longing rivaling anything she ever felt before whenever he came around. The curious emotions didn't feel like hers, but the notion of anything else seemed silly.

Seth gave her exactly what he promised. He acted like nothing happened. Their usual banter continued, taking snipes at one another that would have another person believing they disliked each other, and while she loved that they could move on and fall back into their regular way of life, it felt wrong.

Sexual chemistry aside, the way she felt giving in to him, how still her mind became, wasn't a feeling she wanted to let go of yet. Even when she knew she should.

On a windy Wednesday morning when the sky was cloudy and leeched of blue, promising rain, word arrived requesting their presence at Blackthorn Manor.

Professor Velastra debriefed them on the situation, stating the Oracle had arrived, and now the king wanted to discuss the details of the Order before hosting a dinner to thank Blaire properly as intended. Apparently, King Adrian believed the Oracle possessed a gift that would sniff out a lie and intended to use that in his follow-up questions.

Lukas was understandably angry. Having seen what happened to his Korrena and what happened to him at the hands of the Order, no one could blame him for the brief—albeit loud—fit her threw when Professor Velastra revealed that piece of information about the king's little quirk.

Now, standing in front of the king, Riley worried Lukas would make a scene. Judging by the tense set of his jaw, he wasn't happy. Blaire kept her arm linked around his forearm; that connection was probably the only thing preventing Lukas from saying something he shouldn't.

The Blackthorn Clan sat in the same positions as last time. The liaison made herself scarce after delivering them to the throne room, likely not allowed to know the situation back in the States.

"Thank you all for joining us again. Our sincerest apologies for not gathering sooner," King Adrian said, giving no further explanation for the delay. No one dared ask for one.

"As you know, Adrian intended to host a fanciful dinner for our human friend here," Gabriel said, flashing his white teeth with a cheerful smile. "But our dear Oracle has finally shown herself, so there's a few business matters before we can get fed and bollocksed."

"Gabriel. Must you be so crass?"

Gabriel gave Mariana a faux-innocent look. "What did I say?"

"No one wants to compare drinking to your testicles."

"They might not even know what it means," Gabriel said, petulance in his tone.

Dimitri snorted. "I'd think bollocks is pretty universal."

The king pinched the bridge of his nose, resting his elbow on the arm of his throne.

The Blackthorn Clan behaved nothing like Riley expected. Mariana and King Adrian spoke most like members of authority, but Gabriel acted too laid back, and Dimitri reminded her of a rebellious sibling forced to sit with the family. Mariana's husband Felix seemed more poised—like his wife—and didn't speak enough for her to formulate an opinion.

Another expected absence was the king's rumored anger. Many Vasirian spoke of the strong, and oftentimes explosive, temper King Adrian exhibited. The rumors made it seem that behavior was an all-the-time thing. A fair and just king caring for his people who accepted no less than perfection.

Reality rarely lived up to the hype. Unless more rested beneath the surface.

Riley shifted on her feet, wishing they had chairs to sit in instead of standing in front of the clan like prisoners awaiting execution by firing squad. Uncomfortable and antsy were the only feelings she could identify at being forced to wait.

Seth stepped closer to her side, his arm brushing hers, and she had to fight the shiver his touch caused. She didn't think he even moved with intent.

"Excuse my family," was all the king could manage to say before the side door opened and the Oracle glided into the room.

Simple navy slacks and a lighter blue blouse looked out of place on her when she'd only ever worn elaborate robes on campus. Riley assumed the fashion choice was to maintain a low profile while in London until the dust settled. Her black hair, highlighted with stark silver pieces, was piled high in a tight bun, lifting her facial features. As the oldest known Vasirian at four hundred, she looked good for her age, even by their standards. She would never look older than she did now. At one hundred and fifty Vasirian stopped aging, never looking older than sixty.

Every member on the dais stood, surprising Riley. The deference shown as all but the king lowered their heads was interesting. The Order never reacted that way. Even Dominic stood from his chair on the end, allowing her to take his seat. He stood at her side. When he noticed Riley looking, he winked at her.

Aiden leaned down to whisper, "Still talking to him, then?"

"Shut up," she hissed. "I haven't since you did."

Returning her attention back to the dais, the Oracle smiled with warmth at their group. "I am here to fill in the gaps and provide additional information to King Adrian as needed." Her gentle gaze moved to the king. "You need not fear lies from these students. The trust, conviction, strength, and love found in the bonds they share with one another holds too strongly to allow such a thing. To protect those bonds, they know to be forthcoming with the information you need."

For once, the Oracle didn't speak in a riddle. The gang had spent most of their lives together, outside of Blaire, and it even felt like Riley had known Blaire her whole life, so of course they connected.

King Adrian sat upright and nodded. "Very well. From my understanding of the reports provided, Angelo Moretti, leader of the

Order, believed you"—he motioned to Blaire—"were something akin to a witch, and he wanted to perform a blood-letting ritual to extract said magic? Is this correct?"

Blaire looked at Lukas with hesitation, then Aiden, before settling her gaze on the Oracle, who nodded encouragement.

"Yes, sir—er—Your Highness?" Blaire grabbed at the ends of her long, blonde hair and began twisting them around her fingers.

Gabriel laughed, and even Dimitri chuckled under his breath until the king's low, inhuman growl echoed in the space. The entire room fell silent, allowing him to speak. The king seemed done with the casual back and forth energy at last.

"Use whatever makes you feel the most comfortable. Formalities are unnecessary, especially with what occurred. The important thing is you feel settled enough to not only recall such horrific events, but answer questions related to them. I delved deeper into those documents after your group's revelation about magic and runes last we met, and needless to say, I want to know more."

"Yes, sir."

"Good."

The compassion the king showed Blaire backed the "fair and just king" praise, but power lurked behind his growl, and the way even his own council stilled at the sound, it might take little to lose the kid glove treatment.

"Am I also correct in my understanding they ordered experimentation to reach the conclusion you are a witch?"

"Yes, sir."

"Experiments you volunteered for."

"Under duress," Professor Velastra interjected. "She accepted their requests to test her blood for what could possibly be the reason behind her Korrena status. At that time, we knew nothing of anything magic related. Blaire agreed because her Korrena pair, Lukas, was being held in the dungeons with the threat of exile to Cresbel Asylum for attacking their TA, Vincent Brandt, for his role in drugging and holding Blaire captive for two months."

Dark eyes slid to the professor and back to Blaire, but the king made no other outward reaction to the interruption. He stared at Blaire, waiting for her answer.

"Yes, sir," Blaire said, glancing at the professor.

"Adrian," Dominic stepped forward. "I think you should consider listening to this."

Again, the only outward reaction came from a simple eye shift.

The king had read their depositions, reviewed the physical evidence and other witness statements from the lab technicians and Blackthorn Security, so Riley didn't see where the line of questioning was headed.

"And these experiments revealed magical traits?" King Adrian's head tilted ever-so-slightly as he considered Blaire. "To think the stories of old might hold a grain of truth."

"I don't remember, sir."

"No?"

"What they did was painful—more painful than anything I had ever experienced until the ritual. I rarely stayed conscious long."

"Before those painful moments, can you explain to me what occurred that you remember? We only have the researcher reports from the lab, but as they were so clearly working for the Order, we cannot say for certain these reports are accurate."

"They used these stones. Stones with symbols engraved on them. All they really did was put them on my skin. My arms, thighs… Nothing happened. Not until they added blood."

"Blood?" Mariana asked, her eyes narrowing so her long dark

lashes hid her irises.

"Vasirian blood. My blood. They tried combinations with the stones. Like putting it on the stones. Then the pain started. None of it compared to one time, though."

"What happened?" Mariana's husband, Felix, asked.

Blaire looked at him. "They cut me. Said something about fresh blood from the source. I didn't understand how it differed from my blood in vials or freshly drawn with a needle, but apparently it was. My skin burned from the inside out, and while I struggled for consciousness, they mentioned my Korrena mark appeared like a brand on my skin. I passed out shortly after."

"From what I read, during your time in the dungeons, you didn't have your mark," the king said, and the tension in his jaw made his voice sound strained. Had he thought he caught Blaire in a lie? "Further, there was no mention of such an experiment."

"They said they were going to hide it from Angelo because of what it did to me."

Mariana asked, "You expect us to believe those who worked for the Order wanted to protect you? A human?"

"Mariana," Dominic said with a growl. "It happened. Blaire could barely move in her cell after it occurred."

"Then what of the mark?" she fired back.

"My mark was taken from me in the blood ritual Vincent performed, yes. Something about the experiment made it briefly resurface in fire, and I could smell the burnt flesh, but it didn't stay. I only know it resurfaced because the researchers spoke about it, but I couldn't see anything."

King Adrian sat back and rested his elbow on the arm of his throne, contemplating the information provided.

"What I have a hard time grasping is how a single human found herself in the position to not only be fated to a Vasirian in our strongest bond the gods bless us with, but that she is also magical—when there has been nothing of the sort documented."

The Oracle cleared her throat and smiled at the king with kindness. "This is where I come in." She turned in her chair to face the members of the Blackthorn Clan.

It wasn't a dismissal of the rest of them. They knew what information she planned to reveal to the monarchy about the bloody history of their kind and where Blaire fit into it. It made Riley anxious to think of what the reaction would be. Would they lock Blaire away? Hurt her?

Seth leaned down and whispered in her ear. "Think we'll get out of here in time to grab you a milkshake and me a burger?"

She swung her head to stare at him, mouth agape. They were meant to have dinner with the clan after this meeting, and she was about to snap and tell him so when the Oracle stared at the two of them, so she refrained.

At least she didn't feel anxious anymore. She glared at Seth; the small smile on his face confused her.

The Oracle explained how long ago a balance occurred between select humans and Vasirian. Magic linked the two. Those special humans were the witches and warlocks of old. The magic itself manifested differently for each human, which was a piece of information Riley didn't know, but the Oracle didn't elaborate that part.

These magical humans knew everything about Vasirian like they were one of them, and the magic in their blood called to the magic that stirred the Korrena bond in Vasirian.

"So what happened? Where have these magical humans gone, and where is any of this information outside of the wild legends Father once spoke of?" Mariana said with a scowl.

The Oracle closed her eyes. "The Blood Wars happened." She opened them again, turning her attention to Mariana. "A time where an entire group of beings were snuffed out of existence, out of fear and a lust for power. Such documentation was destroyed in an effort to hide our species' dark history and protect the one responsible."

"Who?"

The Oracle met King Adrian's eyes. "Your great-grandfather, Rosendo Blackthorn."

"There's no record of him."

"That is correct, but it was by his doing. To ensure his secret remained buried, he had any previous history of our kind destroyed lest suspicion arise about only his reign being missing from record."

Professor Velastra straightened. "I have been meaning to ask," she said to the Oracle. "You have said what occurred with Rosendo, and we have documentation of the king's father, Luciano, but I couldn't find anything on his grandfather either, who was after Rosendo. The rule went straight to Luciano, it appears."

"It did," the Oracle confirmed. "Salvador Blackthorn went mad because of what his father did and spent his remaining days in Cresbel Asylum before succumbing to the same method of death as both Rosendo and Luciano. He was very young at the time. He held no position of power to be documented."

With the documentation of their kind before King Luciano's reign missing, no one questioned the kings before him. When the Oracle revealed what King Rosendo did, it was so jarring none of them stopped to question the missing king in between. Riley shuddered at what a younger man possibly may have witnessed his father do and order.

"Wait a minute," Blaire said, turning her gaze on the Oracle.

"You told me before that Luciano was Rosendo's son."

The Oracle looked down with a sigh. "I am sorry for the confusion, child. Salvador had Luciano before the Blood War, but he was but a child when it occurred and when his father was locked away. Rosendo raised Luciano as his own child; and with no records to speak of, no one questioned the gap in the bloodline."

King Adrian muttered something under his breath. Riley could only imagine what it would be like to discover things about your family like that.

Gabriel's brow twitched in apparent confusion. "When you say he snuffed out a group's existence, you're speaking of the magical humans?"

"Yes. Rosendo ordered every warlock, witch, and Vasirian pregnant with a warlock's child to be slaughtered to avoid their power becoming too great."

"How would that be?"

"The children born of a Korrena pair between a magical human turned Vasirian and a Vasirian were the strongest of their kind. From there, a hierarchy of power followed down to Vasirian and humans who knew nothing of our existence. Rosendo feared this power and destroyed it."

The stoic and composed king finally snapped. He rose to his feet in a swift motion. "There will be no such tyranny under my rule." His voice boomed through the throne room at his declaration, his chest heaving as his eyes glowed amber.

The Oracle turned her eyes on Blaire as the king sat and composed himself, continuing as if not interrupted. "Except your great-grandfather didn't realize one witch escaped his destruction, and over the years, only one child came from any birth from that line until Blaire was brought into the world. With the death of your father last January, her magic stirred, and the chain of events to restore the natural balance began."

"Why are you bringing all of this to our attention now?" Mariana asked with narrowed eyes. "You've had hundreds of years to share this information with others. With our father. What changed?"

The Oracle sighed. "My memories. Before Rosendo ordered genocide, he forced one of the very humans he feared to bind my memories in a way I would never retrieve them. The ultimate way to silence the past without killing me."

"How did you finally get your memories back?" Gabriel asked.

"The Celestial Conclave has slowly revealed the information to me."

Dimitri scoffed. "That story we heard from the Order before about 'real creators'?"

King Adrian glared at his half-brother and turned to the Oracle. "So it's true then."

The Oracle nodded and redirected the subject. "I must press a warning I have already given to them, with additional information revealed to me." She looked down the marble steps to where Riley and the others waited. "This broken balance is a large reason our species is not as strong, or as long lasting as it was long ago. The moment the connection severed, a clock began ticking. Only in recent years have we seen the effects because only I was alive before the Blood Wars to remember what we had. Vasirian with special abilities such as compulsion were stronger. They had the affinity to learn and control magic. Our preternatural abilities resonated better. We did not struggle to find our Korrena pair."

The king's fist tightened on the arm of the throne's arm.

"Should the balance not be restored, the bloodline will not continue."

That seemed to perk the king's interest. "So does this mean Blaire and Lukas must reproduce to restore this balance you speak of?"

"No. There are others out there with magic lingering in their blood, but not direct descendants. Born with affinities, but not strong enough to awaken. Their blood lies dormant." The Oracle looked at Lukas and Blaire. "When your father died, Adrian, Blaire was able to awaken, and Lukas found her almost immediately. Others wait, but it will take something much stronger for the remaining to awaken and for the balance to come back to our kind."

"And that is?"

The room fell eerily silent, and Riley shifted toward Seth. His hand linked with hers.

"The Dark Kiss is the key."

Riley sagged and let out a held breath. She expected something different, but it was something they knew. The words were in the cryptic messages the Oracle delivered to Blaire when she first arrived at Blackthorn Academy.

"The Dark Kiss? The human must become Vasirian?" Dimitri asked, looking scandalized, which was comical on the bad boy persona he wore proudly.

Once again, the king ignored his half-brother. "There has never been a case of a Vasirian able to turn a human. They all died. It is why my father enacted a law forbidding it."

"But magical humans can," the Oracle reminded him.

King Adrian turned eyes on Blaire. "When do you intend to become one of us?"

Blaire wrung her hands. "I don't know, sir. I hadn't accepted before when asked."

The same anger that welled up in the king's eyes before came roaring back, though his voice remained calm. "You stand before us, hearing that our kind needs this to survive, and you choose to be selfish and remain a human?" The icy quality wasn't missed.

Blaire stepped back, and Lukas immediately stepped in front of her.

"Stand down, boy. No one will harm your Korrena."

Lukas shifted reluctantly; his muscles were tight, by the rigidity of his movements.

"I demand you accept. I will not allow one human to be the downfall of my kin. I swore to protect and provide them with prosperity, and I intend to see that through."

The Oracle slowly shook her head. "I am sorry, Adrian, but it does not work that way. Unless Blaire accepts of her own volition, the balance will be unstable. Whatever will awaken in Blaire will be unstable."

Surging to his feet, the king glared daggers at Blaire before turning his attention to the others. "You are dismissed. You will be found later for dinner. Do not leave the grounds."

17

Pairs

After the abrupt dismissal, when the king's mood soured at Blaire's indecision—had he listened, maybe she would have explained she was coming around to the idea—they spent the remainder of the day wandering the manor, learning about pieces of history from the liaison and staff members they came across.

The setting sun sent streams of soft light over the top of the forest on each side of the drive leading to the secluded manor. Finally away from the group for time to herself, Riley stood in front of the dragon statue with ruby eyes, admiring the onyx stone that, upon closer examination, held flecks of shimmery bits.

"Ostentatious, isn't it?"

Riley spun around at the sound of Dominic's deep, slightly accented voice. She remembered Blaire saying he was Canadian.

"The statue, I mean." He titled his head forward, hands tucked deep into the pockets of his slacks. "Even though we're in the twenty-first century, the monarchy continues to keep things old school."

"I think it's beautiful."

"Oh, it is. I'm accustomed to simpler things, like a coffee maker that I can operate myself without needing assistance from staff."

Riley kicked her boot on the cobblestone. "Why not make your own, then?"

"I do, but sometimes it's best to stay out of the kitchen if the staff is on grounds. I still remember Ms. Darby caught me making my own coffee and trying to make a sandwich. I'm sure I still have the marks on my ass from the wooden spoon she chased me out of the kitchen with." He shuddered dramatically. "Told me she likes feeling needed. Who am I to argue that?"

That made sense. At least it wasn't forced servitude. If the staff at Blackthorn Manor enjoyed their work and genuinely wanted to be there, how was it different from any other job in the modern-day service industry? Only at a private location.

Riley recalled the times Blaire complained about the awful state of her job at the diner she worked at before joining Blackthorn Academy. It didn't sound like the staff here had the same complaints. They all seemed nice and welcoming. Offering information without prompting.

"Walk with me?"

Pulled from her thoughts, Riley looked up at Dominic. "Sure."

He guided her into the garden in front of the manor along the narrow footpaths lined with beautiful blooms. The perfume in the air grew thicker as they made their way to the center, where a bubbling fountain sat.

"Tell me more about yourself, Riley."

"Um." Her lips rolled in as she nibbled on the bottom one inside her mouth. "I don't know what to say."

"No? Surely there's something you think is worth knowing."

I'm a basket case who can't stop fidgeting, thinking, worrying, and obsessing over my childhood friend who, instead of seeing me as a potential compatible partner, sees me as a project to help. No, thank you.

"Not really." Her hands twisted in front of her as she played with the chain belt hanging in front of her skirt. "I mean, I'm studying to get a degree in fashion."

"Really? What do you plan to do with it?"

That perked her up.

"I want to open my own shop. I want to start my own clothing line for alternative fashion for all ages, sizes, and styles. Like, a lot of the stuff I find is more for my size, but there's not much for really tall people, or plus size, or anything else, unless you pay a fortune. I think it's like that with all clothes, honestly. But alternative fashion is my wheelhouse. Then there's 'age appropriate.' Why do humans think it's right to force themselves to stop dressing a certain way at a certain age? Why can't we have alternative business attire? That's where I come in. I want to make something everyone can enjoy."

The silence following her rambling made her shift her eyes upward to meet Dominic's chocolate stare. Tension settled in her body and disappointment hit hard. In her excitement about something she enjoyed, she probably freaked him out and annoyed him.

She turned and started walking down the path. "I mean, it's silly. Sorry. Just ignore me. You probably weren't looking for all of that."

A gentle hand grasped her upper arm, and she stopped. When she turned toward him, he released her. His eyebrow piercing glinted in the fading sunlight, catching her eye.

"What just happened?"

"Huh?"

"You seemed so happy talking about your aspirations. Which, I can definitely see working for you considering your taste in clothing."

At the sour face Riley made, he quickly added, "You look hot."

His face flushed at her surprised expression, but he pushed on.

"But yeah, you seemed happy, and then you just… I don't know. Stopped."

Riley's arms crossed around herself protectively, cupping her elbows with her hands. She scratched at the fishnet sleeves of the undershirt she wore beneath her T-shirt; the texture and sound of her nails scraping across each hole grounded her.

Taking a breath, she said, "I thought I annoyed you."

"What? Why? You didn't."

"I talk a lot," she said simply, as if it explained everything. It's all he would get.

Attraction or not, they didn't know each other. Her own friends didn't even get that deep into her psyche. At least, those she could hide from. Even her brother couldn't grasp it all, but he knew more than the others.

A brief flicker of Seth's face crossed her mind, and she pushed it out. *Not today, Satan.*

Dominic gave her a lazy smile that relaxed her. "In case you haven't noticed in the times we've been around one another, so do I." He reached up and touched her face, not lingering long. "I enjoy hearing you speak and hope we can talk more. I feel we haven't gotten too much opportunity—"

"Riley," Seth barked.

She turned as Dominic looked up to find Seth striding toward him with a fiery expression. Had something happened while they were in the garden? Guilt hit her hard. If something happened to Blaire while she was chatting with a guy when she should focus on her friend and this situation…

Pushing down the insecurity and guilt, she rushed forward to

Seth. "What happened? What's wrong?"

Seth didn't even look down at her, staring at Dominic with an intensity she didn't understand.

"Seth!"

His gaze dropped to hers, and the fire faded somewhat.

"What is it? Is Blaire okay?"

Lines formed between his brows. "Blaire?"

So she was way off base. She shook her head. "What's going on?"

"Did he do something to you?"

"What?"

"Are you okay?" Seth moved to pass around her, but she grasped his arms.

"Seth, stop. I don't know what you're talking about, but Dom and I were just talking."

"I saw him."

"Saw what?"

"He touched you."

"And? What's going on?"

"You let him? But you were upset."

"Huh? I wasn't—"

"I *know* you, Riley. I *felt* you. I don't know how, but I felt it."

What was he talking about? Dominic touching her didn't upset her. Made her nervous, sure. But upset? That came before. About her own hang-ups. Seth wasn't even here. How would he know?

"I assure you," Dominic said, stepping closer, "I have no intentions of harming her. We were talking about fashion, actually."

"You needed to touch her for that?" Seth all but growled out.

"No." Dominic shrugged. "But it went with the rest of our conversation."

Dominic moved past them, walking toward the manor and leaving it at that. Seth didn't need to know what they spoke about or didn't.

Seth looked down at Riley. "Are you sure you're okay? I swear I will smash his face in if he hurt you. I don't care if he's part of the clan."

Riley's stomach fluttered with excitement that he would defend her. Even as children, he stood up for her when she didn't stand up for herself—and even when she did. He kept her out of messes, sometimes handling the problem for her, sometimes getting her away from it before she got herself in a world of trouble. Something about his protectiveness felt different this time, but it still ruffled her feathers he would hurt someone who only asked about her future plans.

"You need to calm down. He's only trying to get to know me."

"Why?"

"Because as hard is it might be to believe, someone out there might find me appealing." She crossed her arms and *hmph'd.* She sounded bratty, but his attitude brought out a knee-jerk reaction. "Why *wouldn't* someone want to get to know me?"

"That isn't what I meant."

She stared at him with interest, and when he didn't give her anything more, she sighed. "Come on. Dinner will be soon."

The dining hall of Blackthorn Manor looked as elaborate as the rest of the place. The room arched into a dome shape above a long dining table that sat twenty people.

Columns on the corners of the walls led up into beams that cross-crossed in intricate patterns on the dome overhead surrounding an elaborate chandelier over the table dripping crystals that without a doubt were real.

A trio of lancet windows framed the head of the table where King

Adrian sat in a high-backed black chair with ornate flourishes and carvings that matched the other chairs. Like in the throne room, his chair back stood slightly higher than the others.

To one side of the table behind the members of the Blackthorn Clan, a crackling fire warmed the room in a large hearth on the wall made of heavy stone, carved into more flourishing designs befitting the extravagant decor of the manor. An array of flowers and candles in hurricane globes sat on the mantle. A mirror centered above the mantle was part of a massive wall piece of filigree and flourishing designs that crawled up the deep burgundy walls and down the sides of the hearth. A single, large lancet window backed Riley and her friends on the opposite side of the table.

The table centerpiece held fifteen tall, skinny black candles on silver holders surrounded by more of the same foliage and flowers from the mantle.

Around the centerpiece, a veritable buffet spread before them. Two large turkeys, ham, roasted potatoes, vegetables of all kinds, a few dishes Riley didn't recognize but was sure were either local to England or fit whatever culture the king and his family originally hailed from, casseroles, and pastas offered many options to choose from. Wine, juice, tea, and water sat on the table, ready for consumption. Blood packets lay stacked on an ornate silver platter.

The tension from the meeting in the throne room fell away with easy conversation and laughter as they ate, drank, and discussed simple things like college, the history of the manor, sights of London and other areas of Europe. The food tasted delicious, and Riley finally relaxed.

They learned the throne room mostly found use when they needed a formal setting, and only King Adrian, Mariana, Gabriel, Dimitri, and the king's youngest sister, Natalia, who only just arrived from

France in time for dinner, used the space. The remaining council that came and went from the manor, spouses, and even Dominic tended to not join unless needed because of their constant states of travel. The siblings and the one cousin were the true decision makers.

Natalia looked across the table at their group and smiled cordially. “Tell me, are any of you paired?” She looked young, her russet eyes sparkling and shiny, wavy black hair cascading down her back. Her skin had olive undertones like her sister, but paler, as if she kept out of the sun entirely.

“Natalia, if you had been here when the reports arrived and instead of traipsing through the countryside, you’d know the human girl and this young one are bonded,” Mariana said, directing her sister’s attention to Lukas and Blaire, who sat closest to the king across from Mariana and Felix.

“Oh.” Natalia frowned then studied Professor Velastra. “And you?”

“My pair is no longer with us,” Professor Velastra said with calm ease, taking a sip of the wine a staff member poured her.

“Oh, my.”

“I am sorry for your loss,” Mariana said, a genuine look of sadness crossing her face as she reached for her husband Felix beside her, contrasting the business-mode demeanor she held in the throne room. His hand squeezed hers.

“What about you?” Natalia asked with a beaming smile when her eyes met Riley’s.

“Me?” she chirped. “Um. None. No pair.”

When Natalia looked at Aiden and Seth, they shook their heads. “That’s sad. Aren’t you older than me?”

“What? How old are you?” Riley asked.

“Seventeen.”

"We're older, but not by much."

"How much?"

Dimitri groaned. "Does it matter?"

"Of course. I'm curious."

"I'm eighteen. My brother is twenty," Riley motioned to Aiden, who had just taken a bite of potatoes, so he nodded confirmation. "Seth is nineteen."

"I'm sorry you haven't found them yet. I found mine a couple of months ago. Can you believe he was on our very own council?" The giddiness in Natalia's voice made Riley both happy for her and jealous simultaneously. Why couldn't it be that easy?

"Congratulations," Professor Velastra said.

The others continued eating while Natalia chattered away. It reminded Riley of how things usually went when she was with her friends. Her family too, if her mother wasn't around. Even her mother could rival her on the chatterbox train.

Aiden wiped his mouth with a napkin. "Are the rest of you paired with members in the Blackthorn Clan council?"

"Well, you know Mariana and Felix are," Gabriel said. "Natalia and Emil are new. Like your headmistress, my mate left this world after an accident she couldn't recover from." At the horrified expressions on several faces, he shook his head. "I don't know if it was a blessing or curse that we only got a year together. Had it been longer…" He swallowed. "I was younger. I've had time to process."

"While it would be nice, I'm a realist. If I find someone who I want, then I'm happy to have a compatible pair," Dominic said, giving Gabriel a moment. His eyes met Riley's, and she looked down at her plate, not sure what to do with herself.

"Dimitri doesn't have a pair either, but he's your age," Natalia said to Aiden. "But Adrian doesn't either, and he's thirty years older."

"That's such a big gap," Blaire said, and then covered her mouth. "I'm sorry."

Gabriel chuckled. "Don't be, love. In our world, gaps between children aren't uncommon considering how long we live. As you heard, Natalia is thirty-three years his junior. Especially if we take a temporary partner, have children, and later find our Korrena and choose to follow the path with them and have children again."

"They just leave their partner or spouse because their Korrena shows up?" Blaire looked horrified, and it made sense.

Even Riley didn't like the idea of it. The problem came with the pull of the bond when it presented itself. It wasn't always rainbows and sunshine. Sometimes it left heartache in its wake for those who loved the person.

She glanced at Seth, who looked over at her like he could feel her eyes on him. She looked away.

In rare cases, pairs and compatible pairs formed polyamorous relationships and it worked. But she couldn't imagine how that would happen if kids already existed.

"Not always," Gabriel said. "Sometimes they reject the bond. But to do so has devastating consequences on the psyche."

King Adrian snapped, "Must we continue speaking of pairs?"

Everyone froze at the harshness of his voice, even the staff who were mulling about with trays and pitchers. He had said nothing while they discussed Korrena pairs, and now he seemed agitated.

"What's the matter, brother?"

King Adrian's gaze panned to his little sister, and he spoke through clenched teeth. "You know this subject brings me no comfort. I do not relish in continuing."

Natalia pouted then looked at Riley and the others. "He's just mad because the prophecy hasn't come true."

"Enough! You will not disrespect me in front of our guests, Natalia."

She lowered her head in submission and clenched the napkin in her lap. "My apologies, Adrian."

The king shoved his chair back and stood, turning, and leaving the dining room like the hounds of hell were chasing him.

"That bitterness will be the death of him," Gabriel said with a defeated sigh.

Riley didn't know what prophecy the king received, but she knew a sensitive subject when she heard one. Seth hated talking about Korrena pairs too, evident by how he remained silent through dinner once the subject came up and the tense set of his shoulders.

All the surrounding tension didn't help her anxieties. She needed a nice, long bubble bath in the hotel, her book, and junk food. A milkshake, preferably, but room service lacked that.

After finishing dinner and thanking the members of the clan for their hospitality, they made their way out front to the waiting cars that would see them back at the hotel. Gabriel informed them the king wanted to hold an audience with them two days from now on Friday to discuss the fate of the Order, the future council, and Blackthorn Academy's future. Riley didn't see where it mattered if they knew about the future council, but she would not question the king.

"Riley!"

She paused at the open door of the car at Dominic's shout. The others had gone in another vehicle, leaving Seth, Aiden, and her in this one. She turned and walked to meet him halfway.

"I'm glad I caught you," he said, breathing hard.

She smiled at the flush of his cheeks. He must have run all the way to find her. "What's up?"

"I wanted to ask you something." His hands rubbed over the side of his neck and across the back of his head. "Would you consider having a proper date with me?" His smile was tentative.

She'd never been on a date before. She always wanted to go on one, but never had the chance. Recalling her conversation with Blaire, it would be a good thing to do. She couldn't pine for Seth forever, and Dominic seemed like a genuinely nice guy. He deserved a chance if he truly thought he saw something worthy in her. But she didn't know what to say. Her nerves made her palms sweat, and she started picking at the hem of her pleated skirt, scratching lightly at the tights she wore.

Something about her expression must have given him the wrong impression because his face fell.

"Ah, that probably was too much, too soon. You don't know me. I'm sorry."

"Of course I'll go on a date with you."

"Pardon?"

"I said… I'll go on a date with you." She let out a slow breath. "You just surprised me."

The smile on his face was bright when he told her when he'd pick her up before he headed back into the manor.

The time had come. She couldn't become a convenient partner to Seth. With her feelings, and the way he made her feel physically, it would be so easy to slip into that role until he tired of her.

She couldn't do it.

She loved him too much.

She needed to let go and move on.

Time to find a compatible partner and be happy.

18

Resolve

Back at the hotel, Riley climbed out of the car, thanking the driver and heading inside. The lobby was quiet for the time of night, and the receptionist smiled warmly as she, Aiden, and Seth passed on the way to the elevators.

Aiden chatted on the way up, and Riley tried to participate, but something felt off in the air. Seth remained on edge, and she didn't know why. Was he still bothered by the Korrena talk? Normally, he would be over it by now.

Once on their floor, Riley stretched and groaned. "I am so ready for a bath. And junk. Lots of sugar."

"You just ate your body weight in fine dining at the manor," Aiden said, laughing.

"I can always make room for sugar."

"Whatever. You eat like a pregnant five-year-old." He cringed. "That's a terrible mental image. Forget I said that. Just don't come crying to me with a stomachache." With that, he opened his door and disappeared inside.

She remembered the last stomachache she had where she did that very thing. Ate so much ice cream she literally cried. It took fifteen minutes before her preternatural healing abilities kicked in, but it felt like hours.

Before she could continue to her room, Seth stopped her.

"So you're dating him?"

He'd overheard through the open car door. She sighed and crossed her arms. *Incoming protective brother.*

"I'm going *on* a date with him, yes."

"Do you like him?"

"What does it matter?" Her gaze shifted away. She never could meet his eyes when things got too serious. It left her feeling naked and exposed.

"Look at me."

"No."

"Riley. I don't understand why you won't look at me."

Because you'll know.

"Look, it doesn't matter." He clenched his jaw tightly and took a long inhale through his nose. "It doesn't," he said calmer, as if trying to convince himself the words were true. It made no sense to her.

Piercing silver eyes met hers, and she sucked in a breath at the intensity there.

"Just… don't sleep with him."

"What?" Her voice pitched high, and her eyes widened, her cheeks heating.

"You heard me. Don't do it."

Her embarrassment fled as indignation set in.

Did he think so little of her to think she would have sex with a man the first time she went out with him? Maybe he did. He surrounded himself with girls who behaved like that at the academy.

"I'll have you know that just because I'm going on a date with Dom, it doesn't mean I'll jump into his bed." Her hand went to her hip, and she pointed at him with her other hand. "I am not like you."

"What the fuck does that mean?"

"You sleep with everyone."

Seth's entire body tightened, and his fists clenched at his side. "I am so sick of everyone saying that."

"It's true, isn't it? I walked in on—"

"I haven't slept with anyone in months! I *almost* slept with her. I *used* to fuck around, but not anymore."

"It doesn't matter."

"It does. I need you to know."

"Why?"

Seth ground his teeth. "Just leave it at that."

What was she supposed to do with that information? It wasn't like she needed to know. It changed nothing about their relationship and held no bearing on the potential relationship with Dominic.

When she didn't respond, he repeated in a softer tone, "Don't sleep with him."

An order, but not. A request, but not quite. It was enough to clear the frustration she felt.

"I didn't and don't plan on sleeping with Dom," she said. "You know I've never slept with anyone, and I'm not about to start after one date."

Seth's shoulders lowered, and he finally relaxed until she added, "Besides, Dom seems to really like me. I finally have a chance at having a compatible pair."

He frowned, studying her. "Is that so important right now?"

"I don't want to feel the way I feel anymore," she whispered, looking away.

His frown deepened. "The way you feel?"

Riley waved a hand dismissively, her bracelets making jangling noises.

"You know you can tell me anything, right?"

"I do."

Seth licked his lips and nodded. "Then what?"

Choosing to give him part of her concerns, but not all, she said, "I'm not sure I'll ever find my Korrena. Aiden hasn't. Dominic hasn't. You haven't. Even our king hasn't. I don't want to be fifty like him and bitter and angry about it." Her eyes pleaded with him to understand. "I don't want to spend my life alone, Seth."

"So you're happy to settle for some guy you barely know because he showed an interest in you?" The agitation in Seth's voice made her recoil.

"Why are you so against Dom? You don't know him."

Seth's hands went into his hair and gripped tightly. "That's my fucking point! Neither do you!" His hands dropped, and he threw one to the side, lowering his voice to not attract hotel guests from their rooms. "You don't know him well enough to make that kind of commitment."

"Well, that's why I'm going to go on dates. I never said we were going to be compatible pairs. I said I have a chance."

Seth paced the hall, his agitation obvious. Even Aiden wouldn't be this overprotective. Seth needed to learn he couldn't always boss her around like she was a kid. They were grown now.

He stopped and looked at her, and the fire in his eyes froze her in place.

"You know, it didn't seem like it was Dominic you wanted with the way you kissed me, with the way you gave in to me at the pool."

She scowled at him. "You said we would go back to normal. Why are you bringing that up?"

"Because I can't believe you want him when I look into your eyes."

Oh no… No, no, no. Blaire was right. He could see the truth she tried so hard to hide. She closed her eyes momentarily against the burn from holding back tears that threatened to show themselves.

"I don't know what you're talking about," she finally said, her tone petulant, opening her eyes.

Seth stalked toward her, and she stepped back with a squeak. "Don't give me that. I can see it when you talked to him. I can see you're phoning it in. He interests you, but there's no depth. You don't *want* him."

So he didn't see her feelings for him. Still, she didn't enjoy appearing so transparent.

"You don't know what I want."

"I do," he said, his voice lowering to just above a whisper.

He stepped closer, and she moved back again, her back meeting the wall as he came to a stop in front of her.

"What do I want?"

Don't ask dangerous questions.

"Not him." His eyes bore into hers, and she swore there was a faint glow at the edges of his irises. "You want *me*." The growl in those final three words made her entire body shudder.

She turned her head away, no longer able to maintain eye contact. She felt raw. Exposed. Giving in to him revealed too much. Her body had betrayed her and let him know how much she craved his touch. But it still didn't stop the fire stoked low in her belly at his words.

Seth's head lowered and rested on her shoulder as he moved closer, cutting the space between them, posting his arm on the wall above her head.

"Tell me to stop," he rasped, dragging his nose over her neck across the pulse she was sure he could see—or possibly hear—going haywire. She swallowed audibly.

She didn't tell him to stop.

"Riley."

Her name was a command. A plea. His fangs pricked her sensitive flesh, followed by the wet caress of his tongue; his control was slipping fast. She saw it in the glow of his eyes before they reached the wall.

Still, she didn't tell him to stop.

She didn't *want* him to stop.

Panting, she reached up and ran her fingers over the back of his closely cropped hair all the way up into the long strands on top of his head.

The scrape of her nails against his scalp made him shudder, and when he sucked the soft skin at the side of her neck into his mouth and she moaned, it was all over.

A sharp sting was immediately chased away by pleasure like she'd never known washing over her as Seth sunk his fangs deep into her skin and drank from her.

"Seth," she breathed, her eyes rolling back in her head. A long, desperate moan she couldn't hide even if she wanted to followed his name.

She'd never been bitten before by anyone. It wasn't something their kind normally did outside of pairings. There wasn't a need. But now she couldn't understand why that was a thing, because this felt incredible. Nothing like the box cutter incident.

"Seth," she whimpered his name again, clutching his shirt with her hand on his chest. Her other hand still gripped the long strands on top of his head, holding him to her throat as he stayed bent over her slight frame, drinking greedily.

The hand that wasn't above her head on the wall moved to her waist and pulled her body solidly against his. His arousal strained against the front of his jeans. She moaned as his fingers tightened their grip on her side.

"Seth…"

She needed to get him to stop.

While they replenished their blood easily, and anemia wasn't exactly a problem, she still needed time to recover. And if a human caught them in the hall, they would be in trouble. Not to mention she was point-five-seconds away from climbing Seth like a tree in the hallway where anyone could see.

"Seth," she said with a firm tone, finally sounding less like a wanton porn star and more like someone with their wits about them.

It didn't matter, though.

Seth seemed to be lost to bloodlust, and Riley had a hard time seeing reasons he should stop. In fact, she started wondering what *he* tasted like.

Her gums throbbed, the sensation foreign.

Seth rolled his hips against her front and the groan that left his throat was nothing like what she envisioned when she pictured her book boyfriends. When his hand slipped around to slide up her thigh toward the hem of her skirt, blazing a trail toward her backside that made her skin burn, she gave up on reasonable thinking.

She wanted him to touch her again.

She wanted to touch him.

Riley tilted her head enough to not disengage from his bite, but to where she could access his neck.

Breathing heavily, she stared at his skin where his pulse beat fast; her fangs descended. Was she really about to drink the blood of her childhood friend who she'd always… no, she wasn't going there.

Get out of your head.

With timid gentleness, she grazed her tongue over his skin, tasting the saltiness of his sweat. He shuddered and stopped drinking, lifting his head slightly as if waiting, but not meeting her eyes. Emboldened by his response, she pressed an open mouth kiss to the spot she found most sensitive on herself and was rewarded with a groan of pleasure.

"Riley," Seth breathed out as he seemed to struggle with himself.

Swallowing hard, she allowed her fangs to graze his skin, and he immediately dropped his other arm to wrap around her, pulling her body tight to his. Her lips parted, and the tips of her fangs had barely pricked his soft skin when a voice cut through the silence from the other end of the hallway.

"Fuck," Seth said, stepping back and looking at Riley with wide, panicked eyes.

Her blood stained his mouth, and he was hard against his jeans. They continued to stare at one another as Blaire approached, and just before she reached them, Seth turned and went several doors down, disappearing inside.

Before Blaire reached her, Riley swiped her neck of blood and sighed at the sting. Hopefully, Blaire wouldn't notice before it healed in a few minutes.

Riley didn't know what to make of what happened. It was obvious Seth was aware of her physical attraction to him now, but she wasn't ignorant of his attraction. It made no sense. But then again, he said he hadn't slept with anyone in months. She needed to be strong and stop giving in to this sort of thing. While Seth might be willing to explore things sexually with her, he didn't want her like she wanted him. She would not spend her life pining for him.

Nodding, she made an oath to herself. She was over her childhood crush. She would find a compatible pair, even if not with Dominic, and she would be happy.

Now if only she could keep that resolve this time.

19

Confession

After disappearing into his room to get away from Riley before Blaire saw him, Seth realized the silence wouldn't help him calm down.

Giving them enough time to vacate the hall, he slipped out of his room and into the streets of London with no destination in mind. Even with a warm jacket, the night air bit at him as he kept a brisk pace, running from the invisible demons that nipped at his heels.

How he allowed himself to cross a line with Riley not common for their kind was beyond him. Knowing he left his mark, even if it would heal, made a perverse satisfaction warm his blood.

And he knew. Just knew if the opportunity presented itself again, he would do it again.

He wanted to cover her with so many marks that anyone who saw her skin would know who she belonged to. He wanted to own every inch of her.

Did that make him crazy? Probably. Did he care? Not one fucking bit.

Riley wanted him. In whatever messed up turn of events, he knew it. Saw it in her eyes when she looked at him. She might be attracted to Dominic, but it was nothing like what burned between them.

The problem arose with not wanting to just be a fuck buddy. Seth didn't want to take their friendship into that realm. He wanted her physically, absolutely; but not enough to jeopardize what they had. Not when it wouldn't—shouldn't—*couldn't*—be more than a fleeting thing where Riley learned about her own sexuality.

He'd give her that, even if he lost his heart entirely in the process.

Seth's face felt numb by the time he entered the quiet lobby of the hotel hours later and approached the elevators.

He didn't need to be alone now. It was his usual coping mechanism, but if he went to his room, eventually his self-control would break, and he'd seek out Riley. As much as he wanted to mark her, now that he had time to calm down, he knew he shouldn't. Nothing about drinking her blood should have been sexually stimulating for either of them.

Blood was life. Not foreplay.

Standing outside of Aiden's room, he debated his options. He needed to talk to someone. Lukas offered, but Blaire was in the room, and she was too close to Riley. Aiden was Seth's best friend. His brother. But Aiden was also Riley's brother.

It made him feel isolated.

Seth cursed under his breath. For the first time he could recall, he wished Kai was here. His brother would likely give him some dry humor with a scientific approach that would serve to piss him off, but at least he wouldn't be facing this alone.

Since he couldn't reach out to anyone about the situation, he turned away from the door just as it opened.

He turned back to find Riley staring up at him with wide blue eyes. Before he could say anything, she made a sound that reminded him of a startled puppy and rushed down the hall to her door and disappeared inside.

He really screwed up this time.

"Is this 'keep Aiden from sleeping night'?" Aiden said, leaning on the door frame and scratching his chest over his faded blue T-shirt. He chuckled at his own joke, but then stopped, dropping his hand and studying Seth's face with concern. "Get in here."

With a sigh, Seth complied. This somehow felt familiar.

The room was dimly lit by the table lamp next to Aiden's bed, which was already in disarray. He likely had been asleep at some point.

"What happened between you two this time?" Aiden collapsed onto his bed, leaning on his headboard. "Before you say 'nothing,' Riley was just in here acting cagey as hell and wouldn't talk to me. Came asking about everything under the sun and just wanted to lie on the side bed over there. Spent the last two hours keeping me awake. And now you show up looking like someone told you Santa isn't real…"

"He's not."

"You get my point, man. I'm tired. Can't think of a nicer way to say you look like shit. What's going on?"

Seth's jaw muscle twitched, and he dropped to sit on the door of the bed, facing away from Aiden. "I don't even know."

"Don't give me that. Something happened between you two finally, didn't it?" At Seth's silence, Aiden smiled. "I told you there was something there, so you can stop denying how much you want her and how much you two belong together, because it's getting old."

Seth twisted and glared at Aiden. "We don't—"

"Fucking come off it, man. You and I both know it's there. So what if you're not Korrenas? Who gives a shit?" Seth's brows rose at the language. Aiden cursed, but never laid into him with it. "You both have something so much stronger than a pair-bond based in biology. You should be glad since that's the part about Korrena pairs you're so fixated on."

"She deserves someone—"

"She deserves *you*, Seth. Fuck. Don't you see how much she loves you? I do. I also see how much you love her."

Anger stole Seth's breath; resentment at the words his best friend spoke burned through his veins like battery acid. He stood and paced the room like a caged animal.

"You don't know what the fuck you're talking about."

"No? You saying you don't love her?"

Seth stormed toward him, and Aiden jumped to his feet to meet him on an equal footing. Fisting his shirt, Seth glared up into eyes that held no anger, only empathy and sadness. It pissed him off more. He shoved Aiden back, but the strong asshole barely moved, so Seth resumed pacing the room.

"I can't. I can't be what she needs," he said under his breath, but he knew Aiden heard by the sigh behind him.

"You can, but you won't allow yourself to see it. Seth, you *have* been what she needs for way longer than either of you realize. You're like her own personal shadow." Aiden rubbed his face. "I don't even think her Korrena would be so devoted."

"Bullshit."

"It's true. And I don't think she'll be happy without you in her life."

Seth wouldn't leave her life. He didn't think. Could he endure being near her if she went with a compatible partner or found her Korrena? He rubbed his solar plexus roughly, trying to chase away the ache the thought elicited. No, he'd never leave her. That little firecracker owned his heart and soul.

"I'm not good enough for her, anyway."

"Why do you think that?" Aiden's head tilted. "What makes you less worthy than someone else?"

"Look at me. I've always been a loner. A hothead. I thought it was to keep up with you and Lukas when we were kids, but it worked for me. I didn't leave that behind when you two stopped. I'm a pessimist, at best. Riley is a fucking ray of sunshine, and I would darken her skies and drag her down. She doesn't deserve that."

"That girl has held her own with and against you our entire lives. You've never dragged her down. Give me something else, because right now, I don't see a reason you're not good enough."

Both hands held the back of his neck, and he bent forward, taking a breath. When he stood, he pinned Aiden with a look. "You know my reputation. I don't want her dragged into that either."

"Then stop."

"I have!"

Aiden's brow lifted at that.

Seth didn't feel right sleeping with anyone anymore. He wasn't even with Riley, but now, the idea of living the way he had months ago felt like cheating, and he wasn't one of those bastards.

"I haven't gotten laid in months. The most I've done has been with—" *Shit.* He glanced over and, judging by the smug look on Aiden's face, his friend knew what he didn't say. "Even she thinks I'm sleeping with half the academy. I don't want any of them to give her shit."

"Then don't let them. Put them in their place. You're going to let someone else dictate how you live? That's not the Seth I know. Stop making excuses, because they are paper thin. Thinner than those fucking papers you hide behind."

"Then what do you want?"

"For my little sister and my friend to be happy. If I'm mistaken, and you don't love her, then you need to let her down gently, because that girl adores you."

Seth didn't believe it. He didn't dare let hope latch its sweet claws into his heart. But he couldn't let her go, either. The entire situation was so messed up.

"But I will tell you right now. I know you love her. If she knew what you did—"

Seth moved and grabbed Aiden's shirt again. "You don't fucking tell her anything."

Aiden lifted his hands in a placating gesture of surrender. "I'm just saying if she knew what you did, not that I'd *tell* her, she'd see it too."

The sound that left his throat when he tried to speak made him feel weak, and he released Aiden, dropping onto the single bed on the other side of the nightstand. Immediately, the smell of tiger lilies assaulted him, and he wanted to cry. For the first time in years, he wanted to bury his face in Riley's scent and sob like a little boy for all that he would never have.

Instead, he put an arm over his eyes and lay on his back, whispering the words he always knew were true, but never gave sound. A confession that broke the chains he kept binding his heart tightly.

"I love her."

"Then you need to tell her," Aiden said after several minutes of silence. The mattress creaked as he sat on his own bed.

"I can't." Seth's voice was barely a gravelly whisper.

"You can. I know you're stronger than this."

"Why are you doing this? Why are you pushing so hard?"

"Because it's about time I did. I'm sorry I haven't already because I can see it's now tearing you two apart."

Seth lowered his arm and turned his head to look at Aiden. "I don't see how you're cool with all this."

"What? With one of my best friends who I trust with my life being in love with my baby sister? I couldn't ask for anyone better."

Seth swallowed hard, cursing the burn he felt irritating his eyes. He already felt emotional over this situation, but then Aiden had to lay on the sentimentality. He trusted Seth with his life? Seth rubbed his face furiously.

"Besides," Aiden said, his voice lighter, and Seth sensed a joke coming. "There's no one else I think could handle her antics like you can."

"Too bad it won't happen."

"Why not? It makes the most sense." Aiden put his forearms on his thighs and leaned forward. "If you could only get your head outta your ass."

"No. No." Seth sat up, shaking his head. The tense feeling returning to his chest. "I can't."

Aiden's face fell, and he dropped his gaze to the bedding. The next words he spoke held true pain, and Seth felt that same pain in response, but he stuffed it down where it belonged and wrapped it in chains.

"Then you can't complain when someone else snatches her away from you."

20

Lasting Bonds

If she told me to give her the very core of my being, I would kneel at her feet, carve my own heart out, and serve it to her on a silver platter. I would do it without hesitation. If only to see the brief moment of happiness in her eyes at my offering before I sank into oblivion, knowing I'd finally done something to please her in my lifetime. Only then could I accept death.

"You know, it's really hard not to tell you what's happening," Riley said, bookmarking the page she was on.

Blaire sighed. "I know, and you're not making it any easier with the giggles."

"Sorry?"

She wasn't sorry.

"Things get really romantic and deep in the final installment; I'll only say that."

"I don't mind the spoilers too much."

Riley shook her head. If someone spoiled a series she loved when it neared the end, she'd blow a gasket.

Room service had delivered their breakfast moments ago, and Professor Velastra ensured Riley got her morning blood packet. Now she and Blaire were cuddled beneath her comforter, eating, reading, and relaxing while some British comedy show that made absolutely no sense played on the TV as background noise.

Blaire closed her fruit container and looked at her phone. "What time is your date tonight?"

"Dom said he'd pick me up at five."

"Do you know where he's taking you?"

"Nope."

She probably should have asked so she'd know what to wear. But calling him now felt silly. She would err on the side of sensibility and wear dressy-casual. That way, if he took her somewhere nice, she wouldn't be underdressed, and if they went somewhere like a diner, she wouldn't stand out like a sore thumb. Not that she didn't do that already, but it was her first date. Making a good impression felt important.

"I need to go shopping, though. I didn't bring anything date-worthy. I didn't expect to meet a guy in England, of all places." She laughed and leaned against the head of her bed. "He's a nice guy, you know?"

"He is," Blaire said causally, waiting her out.

When the silence started making her antsy, Riley thunked her head against the blue headboard of her bed and closed her eyes. "Why is it so hard?"

"I don't know."

Blaire knew exactly what she meant. They'd discussed it earlier. Riley struggled with her feelings for Seth. She liked Dominic, but why did it feel like she was forcing herself to like him more than she did?

Deciding to change the subject and take the path of a coward, she said, "The king was really pissed about you not giving a straight answer the other day."

Blaire shifted on the bed and took a sip from the mug of tea she held. "I know, but what can I say?" Her dialect slipped, sounding more regional to the Southeast and thicker like Riley's mother when she said, "He didn't give me the chance to tell him what I'm thinking or want to do."

The shift in Blaire's accent showed she wasn't happy about the situation. Blaire fell into loose words and their regional dialect under stress. Not that Riley didn't do it often just because, but Blaire did it specifically in response to frustration. Her stepfamily had trained her to repress it for years prior to coming to Blackthorn Academy.

She wanted to sound understanding and curious, to ease Blaire and give her the opportunity to express her denied feelings. Riley hated when others did it to her. "And what is that? Because I'll be honest, even I don't fully know."

"I'm afraid of dying. Of agreeing to this and it failing horribly, and then what short human life I would have with y'all would be gone in an instant. So not only would Lukas not get hundreds of years with me, he wouldn't get the possible eighty or so I have left naturally. But I feel part of part of this world now in a way I never felt in the one I come from, even before being trapped by the Wilcox family."

"So you want to do it?"

"Yes."

Riley couldn't hide the joy she felt as she launched herself at Blaire, knocking over the empty breakfast dishes that nevertheless left residue from plates on the bedding that housekeeping would have to deal with. Blaire held her cup high to avoid spilling her tea as she laughed and one-arm-hugged Riley.

"Does Lukas know?"

"Sort of."

Riley sat back. "I don't understand."

"I haven't said, 'Yes, let's do this,' but I have told him it's something I'm not against anymore. And with all this going on with the Order and traveling, it's not something we can focus on. But I do plan to sit down with the professor when we're settled and check into something Dom brought to my attention when we were locked up."

"Dom?"

"Yeah. I don't know why I never thought of it, considering we had to do this when the Order nearly killed me once before."

"I don't follow."

"Blood transfusion." At Riley's squint, Blaire explained, "If Lukas attempts to turn me and something goes wrong, since we don't know what happens during the transition, we could use the blood Professor Velastra stored in my blood type for emergencies to save my life."

Riley's jaw dropped. Why hadn't any of them thought of something like that? Turning a human was unheard of, other than in a tome Professor Velastra found and the information the Oracle provided. It made sense now that they knew only Korrena-bound humans could survive it—magical humans—but the process itself sounded extremely dangerous.

It wasn't like in the movies where a vampire bit a human and they automatically turned, or where they had to give the human a mouthful of their blood in exchange. If it were that easy, Blaire would already be one of them.

Lukas would have to drain Blaire to the point of near death, and then give her his blood. She would have to accept the transition for the magic to work, if what the Oracle said the other day in the throne room was true. After that, Blaire would fall into a coma-like slumber. They knew nothing about the transition because no information was available, so from that point it was a blind guess. The tome only said a human would sleep then awaken a full Vasirian without humanity.

Blaire and Riley shared the hope that the Oracle would recover more memories to tell them what might happen during the sleep and how long it might last.

"I'm behind you whenever you're ready." Riley sniffled, overcome with emotion. "I'm just so happy you're not leaving."

"I'm not going to leave you."

Riley knew it logically. But the idea of spending hundreds of years without her best friend hurt. It was a loss she couldn't bear to think about. She felt connected to Blaire in ways she could never explain.

Blaire set down her mug and pulled Riley to her into another side hug. Riley pivoted and collapsed on the bed, wrapping her arms around Blaire's waist, resting her head on her leg and closing her eyes. She reveled in Blaire's comforting presence after how long she'd been gone.

They embraced in companionable silence for a while before a knock on the door interrupted.

"Who do you think that is?"

Riley rolled onto her back and groaned. "Probably Lukas tracking you down like a bloodhound."

"He is not that bad." Blaire crossed to the door and laughed as she pulled it open. When her laughter cut off abruptly, Riley sat up.

"Ah-ha!" She pointed. "Called it!"

Blaire burst into laughter again at Lukas's confused expression. She patted him on the chest over his leather jacket. "What are you doing here?"

"Looking for you."

Riley snorted from her spot on the bed.

"What the hell happened in here?" Seth asked.

Riley shot up into a sitting position as Seth came into the room, followed by Aiden.

Blaire looked back at the scattered mess of dishes on the bed. "Breakfast in bed might not have been such a good idea."

Aiden laughed. "Did you have to wrestle it onto the plate?"

Blaire raised an eyebrow at him as Riley stood. "No. It was an accident."

Riley had actively avoided Seth since the night in the hallway. She'd seen him during meals with everyone, of course, but didn't stay close for long. She sat next to Blaire then went back to her room early—and he'd let her.

Seth didn't push to talk about it—which she expected. He didn't look at her. Didn't say much of anything at all. Even their usual sniping was replaced with uncomfortable silence. It was as if everyone knew what happened, but no one did. She didn't tell anyone, and Seth wouldn't have either. He wouldn't talk about that stuff.

Riley protested. "Why is everyone in my room? I gotta get ready, and I can't do it with y'all in here."

"Lukas was looking for Blaire, and we were with him." Aiden crossed his arms. "Get ready for what?"

"Her date," Blaire said with a grin, and Riley grimaced, glancing at Seth out of the corner of her eye. His expression remained impassive. Maybe he didn't care anymore.

Lukas blinked. "Date?"

Aiden glanced from her to Seth and back again. "Y'all going on a date? About damn time."

"No!" Riley shouted at the same time Seth said, "*We're* not."

"I'm confused."

"She's going on a date with Dom tonight," Blaire clarified.

Aiden cursed under his breath and rubbed his neck. "I'm sorry. I shouldn't have said that."

Ignoring the awkwardness, Riley said, "I need to get ready to go shopping. I didn't bring anything to wear."

Seth snorted. "You have plenty of clothes."

Riley frowned at him. "Not date appropriate." Did none of them get fashion?

"If some douche canoe can't be happy with your style, he doesn't deserve you."

"It isn't about that." Riley rolled her eyes. "It's about looking nice for a special occasion. You know, like when we go out to Haven."

Seth always changed his usual style when they went to the local nightclub. His style always went darker. Wearing button-down black shirts or a black Henley with black jeans or slacks. She imagined that's what he wore on dates but didn't know how often he dated anyone.

"It's just dinner," Seth muttered, sounding tired.

"Maybe. Maybe not."

"What the hell does that mean?"

"Huh? Oh, I'm just saying I don't know where he's taking me and what we're doing."

"Hell no. There's no way you're going off with a guy you barely know in a city you're not familiar with and not even knowing what you're doing."

Riley's hackles rose. "Listen here, Mister, I'm a grown woman and can go wherever I want with whoever I want."

Seth looked from Lukas to Aiden, his eyes downright pleading for backup. "Tell her I'm right. This is ridiculous. She's gonna get hurt." The desperation in his voice made Riley's indignation at his words settle. He was worried about her.

"Dom wouldn't hurt her," Blaire said, her eyes narrowing at Seth. "He didn't even hurt me when suffering from *sanguis manie*."

That statement alone made Riley trust Dominic more than she would a random stranger. *Sanguis manie* meant death for their kind. It started after a prolonged period without blood's nourishment. The time frame varied from Vasirian to Vasirian, but the symptoms and progression were mostly the same. First came lethargy with slight tremors, followed by paleness. Then the heavier shakes, motor functions becoming harder to control, the sweats, weakness, and poor balance. Anxiety wasn't unheard of, nor were hallucinations. Anger was a definite. Then finally, the body gave in to a sense of mania, the mind finally breaking.

A Vasirian in mania reverted to nothing more than a primitive beast with the desire to feed and feed until caught and put down like a rabid animal, because once the mind broke, there was no escaping the clutches of *sanguis manie*—blood mania.

For that reason alone, Vasirian remained vigilant in not testing the limits of how long they could last without blood. Tempting fate could be a death sentence.

"Blaire's right," Lukas said. "I trust him."

"What the fuck?" Seth turned to Aiden. "Aiden?"

"I gotta go with Blaire on this one. Sorry, man. And if you were thinking rationally, you would too."

"Rationally?" Riley looked between her brother and Seth. "What's going on?"

The muscle in Seth's jaw spasmed. "Forget it." Looking into Riley's eyes, he said, "If he hurts you, I will kill him." He stormed out of the hotel room before she could respond.

Blaire gaped. "Did he just threaten a member of the Blackthorn Clan?"

Aiden looked down at her. "I guess he did." Lips pressed tight, he looked back at the door.

21

Compatible Pairs

Soft music filtered through the restaurant, which had a stunning view of the sun setting over Hyde Park through the massive floor-to-ceiling windows.

Her choice of a black jumpsuit with chunky heels with tiny silver spikes on the toe piece and a matching spiked bracelet with thin black bands allowed her to look date appropriate without giving up her style. Judging by the appreciative glances Dominic kept shooting her way, he approved. She also chose a statement necklace to draw attention from her bust because she felt self-conscious in the lower cut. A handful didn't make for much cleavage in an outfit like this without a push-up bra, and she refused to buy special underwear for one date—especially when she didn't intend to be seen in her underwear at the end of it, in spite of being on the twenty-eighth floor of a fancy hotel.

"Riley?"

"Huh?"

"Alright? You kind of spaced out there on me."

Of course I did.

She forced a smile. It wasn't hard to wear the mask. She perfected it. He didn't have to know. "I'm good. The sunset is just really pretty."

"It is. That's why I picked this place. I'm not one for overly lavish places like this, but I thought since it's your first time in London—wait, it is your first time, right?"

Riley laughed at the panic on his face. "Yeah, you're good."

"Well, I thought it would be worth the pretentious menu if not for the view alone." He gave her a crooked smile.

It relaxed her to know his choice was rooted in a desire to share something beautiful with her and not a need to flash money to impress her. To be honest, it had rubbed her wrong, and she felt bad now for assuming.

"You look nice," she offered, trying to recover from the thoughts she had.

It was true. Dressed in finely-tailored black slacks and a smokey-purple button-down that made his silver hair look amazing in contrast, he looked incredibly handsome. He'd changed his silver brow piercing to a solid black barbell, and his earrings were black to match. She wondered if his hair was as soft as Seth's.

Don't think about him.

"Thank you. As I said when I picked you up, I think you look amazing."

Her phone buzzed in the clutch she bought to accessorize with.

"You really do have an eye for alternative looks, no matter the occasion."

Another buzz.

"Is that your phone?"

"I think so. I'm sorry. One sec."

"No, it's fine. I'm going to run to the washroom while you check that. They should bring the first course of the tasting menu soon.", Dominic had suggested that, not knowing what she would like; she agreed the choice was brilliant. "Would you ask the server to bring me a water refill? I'm not into the wine." He took one step away then paused. "Don't tell him that last part." He winked before disappearing across the room.

She hurried to open her clutch once he left and pulled out her phone, worried something was going on with her friends.

Seth:
where r u
Seth:
did he take you to dinner?

Really? Riley rolled her eyes and looked at the ceiling, praying for patience. She debated not answering, but gave up on that because he either wouldn't stop texting or she wouldn't stop thinking about it.

Riley:
Noneya. And yes. And again, your texting is terrible. :P

Before she could even put her phone away, it buzzed in her hand with a new message.

Seth:
I'm serious Riley. Tell me.
Seth:
That better?
Riley:
Much.
Seth:
Riley…

She giggled and put her phone away as Dominic returned to the table.

"What has you so happy?"

"Happy?"

"You have this beautiful smile on your face and you're giggling."

Her cheeks burned. She hadn't realized.

"Everything okay?" He nodded toward the clutch she left on the table.

"Oh, yeah. Nothing major." She twisted in her seat and looked around the beautiful restaurant with its round tables with crisp white linens. "No one came by while you were gone."

"Oh, that's fine. I caught them on my way back." He laid his napkin across his lap as the server brought their first item and placed it in front of them.

Riley studied the dish. "What is the white stuff?"

"*Stracciatella di bufala.* A soft Italian cheese. It isn't half bad with the peach, but I'm not a tomato fan."

Riley was used to new and unusual foods, as her eldest brother was a chef with his own restaurants in Korea, but she never understood the flowers and leaves on food. Not that this dish had flowers, but she saw it on other tables. Her brother tried to explain, but the nuance was lost on her. His passion was food, hers was clothes. She would be just as content with a burger, basket of cheese fries, and a milkshake instead of a five-course meal that would probably have less sustenance and be triple the price.

But she wouldn't complain. She wasn't complaining.

This was nice.

Dominic was nice.

Her phone buzzed again, and her lips wobbled.

"Excuse me," she said softly, trying to keep her voice steady as she rose to her feet and made her way to the bathrooms.

Once inside, she placed her clutch on the marble surface of the counter and peered into the round illuminated mirror. Her eyes appeared glassy, and she swallowed down the emotion, hoping it would push away the obvious feelings reflected at her.

It wasn't fair to Dominic for her to act this way. She didn't even know why it was happening. Something triggered the anxiety that crept up and wound itself around her throat and gripped her head in a vise.

It wasn't the restaurant.

It wasn't the food.

Something felt off, and it made her feel off-center. Feeling off-center always made her panicky.

When her phone buzzed again, she opened the clutch with trembling fingers.

Seth:

fucking hell riley tell me where u r

Seth:

do not make me go all over London to find u

Riley laughed; her shaking eased as she read the frustrated messages.

Riley:

He took me to a place overlooking the park.

Seth:

that could be anywhere

Riley leaned against the counter and debated how to answer. She didn't want Seth showing up and ruining their dinner. He wasn't acting right, and she couldn't understand it. She didn't want him getting in trouble with the monarchy, and she didn't want him taking out on Dominic whatever foul mood he found himself in.

Seth:
Aiden just told me ur at some place at a hotel???
Seth:
wtf Riley! dont do this. dont sleep with him
Seth:
please
Seth:
I only wanted to know where u were so I could find u if u needed me

Riley stared at the phone in her hand in shock. His incessant texting had all been because he wanted to ensure he could find her if something happened?

Her chest swelled with happiness at his care and concern, the earlier anxiety gone. To know that even if he was irritated by her choosing to date someone he didn't approve of, and even after what happened in the hallway, he still would look out for her as he always had meant the world to her.

She didn't understand why he was begging her not to sleep with Dominic. It wasn't like they weren't two consenting adults, and Seth wasn't her boyfriend, so she wasn't cheating on him to have dinner with the guy. It was innocent. So why did it feel so wrong?

Because you love him.

She sighed, shoving down her intrusive thoughts. Loving someone and having them and loving someone and not having them were two different things. Again, she reminded herself she couldn't wait forever on a possibility.

Sending a quick text back reassuring Seth she had no intentions of doing that, she gave him the name of the restaurant in case she needed him. She followed up the information with a quick lecture on not spending the rest of the evening blowing up her phone so she could enjoy her date.

Heaving a sigh, she powered down her phone for good measure and tossed it into her clutch before returning to Dominic, who sat staring at the lights of London against a dark canvas.

"They brought out the next course, but I didn't want to start without you. You hadn't touched the first." He smiled at her. "Listen, since the sun has set, the major draw of this place—for me at least—is gone. Not sure about you, but I could go for something greasy and bad for me. Sounds like a better plan, eh?"

"Oh, thank the gods. I don't get these tiny portions of forest food."

Dominic's boisterous laughter made a few couples glance over at them with disapproving stares.

"Pardon me," Dominic said in an overly posh accent that suited him because it brought out his Canadian accent as he pulled her to her feet by her hand. "We shan't disturb your evening any longer."

Riley tucked her head and bit the inside of her cheek to hold back the laughter bubbling until they paid and left. Once in the elevators to the ground floor, she let loose until tears ran down her face and she could barely breathe.

When she finally calmed down, she looked up to find Dominic staring down at her. "You're really beautiful when you're open like that."

"Huh?" She straightened, confused.

"I know I don't know you that well, but I get the distinct impression you haven't been yourself around the manor." His smile was sad as he added, "Or around me."

Riley leaned against the back wall of the elevator as it descended the long journey from the twenty-eighth floor. "I suppose you're right." She would not lie to him. "I've had a lot on my mind, and all this is new to me. Coming to London, meeting the Blackthorn Clan… You—this."

"What do you mean?"

"I've never really had a relationship before." She shrugged, not intending to share the lengths of her inexperience with him like she had Seth. "This is my first date," she said shyly.

"Really?"

Riley met his surprised expression and laughed. "What?"

"I would have thought…" He shook his head. "You're so pretty and have this air about you that draws people like a magnet. I see it. It drew me."

Riley flushed and looked down at the little spikes on her shoes. She couldn't say anyone seemed drawn to her, especially with such a tight friend circle, but she made friends easily. In the last year alone, she became friends with Blaire, Rue, Charlotte, Layla… Maybe Dominic was right. Aiden told her once that Lukas said she could make friends with a houseplant if left alone with it. She smiled at that.

But she didn't see where that talent helped with a romantic relationship. If she were honest with herself, she hadn't been looking very hard for anything more than her Korrena because of her attachment to Seth.

"I will say, I think I have seen glimmers of the real you."

"What do you mean?"

"Moments ago, when you were laughing. How you responded at the end of the 'meal' we didn't even eat. When I came back from the bathrooms. In the garden at the manor, when you were so animated about your dreams for fashion."

"My yammering really didn't annoy you?"

"Not at all. You were so alive and happy. I like happy people. Why in the world would you think it would annoy me?"

Riley sighed. While her tight friend circle and immediate family accepted her, it didn't always work out that way. Growing up, she was often scolded by teachers for hyperactivity, and her mother frequently attended disciplinary meetings for it. Other students treated her like an outcast because she wasn't like them. Childish, emotional, annoying, weird… the different words both teachers and students used stayed with her. Those who did find her behavior endearing didn't stick around long. The novelty wore off, and they couldn't handle the constant "on" behavior.

If it weren't for the support of her family and close friends, she might have become a different person. But it didn't mean emotional wounds and insecurity weren't left behind.

They reached the bottom floor and went out into the night. The temperature was low, so they put on their coats before Dominic led her down the street. If not for the unfamiliar sights grabbing her attention as they approached their destination—one she recognized immediately by the classic logo on the awning—she would have found the momentary silence awkward.

"Figured somewhere like this would be more your speed."

"Yeah," she said with a dreamy sigh, smiling at the Hard Rock Cafe sign. She knew a milkshake was within reach.

"Well, that's not the reaction I expected."

"Huh? Oh. I just really, really like milkshakes." She looked away.

Long fingers took her chin and turned her face back around. "Hey, I'm not saying it's a bad thing. It was pretty cute, actually."

"Oh."

After polishing off a side dish of twisted mac and cheese, Tupelo chicken fingers, and a delicious vanilla milkshake with extra whipped cream, Riley sat back and patted her food baby. Hoovering her food probably wasn't proper date etiquette, but after Dominic loosened up after her bathroom trip at the high-rise restaurant, she felt more comfortable to be herself—or at least the extent of herself she shared in front of others. It seemed to come down to a time thing between them. Familiarity to reach comfort.

Finishing his beer, Dominic sat back and set his empty bottle on the table. "I had a good time tonight."

"Me too, but you might need a wheelbarrow to haul me back to my room. That was some good food."

He chuckled and propped his elbows on the table, sitting forward. "I wanted to talk to you about something before the night ends."

Riley groaned. "Don't do that. Nothing good ever comes from the 'I want to talk to you about something' bit."

His smile was lazy and understanding as he laid his warm hand over hers. "I want to ask you what you think about compatible pairs. You know, after the discussion about Korrena pairs back at the manor."

"I know it's not for everyone."

"But what about you?"

Her heart thumped. She debated how to answer. If she were true to herself, she'd go in-depth about her feelings and plans entirely. But if she were careful and gave what was probably expected of her, she would just acknowledge her lack of aversion to it. The thing was, Dominic wanted her to be herself. How could she say she gave him a fair shot if she didn't at least meet him part of the way?

"I want my Korrena pair, but if I never get lucky, then I want a compatible pair. I don't want to be alone. Like, I have a big family, but everyone but my mom and brother are scattered miles and miles away. I want to create my own big family."

"Can't say I don't like that idea."

She looked up from the glass of water on the table she had been staring at when she made the confession.

Dominic tightened his hold over her hand and met her eyes. His soulful brown eyes looked so earnest as he spoke. "I want to make a proposal."

She startled, and he laughed.

"Not that kind of proposal. I suppose the topic would make you think that." He shook his head. "This proposal is not something you have to answer right away, and not something we have to dive into immediately."

"Okay…" She dragged out the word, unsure where he was going with this.

"Neither of us has found our Korrena pair. I'm twenty and you're eighteen. I know it might be a little different for you, since you're at the edge of that coveted age, but I don't want to miss out on this chance."

"What chance?"

Her heart sped up, and when she reached for her stockings, she cursed herself. She had on an outfit with no quiet accessories to fiddle with.

"To see what we could have. I like you, Riley. I can tell you're attracted to me. We can take it slow, but I would like to begin seriously seeing you with the intentions of that being the endgame."

"'That.'" She cleared her throat and grabbed her water, breaking his hold to wash down the nerves and dryness making it hard to speak. "'That' being we'd become compatible pairs."

"Yes."

"Why me, though?"

"Aside from all the reasons I've told you that draw me to you? There's something else I can't explain. Something that tells me I need to be around you. If I understood it more, I'd tell you."

Riley didn't know what to think of that. She understood people could feel drawn to another person without understanding why; she felt that way toward Blaire, but it seemed absurd for someone to feel that way toward her. She wasn't special. Wasn't a magical human who defied death itself.

Sighing, she looked at Dominic. "I just don't know." When his expression broke and he wasn't quick enough to school it, she added, "I need to think about it."

"I understand. This isn't a quick decision. I've spent a while thinking about it. Before I thought dating might be enough, but I don't think so anymore. I think you're meant to be in my world long term."

A week ago, Riley was prepared to move on and find a compatible pair and forget her childhood love, but now it felt strange. Something held her back from accepting what she wanted for her life. To not be alone and possibly have a big family she could love.

22

Rabbit Hole

After Dominic made his intentions clear, he left Riley to process without pushing the subject, and the conversation turned comfortable again until he saw her back to the hotel. She respected him for not pressuring her, but also didn't entirely favor how passive he acted around her. Though passive might not be the right term. He met her on equal footing, despite his position, and she needed that, but she also wanted something else added to the dynamic—something she needed.

An image of Seth in the pool with his hand around her throat came to her mind. *"But we both know that sometimes you need that."*

Closing her eyes, she took a deep breath and shook her thoughts away.

Inside the lobby, she found Blaire at the front desk with a paper in her hand and a pinched expression on her face.

"What's up?"

Blaire looked up in surprise. "I just received this letter from the front desk."

"Who's it from?"

"The Oracle."

"Another message?"

Blaire shook her head. "No, nothing like that."

Riley peeked over Blaire's arm to get a better look. "So what's it say?"

"She wants to meet at a pub down the street."

Riley lifted her head to meet Blaire's eyes. "A pub? The Oracle? That doesn't sound like her." She couldn't imagine someone like the Oracle hanging around in a local pub in the middle of the night.

"It's not the same parchment and lacks the wax seal, but what if it's the same as the other messages from the Oracle back at the academy? I mean, I doubt she's carrying a stamp, wax, quill, ink, and parchment paper everywhere she goes."

"But you said it's not a message, just an invitation."

Riley didn't think wandering through a foreign city in the middle of the night seemed smart. She had to admit curiosity poked at the back of her mind, but she also knew what people said about consequences for curiosity.

When Blaire didn't say anything, Riley asked, "Are you going? Are you sure this is a good idea?"

"It's a pub in the middle of the city. It'll be fine. I looked it up, it's not far." Blaire shrugged, looking toward the doors. "I wouldn't go if it was somewhere rural without people."

"Where's Lukas?"

"He's already crashed, and I really don't want to wake him or anyone else when it's probably a harmless conversation about what happened at the manor. I did at least text Professor Velastra." Blaire paused. "Not the group text because I don't want Lukas freaking out, but directly. She didn't respond though. She's probably asleep."

Riley didn't like that. Blaire wasn't like them. If something happened to her, magic in her blood or not, she couldn't recover the way they could.

"How about I go with you?"

"Why?"

"Because it's been a long night and I'm not ready to sleep." At Blaire's questioning look, she added, "Plus, I had a lot of calories and should walk them off."

"Do you want to change first? I was about to put on pajamas when the desk called; glad I didn't."

Riley looked at Blaire's comfortable black leggings, deep indigo sweater dress with a cowl neck, and tall black boots and shook her head. There wouldn't be time for any of that if the Oracle was waiting for them. It was extremely disrespectful to leave a woman of her stature waiting long.

"I'm good. It's just a pub. I'm used to chunky heels, and I have a coat. You sure you won't leave a message for Lukas?"

"Nah. We'll be back in no time. Why stress him out and cause an argument when he wakes up? Because you know he'll get all pissy if he finds out I went out into the city without him."

Riley understood her logic. Seth reacted the same way, and she wasn't even his Korrena pair or human.

Blaire looked at the paper again. "It says the pub is about a five-minute walk. But at least there's directions."

"Then let's go."

The streets around the hotel were nice, even in the night light. The entire neighborhood seemed higher class, and it put Riley at ease as they made their way along. Blaire mentioned how the letter didn't give the name of the place, but she thought it was one of those exclusive, private bars hidden away like a local gem only the most in-the-know denizens of society would find, since they had to give their names to enter.

As they rounded the corner and entered an alleyway, the temperature dropped significantly in the darkness. Not much streetlight filtered in, but Blaire assured her they were going the right way, and the alley was a shortcut. How could she even tell in the darkness? The paper had to be nigh unreadable. She much preferred the idea of staying out in the open where people were when it was this late.

"Are you sure? Would there at least be people outside if it's a high-end bar? Lights? Music? Something?"

"Just down here on the end. That door up there." Blaire gave her an encouraging smile she could barely see, but it wasn't hard to catch the faint glimpse of apprehension there.

They looked up at the heavy-looking metal door.

"Maybe it's soundproof?" Riley asked.

Blaire laughed nervously. "Maybe."

Before they could knock, a sliding panel on the door opened and a set of eyes peered down at them. *What is this? Some cheesy movie?* She didn't know places still did the whole shady peek-a-boo with clientele.

"Um. Someone is expecting us," Blaire said, tossing her long hair back and straightening her shoulders in an attempt at bravado. At least, that's what Riley thought she was doing. Maybe she did feel confident.

"Names," the gruff voice on the other side of the door said.

"Blaire Wilcox and Riley Easton."

After a moment, the eyes returned to the peep slit. "She's not listed."

"Last minute addition," Blaire said with a smile.

Those eyes that looked black in the darkness narrowed on Riley for a long moment before the latch released with a harsh click. Only then did Blaire's shoulders fall as she exhaled. Riley's heart sped up at the realization Blaire was afraid. If they denied Riley entry and she had to leave Blaire alone, it would have made her sick.

Riley knew something was wrong the moment they stepped through the door.

The entryway was dark, and no music played. The smell in the air was stale and metallic, like nothing was in the place except the piping and exposed interior construction they couldn't see. She expected at least the scent of alcohol to permeate the air.

Movement to their right grabbed her attention as a man built like a truck stepped forward, glowering at them. He was not an attractive man. His head was shaved to the skin and covered in tattoos, and he had several facial and ear piercings along with huge, gauged earlobes that made the skin dangle. She liked the gauged look, but not so much it made floppy ears. The muscles of his upper body bulged against the dirty T-shirt he wore, and his arms were covered in a thick layer of coarse hair the color of cinnamon. She still couldn't make out his eyes, but his displeasure at Riley's presence was obvious in the hard expression he gave them. Especially her.

"Blaire," she whispered, grasping the sleeve of her friend's sweater. "I think we should go."

"This way," the burly man said, either ignoring Riley or not hearing her.

"It'll be fine. If we get in there, and it seems weird, we'll leave. Someone has to be inside."

It felt bizarre hearing Blaire be the voice of foolish optimism instead of her. Not that Blaire wasn't optimistic or foolish—though she questioned her decision to traipse about in the middle of the night to parts unknown. It was just usually Riley who kept up with reassurances for others. It felt like she'd fallen down a rabbit hole like Alice did in *Alice in Wonderland*. Nothing was what it seemed.

The stress of the last couple of months was finally catching up with her.

Her hands tightened on the clutch bag she hid beneath her coat. Thankfully, it had a strap to carry it cross-body, so if they had to run, she wouldn't lose it.

She considered trying to text Seth, but she had turned the phone off back at the restaurant to avoid being bombarded with his texts and annoying Dominic. Right now, she regretted not turning it back on after dinner. The guy might get pissed if she made a move for the phone, especially if it made noise when she powered it up and more texts came through.

Riley released a shaky breath. Blaire was right. She needed to calm down and get out of her head thinking such ridiculous thoughts. She'd watched way too many horror movies, and it didn't help her think rationally.

That had to be all this was.

Right?

She cursed her hopeful thoughts as a bag was pulled over her head, and the pungent smell of chemicals assaulted her senses before a hard impact smacked the back of her head.

She was unconscious before ever hitting the ground.

"—end to a problem," a thickly-accented, distinctly British voice rumbled, rousing Riley from blackness.

Her mind felt fuzzy, and the room spun as her head throbbed.

"Riley, wake up. Please wake up."

Blaire?

The sound of metal clinking reached her ringing ears. She cursed, willing her healing abilities to hurry up. Whoever took them probably thought drugs wouldn't work on her, but she smelled a harsh chemical in the air. Whatever they used wasn't a standard kidnapper tactic—wasn't chloroform supposed to smell sweet?

Something warm ran down her forehead. Blaire cried out her name again.

Focus.

Squinting against the harsh lights that greeted her as she opened her eyes, she realized they weren't in the same location as before. It was larger, like a warehouse. A few lone machines sat around the edges of the place, and scaffolding butted against the walls, but the main area of the room only held dirty, empty, concrete floors. From the look of the busted windows coated with grime in the upper areas of the walls, the place appeared abandoned.

"Riley, are you okay?"

Finally coming back to her senses, Riley tasted copper on her lips when the warmth running down her face reached the edge of her mouth.

While Blaire's hair was a wild mess—likely from the bag over her head—and her clothes dirty, she appeared fine. Shaken, but physically fine.

"Yeah, it'll heal. Are you okay?"

Just because Riley didn't see a wound didn't mean it didn't exist.

"I think so. They drugged me, so I'm really dizzy."

Blaire's posture appeared wilted, and she kept having to right herself as she tipped to the side. Riley's concern grew. She was going to tear this bastard's head off for hurting her friend.

She wiggled in the metal chair, but her cuffed hands only rattled behind her and drew the attention of the short, slender man standing in front of her. He wore a vest over a button-down white shirt rolled to his elbows, and tweed, army-green chinos, every bit the polished man she would expect upon hearing his accent.

He turned from the small rolling table that looked like a dentist's table for their tools. "Well, it appears the third wheel is awake."

"What do you want?" She continued trying to break the cuffs, but they wouldn't budge. Even with her preternatural strength, they weren't breaking.

The man's wicked grin widened at her struggle. "It won't work, so there's no use continuing your struggle." At her confused expression, he said, "Your preternatural abilities have been suppressed."

The chemicals? She thought they were for Blaire.

As if reading her thoughts, the man said, "We used basic methods to put the human to sleep, but a little injection took care of you after a knock to the noggin' so you weren't a threat." He rapped on the side of his head with his knuckles.

So that's why her head still throbbed, and she kept feeling blood trickle from the wound. She wasn't healing. She had no idea a substance that could suppress Vasirian abilities existed.

"How?" she finally asked, unable to mask her genuine curiosity. She didn't exactly expect the bad guy to reveal all his dastardly plans, but it was a nice thought.

"Never you mind, love." He turned back to the table. "All you need to know is you're to sit there while I take care of this little problem we have."

"What?"

The man picked up a scalpel. "We're going to need to take samples before I carry out my contract."

Riley's eyebrows knitted in confusion until she realized the man wasn't speaking to her anymore. He spoke to Blaire.

"What do you mean?" Blaire asked, blinking a few times. Her vision probably wasn't the best.

"I was instructed to exterminate you as if you were a common pest, but I simply find your existence fascinating." He pointed the scalpel at Blaire. "A human witch who bonded as a Korrena? Marvelous!" He spun to look at Riley, his eyes glittering as a manic giggle bubbled from his throat, looking every bit the part of the Mad Hatter with his behavior. "Isn't she just a fascinating specimen?"

Riley wanted to scream for allowing herself to be stuck in a position where she couldn't help Blaire, when she'd vowed to do whatever it took to help her after what she'd been through. "She's not a science experiment!"

Riley kicked out at the man, but her short legs didn't even get close to him.

"Well, I was told I could do whatever I wanted as long as I ensured she never left this place." He shrugged casually, the maniacal giddiness gone. "I think I deserve to have something for saving the Vasirian world from what this parasite will bring about."

What the hell is he talking about?

Before Riley could ask him to elaborate, several Vasirian approached across the empty floor.

"Gentlemen! Ladies!" The weird man spun and faced the group. "Come to witness the show?"

The tattooed bald man from earlier led the group and closed the distance while the rest hung back. "No," he grunted. "Boss needs you."

"But I haven't even started."

"Yeah, well, you're the only one capable of removing bullets."

The man put his hand on his forehead and sighed. "Can't you idiots go one day without mutilating yourselves in some way?" He heaved a sigh and turned toward Riley and Blaire. "Excuse me, ladies, I'll return as soon as I'm done. Can't have those bullets moving around once our friend heals and hitting a vital organ. Might bleed to death before we can do anything."

Without another word, he turned and followed the group from the room, leaving Blaire and Riley alone.

Sweat from the bright lights aimed directly at them ran down Riley's forehead and got in her eye, making her squint. She felt terrible. Her body wasn't burning the drug away, and her head hurt. The foreign feeling of not having her body in tiptop shape scared her. Focusing on how to get Blaire out of the situation was the only thing keeping her from crying.

She looked at Blaire, who hadn't uttered a sound in a while, to find her passed out again. That couldn't be good.

Riley's head dropped forward. The dizziness swirled around, and she needed a moment for the world to orient itself.

"Riley! Blaire!"

She opened her eyes and gaped at the sight of Dominic running across the warehouse floor to them.

"Dom? What are you doing here? How did you—"

"I came back to the hotel to ask about another date, and the concierge told me you and Blaire left, but I had just missed you. When I went outside, I saw your pink hair as you rounded a corner, so I tried to catch up. When you both disappeared down an alley, I lost you completely, until after a while I saw you two carried out with bags over your heads."

His hands shook as he came around behind Blaire's chair, breaking her cuffs.

"I had my driver follow, and thankfully got the opportunity to get in here when that group left." He crouched in front of Blaire. "What's wrong with her? Why are you still cuffed?"

"They drugged us. She's only been given something to put her to sleep, I think. But the guy, this weirdo with a scalpel, said they gave me something to suppress my preternatural abilities."

Dominic's brows crashed together. "Folinarin?"

"Huh?"

He stood and moved over to uncuff her. "A black market drug rogue Vasirian have been trafficking all over Europe, the East, and Oceania. It hasn't made it to the Americas or Africa, but it won't be long if we can't find the root of the trade."

Riley rubbed her wrists and beelined toward Blaire, who sat slumped in the chair. "So what? It suppresses our abilities?" She gently put a hand on the side of Blaire's face and tapped her cheek in an effort to wake her. "Why are they using it?"

"Same as any other weapon. To control and build numbers. Gangs want territory. If they make their enemies helpless then seize what they want, it goes easier. Want to just eliminate the problem? One shot of Folinarin followed by a stab wound or gunshot that would be fatal to a human that we'd normally survive, and Bob's your uncle."

How had something like that gotten out into the world without the Vasirian population being aware? Was it simply because it didn't affect their side of the world yet? Riley had so many questions, but they didn't have time.

"I overheard them saying they had to drive out to Watford, so we've got a while. It's just over an hour out one way, and they still have things to do and come back. But there's no telling if they might come back or send someone, so we need to get out of here."

Riley moved out of the way when Dominic approached and lifted Blaire into his arms.

"Come on, I've got a car waiting. I'm going to take you both to the manor."

"What? Why?"

"Because it's too risky at the hotel. If someone lured you away from there, they know where you're staying, and they might come looking for you. It'll just be us three and the staff. Adrian is currently in Hong Kong and will return tomorrow. The rest alternate their time between the manor and their private homes. Mostly their own homes. Adrian lives at the manor alone."

Commotion near the door grabbed her attention.

"I told you I saw the fucking half-breed lurking outside!"

Half-breed?

"Speak of the Devil, and he doth appear. Or in this case, devils." Dominic hoisted Blaire higher in his arms. "Time's up! I hope you can run in those."

Riley didn't feel too stable on her feet, and not because of her shoes. She ran in platforms and chunky heels all the time. But she didn't have time to overthink it with several pissed off Vasirian heading their way.

They made it out the other side of the warehouse, through the opposite doors, and into a neighboring warehouse before the rogues cleared the door in pursuit.

Dominic set Blaire against the wall inside the smaller building. It was pitch black inside, not a window for the moon to filter through.

"If you find the half-breed, inject him and kill him!" After a pause, the same voice yelled, "I don't give a shit if he's part of the monarchy!"

Riley looked at Dominic. What were they talking about?

Dominic felt around until he found a steel pipe that he used to secure the door. It wasn't much against Vasirian strength, but it would keep a group of rogues at bay long enough to give them a head start.

"If they find my driver, we're hooped."

"Hooped?"

"Screwed. Up the creek without a paddle. Royally fucked."

She couldn't see his face in the dark, but the concern in his voice shone clear. He wasn't confident they were getting out of the situation.

"Master Dominic," a hushed voice called from somewhere deeper in the building.

"That brilliant bastard. Come on."

Dominic hefted Blaire into his arms again and crept through the building with Riley holding the back of his shirt to make sure she didn't bump into anything.

On the other side of the building, a half door stood open with moonlight shining into the space. The same driver from their date waited at the door, his gaze fixed outside to watch for threats.

"I'm glad to see you, Roger."

"I'm happy to be of service, Master Dominic."

Clearing the building, the driver led them through a maze of shipping containers to where his car sat in shadows.

Scrambling inside, Riley asked, "What are we going to do about everyone else?"

Lukas needed to know what was happening with Blaire, and Seth and Aiden would want to know about both of them. Professor Velastra needed to report the incident, most likely. She nearly toppled into the seat as the car began moving, and a throbbing pain ricocheted through her head as dizziness washed over her. She couldn't even think straight without feeling off-kilter, and the fleeing for her life thing didn't help.

Dominic finished securing Blaire in her seat belt; she'd been in and out of it as they escaped. It reassured Riley that Blaire would pull through. If she hadn't woken up any, Riley didn't know what she'd do.

"I'll call them in the morning. Right now, both of you need rest.

I need to tend to your head wound. Hopefully, the drug will be out of your system before morning. I don't know enough about it to tell you, but we'll find out." His jaw clenched. "I won't let anything happen to either of you."

Riley hadn't even considered contacting them herself. Her head hurt and it made focusing difficult, so if Dominic thought it best to wait, she would wait. She didn't want to make any more decisions, and the strain from running and her head injury weighed on her physically in ways she never felt before.

Riley sighed, setting a glass of water on the bedside table next to the bottle of Ibuprofen and the now empty blood packet Dominic gave her. Her head hurt so badly she couldn't even appreciate the luxury of the room. Though she couldn't see much with the black curtains drawn.

Soft light spilled across the king bed she sat on. Blaire was finally alert, and they both leaned against a velvet, diamond-tufted, padded headboard with a flourishing, dark wood top that swooped and came to points in the center and each bedpost.

Dominic insisted they sleep, taking up residence in a chair beside their bed to watch over them. Despite feeling terrible, Riley's brain whirled with curious questions.

"I don't understand what happened tonight."

She explained to him the things the weird man with the scalpel said about Blaire and the contract, but she couldn't understand why rogues had targeted her, or what any of what he said meant.

Dominic sighed. "We've been receiving intel about our meeting being leaked. Which sounds absurd, considering the limited number of people in the throne room at the time." He shook his head. "We have come to learn there were already groups of Vasirian who felt a strong opposition to Blaire being not only a Korrena, but allowed to live with the knowledge of our kind."

"But why? I wouldn't hurt anyone."

"We know that. The clan knows that. Others don't. With rogue groups emerging more and more each day, they keep the fires of animosity stoked. Hell, maybe the groups were always there, and we were too blind to see." He ran a hand over his mouth. "I'm also concerned the inhibitor drugs have made it into North America."

"Why?"

Dominic looked at Blaire.

When she had woken up fully, they gave her the rundown on what took place and the new information. At first, Blaire's only concern had been for Riley, which warmed her heart.

"Because I recognized a few of those guys, and I know for a fact they live in Canada. One of them used to be a friend. Haven't spoken in years."

"They called you a half-breed. What was that all about?"

Dominic put his elbows on his knees and rubbed his face before sighing. He looked tired. "While I'm not necessarily 'half,' my family knows somewhere down our line there existed a human/Vasirian pair offspring, and I'm descended from that."

"How is that possible? Like, how can you know? How *did* you know? We just found out that it could happen, and Blaire is the only surviving descendant of those humans."

"See, that's the weird thing. The Oracle told my parents this when I was a baby, and she doesn't remember. It's like she had a recollection of something and lost it, so we couldn't get more information. It's been a point of frustration and unrest in the clan my entire life. No one actually believes it, but other children ridiculed me often for it, as if I was defective. Leave it to the rogues to think so too."

His laugh lacked his usual humor. Clearly, it bothered him, and she couldn't blame him. Not knowing who you are, feeling like an outcast, and being treated poorly for being different. She looked at Blaire. She couldn't imagine the life they each had led, but she could at least relate to the emotional damage. Not that she had it all together, but she knew on a biological level what she was—they didn't.

Dominic sat back and crossed his ankle over his knee. "The entire situation has gone far beyond what I ever could imagine. The entire Vasirian world is buzzing with the knowledge of what happened. They know the information the Oracle shared." He scoffed. "Like, who shared that? Is the throne room bugged? It infuriated Adrian. And believe me, after tonight, I'm angry too. Knowledge is one thing. Killing someone over it is another."

Blaire closed her eyes and muttered, "Wouldn't be the first time. Even before I found out Vasirian existed."

"I don't think they'll stop, though." Dominic sucked in his cheek and exhaled through his nose heavily. "They won't stop until they kill you to prevent the reawakening of the magical bloodline."

"No way," Riley said. "Isn't there anything we can do?"

Pained brown eyes met hers. "Restore the balance sooner rather than later."

Blaire gripped the lush comforter in her hands. She already planned on doing that. The problem rested with getting into a safe enough situation to give her the time to make it happen. As long as rogues, kidnappers, and councils of madmen who craved power continued interfering with Lukas and Blaire's Korrena bond, it would never happen, and the Vasirian world would be doomed.

"What I don't understand is why there are Vasirian against it. If our species is in trouble without it…" Riley shook her head.

"This is why I'm not so quick to think the throne room is bugged. Either that, or whoever passed on the information left that part out. If word is spreading that the one human who bonded with one of our kind has magic in her blood that not only drove another Vasirian to insanity but also has the power to restore the original bloodlines when she becomes like us, allowing people who would ultimately be more powerful than them to exist again, it isn't a surprise some folks are afraid."

Blaire looked down.

"Then, there's the small matter of discovering there were Vasirian in remote regions in Asia and Africa who knew of our history prior to Luciano's reign. All records weren't destroyed after all. The past few days have been busy while the council has traveled for information. No one has additional details beyond retelling the legends of the Blood War and knowledge we once held a connection to humans prior to that. Many are distraught about it. If they'd known of the prophecy, and that the bloodlines would be restored and awaken the bloodline to save us, they would have come forward. Many live so remotely they didn't know the clan wasn't aware of the same things."

Blaire cleared her throat. "If they're in remote locations, are they tribal?" Her voice sounded raspy, which would be expected from the chemicals burning her throat.

"Not like human tribes," Dominic said, handing Blaire a glass of water when she coughed. "These Vasirian, while they live a primitive life and rely on the land, are educated, and some have chosen to take up the simpler lifestyle after many long years in normal society."

Riley didn't know what to make of it. She understood how Vasirian might fear what Blaire's existence might mean for their world, but to lash out in fear of that power? If she thought about it, was that not the very thing Rosendo Blackthorn did?

Took innocent lives all in the name of fear.

23

LOVE

He was going to kill her.

As soon as Seth found Riley, he was going to kill her.

First, he would make sure she was okay, then he would kill her himself. Those driving thoughts kept him from panicking as he blazed a trail of fury through Blackthorn Manor, ignoring the staff along the way.

After Riley stopped responding to his texts, Seth took up vigil outside her room, sitting on the floor next to the door waiting for her return to ensure she got back okay. He resisted the urge to continue texting. She told him not to. But when the small hours crept in, he couldn't handle it. Had Riley actually gone home with Dominic? Slept with him? The thought filled him with a mix of overwhelming emotions. Anger, jealousy, sadness, loss, all waged a war in his mind, and it was all he could do not to scour the streets of London to find her.

Shortly after daybreak, Professor Velastra found him half passed out in the hall and told him they needed to all meet right away. The look on her face did nothing to reassure him. The warning bells in his head that hit him in the middle of the night were nothing short of an ominous sign that something was wrong. He didn't know how he knew, but Riley was in trouble.

Professor Velastra had gathered them in Blaire and Lukas's room, but Blaire was missing too. Lukas woke up and immediately panicked. It wasn't abnormal for Blaire to leave the room to visit Riley before Lukas woke, so his distress added another layer of confirmation to the sinking feeling that hit Seth.

The professor told them Dominic had called her. Blaire and Riley had been kidnapped, drugged, and were sleeping it off at the manor. This set off a flurry of things at once. Before she could relay more than the basic facts, Lukas was throwing on clothes. Aiden disappeared to his room to get dressed, and Seth went to the lobby, where he paced in agitation until they all met there. He didn't care that other patrons gave him a wide berth.

All that mattered was finding Riley.

Seth shoved the heavy bedroom door open with more force than necessary, and it hit the wall with a crack that damaged the manor walls.

Blaire sat in bed talking quietly with Dominic, who sat in a chair beside the bed. They both looked up, startled at the noise.

Lukas shoved past Seth and made a beeline straight for Blaire, putting his hands on her cheeks and kissing her deeply. Seth couldn't hear what he said to her because when Seth's eyes landed on the small lump on the other side of the bed, all sound ceased to exist.

He slowly moved to the side of the bed and pulled the cover away enough to see Riley's upper body. His knees grew weak at the sight of her blood dried on the shaved part of her head. He didn't crave her blood then. No, fear made him feel weak. Fear he never felt before.

"They used Folinarin, an inhibitor that suppresses our preternatural abilities. I still don't know how long it stays in the system. It doesn't look like it's gone." Dominic motioned to the wound on Riley's head. "There's still an actual laceration from where they knocked her out. Blaire told me about concussions in humans, so I've been waking her every hour or two to make sure she's alright."

Aiden sat at the foot of the bed on Riley's side, studying his sister and then Blaire, obviously looking for signs of damage.

"I have never heard of such a thing," Professor Velastra said, moving to sit at a side table near the window to not crowd the bed more than the boys did.

Seth didn't know what Dominic was talking about. Never had he heard of anything capable of suppressing their abilities.

"Who did this to her?" He couldn't keep the growl out of his voice. In all the years he fought, never had he felt the murderous rage he felt in this moment. "What else happened to her?"

"Rogues. They were after Blaire—"

"What? Why?" Lukas asked, holding Blaire to his chest like she would disappear if he released her. Seth couldn't blame him. Circumstances and kidnappers had taken her from him before.

Dominic looked at Lukas. "Somehow, word has gotten out of the Oracle's revelations about our history and Blaire's role in it. They wish to stop it. Either it's not revealed, it will save our kind, or they don't care. I have yet to understand."

Seth clenched his jaw and gently lifted Riley's small body into his arms, careful not to shake her head. He settled against the velvet headboard and placed her in his lap. He wrapped his arms around her and rested her head against his chest. Straight away, she snuggled into him and exhaled, mumbling words he couldn't hear. He pulled the thick comforter over them.

Dominic turned, clasping the back of his neck. Seth didn't care. Riley didn't belong to him. *She doesn't belong to you either.* He couldn't stop the rumble in his chest as he fought with himself. As if to soothe him, Riley placed a hand over his chest.

"What else happened to her?" he repeated, needing to focus on getting answers and not on the twisted jealousy gnawing at his insides.

Dominic took a seat at the table next to Professor Velastra.

"Other than the head injury and drugging? She said nothing else, and Blaire wasn't coherent enough, or conscious, for most of it to know."

Dominic's gaze lay heavy on Seth holding Riley in his arms.

Seth's tone was cold and accusatory. "Why didn't you call us last night?"

"They needed to rest. Blaire took a while to come around, and Riley had a lot of blood on her face and head I needed to clean to check for injuries. Once I got them settled in bed, we started talking. It was so late. I didn't want to keep them up longer to wait on you all to travel out of the city to here."

Reasonably, it made sense. But to Seth's distressed heart and current state of mind, the delay made things worse. Who was this guy to say what was best for Riley? Grinding his teeth, he resisted the urge to snap at Dominic. The guy only tried to help, and he looked exhausted.

See, I can be diplomatic and rational too. Go me. Personal progress and all that.

"Thank you again for taking care of her when I couldn't be there," Lukas said, kissing Blaire's temple. He looked at Riley. "For looking out for both of them."

Seth clicked his tongue against his teeth. The Lukas from a few months ago would be worse off than him. Dominic would likely be picking himself up off the floor. Now that Lukas sorted things out with Blaire, he acted rationally—for the most part.

Show off.

"Seth?"

Every muscle in Seth's body tensed at the sound of his name whispered against his T-shirt. He shifted and placed a hand on Riley's cheek, tilting her face upward.

"Yeah, Firecracker, I'm here."

Her grip tightened on him. "Stay." His heart swelled as she breathed him in. "Sorry I didn't text you," she mumbled, her eyes still closed.

"It's okay. All that matters is that you're safe." He couldn't hide the thick emotion that crept into his voice.

"Mmkay. I don't think the drug is gone," she said sleepily. "Head still hurts."

Seth cursed and looked at Dominic, who had been watching them the whole time with curiosity in the furrow of his drawn brows. "How long does this stuff take to wear off?"

"I don't know. I thought after sleep she'd be fine, but she's petite. If they gave her a lot, it might take longer to burn off."

"Should we call someone?" Aiden spoke up in concern. "A doctor?"

Dominic tapped his fingers against the surface of the table. "Even if we were able to bring a Vasirian doctor to the manor, Folinarin isn't well known. They wouldn't know what to do. It's all a guessing game until the clan's research team can field test it. Unfortunately, tracking shipments is difficult. Most trafficking remains with the rogue groups that stay mostly incognito."

Seth looked down at Riley. Her eyes were closed again, her

breathing steady.

"I don't think they used anything like that on me," Blaire said. "I feel fine."

Dominic shook his head. "Likely not, with it designed for one purpose only."

Professor Velastra turned a severe frown on Dominic.

"So what are we going to do about it?" Aiden asked.

Dominic looked at him. "About the drugs?"

"No. That's not my business. I'm talking about Blaire." His hand reached out and gripped Blaire's foot over the covers. "These pieces of trash keep coming for her in some way or another, and I, for one, am sick of it. They even hurt my sister this time."

Blaire reached for Aiden's hand. "Hey, it's okay."

"No. It's not. You've been kidnapped and tortured off and on over the last… what? Four? Five months? Six? I can't even keep up with it, because the Order had been messing with her since she arrived at the academy." He slumped forward and held his head in his hands. "They won't stop until they kill her. We need to do something."

Seth looked from his best friend to Blaire. So far Blaire resisted the idea of becoming a Vasirian. She almost left the academy because of her fear. Everyone agreed to back off about it, but he wondered if she would ever change her mind. He hadn't heard of any change in her opinion. As far as he knew, she had no intention of becoming like them. Which, according to the Oracle, spelled disaster for their kind. Had that changed things for Blaire?

Riley whined and tucked her face into Seth's chest, burrowing deeper. He put his hand over her ear to shield her from the noise.

Dominic went through a door on the side of the room and returned moments later with a glass of cold water, setting it on the bedside table next to Seth. "She had Ibuprofen not long ago, but when she needs it, here's fresh water." With a final scrutinizing look, filled with what looked like curiosity and regret, he turned and looked at the others. "I think we need to let her rest. If her head still hurts, this noise isn't helping." He looked at Blaire. "You feeling like eating?"

Aiden promptly snorted, and Lukas rolled his eyes.

"Oh, screw both of you," Blaire said, scoffing.

"She could be missing a limb and still be up for a meal," Aiden said, laughing.

"Yeah, I remember her relationship with food from when we first met. Wouldn't even share the crab rangoon with me."

"I did!"

"Only after I made you feel guilty."

Blaire shrugged and nudged Lukas. "Let's go."

Lukas helped Blaire to her feet, and Aiden stood. "You got her?" he asked, looking at Seth.

"Always."

Aiden shook his head slowly and followed everyone out of the room.

Before shutting the door, Dominic said, "I can either have staff bring breakfast, or you can come later. Preference?"

The guy was too nice, and it made it difficult to be angry at him for liking Riley. If that was even the right emotion to label it.

"In here sounds good. Less noise." Seth looked down at Riley sleeping soundly, and then sighed. "Thanks… for um, looking out for her. You're a good guy."

Dominic didn't say anything to that, gently shutting the heavy door to avoid waking Riley.

The steady thump of a heartbeat stirred Riley from slumber. The smell of warm, fresh baked sugar cookies blanketed her senses with its vanilla goodness; a faint cologne mingled at the edges, making her toes tingle.

Opening her eyes, she paused. She remembered being in a room at the manor and the events from last night, but she couldn't remember Seth getting into bed with her. Now, he held her in his arms, asleep with darkness beneath his eyes as if he hadn't slept last night. His arms held her loosely, so she tried to move to give him space. He immediately tightened his hold and pulled her against him. Again, she could hear the steady thump of his heart.

Her headache was gone, so at least that had improved. Reaching up and touching her scalp, she found dried blood, but no sting of a wound. She suspected the drug finished its course through her body.

A light knock on the door came before it was pushed open and a short young woman peeked into the room wearing a black and gray dress with a matching apron over the top and her coal-black hair pinned in a tight knot.

"Oh, good. You're awake." She smiled and opened the door wider, rolling a cart into the room and stopping at the side of the bed where Blaire slept before. She nodded at Seth sleeping. "I came earlier, but you were both asleep, so I kept breakfast warm for you," she said in a soft voice to not wake Seth. "I'll leave this here. Is there anything you want from it before I go?"

"Where is everyone?" Riley asked, with a scratchy throat from sleep.

"They have had their breakfast and are waiting for the clan to arrive. There is no rush, lovey," the woman said, pulling a carafe of orange juice from beneath the cart and bringing a glass of juice to Riley. Once Riley finished, she set the glass and carafe on the cart again.

"Thank you."

"My pleasure. If there is anything more you need, please ring the bell."

"Bell?"

The woman pointed to a silver rope hanging by the headboard with a tasseled end. "It's connected to a system that rings the staff quarters."

Riley nodded her thanks, trying to avoid saying too much and waking Seth.

Once the young woman disappeared, leaving them alone again, Riley peered up at Seth's sleeping face.

Other than the shadows beneath his eyes, he looked peaceful—content. His breathing came slow and soft; his lips parted. She slowly reached up and gently touched his bee-stung lower lip. His tongue ran over his lip in response to chase away the sensation. The shininess left behind tempted her.

A light layer of stubble on his jaw added more evidence to the not slept appearance he carried.

He still wore his clothes from yesterday.

The thought he might have waited up for her both warmed her heart and made her sad.

Seth cared for her, and while she would give anything for it to be more than the moments of lust that blinded them, she knew their relationship wasn't meant to be more than family. She simply needed to convince her libido of that.

Your heart too.

Shut up.

Great. Now she was arguing with herself.

"What are you thinking about?"

Blinking away her thoughts, Riley looked up into Seth's heavy-lidded eyes. "Nothing really."

His eyes narrowed slightly, but he didn't call her on the lie.

When she pushed up from his chest to give him space, his arms tightened again, and she froze. Whatever he read in her response made him release her, but this time, she didn't move. Her hesitation stemmed from the uncertainty behind the action's motive. *Why* did he hold onto her? But it really didn't matter. She craved his warmth, scent, and touch as much as her next breath. After a moment's hesitation, she relaxed, and he wrapped his arms around her again.

Her nose wrinkled as she looked at him. "Your clothes stink." *No, they don't.*

Seth's soft chuckle sent a shiver up her spine. "I have worn them for two days," he said, voice raspy from sleep. The sound went to places she shouldn't be thinking about while in bed with him.

Morning Seth was a dangerous Seth.

"Breakfast!" She sat up so quickly, his hold slipped away. "They brought breakfast. Want some? I had some juice. You sound like you need some juice. Your voice is all… you need some juice." She crawled across the bed and sat on her heels next to the cart. "Apple or orange?" She looked back at him and instantly snapped her attention back to the cart when she got an eyeful of him sitting against the headboard, one leg bent, forearm propped on his knee. His hair was a wild mess, as if he'd been running his hands through it all night. His rumpled shirt lifted enough to show his tight lower abdomen—skin she'd just lain against.

Seth Emerson looked like he'd just had the wildest, hardest sex imaginable. The kind so passionate clothes didn't completely come off, only what needed to be undone to complete the act.

The sight literally had her panting as she tried to make herself seem smaller.

Another chuckle reached her ears. Her cheeks flamed hotter. Why did it feel like he could see right through her? Could he? She shifted her body weight from side to side on her heels, nervous under his searching stare.

"Apple."

As she poured the glass with trembling fingers, his arms came around hers and she jumped when he took both the carafe and glass from her hands.

Seth whispered against the side of her head, "Easy. Still feeling out of sorts?"

He set the carafe down and pulled back from her personal space, sitting on the bed and taking a long drink of the juice. His Adam's apple bobbed as he swallowed.

He still thought she was drugged.

If only she could chalk her behavior up to that.

"It's out of my system."

Finishing the juice, he raised a brow in consideration. "Hungry?"

She was. "I am." *There. No need to lie.*

Seth slid around her side and removed the lid of the tray on the cart. A platter with fluffy scrambled eggs, linked sausage, ham, bacon, pastry puffs, toast, several jellies, a bowl of fruit, and even a couple of blood packets lay before them. Riley's stomach growled in response.

"Don't worry," he said with a chuckle when she tucked her head embarrassed by her rumbling stomach. "I haven't eaten since lunch yesterday."

"What? Why? Why didn't you eat dinner? Have you had blood?"

Seth's hand stopped her from reaching for the blood packet. "I haven't, but I've been worried about you." His other hand grazed over the spot on her head where the wound used to be.

Sighing, she said, "Seth… it's been hours. You can't risk it."

"I'm fine."

"Drink it."

Seth shook his head. "Stop worrying so much."

"Stop making me worry so much."

"You should worry more about yourself."

"Seth, I swear to…" Huffing an exasperated breath, she said, "If you won't drink the blood packet, then take mine. Stop being stubborn." Her hand stilled in the process of reaching for a blood packet. Had she said what she thought she did?

Slowly, she turned her head and winced at the squirrel-staring-down-the-barrel-of-a-shotgun expression on Seth's face. She definitely said what she thought she did.

"Seth?" she hedged, then waved her hand in front of his face, only to gasp when his hand thrust out and grabbed her wrist.

Glowing silver eyes met hers, and her lips parted in surprise at how white they looked from their intensity. She'd never seen his eyes glow so strongly.

"You'd let me…" His throat worked again as he swallowed; his voice sounded strained and gravelly. "Willingly let me…"

Riley couldn't drop her gaze. She knew what he was asking without completing his sentence.

"If it will help you," she whispered.

He didn't need her blood. Two blood packets sat right behind her on the tray. So why was she playing along like this was a game? He knew they were there too, right? Unless he really was in the early stages of *sanguis manie* and couldn't think coherently. Maybe he needed her help in ways other than blood.

Seth brought the wrist without bracelets to his mouth and licked the thin flesh there. She whimpered.

"What if I don't need it to help me?" he whispered across her skin.

"What if,"—his fangs grazed over her inner arm—"I just want your blood instead of those packets over there?"

There goes the theory of sanguis manie.

"Why?" was all she could manage to say, her breath coming in quick puffs. Her heart hammered in her ears.

"Didn't it feel good before?" He kissed her wrist. "I know it did."

It was too much. Way too much.

Riley would have an anxiety attack or self-combust if this kept up. She needed something to help her calm down. She didn't know how much Seth was in his right mind, and that thought drove her anxiety. If he wasn't, he could be in trouble. Even if he wasn't deep into *sanguis manie*, she'd never seen him act like this—except once, but she wanted to bite him too. What was the difference? Was it her worry for him?

Her breath caught when he cuffed her throat gently with one hand, thumb pressing lightly enough to get her attention and then releasing, snapping her out of her thoughts that spun round and round like a carousel.

She stared up into gunmetal eyes that held a faint glow at the edges.

Stroking the column of her throat with his thumb tenderly, Seth said, "Stay here with me. Don't be afraid." His voice still held a strained quality, but the way he looked at her with concern and care… the way he touched her… he was in his right mind.

His hand fell away once her full attention was in the present. She tried to ignore the pang of disappointment that passed through her at the loss of the possessive gesture he only did when it was the two of them. *A gesture to help you focus; it's not possessive,* she reminded herself. It still didn't change her body's response to it and craving it for its intended purpose… and more. She wanted to belong to him.

"I'm not afraid," she finally said.

"Then what?"

"I worried for you."

Confusion creased his forehead. "Me? Why me?"

"That wasn't like you," she whispered.

Seth cursed under his breath, looking at the platter of food long since cold. "I'm sorry. It was out of line."

"No!" She grabbed his arm, surprising them both.

His eyes met hers, and she released him.

"I mean…" She played with the comforter they sat on, watching her twiddling fingers. "I thought not having blood made you act that way. That's why I worried. Not that the way you acted worried me."

She wasn't as concerned about how he knew she was worried. They grew up together; he knew her. Understood her.

"You didn't mind what I did?"

Her shoulders lifted a fraction.

"Riley." He used his tone that brooked no argument and demanded a response without hostility.

"Fine. No. I didn't mind. Happy?"

"Honestly? No."

Her head snapped up to look at his face. She hadn't expected that response.

"Don't look like that. Why would I be happy if you were fine with it and nothing happened?"

"Oh."

"Yeah. *Oh.*"

"So, um, do you want…" Riley twisted and grabbed the packet. When she turned back, Seth looked at it in her hand then up to her face, gaze sliding to her neck. "No, you want…" She swallowed.

"I'm not doing it without your full consent. I bit you before, but it was dubious at best then." He dug his fingers in his eyes. "I'm sorry for that, by the way." His hand fell into his lap. "I don't know what came over me, or why I want your blood so bad now, but I won't lie to you and say I don't. Your blood tastes sweeter than anything I've ever tasted."

"Maybe it's because it's from a live source."

"Fuck if I know, but it's addicting, and it's driving me mad."

The confession stunned her. She didn't know what live, warm blood tasted like, outside of her own. It tasted coppery, similar to the blood packets of human blood. Nothing to write home about. But maybe that was why human blood from the source was forbidden. Other than Korrena pairs, blood that was addictive or tasted different from what they drank from the packets was unheard of.

Usually in pairs, the blood held whatever taste appealed strongly to the pair tasting it. She didn't understand it, but that didn't apply here. They weren't Korrena paired. The fact that the last time he bit her the wound took ten minutes to close was proof of that.

One lick from a Korrena sealed their bite on their pair, a biological design of a Korrena's saliva. They couldn't close other wounds like that, only their bite.

She studied Seth, and he studied her. The silence weighed thick and heavy in the room, like a blanket.

If she let him drink her blood again, it wouldn't do much for the future. She couldn't let him continue to use her as his source, nor could she occasionally let him have a taste.

Could she?

It wouldn't be fair to anyone they might form a relationship with. *Like Dominic.* She sighed. She needed to figure out what she was going to do there. She liked the guy, but that spark she so desperately wanted was missing.

"Just forget it," he said gruffly when she took too long to say anything, reaching for the packet.

Riley leaned back and held it away to keep him from grabbing it. "No, hang on."

"Riley, give it to me."

He leaned forward and crawled over top of her to get the packet but froze when his hand closed over hers. Tilting his head down, he studied their position. He cursed under his breath and sat back.

The movement stung, but helped remind her that in his right mind, Seth didn't think of her that way.

"Can I have the packet now?" His gaze drifted to the platter where the other packet lay.

Riley immediately lunged for it.

"What the fuck, Riley? First, you're worried about me not having blood, and now you're denying me?"

Riley sat back on her heels, on her knees, with both packets in her hands. He was right. She was acting ridiculous. She couldn't explain what had gotten into her, but she didn't want him to have the packets anymore.

Not when she was available.

Tossing both packets to her side of the bed, she moved closer to him and sat right in front of him on her heels. "Do it."

"What?"

"It didn't hurt before. Do it."

"Are you positive?" The glow slowly illuminating his irises made her shiver.

"Positive."

"If it's too much for you, push me away. Hit me if you have to so I don't take too much if I lose control." The pained look on his face made her heart break.

"You won't hurt me. I trust you." She shifted her weight on her knees. "How do you want to do this?"

This situation wasn't like the last time, where a wall at her back supported her. Even then, it felt like she could barely stand. She could lie down, lean against the headboard, or—

"Come here." Seth pulled her forward and sank his fangs into the side of her neck with no warning. She was so caught up in her thoughts, she hadn't prepared herself. She whimpered at the initial pinch, but sagged as the pain faded and pleasure made her toes curl.

Seth kept his arms locked around her as he sucked from the wound, and when she moaned at the wonderful sensation, he growled in response.

Hands roamed—both hers and his. One arm remained banded around her while the other moved to cup her backside and pulled her forward to straddle his lap. Her hand went up the back of his head into the long strands on top of his hair, while her other fisted his shirt.

In a move she didn't expect, he pushed up on his knees and forward, taking her to her back on the bed, placing himself between her legs.

His hardness pressed against the thin fabric of her jumpsuit, but she fought the urge to writhe against him and take the pleasure she wanted.

He braced himself on his arms, staring down at her, panting, his eyes alight and wild, brows knotted.

"Not enough." He groaned and fell forward, latching onto her neck again, moaning when her blood coated his tongue.

The pull from the wound drove the simmering in her lower belly from earlier into a full-blown boil. Trying to rub her thighs together only served to cage him against her body, but she desperately needed friction. Her pulse thrumming between her legs was maddening.

As if he could sense her needs, he rolled his hips in a slow and delicious grind that made her eyes roll back in her head.

Seth's hand blazed a trail of fire over her hip, across her stomach, and between her breasts to her throat where he held there. She wasn't lost in her thoughts, and she realized he wasn't drinking.

"Do you have any idea what you do to me?" He sat back on his heels, dragging his hand down to rest on her stomach. "Any idea how much you torture me? How long you've tortured me?"

"I don't understand," she whispered, her eyes heavy as she warred against the haze of desire taking over her senses to listen to him properly.

"It doesn't matter," he bit out, and leaned in, taking her mouth in a slow kiss flavored with her blood on his tongue.

His fingers worked the straps of her jumpsuit down her arms slowly, giving her the chance to stop him, but she didn't. She pulled her arms free so he could pull the fabric down to her waist.

Once bared to him, she folded her arms across her breasts, too aware that she was now vulnerable and had given him more than she ever gave another. At least at the pool she was half out of her mind and her swimsuit bottoms partially covered her. His head dipped until she looked up at him. Gentle hands ran across her arms and to her hands, coaxing her to remove her shield.

Biting her lip, she looked away, nervous about what he thought of her.

"You're so beautiful," he said in awe, staring down at her bare breasts, nipples hardening in the air. He lightly ran his fingertips across them, and Riley moaned in response. "So sensitive." He leaned forward and kissed around the soft skin of her breast before swirling his tongue slowly around the nipple. Her answering whimper made him smirk. "And so responsive."

Trailing kisses down between her ribs and over her flat stomach, he stopped at the waist of her jumpsuit and looked up at her through heavy-lidded eyes.

Gnawing at the edge of her lip nervously, she looked at his hands.

Seth rose to his knees and shucked his shirt, tossing it aside, making her feel immediately more relaxed that they were on the same playing field in their states of undress. His hands hesitated on the button of his jeans, and he looked at Riley with a silent question.

Don't think.

Don't think. Just do.

She nodded, and he unbuttoned and unzipped his jeans. When he pulled them off and tossed them aside, revealing the outline of his cock in his navy-blue boxer briefs, her heart hammered in her chest.

What if he didn't fit?

He wasn't a monster, but she hadn't had anything inside but fingers, and he wasn't exactly small looking. In fact, he was bigger than some pictures she'd seen on the internet.

"Riley?"

"Huh?"

"You okay? Still with me?"

She cleared her throat. "Oh, yeah, just… that's a lot." Her eyes fell again to his obvious arousal. No wonder girls liked him. *Stop that.* The realization of what she said hit her. "Not that *that's* a lot—well, it *is*—but I mean, this is a lot." She covered her face with her hands.

Seth grinned, clearly pleased with the compliment as he moved over to her again. "You are adorable." He kissed her ribs before gently pulling the rest of her jumpsuit down and off, along with her panties. When he had her completely naked, his eyes fell shut, and he cursed softly. She had no idea what it meant.

Feeling under the microscope, she reached out and tentatively grazed her fingers down the length of his cock through the fabric, and he hissed. Her hand moved to his lower stomach and sat on the waistband of his boxer briefs.

Taking the hint, he lowered and tossed his underwear to the side with the rest of their clothes.

Riley couldn't hide the little gasp that betrayed her apprehension when his cock sprang free, thick and pointing at her, glistening at the tip.

Shaking, she reached out again and touched him. His shuddering breath made her feel more confident, but she couldn't hide the tremor as she gripped his shaft and stroked a few times slowly.

"Fuck, Riley."

Seth groaned low, and his thighs tensed when she twisted her hand at the head of his shaft. The more she pumped him, the easier it became; his natural lubricant made her strokes slippery.

Watching with rapt attention to his every reaction to her ministrations, she reveled in knowing she reduced him to a shuddering, moaning mess.

"Riley, stop. Wait."

She instantly released him. "Did I do something wrong?"

He chuckled and shook his head. "Quite the contrary. If you don't stop, I'm going to come."

"Isn't that kind of the point?"

He growled and moved between her legs, lowering his upper body. "Not before you," he said before leaning forward and swiping his tongue straight up her center from entrance to clit.

She arched her back on a strangled cry. "Holy hell!"

His rumbling laughter sent ripples of sensations through her core as the sound vibrated against her most sensitive areas.

"Good?"

"Yes," she said, panting. "Unexpected."

"More?"

"Please."

Who was she? Riley was not the kind of girl who begged for sexual attention, but here she was, legs spread and asking for it. Sex did things to her head. No. *Seth* did things to her head.

Wasn't this supposed to be about feeding? Did she even care anymore? Nope. Not at all.

Seth hooked his arms over her trembling thighs as her hips squirmed on the bed when he made a figure eight with his tongue around her clit. When he sucked it into his mouth, she bucked against his face with another mewl of pleasure.

He dropped one arm and brought his fingers to her entrance while continuing his assault on her nerves. She was going to combust, and nothing would stop it.

He lifted his head and their eyes met. His glowed a beautiful icy silver, and for a long moment she questioned what this meant to him. Was this from the arousal they didn't know was a thing with feeding on a live source, or did he want her—at least a little bit?

His brows furrowed like he could sense her mind wandering away. He lowered his face to her thigh, whispering against her skin, "Stay with me, baby." A deep bite into her flesh punctuated his words. He slipped one finger into her channel and curled it at the same time.

As he drank, her back arched and a supernova exploded behind her eyes.

When she finally came back down from the euphoric high of being fed on and given another mind-blowing orgasm concurrently, he was kneeling between her legs, studying her face with a soft expression.

Riley smiled sleepily, still feeling out of sorts, until her eyes lowered to see he still was hard and probably needed to finish too.

Did she take this step with him?

What if it ruined everything?

It was so much more than hands, or even a mouth—though, she wasn't sure if she'd be any good at that. Maybe things were already messed up. But she trusted him. She wanted him to be her first, but she wondered if her heart could survive it.

A battle between desire, her heart, and fear of losing one of the people who mattered most waged in her mind. It must have shown on her face, because Seth moved from between her legs and pulled on his boxer briefs before coming close to her and laying a final, gentle kiss to her lips, whispering, "Your pace." She tasted herself on his lips.

Seth helped her sit up and passed her clothes to her while grabbing his own and dressing. He reached over and grabbed a blood packet to give to her once she had her clothing situated.

Riley expected him to leave, to possibly be mad, but he sat there taking care of her with no trace of frustration in his features.

"A-are we okay?"

He turned from where he'd started eating an apple slice and gave her a half smile. "Why wouldn't we be?"

She gave him a flat look.

"Riley, you allowed me to do something most people don't do to one another. You also trusted me. I saw you weren't ready for more than what we did, so I stopped. I'm surprised we did what we did. Giving you your first orgasm with my hand was one thing, but this went beyond that. I got carried away, and if I went too far, I'm sorry."

"You didn't," she mumbled.

She didn't understand why his expression looked pained, but the tense set of his jaw, narrowed eyes, and tight lips spoke volumes.

Finally sighing, he put down the apple piece. "Did I read it wrong?"

"Yes, I mean, no, not exactly." When he said nothing, giving her the chance to elaborate, she added, "I… wanted to."

"Wanted to what? There's a lot that could mean. A lot that can happen." He gave her a pointed look. "A lot more than one finger, my mouth, your hand."

From the heat crawling over her face, her skin was likely as pink as her hair. "To go all the way." In a quieter voice, she added, "For you to be my first." He would take care of her, not rush her, and make it feel good.

Seth turned his head away and muttered what sounded like "Fuck" under his breath. He turned back to her and asked, "But?"

"But what?"

"You wanted to, but there was hesitation. Why?"

It was a fair question. She needed to give him an honest answer.

"Because I don't want to ruin what we have." Her voice broke as she said, "I don't want to lose you." Tears welled in her eyes against her will, and Seth's face crumpled at the sight.

"Hey," he said softly, reaching for her and pulling her into his arms. "You will never lose me. No matter what dynamic our relationship takes on. If nothing ever happens again, fine. If it did… if you wanted me to be the one to show you…" He took a shuddering breath she didn't understand and cleared his throat. "I can be whatever you need. I will be whatever you need. If you'll have me."

Riley wrapped her arms around his waist, squeezing tightly. She buried her face in his chest to inhale the sugar cookie scent that calmed her.

"I love you so much, Seth," she whispered.

He stiffened at her words, and she wondered if she messed up by saying them. She hadn't meant them to bind him. The words were true in all ways they could be. Family, friends, and more. So much more. But that confession would stay locked away. She could tell him she loved him and mean it without ruining things.

Seth kissed the top of her head and relaxed. “I love you too, Firecracker.”

How she wished his words meant more than hers did in that moment.

24

Bloodlines

When Seth led Riley through the heavy doors into the clan hall, they were met with chatter and frustrated voices.

Everyone was waiting on them, but he needed to take care of Riley first. She needed rest, a shower, and food. Once again, she gave him a piece of herself he could never return, and once again, he took it farther than it should go.

He felt disappointed in himself that things got out of hand, turning an act of drinking blood into something sexual, but how could he not? Riley's blood was an aphrodisiac that held his heart—and cock—in a white-knuckle grip he couldn't escape.

The indecision that swirled in her eyes when he'd been ready to sink himself inside her made him stop. He couldn't take from her something so precious with that much uncertainty.

But hearing she wanted him to be her first? Trusted him? Him of all people, when he didn't feel worthy of her? The pride her words prompted was heady.

Still, it wasn't the time. Making a choice like that based on lust alone wasn't enough. She needed to make the choice without simply going along for the ride. So far, their interactions had been by his lead. While she might need that going in, he wanted her full awareness of where it would lead—full consent. Only then would he cross that line. If only to teach her and let her go. He would be whatever she needed.

As they approached the dais, Riley smiled at Aiden. "Thanks for bringing me a change of clothes." She smoothed her hands down her stomach over the black T-shirt with a logo of a band Seth hadn't heard of before on the front. "The dirty warehouse kinda ruined my jumpsuit."

Aiden hugged his sister close and kissed the top of her head. "Glad you're alright now. We were worried about that drug. I've never heard of anything like it." He released her and stepped back, looking at Seth. "Good?"

Seth nodded sharply; his jaw tightened so much it made his teeth ache.

"Is the girl well?"

They all turned toward King Adrian, who sat on his throne studying them.

For all the rumors about his temperament leaning toward fiery, he seemed polite and accommodating so far. At times Seth had seen a flash of something more. Something he recognized. Like calling to like. Especially at the dinner table when they spoke of pairs.

"I am," Riley said brightly. Her big smile sent a shot of serotonin straight into Seth's veins.

"I can assure you we have our best looking for the rogues responsible for what happened to you and Blaire. This is unacceptable on many levels and breaks more laws than is redeemable." His dark eyes moved to Dominic, who sat at the end of the lineup watching Riley.

Seth moved closer to her back and was pleased when she automatically leaned against him. He didn't think she did it consciously. It made him question Aiden's words. If maybe there might be something more than physical desire and family that continued to draw them together.

"How did you know where to find them?" the king's sister asked.

Dominic broke his stare and turned his attention to Mariana. "After my date with Riley," he said, and the king raised a brow but said nothing, "I left but returned to ask her for a second. Maybe presumptuous of me, but here we are." He laughed, but no one else did. The situation was too serious for a joke. When Dimitri rolled his eyes, Dominic sighed.

"When I went inside, the concierge told me I just missed them, which was odd. I started outside but heard a couple of men near the doors inside talking about taking the human." He looked at Blaire. "I left this part out before."

Gaze drifting from everyone in attendance, he continued. "I was torn whether to go warn Lukas or find Blaire and Riley. I stepped outside to see if I could see them first, and that's when I saw a flash of pink hair and followed them. I lost them for a bit then saw them dragged out of the alley with bags over their heads."

The stereo growl coming from Lukas and Aiden would be amusing if Seth's chest weren't also vibrating with a rumble. Riley entwined her fingers with his, and the strangest sensation of calmness cocooned him, his agitation leaving him. He was too far gone on this girl.

Dominic glanced between Lukas and Aiden as they calmed themselves. "I kept a safe distance so they wouldn't notice me—or so I thought. When they left the warehouse they'd taken the girls to,

I snuck in to free them. Apparently, someone had noticed me, so we had to run for it. I brought them here, thinking it safest since they knew the hotel the girls stayed at."

"Wise choice," Gabriel said.

"With Folinarin in Riley's system, along with a head injury, as well as Blaire not being in top shape either, I thought it best to let them rest before everyone arrived."

King Adrian nodded, satisfied by Dominic's recount of the events and how he handled them.

Seth grasped for patience to ask, "Why didn't you come back to the hotel and get us when you saw them taken from the alley? Or at least call someone while tailing them?"

Dominic met Seth's eyes and shook his head. "I didn't come back because I didn't want to lose track of them and thought it'd be too late for them if I waited on others to arrive before taking action." He leaned forward in his seat and pressed his hands together in front of him, forearms resting on his knees. "I didn't think the rogues would recognize me, seeing as I'm often overlooked in spite of my status in the Vasirian world as part of the clan—albeit more advisor than anything."

"Why would you think that?" Riley asked.

Dominic blew out a breath and sat back. "Because I'm not a full-blooded Vasirian." At the surprised look on Aiden and Lukas's faces, he added, "Supposedly, somewhere down my family line that isn't connected to the Blackthorn Clan is a human and Vasirian pairing. According to my parents, that is. How much is true, I don't know. But it's enough to change opinions, and when you're in the monarchy, everyone knows your business."

The dark chuckle that followed Dominic's admission didn't suit him at all, from what little Seth knew of the guy.

However, no one in the clan looked surprised by the admission.

Professor Velastra stepped forward, her nude stilettos echoing on the marble floor in the spacious throne room. "If you are descended from the ancient bloodline, then why do you not also possess magical blood?" She crossed her arms over her slim waist as she looked at the floor in contemplation. "In fact, by your admission, the entire foundation of the Oracle's words crumbles. I spoke further with her in this after our last meeting to learn more. The existing beings with magic in their blood are human, and it's dormant in their blood. Humans who continue to be born into our world but have lost their connection to the original source of power—the original bloodline." Her eyes briefly met Blaire's. "This is why they cannot awaken."

Dominic nodded. "The Oracle confirmed only humans who became Vasirian themselves had the most powerful children. Offspring of a human and a Vasirian pair had magical blood, but it was powerful. But I don't even fit that, as I'm a descendant of that. Only Vasirian are in my family tree until we ran out of records back at the start of Luciano's reign."

"Shortly after the records of our people were destroyed," Gabriel said with a solemn expression.

Dominic nodded. "Considering how many centuries have passed, it's doubtful I have any trace in my blood worth noting."

Blaire shook her head, a knot of concentration between her eyebrows. "Something's weird about that, though."

"What do you mean?"

"Well, when you were suffering from *sanguis manie* and I shared my blood with you, you didn't go mad like Vincent did."

Mariana made a sound of disapproval.

Blaire continued, "If your blood isn't magical, then how did you not suffer the same fate?"

Seth wondered the same. He remembered how unhinged his cousin Vincent behaved at the trial after they rescued Blaire from the diplomat wing. He'd held her prisoner for two months under some sick delusion he could claim her as a compatible pair via Stockholm Syndrome. Seth always thought his cousin odd, but not disturbed. Feeding on Blaire's blood exacerbated the issue until he became feral.

"Considering the timeline," Gabriel said, sitting back in his seat, "and the fact Dominic's family only consists of Vasirian—as he said—it is likely his blood has become diluted over time, that while traces remain, he has no power himself. Likely the same applies to his children and those before him. Which attests to the uncertainty of his claim to being half." He held his chin between the curl of his index finger and thumb, leaning on his elbow. "It's likely what made him immune to whatever is in your blood, love." He winked at Blaire.

"Of course," Felix chimed in from his position between Gabriel and Mariana. "Having magic in blood that is dormant can still result in peculiar things occurring within the host, I suspect. Otherwise, based on the reports of what happened to the other student, I believe Dominic would have met the same fate." Rarely did the man speak, begging the question what role he played in the clan other than being Mariana's husband and pair.

The entire situation made more questions arise than quelled them.

Riley released Seth's hand and turned to Blaire. "But I thought you said there *was* a physical response between y'all."

Her lips turned down, as though regretting being indiscreet about what happened between Blaire and Dominic after Blaire gave her blood to save him.

With Vasirian able to release chemicals that triggered pleasure in a willing human when they bit them, it wasn't surprising a pleasure response happened. Combined with the connection they built while mutually surviving, it would seem strange if nothing happened at all.

Judging by the apprehensive expression on Riley's face as she looked between Blaire and Dominic, she questioned whether Dominic was jumping from one girl to the next when it didn't—couldn't—work out with him and Blaire.

Had she forgotten Blaire told them Dominic didn't see her that way?

The need to reassure her obvious concern and his selfish desire to allow the rift that train of thought might create fought for dominance. But once again, his need to ensure Riley's happiness won out, and he leaned down to whisper in her ear, "He doesn't want her. He didn't. It was only an emotional situation and a response to stimulus."

He tried to keep his voice even and the explanation concise the way his brother would, to avoid his own emotions creeping into his words. Judging by the way her shoulders relaxed, he succeeded.

All eyes were on Dominic as he explained. "Yes, the stimulus of Blaire's blood, combined with our proximity to each other, and her biological reactions to the chemicals released with the accepted bite all played a catalyst to my desires."

The look of sincere regret and discomfort as he met Lukas's eyes spoke volumes. "I am truly sorry. I have no romantic intentions with Blaire, and never would I ever try to come between Korrenas who've pair-bonded." To Blaire, he said. "We grew close, yes. But I see you as merely a friend."

Lukas long since forgave Dominic, and as Dominic physically relaxed under Lukas's watch, Dominic clearly saw the forgiveness in his eyes. Maybe he needed that public acknowledgement along with the gratitude Lukas had already shown. It made sense. Touching someone's Korrena was the ultimate betrayal.

Knowing the truth about the dopamine reaction from a Vasirian bite, remembering the teachings of how they affected humans, Riley was surprised to be so disappointed to hear Dominic declare he saw Blaire as only a friend.

It made little sense for her to feel disappointed not to have an easy reason to reject him. Not that he was a bad guy. She liked him. But he wasn't the one for her, and she couldn't lie to herself after what happened with Seth in the bedroom. Not that what happened meant Seth was the one. It meant her heart wasn't settled enough to choose Dominic. She needed to tell him.

It was only fair.

Dominic's eyes met hers as he continued his explanation, and her stomach twisted at the softness in his eyes. "I meant what I said on our date."

When she looked down, Aiden asked the question probably on everyone's minds. "What did you say?"

Both the king and Gabriel turned their attention to Dominic with eyebrows raised.

Never taking his eyes from Riley, Dominic said with conviction, "I want her to consider becoming my compatible pair."

Seth exploded at her side. "What the fuck?"

Riley twisted to face him.

His loud bellow didn't fully express the anger rolling off him in red-hot waves of molten fury.

"When did it become like that?" He gaped at Riley in disbelief. "Were you ever planning to tell me you were going that far? That's not some simple dinner date."

"For your information, it was a simple dinner date. Dominic asked me how I felt about compatible pairs. If I was open to the idea." She looked at Dominic and back to Seth, unable to hold either guy's eyes, but not backing down from Seth's attitude.

"With him?"

"In general."

Seth narrowed his eyes in suspicion. "Then how the—"

"*After* I told him I was open to that type of relationship, he proposed seeing where things might lead with us. He didn't outright ask me to be his compatible pair." Again, she looked at Dominic. By bringing it up in front of everyone, he must be asking now. "But he asked me to consider it because of our age and mutual desire for a partner."

"You're only eighteen! You're not past the final average year. What the hell, Riley! Are you that desperate for someone that you'll accept anyone who comes along?"

She shrank back, and Aiden immediately stepped to her side. "Calm down, man."

"Calm down? How the hell am I supposed to calm down when he's laying a claim like that? When she was just—"

"Just what?" Dominic asked, rising.

"No. Nothing. Clearly it was nothing."

Riley set her jaw. Did the private sanctity of what happened between them in that bedroom mean nothing to him?

Aiden shook his head. "That was uncalled for. You know Riley doesn't mess around."

"I didn't mean—" Seth's remorseful eyes met hers. "I didn't mean it to sound the way it did. I know you're not like that."

King Adrian cleared his throat and sat up, having been silent for the exchange and thorough explanation of events, taking in everything with keen eyes over using excessive words and questions.

"As entertaining as this display of hormonal posturing is," he started, his tone dry and sarcastic, "can we get back to matters at hand and not your desire to pair with one girl?"

Dominic fell into his seat with a heavy sigh. Riley stayed next to her brother, not knowing what to say to help Seth. She didn't understand the level of anger he exuded. Wouldn't he want her to be happy with a pair? It hurt that he didn't approve, even if she had decided to let Dominic down gently.

"If we are back on task, I question the motives of the rogues who attacked Blaire. Harming a human is forbidden. Why would they risk banishment to Cresbel Asylum?"

Dimitri smirked. "Not everyone follows the law."

"The Order is a prime example of that," Gabriel added. "They wish to halt a prophecy long in the making. I sincerely doubt they care what laws they need to break to stop it from coming to pass."

King Adrian nodded and swept his eyes over the lineup in front of him. "It appears Blaire may be in more danger than she ever was with the Order, if there truly are Vasirian in opposition to the restoration of the original bloodline."

That Blaire could once again find herself at the hands of mad Vasirian crazed enough to want to destroy her made Riley sick. She felt guilty for even thinking of things between her and Dominic at a time like this.

"If you'll excuse us." Mariana stood, her husband Felix taking her arm.

Riley wondered if she has missed part of the conversation.

They both made their way out the side door, leaving the rest of the court, Riley, and her friends to digest the new information about the rogues.

Professor Velastra looked at King Adrian. "What has happened to the Order during all this? Were we not set for trial?"

"Considering recent events, they have been exiled to Cresbel Asylum, save for Tobias, who acted as our mole. They will likely remain there without trial, as new information came to our hands of their involvement with rogues in the Americas. Between that and the mountain of evidence provided by not only you all, but Tobias from his time in service with them, eyewitness accounts from researchers, and members of Blackthorn Security, this is an open-and-shut case." He rested his hands on both arms of the chair and looked at Blaire directly. "I feel for your emotional wellbeing it best you do not suffer through a trial."

Blaire smiled, and Lukas took her hand, squeezing it.

"A new council will be appointed to handle overseeing the Vasirian population in North and South America. They will still use Blackthorn Academy as their base of operations if for no reason but accessibility and familiarity, but they will not function as the overseers of the students there. I feel my father continued a tradition that doesn't fit with modern times."

Professor Velastra stepped forward when he motioned for her.

"I am appointing you the de jure headmistress of Blackthorn Academy, should you choose to accept it. You've done an exceptional job in this short time, and Tobias has provided excellent feedback on your time as student liaison. You practically ran the school already. With this, you will not face the opposition of the Order should something need done."

"If you feel I am a proper fit, I humbly accept your offer."

"Excellent. For the branch schools, I will appoint heads for each to keep the new Order out of their halls as well."

Professor Velastra stepped back as King Adrian's serious gaze settled on Blaire again.

"As far as this magic blood business is concerned, you need to think long and hard about the future." His gaze hardened. A chill went up Riley's spine. "For all our sake."

Before Blaire could say anything, a blast splintered the heavy doors behind them like cheap plywood. Riley screamed and covered her ears.

25

Under Attack

A shrill alarm filled the throne room moments after the explosion. The sound should be louder, but the ringing in Riley's ears muffled it. Soon, her preternatural healing would repair the damage, but until then, the shock threw her equilibrium off balance. The voices around her shouting in panic and anger sounded like they came through a pillow.

Looking at Blaire, awareness hit her. Could she handle the lasting effects? Lukas held Blaire to his chest, covering her ears as they backed toward the dais.

Once the smoke settled, it became clear this wasn't a one and done explosion.

Down the long corridor, dozens of rogue Vasirian headed their way, weapons in hand. Riley didn't know how it happened, but rogues had invaded Blackthorn Manor.

King Adrian rose to his feet.

"Clear the area! Take the side doors and head toward the staff quarters. Libby, show them where to go. Quickly!" He turned as a tall woman approached dressed in the same dress and apron the other lady had worn before. "Where is my security detail?" he bellowed.

"Hurry! Quickly!" The woman motioned for them, and Lukas led Blaire—still covering her ears—through the side door. Professor Velastra, Seth, and Riley followed through the door, with Aiden bringing up the rear.

A couple of rogues converged on them before they could get through.

Aiden turned panic-filled eyes to Riley then Seth. "Get her out of here." He shoved Riley into Seth's arms and pulled the door closed.

Riley screamed. "What? No!" She squirmed as Seth hoisted her up, arms banded around her from behind as she kicked out, trying to dislodge herself from his strong hold. "Don't you leave him!"

"He's not alone! The clan is in there too!"

She continued to thrash. There were too many rogues. She wouldn't abandon her brother.

"Riley." The commanding tone of his voice next to her ear made her freeze. Seth's hand cuffed her throat and held her against him as she panted. He whispered calmly, "We're not abandoning him. He's going to be right behind us. He wanted me to get you out of here. I'm getting you out of here." With that, he flipped Riley over his shoulder and turned to the others.

Libby led them down a corridor into the staff kitchen, where they stopped and waited, listening to the alarm in the distance. A red light flashed over and over across the kitchen, obscuring any detail of the room. Riley closed her eyes against the strobing effect then stared at the checkered pattern floor, still dangling from Seth's shoulder like a sack of potatoes.

"What is happening?" Blaire asked, uncovering her ears at last.

Libby looked from the door they passed through to Blaire. "It seems we are under attack, my lady."

"I understand, but how? Where's Aiden?" Blaire looked around in confusion. With Lukas covering her ears and taking the lead, they missed Aiden's choice to buy them additional time.

"Indeed. How? That is the question of the bloody hour," Gabriel said, pushing the staff door open harshly. Dimitri, Natalia, and Dominic followed. He strode across to the center island, resting his hands on the counter. "Blackthorn Manor is typically well secured with armed guards, yet not a one can be found? Rubbish."

Seth placed Riley on her feet, and she threw herself at Blaire, her arms wrapping around her friend's waist as she sobbed into her chest. "Aiden chose to stay and fight. Rogues were right on our heels; they would have followed us through otherwise."

Blaire looked at Lukas, and tears formed in her eyes too. Riley's brother was in trouble, and no one would acknowledge it aloud.

In fact, no one said anything for a long time.

Only the sounds of Riley softly sobbing and the faint alarm in the distance kept them company until the door rattled. Libby jumped away with a startled gasp as Aiden burst through.

He put his back to the door, pulling in heavy breaths. Blood stained his T-shirt and arms. Blaire gasped.

"Aiden!" Lukas stepped forward.

"It's not mine." He put his hand up. "I'm okay," he said before moving to the sink and washing his arms then sticking his head under the sink to drink from the faucet. When he turned, whatever he saw on Riley's face made him hold his arms out. "Come here."

Riley ran at him, her body slamming into his as she clung to him and wailed. She could only remember one time when she cried so hard since growing up, and that was when she thought Blaire was gone.

Gulping down air, trying to steady her hysterical cries, she said, "You… stupid. I hate you!" She hit Aiden's chest. "Don't do that to me!"

He grabbed a cloth from the counter and wiped away the snot on her nose and pulled her back to him. "Hush now. I'm here. I'm okay. We're okay."

"Where's King Adrian?" Professor Velastra asked.

Natalia frowned. "He went another way to find the status of security."

"Alone?"

"My older brother is nothing if not stubborn."

Riley glanced up at Aiden, glaring through the tears still sparkling in her eyes. She could relate. She hit his arm again for good measure.

"Hey! Next time, I won't give you a head start." He hugged her again and kissed the top of her head before finally releasing her.

After what felt like hours of waiting, the noise in the hall drew their attention, and they moved away from the door. Moments later, King Adrian burst through.

"They are closing in. We must go now," he rumbled.

Natalia stepped forward. "What about security?"

"There's no one!" he roared. Natalia shrank away at his outburst. Softening his tone, he cupped his little sister's face. "The manor has been mostly abandoned. I can't even find Mariana or Felix."

Natalia nodded, swallowing and taking a sharp breath in through her nose as if to steel herself. He released her when it looked as if she were composed.

Gabriel pulled a large chef's knife from a magnetized strip over the sinks. Dimitri grabbed a metal pipe leaning on the wall next to a few buckets and hoses.

"The back halls lead only from here to the ballroom. Unless

they came from the ballroom, no one should be there," Libby said, motioning to a small door on the other side of a massive refrigerator.

Natalia nodded. "There are several guest rooms along the corridor to take refuge in. We would do well not to dilly dally here. Libby, go to your room and hide in your wardrobe. Do not come out until one of us comes for you. If you see any other member of staff, instruct them the same."

"Yes, Your Highness."

Libby disappeared through another door opposite them, and King Adrian took charge, leading them into the extremely long corridor lit by heavy beams of bright sunlight filtering in through large windows all down the left wall. To the right, at least seven doors led into the guest rooms Libby referenced. Small tables and large vases filled the empty space along the walls all the way to the end, where an enormous set of double doors loomed, leading to the ballroom.

"Wait," Dimitri said, walking farther into the hall. "The guest rooms will make us sitting ducks with no place to run. We should move to the ballroom, where we at least have a place to stand our ground."

"You want to wait on the rogues to come to us in a big empty room, and then what? Fight them?" Gabriel scoffed. "You want four students, a headmistress, and your family to fight rogue Vasirian who are likely blitzed on narcotics?"

"They aren't human," Dimitri said, pointing the metal pipe at the group. "*We're* not human. It's not the same."

"You'd risk your family? Your little sister?" King Adrian snarled at his half-brother. The laid-back demeanor of the king was long gone, and the simmering rage he masked well had surfaced.

"We don't have time for your sibling rivalry!" Gabriel shouted as the staff door opened and rogues filed through it.

"Go!"

Riley wasn't sure who shouted it, but they all responded, fleeing toward the alleged safety of the ballroom as more rogues poured in behind them.

Breaching the doors of the ballroom, they came to a grinding halt.

Waiting in the center of the room beneath a massive chandelier that easily held hundreds of crystals of various sizes, casting the marbled flooring beneath in amber light, stood at least a dozen Vasirian men and women. Some were dressed in casual clothing, others in more refined fabrics.

These weren't rogues.

Gabriel, Lukas, Aiden, Seth, and Dimitri braced themselves against the door as it banged, echoing loudly across the lavish ballroom.

King Adrian marched forward, arms thrown out in welcome. "It is good to know you are safe. How did you get here?"

Natalia leaned down with a conspiratorial whisper to Riley. "These are members of the Blackthorn Clan. Extended council who live throughout the area and come to the manor often. They must have responded to the alert system."

"How?"

"Every member connected to this manor has a built-in system on their phones to alert them of any breach in our security. They are to come immediately upon this alert to protect the monarchy. To protect their king."

Riley glanced at the members of the council standing before the king. Some held weapons like swords, long sticks, and even pipes like the rogues carried. Surprisingly, no one had any firearms. Surely, they wouldn't have issues obtaining them legally or otherwise, even in England.

She recognized the pale blond on the end with alabaster skin. Tobias Nilsson, a mole planted twenty years ago in the Order at Blackthorn Academy. If not for his actions, Blaire wouldn't be here with them. She didn't recognize any of the others aside from Dominic, who joined them as part of the council.

"Natalia, take the headmistress, Blaire, and the pink-haired girl to the throne area out of the line of fire," King Adrian said, turning to them.

"The pink-haired girl has a name," Riley sniped, before marching across the floor.

A single dark eyebrow rose at the comment, and Dominic gave a low chuckle. She didn't look to see if anyone else responded. She probably shouldn't make a habit of angering members of the Blackthorn Clan.

Natalia led them across the beautiful floor beneath smaller crystal chandlers to a set of five stairs that led up to a dais. A large throne sat in the center similar to the one in the throne room. All black with high and low peaks along the back to give it a sharper design, but with beautiful rubies inlaid through the scrollwork and black velvet upholstery. Two smaller thrones of similar design sat to each side, likely for the king's sisters, his half-brother, and cousin Gabriel, if their positions in the other room were any indication. On each side of those, three smaller versions that would pass as grand high-back chairs finished each end, likely for members of the council who visited, like Dominic or Tobias. Riley didn't know what they did when the entire council joined an event.

"We can take shelter behind here." Natalia motioned to the thrones, crouching on the floor.

The area behind the thrones was shadowed with long black and burgundy drapes in both opaque and sheer textures sagging from the ceiling and cascading in tiers on the wall. A few large wrought-iron candelabras made the fabric look nice without being a fire hazard, but they weren't lit.

Dominic rushed up the stairs to check on them. "Alright?"

Blaire nodded.

"I don't like the idea of my students out there," Headmistress Velastra said, peering out to where Aiden, Seth, and Lukas were attempting to help hold back the invaders.

As if her words alone could summon the worst, the door finally gave, and the men holding the door were forced to retreat into the room as the rogues swarmed. So many more than they'd seen before came in, and they became outnumbered quickly.

Riley could only hope they were on drugs to impede their performance. Stars help them if it helped instead.

"Don't worry, the other doors leading into the ballroom are secure. The council took care of that once they arrived to set up a bottleneck to that door alone." Dominic peeked out as a rogue went for Tobias with a rusty machete, but Tobias ducked and ran a slim, long blade into his chest. The move was designed to kill. Even Vasirian couldn't survive their heart being impaled. It spelled instant death.

"Gotta go. Stay hidden," Dominic said quietly, trying not to draw attention as he moved into the fray.

Lukas and a stout rogue with long hair of a similar color battled one another for dominance on the other side of the ballroom near a set of doors. Lukas's teeth were bared, and he barely missed having his throat ripped out by the rogue on top of him. They rolled. Lukas broke away from the man and stepped back as Gabriel drove the chef's knife into the Vasirian rogue's chest. Then Lukas moved on to other threats.

Riley sought out Seth in desperation, needing to know he was alright. When she caught sight of him just as he ducked to avoid a crowbar connecting with his head, she had to cover her mouth to keep from yelping loudly.

"We can't just wait like sitting ducks," Blaire said.

"We must stay hidden." Natalia's tone was sharp. "You are too important to our kind and its future to put you in harm's way."

As much as Riley wanted to join the others and help, Natalia was right. Riley's job was important. Protect Blaire at all costs.

King Adrian moved with a grace unexpected of someone his size. He swung a short blade one of the council members gave him to behead one rogue, the blade slicing through their flesh like butter. Before their head even hit the floor, he spun and gave the same treatment to another approaching from behind.

Someone had given Aiden a pipe similar to the one Dimitri wielded, and he swung it like a baseball bat trying to dispatch rogues long enough for council members to strike fatal blows or restrain them for questioning.

Riley didn't think many would end up in custody, not with the slaughter happening.

Watching her brother, Seth, Lukas, and the others fight to protect them made Riley anxious. It felt wrong to sit and wait for them to handle it, but what could they do? Blaire wasn't capable of facing Vasirian strength, especially without a weapon. Riley needed to protect her. Instinct made her move closer, and Blaire reached over and grasped her hand.

"We're gonna be okay," she whispered, eyes never leaving Lukas as he fought off any rogue who came near him. Her fingers trembled in Riley's hand.

Rogues dropped, one by one, but it was obvious those not in the council were growing weary. Did the council have some form of combat training? It seemed likely to protect the monarchy.

While Riley's thoughts swirled with possible scenarios, she missed the initial impact, but Blaire standing abruptly and screaming Lukas's name as he was launched across the room and slammed into a pillar did not go unnoticed. By her or the rogues.

Several sets of eyes turned toward Blaire—their actual target.

"We have to go. Now!" Riley stood and grabbed Blaire's wrist, running toward one of the other doors, hoping it could open from this side. Aiden quickly joined them, restraining a panicked Blaire.

"We need to get Lukas! We can't let them kill him!"

"Blaire. They are after you. They won't focus on him. He's gonna be fine. We need to get you out of here." Aiden moved with them to the door.

Riley desperately tried to open the doors, but nothing worked. "Something's wrong. They aren't just locked from this side. Try the others!"

A small group of rogues not occupied by the council moved toward them as Seth met them at the next doors, breathing heavily with blood splattered across his face and clothes. He yanked and banged on the doors, unable to get them open. His preternatural strength could aid in breaking the doors, but it would take a while and cause injury they didn't need—even if it would heal. The time it would take to break through and heal might get them killed. Their strength was greater than humans' but not without limitations.

Blaire squealed as the large, tattooed rogue from the alleyway pulled her from Aiden's protection, while another rogue held the barrel of a gun to Aiden's temple.

Seth slowly moved from the door, his arms locked around Riley's waist. She didn't fight him, frozen in terror at the sight of a gun held to her brother's head.

The tattooed man slammed Blaire against the wall so hard blood spittle burst from her mouth onto his face. His eyes flashed with a muted green glow, and Blaire's body seized into a frozen position.

Blaire's eyes frantically darted around, locking on Aiden as pure terror flickered through them at finding him held at gunpoint by a different rogue—but she couldn't move. Couldn't scream.

The burly rogue from the alleyway had the ability to compel.

Compulsion froze a victim against their will, unable to do anything but breathe and move their eyes around. Along with that, the mind became vulnerable to suggestion, memory alteration, and complete control by stronger Vasirian.

They discovered not long after Blaire came to the academy that her mind wasn't like other humans'; she didn't fall prey to any manipulations of compulsion beyond being unable to move. Riley suspected the magic in her veins had something to do with that. Unfortunately, the same shield didn't protect her body.

Seth's hold tightened on Riley when she fought to get to Blaire. He whispered, "We need to get to Lukas. We can't do anything like this. Look at your brother. We don't have a weapon."

Tears filled Riley's eyes as she sagged against Seth, and he moved her back farther, inching toward an unconscious Lukas.

With the others occupied, no one could intervene, and the more they tried to make their way to where Blaire was, the more rogues descended on them.

"Now, little human. We're going to take you with us one way or another, and there's nothing that lot of fools will do about it. Doc wasn't finished experimenting on you. But I'm thinking"—he wiped the blood spittle from his cheek, licking it from his dirty, thick fingers and groaning at the tiny, diluted taste—"that I might take a sample first."

"No!" Aiden panicked and lunged for the large man, only to be snatched back by his hair by the rogue with the gun who easily matched Aiden's size.

The man dragged Aiden down onto his knees, crouching level with him, still gripping his hair tightly and shoving the gun beneath his jawline. "*Not* a smart move," he sneered near Aiden's ear. His descended fangs were visible from where Riley stood. "We're takin' the little human, no doubt about that, mate. But you coulda made this so much easier. Coulda saved yourself. Avoided being the *hero*." He spat the last word as if it offended him.

"Seth. Let me go. Let me go now!" Riley squirmed and kicked Seth's leg, only to be grasped tighter by both Dominic and Seth at the same time. "My brother needs me!" Her voice cracked on her broken plea for release.

"We'll help him and Blaire, but we need to get you safe first. There are still too many for you to be alone," Dominic said, trying to sound calm, but his shaky voice betrayed him, his eyes darting to Blaire and Aiden repeatedly. The sounds of the fights in the middle of the ballroom continued.

"Know what we're gonna do with our little human before the doc starts filleting that pretty flesh?" the man who held Aiden sneered, licking his lips noisily. "Gonna show her how real Vasirian men can please her. Not some schoolboys or Korrena lovey dovey crock of shit. I bet she tastes like peaches." He spoke louder. "What do you think, Jude? Peaches? What's her blood taste like, mate?"

Aiden ground his teeth as the revolver dug into his neck. He glared at Jude standing over him, who adjusted himself brazenly. A tear slipped down Blaire's cheek.

"Can't say, George," Jude said with a negative jerk of his head, looking down at his buddy who crouched on the ground next to Aiden.

"Too diluted, but we'll know soon enough, won't we, little human?"

George chuckled darkly. "That and so much more before we rid the world of this parasite," he said ominously, rising to his feet, keeping a firm grip on Aiden's hair with the gun positioned at his temple again.

Aiden and Blaire's eyes met. "I'm so sorry," he said.

Riley's drew in a breath. *No.*

With a thick swallow, Aiden looked at Seth, and then Lukas, who roused to consciousness behind them. His voice was hoarse as tears streamed down his face. "Take care of Riley," he said to them both.

No, no, no.

Aiden's gaze moved to Riley's face, and she stopped thrashing, her breaths rapid and painful in her chest as she stared into her brother's eyes. He said, "I love you."

No, no, this can't be real.

The gunshot echoed off the walls of the ballroom, and her entire body flinched at its concussion as if she'd taken the shot herself.

Time slowed to a crawl.

It didn't happen like the movies.

There wasn't an arc of blood and an immediate jerk of the body from the massive force of a gunshot or a spray of brain matter. No. Aiden remained on his knees, head slumped to the side as blood poured from the wound on the side of his head. If not for the blood and angle of his neck, she wouldn't have thought anything happened.

But it happened.

No.

The crimson liquid spilling down the front of his white T-shirt seared into Riley's brain and her breathing quickened.

George roughly kicked him in the side, forcing Aiden to slump to the floor in a heap. He stepped back howling in laughter, but Riley couldn't hear it.

Why couldn't she hear anything?

This isn't real.

Watching the spark of life fade from her brother's wide, forest green eyes froze her to the spot.

She couldn't look away.

George had held the revolver so tightly pressed to Aiden's temple that only the singed imprint of the weapon and blood showed on his temple. The blood on his shirt came from the exit wound, where his head tilted to the side.

Someone was screaming.

The surrounding fight long faded into muffled thumps and mumbled voices as blood rushed through her ears; her heart raced to the point of pain.

The moment Aiden's body crumpled to the floor in a lifeless heap, his blood pooling around his body and seeping into the cracks of the pristine marble floor, she lost her entire world.

Her brother was dead.

Gone.

Never to tease her again about her fashion choices. Never to have movie night with again. Never to—

A deafening shriek snapped her back into the present moment with the force of a car crash.

Her head snapped up from her brother's lifeless body to see Blaire breaking free of her invisible bonds, throwing herself at George, using the momentum of her body falling from the wall to catch him off guard and bring him to the ground.

The gun skittered across the glossy marble.

Riley took advantage of Seth's shock and broke free, clearing the distance to get to Blaire. She launched herself at the burly man named Jude before he could grab Blaire and help his friend George, but her petite body wasn't a match for his massive bulk, and he tossed her away like a gnat. She slid across the floor until her back crashed into a soft embrace. Dominic peered down at her with concern briefly before looking up as the hulking man came toward them.

Before Jude could do more than take a few steps in their direction, two members of the council descended on him, dragging him away. With the other council members occupied, that left them to face George on their own.

Riley looked toward Blaire, where Lukas now ran to try to help her with Aiden's murderer. His steps faltered, and Riley's eyes widened when Blaire picked up a knife that fell from George's hand. Likely he intended to use it on her and had unsheathed it in the struggle to get her off him.

Straddling him, Blaire didn't hesitate. Repeatedly, she sank the blade into George's chest over and over in blind fury and sorrow. The manic look on her face implied she didn't even know what she was doing.

Blood gurgled from the rogue's mouth, and his body stopped twitching beneath her, but she kept stabbing, soaking herself and the floor in his blood.

Lukas moved in and covered her eyes with his hand, banding his other arm around her torso, pinning her arms to keep from being cut. She dropped the blade straight away, finally cut off from seeing the source of her shock-induced frenzy.

He kept a firm grip on Blaire as he stood with her and moved her away from the mutilated corpse before sliding down the ballroom wall to cradle her in his arms, staring at his best friend, who didn't move.

26

Reflection

Seth stared at Riley clinging to Aiden's lifeless body lying in a pool of his own blood. The onslaught of emotions threatened to drown him in their intensity. His own heartbreak at losing his best friend. Riley's pain that he could practically taste in the air it was so potent. Lukas's state of shock as he held Blaire. And Blaire, so far gone she obliterated the trash responsible for ripping away the guy who was the rock of their group.

Aiden was the protector. The big brother. The person who would both call you on your shit, and then turn around and hug you and tell you it would be alright.

But it'll never be alright again…

The sickening, absolute truth that life would never be the same dug in with no regard whatsoever to the damage it caused and fused itself to his soul.

Seth dropped back onto his backside, his hands dangling between his knees as he sat with his legs spread, feet flat on the floor. His head hung forward as the tears burned his eyes, but this time, for the first time in a long time, he let them flow freely.

His brother was gone.

For so many years he followed Aiden like a lost puppy, never really fitting in with his own brother Kai. Aiden was there for it all. Skinned knees, his first fist fight, where he tried to be like Aiden, his second where they fought each other. Aiden lecturing him on safe sex and chastising him for using it as a coverup for his feelings for Riley.

Fuck—Riley!

Aiden would never see his baby sister find her Korrena or a compatible pair. He wanted her to be happy. *Wanted her to be with me.* Shame forced a tremor through his body, and more tears flowed. If he hadn't been such a failure, maybe he could have fulfilled Aiden's wish before they lost him.

An eternity passed as he listened to the continued cries of the girl he loved more than life itself, yet he couldn't find the strength to go to her.

The council had carted away the living rogues into custody, but the ballroom was a bloodbath, riddled with corpses. Thankfully, none from their side of the line that he could see.

Except one.

Before the crushing agony could pull him under again, Blaire's mournful keening startled him.

She fought against Lukas's hold until he released her, allowing her to crawl across the marble floor to Aiden's side where Riley already sat bent over his limp body.

"Blaire, no! Please," Lukas called after her, his hand extended, but his body lacked the strength to do anything more now that Blaire was physically safe.

Seth understood the feeling all too well. Once he knew Riley was out of harm's way, his body revolted against him, and the shock of losing his best friend rushed over him like an ocean wave, pulling him out into a riptide he couldn't overcome.

"You can't leave me. You promised," Blaire cried in misery, burying her already bloody face into the saturated fabric of Aiden's shirt.

Riley kept her head on her brother's hip, her own tears streaking through her brother's blood on her face.

Blaire had only known Aiden for a year, but they had become so much more than friends. Their bond confused all of their friends, but they never questioned it. It fit. Now the bond was severed; Riley didn't know if Blaire could cope with the damage left behind. Not after everything else she'd been through.

Riley turned her head to the other side to look at Lukas, not daring to move away from her brother while he was still warm. He was gone, but it felt like he hadn't left them yet. It would have to be enough. She couldn't fathom anything else.

Lukas. Aiden's best friend. Brother without blood. As devoted as Lukas was to Blaire, he couldn't even bring himself to aid her, caught in the maelstrom of his own grief. Riley couldn't blame him. She wasn't any good to anyone else, either.

What would she tell her mother and father? Their siblings?

Would they be mad at her for not saving him?

If only she could have gotten away from Seth and Dominic.

Her breathing quickened as the panic settled in her chest. She gripped Aiden's arm, but already the warmth had faded. Her broken cry at the realization was cut off as arms embraced her from behind and pulled her back. The smell of sugar cookies hit her nose, and she collapsed into the warm body where comfort and safety were found.

Seth clutched her face to his chest with one hand on her head, the other arm locked securely around her waist as he held her between his legs on the floor. She gripped his shirt in her fists tightly as another round of tears fell from her eyes.

Memories of her brother and growing up with Lukas and Seth played through her mind like an old school movie projection. Flickering moments of laughter and tears.

Throwing flour at each other in the kitchen while her mother tried to make buttermilk biscuits. Scolding both Aiden and Seth when they tracked mud into her bedroom after tussling in the dirt fighting with a classmate. Visiting Aiden when she had nightmares and him chasing all the monsters away with bedtime stories.

Fighting, yelling, dancing… so many memories with no way to create more.

That was how loss and memories worked. A lifetime of love and happiness could be easily snuffed out like a candle's flame, leaving only memories. For some, only then was it possible to see if the life they lived with their companion had truly been worth living. For others, they knew while they made the memories. Loved enough to notice the memories they created together as they made them. Those were the people who found happiness.

The question remained: Which type of person hurt the most in the end? The one who didn't see what they had until it was gone, or the one who lived the moment and relished in what they had?

Riley liked to think she fell into the latter category.

She sighed as her tears eased and her thoughts drifted to that place where she became contemplative and disconnected from what happened around her. For once, she welcomed it.

Footsteps echoed on the marble, and Riley finally looked up from Seth's chest.

The members of the Blackthorn Clan who entered the ballroom with them stood watch with Professor Velastra, all with varying degrees of injury—even the king.

At least he's *alive.*

Riley pushed the bitter thought away as her eyes welled with fresh tears.

King Adrian lowered his head in deference and broke the silence. "He will receive a hero's burial." The others all lowered their heads in turn.

"No!" Blaire yelled, lifting her head and glaring at the king.

He gazed back at her with pity, not with anger at her disrespectful outburst.

"You can't!" she cried, grabbing hold of Aiden's shirt before turning him onto his back. Several members turned away from the sight. "You said you would always watch out for me!" Anger and sadness filled her broken voice. "You said you wouldn't leave!"

Lukas approached her like a zookeeper handling a wild animal—slow and deliberate, so as not to startle her—his hands coming to touch her upper arms. "He's gone, Blaire." Clearing his throat, he repeated. "He's gone."

Riley's eyes widened when Blaire twisted and glared at Lukas. He stumbled back at the sight of her eyes glowing bright gold that overtook not only her irises, like a Vasirian's glow, but her sclera as well.

Blaire turned back to Aiden, and the clan took a step back when they saw her eyes. She cradled Aiden's face, burying her face against his chest.

The temperature in the room dropped so quickly Riley wondered if she was slipping into shock. Glancing around, the others also noticed something off in the air.

It started small, a faint red mist that glowed and wound like a ribbon around Aiden's limbs. It settled on his skin, creating a shimmering surface that glittered like tiny rubies, but the mist writhed and moved like a living force.

As if in response to the red magic settling, a brighter golden glow engulfed Blaire's entire body.

Gasps echoed through the room at the display of magic before them. Proof of everything the Oracle said.

The golden light wrapped her body in its embrace. Her long blonde hair lifted and blew about wildly in the windless room from the power the beautiful light held. Shimmering golden pieces of stardust danced in the surrounding air like glitter and diamonds.

Energy surged in the room as Blaire's power grew, before the light slowly began trickling away from her body in soft streams of light, weaving with the red light that still hovered above the ruby-like surface cocooning Aiden.

The gold and red twisted and flowed like water down a creek to and from Blaire, and over every inch of Aiden's body. With a cry of anguish that startled the hushed parties in the room, Blaire collapsed onto Aiden's chest at the same moment he sucked in a gasp of air, eyes flying open.

When their eyes connected, Riley gave in to the darkness that crept into her vision.

Riley sat against the headboard in the same room she shared with Blaire earlier, except this time the massive king bed was more crowded. Seth lay at Riley's side with his arm slung lazily over her lap, while Lukas lay in the middle of the bed with his back to Seth, arms wrapped around Blaire from behind.

Blaire still hadn't woken after passing out in the ballroom, but after her last display of magic it took her almost a full day to come around, so Riley wasn't scared. Lukas had washed off all the blood and changed her clothes. After the rest of them showered and changed, falling into bed together after what they went through didn't feel wrong. They all needed comfort and were family.

Bonded in both life and death.

King Adrian even ensured the staff continuously brought food, beverages, and anything else needed for them to remain in the safety of the nest they built until Blaire woke.

After coming back from her fainting spell, Riley found reality really was as good as she imagined. Aiden *was* alive.

It'd taken Seth and Aiden both hours to calm her down. She kept expecting to wake up from her fainting spell to realize what was happening now was merely a sick dream. But it wasn't. A day later and still nothing changed. This was reality.

Her eyes and face looked like she had an allergic reaction judging from how puffy and red her skin was, but the happiness swelling in her heart was everything. This reality was perfect. The joy of seeing her brother alive, even simply dozing in the chair beside the bed next to Blaire, was enough to make her want to crow to the sky. Everyone needed to know.

Whatever special gift that flowed through her best friend's blood saved her brother, and she would never forget that. She could never repay Blaire for giving her the gift of her brother. It didn't mean she wouldn't try. She'd fight tooth and nail until the prophecy was fulfilled—and if Blaire didn't want to she'd defend her right to that and protect her from those who would seek to harm her.

Libby, the sweet young girl on staff, had just delivered three carts stacked with covered dishes for dinner when Blaire stirred in Lukas's arms.

Aiden rubbed his eyes as he got his wits about him, watching with apparent anxiety as Blaire woke.

Riley leaned to get a better look. "Blaire?"

Lukas immediately shot upright, alert as if he hadn't been asleep at all. His hand cupped her cheek as she blinked several times. Easing her into a sitting position, he pulled her into his arms as Seth stirred awake.

"What's going on?"

"Blaire's awake," Riley said. "Dinner's also here. Get up."

Seth groaned and stretched out like a big cat before scooting up the bed to sit beside Riley.

"Blaire?" Lukas coaxed softly as she rested against him, eyes closed.

"Mm?"

"Can you wake up for me?"

"Mm."

Aiden chuckled. "Gonna need more than that."

Blaire's eyes flew open, and she turned her head so fast she winced and reached up to cup the side of her neck.

"Easy," Lukas said.

"Aiden?" Liquid emotion filled Blaire's eyes as the broken word came out hoarse, sounding more like a plea than a question.

"Yeah, it's me."

Blaire moved so fast, squirming out of Lukas's hold and throwing the covers back, that Aiden almost wasn't quick enough. He caught her as she threw herself at him, embracing her as he stood and her knees rested on the bed. The anguished moans as she wept against his neck rang loudly in the room, but no one stopped her.

Everyone had cried for Aiden.

Mourned his death and celebrated his life with just as many tears.

Blaire was entitled to her moment.

And then some.

Aiden lowered himself to sit in the bed and pulled Blaire into his lap with a glance at Lukas, who simply gave him a reassuring smile. Aiden was probably the only guy Lukas would, or could, tolerate holding Blaire in such a position—and it took a long time to get to that point.

Blaire sat back as her cries became sniffling hiccups, her hands roaming Aiden's face, fingers grazing his temple.

"How are you alive?"

No Vasirian survived a gunshot to the head. In rare cases, just as with humans, it might be possible, but they all knew the shot was fatal.

"You saved him," Lukas said, voice thick with emotion.

"What?"

"You don't remember anything?"

"I remember crying. Aiden on the floor of the ballroom. I was so angry I was yelling." She looked at Lukas. "I remember you tried to pull me away, and then everything went dark. I can't remember anything after that."

"That's when the magic started," Riley said, and Blaire blinked at her with her mouth parted as if not sure what to say.

"I felt it," Aiden said, and Blaire turned her attention to him. "I remember the moment I was shot."

He looked over as Riley's breath hitched on repressed sobs that threatened to overtake her again at the reminder. Seth looped his arm around her shoulder, pulling her to his side. She snuggled in, seeking his comfort.

"Then there was this sensation of floating. I don't know where I was or how I got there. I felt no pain. It reminded me of the aurora borealis. Swirls of light and stars were off in the distance as I floated in an endless river of night sky. Then I could finally hear the faintest sound. Soft and distant, crying."

"It could have been any of us. We were close enough to you. Not ashamed to admit it. We were all crying like babies," Seth said.

Aiden nodded, his eyes turning soft as he looked at the faces around the room. "I just knew I needed to get back to that sound, but I couldn't. I was trapped floating in that stream of light, and nothing I did allowed me to move. Then the temperature dropped, and I thought I was going to freeze."

Riley remembered the moment the temperature fell as Blaire's magic descended on the ballroom.

"At least, until I was swaddled in a blanket of red light and glittering rubies. You should have seen it. It was spectacular."

"We did," Seth said with a grin.

"The golden light?"

"Mmhm."

"The shimmery stuff like diamonds?"

"Yeah, man. We watched it flow between the two of you like some weird lava lamp, just less bulbousy fluid and more ribbony. Something like that."

Riley smacked Seth on the arm as Aiden stared at him in awe. "You had to take the moment away from him, didn't you?"

"What? What'd I do?"

Blaire frowned and looked at Lukas. "I'm confused."

"About what?"

"My memory being gone."

"I don't know. Maybe we can talk to the Oracle. Maybe she'll know something."

Lukas looked at Riley, and she understood his concern. If Blaire's memory was sketchy, did she remember what happened when the compulsion broke?

Riley feared what would happen to Blaire once the shock wore off and she realized she had taken a life, especially in such a brutal manner. Not that Riley was opposed. If Blaire hadn't done it, any of them would have. The rogue Vasirian who murdered her brother didn't deserve another breath. He got what was coming to him.

But at what cost?

Would this damage Blaire's psyche further?

"Do you remember what happened when the compulsion broke?" Riley asked, still unsure how Blaire overpowered Jude's mental hold to even do anything.

Blaire tensed and squeezed Aiden's arm. She softly whispered, "I killed him."

Aiden tilted his head to get a better look at Blaire's face through the curtain of blonde hair. "Killed who?" He looked at Lukas. "What happened?"

"When you fell, Blaire broke her binds and attacked the man who shot you."

Aiden's eyes rounded. "You what? Why would you do something so dangerous?"

Blaire tucked her hair behind her ear and looked at Aiden with a pinched expression. "I wasn't thinking. I just acted."

"You can say that again. She was like a wild animal clinging to him, and even with his strength, he couldn't dislodge her," Seth said, crossing his arms. "The part that's shocking is when they fell to the floor, he dropped a knife he must have pulled out in the struggle to use on Blaire, and she grabbed it and just..."

"Stabbed, and stabbed, and stabbed," Riley finished when Seth couldn't.

Blaire slowly looked up at Aiden's face. He sat with the blankest expression, mouth parted, as he stared back at her.

Riley glanced at Lukas. "Only when Lukas shielded her eyes from the man did she drop the knife and lose whatever trance she went into."

"I think what you're looking for is shock. There's no other way to describe what happened. Blaire's no killer," Lukas said with conviction, and Seth nodded his agreement.

Riley nodded. "I think so too."

Blaire looked at her. "You're not judging me?"

"Hell no. None of us are. If you didn't do it, one of us would have. You were just a lot flashier in your method of execution." Riley said this lightheartedly, but frowned when the words fell flat. *Not something to joke about. Got it.*

Aiden tightened his hug on Blaire. "Thank you, but don't ever do something so reckless again."

Blaire tucked her head and hugged him back.

Maybe with the understanding no one judged her, and there would be no legal repercussions for her actions, Blaire wouldn't suffer long-lasting consequences—at least for the murder of the rogue.

It was bad enough they all needed to process Aiden's death. Despite his current state of existence, they all suffered the loss, the trauma of watching him get shot, seeing him bleed out… feeling his body cool. They couldn't simply say, "Oh, he's alive? Great!" and carry on like nothing happened.

Aiden's death, albeit short, made each of them face something. It made Riley face a lot of things. Made her feel many things. There was no way the others didn't experience something similar. She foresaw frequent visits to the psychology department back at the academy in her future.

Lukas sat forward and reached for Blaire, apparently at the end of his generosity in sharing his pair with his best friend. "All that aside, you need to eat something. You've been out a full day. And like last time, the IV they gave you with fluids isn't enough. You need real food."

Blaire looked down at her bandaged hand. They'd given her two bags of fluids during the last twenty-four hours to make sure she stayed hydrated and well.

Lukas climbed off the bed to assemble a small plate from the platters provided for Blaire.

"What the hell, Riley?" Seth protested as Riley crawled over his legs to take Lukas's spot and wrap her arms around Blaire.

"Thank you," she choked out, squeezing her eyes shut. "You saved my brother's life."

"Or more accurately, brought him back from the dead," Lukas said, sitting at Blaire's feet and handing her a plate with rotisserie chicken, sliced cucumber, pasta salad, pear and cheese salad, and sautéed mushrooms. Blaire's stomach growled in response, and Aiden snorted.

"You know," Riley said. "the whole situation sounds a lot like that letter the Oracle sent you."

"Which one?" Blaire asked, before scooping up a bite of pasta salad.

Lukas pulled his phone from his pocket and tapped on the screen, bringing up a photo and turning his phone for everyone to see. "I took photos of the letters to keep track of them."

They crowded around to read the letter.

The stars have revealed new truths.
A danger to both your kind and mine.
The balance and restoration are at risk,
saved only by a friend's sacrifice.
An untapped, lost power is the conduit
for a bond deeper than that of lovers
to overcome even death itself.
But the heart must be open.

"'An untapped, lost power is the conduit for a bond deeper than that of lovers to overcome even death itself.'"

Riley let the words hang in the air before she looked at her brother. "We all know there's something between you and Blaire, and it goes way beyond the Korrena bond. Lukas wouldn't be able to tolerate your connection and intimacy like he does if there wasn't. You have to realize that."

Lukas crossed his arms and sighed. "As much as I hated it in the beginning, I can't dispute it. You two have this strange connection I don't understand. But I know it's not romantic."

Seth asked, "When did you get that letter?"

"After we saved Blaire from Vincent," Lukas said, glancing at him. "Why?"

"So before we knew Blaire had magic and she used it to bring herself back from the dead?"

"Yeeeah." Lukas tilted his head with interest.

"Then yeah, it probably does reference this, because at the time of the letter, Blaire's magic was an untapped conduit of power."

"So what does the open heart mean?" Blaire asked after swallowing another bite of food.

"The intensity of you breaking and mourning Aiden was hard

to watch, even with my own crushed heart," Riley said. "Your heart couldn't be more open than in that moment."

Silence settled as they digested the information they discovered. A full prophecy fulfilled. But so much more to go.

Riley climbed off the bed and stretched. "Now that Blaire is awake, I'm going to my room to rest. I haven't slept well worrying."

King Adrian allowed each of them to take a guest room at the manor and had their things delivered from the hotel, since that location was compromised.

He assured them security would not be lax again. Apparently, a scheduling mix-up occurred, and the entire security detail had the night of the attack off. Suspicious was a light way of addressing how most everyone felt about the oversight, but no one knew who made the error.

Riley wrapped her arms around Aiden's neck. "I love you. I'm so glad you're still here."

He squeezed her, and she stepped back.

"Besides, I don't want the responsibility of explaining to Mama what happened." She gave an exaggerated shudder as Aiden swatted at her.

His laughter followed her out of the room, and it was the sweetest sound.

Maybe now she could sleep.

27

Rejection

Moonlight streamed through the window into the darkened, unfamiliar guest room, creating long shadows across the floor from the ornate furniture that filled the space.

He couldn't sleep.

Every time Seth laid his head down and shut his eyes, his best friend's lifeless gaze stared back at him.

Earlier, when they were all dog-piled into the bed next to Blaire in her magic-induced coma, he slept fine. Curled against Riley, smelling the scent of tiger lilies, and feeling her warmth, kept away the demons plaguing his mind when he tried to sleep.

He didn't know if he'd ever be able to sleep normally again.

It wasn't for lack of trying, either. This was the second night in a row since Blaire woke that he lay awake, fighting to sleep.

The silence and sleeplessness drove him crazy. He'd studied every decorative flourish on the hand-painted mural over the bed on the ceiling. At one point, he swore the naked flying babies with golden curls turned their heads and winked at him.

He considered leaving the manor house to roam the gardens and other areas of the landscape surrounding the large mansion, but with the attack so recent, he didn't want to risk it. The rogues weren't playing around. They would do whatever was necessary to get to Blaire. Even kill their own kind.

Squeezing his eyes shut, he forced the image from his mind again.

His body ached with exhaustion, his eyes burned with dryness, and his brain wanted to give up the fight, but again and again images of Aiden's final moments assaulted him.

Not his final moments. He's alive.

Seth threw an arm over his eyes and fought against the overwhelming urge to seek out Riley for comfort.

With everything that happened, he didn't want to confuse her, but he made his mind up sitting on the floor of the ballroom.

He would take the risk.

Lay himself bare.

Tell her his truth and pray she didn't find him lacking.

The idea of Riley rejecting him made him physically ill, but he had to try.

Life was too short, and as recent events showed him, in the most brutal way possible, it could be taken away like the snap of his fingers.

Seth was tired of wasting his life pining and merely existing from day to day, fighting, and orbiting Riley without feeling secure in his position.

He might not feel good enough for her, but he would damn sure try to be. Aiden thought he was worthy. That had to mean something.

He also needed to know where she stood with Dominic. Did she intend to accept his proposal for more than a dating relationship? He needed to know, but it wouldn't change the truth he would still offer her from his heart.

He released a frustrated breath into the silence of the room. There would never be an opportune time. It was likely the scars of what happened three days ago would linger for a long time, and he didn't have the patience for that time to pass before he said what he needed to.

He would tell her the truth.

Explain what he wanted, and what he'd done, and hope it was enough.

Throwing the covers back, he stood and went to the wardrobe, opening it to find a simple white T-shirt to throw on with his black sweats.

He knew himself.

If he waited, he'd build up his walls again, and he'd never tell Riley how he felt. Watching Aiden die obliterated those walls and left him feeling raw and exposed, so it was time.

It was now or never.

Despite his resolve, uncertainty churned in his gut, making him want to vomit.

He walked down the quiet hallway through the shafts of moonlight spilling onto the checkered marble floor of the corridor until he reached the room near the end where Riley was staying.

It hadn't been long since dinner, so he suspected she would still be awake. The light filtering into the hallway from the crack beneath the door confirmed his suspicion was correct.

Pushing open her door open, he said, "Are you seriously considering being compatible pairs with Dominic?" Not the best start, but it'd have to do.

His mouth opened again, but any words he would have uttered

died a swift death in his throat at the sight of Riley nearly naked, fresh out of the shower.

She hadn't noticed him, likely due to the earbuds in her ears.

As soon as Riley removed her towel and tossed it to the bed, he saw it. Their mark. A beautiful horizontal S edged with lines and spikes that expressed them both perfectly. The force of its meaning lanced through his chest and gripped his throat in a chokehold so vicious he nearly fell to his knees.

His blood rushed through his ears at a deafening pace as his body thrummed with restless energy.

Riley didn't have any tattoos and hadn't had the time to visit a tattoo parlor in London to get one. She wanted one, but not this one. Not one in the same place she claimed he had one he certainly did not.

Aiden was right.

Of course he was right.

Seth's mind rioted as he flashed back to when he was sixteen and the pull of the Korrena bond drew him to Riley, but with her lack of recognition, he didn't believe it. Now he couldn't refute it.

The girl he spent his entire life in love with, *obsessed* with to an unhealthy degree, was his Korrena.

A sharp squeal ripped him away from his shocked state to Riley's wide blue eyes and flushed cheeks.

"What are you doing in here?" she shouted, ripping out her earbuds and tossing them on the bed. She grabbed the towel and held it in front of herself. "Why didn't you knock?"

Seth cut the distance between them in a few strides. He wrapped an arm around her lower back before she could say anything and cupped the back of her head with his other hand, crushing his lips into hers in an all-consuming kiss that stole both their breaths.

Riley moaned, and his tongue slipped between her lips as if

invited by the sound. His fingers held tightly into her soft flesh as their tongues danced together.

With a whine, Riley shoved him away, the towel falling once again.

The mark was gone, but he'd seen it. Only once they claimed one another in body and blood would the mark remain permanently, like a tattoo. One they shared. Same spot. Same symbol unique to their pair-bond, no other. That knowledge satisfied a primal part of him that longed to possess Riley body and soul.

"What are you doing?" she demanded, picking the towel up and wrapping it around herself, tucking it tightly so it would stay on.

"Can't you feel it?"

"What?"

Seth closed his eyes to steady his fast breathing, willing his heart to stop its discordant beat and return to normal.

"Look, Seth. You can't keep doing this."

Opening his eyes, tiredness filled Riley's expression that he could also feel through a faint empathic link. A link that would become solid and strong once fully bonded but would intensify gradually when they both acknowledged they recognized who they were to one another. The thought of it sent a thrill through him momentarily that he didn't understand.

For so long he'd been adamantly against a Korrena, but at last he accepted it was more than biology. He'd loved Riley long before they knew what Korrena pairs were. Before they could even read. The benefits of the bond would only strengthen that.

The tiger lily perfume that drove him mad now made sense. Which meant her sugar cookie obsession that neither he, nor anyone else, could smell was his special brand of pheromones designed only for her.

He cursed under his breath and put his hand on his forehead. How did he not see it?

For months, he'd picked up on more of what Riley felt, but he thought it was their normal dynamic. Their familiarity with one another. But no, that wasn't it. It was the growing bond. How long had it been growing? Since he recognized it three years ago? When had she awakened to it?

He shook his head, forcing himself to listen to her words. He didn't understand. What did he keep doing? "Do what?"

"Coming to me and confuse my heart."

"I don't understand."

"I can't keep being physical with you. I thought you teaching me was enough to sate this, but I can't ignore how much it hurts."

"What are you saying?"

"It has to stop."

Her words stunned him. He didn't think in his wildest dreams his actions hurt her. She consented and even asked for what they shared at times.

Had it all been a lie?

Had she felt nothing like he did?

Riley's arms wrapped around herself as if she were cold and she looked away. "I don't understand why you're hurting," she whispered.

Did she not realize what she said?

"You *do* feel me then?"

Her eyes rounded, her gaze snapping to his as she startled in realization, and maybe what it possibly meant. She felt his pain. He didn't tell her the thoughts that it had been a lie, and that her feeling nothing hurt him—but it did hurt. Badly.

Seth stared at her, willing her to see the truth, to *feel* the truth.

Slowly, Riley shook her head as tears filled her eyes and spilled over her cheeks. "It doesn't matter if I can," she whispered so faintly that if he hadn't been so close, he wouldn't have heard her. "You can't do this to me now. Not after all these years."

"What do you mean?"

Her eyes closed, and she leaned into his touch when his hand gently cupped her cheek. His thumb caressed her skin, wiping away tears.

"Tell me, Riley."

"It doesn't matter. None of it matters."

"It matters to me," he said, dropping his hand. She looked up into his eyes. Pain sparkled in her beautiful stare, but he didn't know why she hurt so much.

"I can't do this."

"But you're my—"

"Don't say it." The sharpness in her demand surprised him. "I can't handle it."

She didn't even want to hear him say what they were to one another.

"Talk to me."

Riley spun and walked across the room and started throwing clothes onto her bed. He watched her, saying nothing in hopes if he waited her out, she'd give him something, because this was not going the way he envisioned.

Not that he thought they would be together without a few bumps, but he'd discovered she was his Korrena. The one thing she wanted most! Being met with resistance to conversation about it… he never could have predicted in a million years.

Riley tossed the clothes on the bed with a frustrated huff and turned to him.

"Do you realize how long I've wanted to be with you?" Her eyes brimmed with tears again, but anger mingled with sorrow in her tone. "How many years I've longed to be more than just your stupid little sister who can't keep her thoughts in line?"

Seth's brows shot up in surprise.

At most, he thought from time to time there might have been a lingering crush growing up as she discovered boys, but nothing more than that until recently. Again, nothing more than the curiosity that came with discovery and the comfort of unwrapping that part of herself with someone familiar. Never had he imagined she could feel the same as him, no matter how much their friends joked and pushed.

Aiden saw it all along.

Seth moved toward her, but she threw up both hands to stop his progress. He froze, indecision warring in his gut about what to do.

"Riley."

"No, Seth. I can't."

"*Please.*"

"Just go."

"I can't leave you like this."

"Get out!"

The venomous tone he wasn't used to hearing from her mouth made him cringe.

He wanted to tell her no. Demand she hear him out. But he couldn't do that.

Seth vowed to be what she needed and nothing more. He wasn't about to break his promise, or her trust in that promise, for his own heart's desires.

With one last look, he turned and left the room, feeling more lost than before he stepped inside to confront his feelings.

The moment the heavy bedroom door closed with an echo that implied a suffocating finality, Riley collapsed to the floor and reached for the edge of the comforter that hung from the bed. Burying her face into the thick fabric, she screamed her sorrow until her voice broke and she could utter no sound.

If she hadn't muffled the sound, Seth would have run back into the room, and she wouldn't be able to survive seeing his face again so soon.

Turning on her side, she curled into a small ball, wrapping her arms around her shins and pulling her knees to her chest.

Of all the ways fate chose to mess with her… She didn't understand why any of it was happening to her.

First her brother and now Seth?

What had she done to deserve the universe playing such a sick and twisted game with her heart?

Seth was her Korrena.

The one thing she dreamed of since she learned of the Korrena bond as a child was within her grasp, but she couldn't take it.

He didn't have to even say the words—she wouldn't allow him to. His emotions rang through her so powerfully it made her knees weak. To hear the words from his lips would have crumbled any resolve she tried to build before him.

And it wasn't the first time.

With the evidence right in front of her, she realized with startling clarity the signs had been there for months.

His new scent that only she smelled. Sugar cookies that comforted her and calmed the noise in her head.

Times she knew what he felt that went beyond their lifetime of familiarity.

What a cruel joke fate made pairing her with the one person who didn't want a pair-bond. The one person who hated the idea of it with his very being. Someone who vehemently rejected even the notion it could be more than mere biology.

She should be jumping for joy and celebrating, but she wouldn't be selfish.

Riley couldn't seal a bond with someone who saw it as imprisonment. She would never shackle someone to her who didn't want that. Even if he thought he did right now, he would grow to resent her when the high of the new connection faded.

Seth didn't love her.

Seth didn't want her.

Not like that.

Riley lay on the floor staring blankly at the cracks in the hardwood until her tears ran dry, but even then she couldn't bring herself to get up.

The floor was cold, and her body chilled in nothing but a towel, but she felt dead inside.

Even her rampant thoughts were silent, and her hands still. For the first time on her own, she didn't feel the need to move. It was the opposite. This time, moving made her want to crawl out of her skin, so she lay there in silence.

Hours passed. The moonlight moved across the floor from the window on the other side of the room, and the blue hue turned warm as the sun rose before her phone rang.

Dragging herself up from the floor, her feet felt like lead weights as she made her way to the bedside table where her phone lay charging. She couldn't lie on the floor forever, and if the call was about her brother, she wouldn't miss it.

Dropping onto the edge of the bed with a heavy exhale, she lifted the phone and looked at the screen.

Dominic.

She wasn't mentally ready for what the conversation with him would entail, but she already intended to cut things off in fairness to him before Seth derailed her entire night. She sniffled, swiping a fresh tear that trailed down her cheek.

The phone stopped ringing, but she decided to call back. Putting the phone to her ear, she waited.

"Riley?"

She hummed an acknowledgment.

"Did I wake you? I'm sorry if I did. You can go back to sleep, and we'll talk later if you want."

This guy is too sweet. He deserves happiness.

Clearing her throat, she shook her head, and then pressed her lips tight, frowning that he couldn't see her.

"No, no. I'm awake," she said. Her voice sounded like she'd raked her esophagus with glass.

"Are you okay?"

"Mmhm." Thc sound was bright and airy, and cntircly put on.

Dominic called her on it immediately. "Please don't lie to me."

Riley sniffled. "I'm sorry."

"I'm not mad," he said with his usual kindness.

"No, not about that. About…" She took a deep breath, steeling her resolve. "Dom, we can't do this. I can't be your compatible pair."

"Is this about Seth?"

She gasped, and he chuckled.

"You know, I'm surprised you two aren't a pair with the way you are with one another."

Her muscles tensed, and her body screamed in protest after lying on the floor all night.

Should she tell him?

She wasn't ready to tell anyone.

"I'm not upset—well, not in the way you'd think. It's disappointing. You're a beautiful girl, fun, and I enjoyed your company. That being said, just because we're not dating, doesn't mean I wouldn't like to still be around you. As friends. If you'd like, of course."

"That sounds nice."

"Then there's no problem. We never took things to a higher level, so we can continue to enjoy each other's company with the intent of only that."

"I'd like that."

One thing she would never turn down was more friends. As long as they didn't find her annoying. People could either keep up with her antics or not, but she wouldn't change to suit others if it didn't hurt anyone.

"Though I suppose that's what we should have done all along, eh? Maybe that's another reason it wouldn't have worked. It typically doesn't if you have to try too hard. When we gave up that and went to the Hard Rock Cafe, I had the best time with you, and I think that's when you did too."

"You're right, actually. I was afraid to be myself for a while."

"See? I don't want you to feel like that. If it takes being your buddy instead, that's what I'll be. Besides, you're one of the few who'll listen to the stories of my adventures back home."

Riley laughed and shook her head. He made her want to see what the Canadian wilderness was like.

"Listen, I need to go file some reports for Adrian, but I will see you at breakfast, yeah?"

"I'll be there."

Disconnecting the call, Riley fell back onto her back and stared at the mural of several dragons soaring through fluffy clouds with a lavender, pink, and orange background like the softest sunset.

Now sadness took a backseat to anger as Riley reflected more on the situation.

Seth ruined everything.

She felt more confused than ever, and it was his fault.

All Seth had done for the past couple of years was sleep around, and in the last half year, kept her in a push-and-pull that toyed with her heart when they'd always been close. Did he even realize the choices he made did that?

You're not innocent either.

She groaned. It was true. She could have told him it was too much. Told him she didn't want to do the things they did. The problem was, she *did* want to do them. Even if every touch and every kiss hurt her as much as it soothed her aching heart. For every crack it repaired, a fissure formed.

She couldn't blame him for that.

But she still couldn't complete the bond with him. She had to stand firm in rejecting their pair-bond.

Seth believed Korrena pairs were a joke.

Riley wanted someone who would take it seriously.

He wasn't that person.

28

Secret Bonds

Coming back to the States to the warmth of April should have made Riley feel better, but it didn't.

Separation from where so many sudden changes happened for her did nothing to quell her grief.

She couldn't even bring herself to visit her mother.

Annie Easton would tear her a new one if she knew she had rejected Seth. From childhood, her mother always doted on Aiden, Lukas, and Seth, but Seth held a special spot more so than Lukas. Maybe she could see something they hadn't.

The situation with Seth tainted Riley's interactions with everyone, and she couldn't hide that something was wrong.

The happy-go-lucky girl who rolled with the punches seemed so far away, and Riley didn't know what to do to get her back. But it wasn't really her to begin with—not completely.

It was part of her identity. But she also used it as a mask to hide the conflict inside about Seth, insecurities about her looks or if her friends found her annoying, self-consciousness about whether she would ever be good enough at anything she tried when she found it hard to focus as often as she hyper-fixated on something.

Genuinely, she felt the hyper, happy stuff, but sometimes she had to try hard to keep it up. Those were the times she stayed in with her books until she could recharge.

After traveling and being in close quarters with everyone, she couldn't do that.

The time leading up to their flight back was short, and she stayed in her room when not at mealtimes, refusing guests—even Blaire. Her excuse? Fatigue, and the need to process things. Both true, but it felt disingenuous all the same because everyone but Seth likely assumed it was her brother on her mind. Which was true, but not as much.

The looks of pity and concern on the flight back and drive back to Rosebrook Valley from Atlanta made her want to scream and jump from the vehicle on the interstate while the car was still in motion.

Seth hadn't tried to speak to her once.

Why did that disappoint her?

It was what she wanted.

Now, back at Blackthorn Academy, she still couldn't be alone because business wasn't finished.

After unpacking in the safety of her dorm room, she moved to the door to once again face her family, friends, and the one man who owned the shattered remains of her heart. She sighed. The dorm room was a haven for her when life got too hard, and right now life was as hard as it'd ever been.

How she longed to curl up beneath her fluffy comforter in Seth's shirt, drowning in sugar cookies—*no.* She couldn't think like that anymore. *No more borrowing Seth's scent.*

Riley crossed the cobblestone courtyard past the familiar, large, bubbling fountain at its center to the looming administration building she hadn't been inside since they rescued Blaire from the temple beneath the school they hadn't known about, accessible only through the administration building's lower levels.

The sun shone warm in her face, and the air carried the scents of spring's budding flowers, and pink and white petals scattered through the air from dogwood trees nearby.

Georgian sunshine felt nice after the chillier weeks spent in London, but it wasn't tempting enough to make her want to avoid her room when this meeting ended or the other meeting she planned.

Her stomach cramped just thinking about that one. Maybe she should go see her mother instead before making any drastic decisions.

Voices drifted out to meet her when she pushed open the heavy double doors at the top of the stairs leading into the building. Once inside, she found Aiden, Seth, Blaire, Lukas, Profess—no, Headmistress Velastra, and, to her surprise, Dominic.

"What are you doing here?" she asked, approaching the group and trying to act more normal than she felt.

"What? Can't come visit one of my new favorite people?" Dominic held his chest as if having a heart attack. "I can't believe you don't want me here."

The laugh that fell from her lips surprised her. But guilt made her face fall into a frown.

Her friends worried about her, and her newest friend was the one to make her laugh. What did that say about her? *You're overthinking again.*

Refocusing her attention on Dominic, she said, "I never said that. But you weren't on the plane with us."

"Oh. Well, that's easy to explain. I had a later flight on a private jet." He shrugged as if it made all the sense in the world.

Blaire glanced at Riley, and if she wasn't mistaken, relief flashed across Blaire's expression when her eyes softened. That alone let Riley know she'd been isolating herself too much. If a few exchanged words made her friend express such heavy relief, the days of silent stewing needed to end.

"By King Adrian's orders, Dominic will join us at the academy for the foreseeable future as a student to keep watch over Blaire," Headmistress Velastra explained.

Lukas bristled, his indignation clear as he said harshly, "She doesn't need someone to watch over her. She has me. Fuck." He slung his arm out, directing his hand at Aiden. "She has Aiden. She has all of us."

"Does another actually hurt?" Dominic asked calmly, not at all bothered by Lukas's posturing.

Lukas wasn't against the idea of Dominic being here and looking out for Blaire. It likely came from fearing he wasn't enough to protect her. He felt that a lot about the things that happened to Blaire.

When Lukas said nothing, Dominic said, "Listen, I'm not here to mess up the status quo. I'm here to be another person on her side—on *your* side." He gave a pointed look to Lukas that Riley didn't get. "More to the point, I'm a direct line to King Adrian and the rest of the clan without having to follow a chain of command. In fact, for some decisions, you won't have to go any higher than me. With the growing threat of the rogues and their clear agenda when it comes to Blaire and stopping what the Oracle prophesied, that might be a good thing. It's mostly for that reason Adrian wants me here. He doesn't believe this is the last you'll see of them."

Aiden put his hand on Lukas's shoulder. "He makes a good point." He crossed his arms and turned to Headmistress Velastra. "So what are we doing in the admin building? I never wanted to see this place again."

Lukas kept his hand on Blaire's lower back as if the touch calmed his ire. "You can say that again."

The headmistress sighed, clasping her hands in front of her waist. "I know it's difficult for you all to be here, but the Oracle has requested an audience with you alone. With no formal council in place, the Order's hall at the top of the building is vacant, so we will have no interruptions. She insisted we meet in a secure and isolated location."

Everyone exchanged wary looks, and Riley couldn't ignore the zing of anxiety that skittered up her spine.

With the scent of warm vanilla and the pressure of a body at her back, she relaxed immediately, only to tense again when she realized her mistake. She looked over her shoulder at Seth.

He felt her anxiety.

Clouded gray eyes full of pain and uncertainty met hers, and she had to look away.

As everyone moved down the corridor toward the stairwell that led to the top of the administration building, Riley missed the rest of the conversation, caught up in Seth's emotions.

She couldn't do this right now.

Not giving opportunity for him to speak, she took off after the group in a dead sprint. She couldn't avoid being alone with him forever, but she could damn sure try.

It wasn't long before she entered the spacious, familiar room with gold-veined marble flooring and a massive, round, stained-glass window depicting a murder of crows flying over blackened brambles that threw crimson light onto seven empty black-stained wooden chairs with burgundy upholstery perched on a high dais like thrones.

Normally the Order sat in those chairs in their robes, lording over the students of Blackthorn Academy and the Vasirian of the Americas with their corrupt decisions, but that was all history now.

A vaulted ceiling of carved wood timbers rose high above them, creating a domed chamber for the room. The tall, wrought-iron candelabras with red and black candles sat unlit, making the entire room feel abandoned and cold. The drapes of black and burgundy covering the walls did nothing to help the radiating cold of the abandoned room, despite the floor-to-ceiling window overlooking the forest at the back of the school. The deep stain of the glass dimmed even direct sunlight.

Once everyone moved to the center of the room, the Oracle stepped from the shadows to the side of the row of chairs on the dais.

Now that they were back on school grounds, she wore her signature burgundy robe with black feathers embroidered at the bottom as if they'd fallen from her knees. Simple, dainty silver chains draped in swooped patterns around her waist and straight down, with small rubies glittering at their ends that swayed as she walked. Black filigree lined the bell-sleeved wrists and hood of her robe.

"Thank you for meeting me here. I understand if this is not the place you favor, but soon this place will come to be more than a room for the unjust and vile."

Riley wondered how the Oracle knew they weren't comfortable with the meeting location but didn't ask. Something about the energy in the air, and the serious look on the Oracle's face, made her spine straighten and her senses go on alert.

This wasn't an ordinary meeting.

By their sobriety, the others sensed it too.

Stepping slowly down the marble steps, the Oracle brought herself to their level away from the opulent chairs that taunted them with bad memories.

"I have called you all here to reveal more truths that the Celestial

Conclave has seen fit to bestow upon me."

"Celestial Conclave?" Dominic cocked his head to the side, his eyebrow piercing catching the sunlight. "You mentioned them back at the manor. What is that? I've heard of no such organization."

Blaire had already shared with the others about the Celestial Conclave and many other secrets the Oracle had revealed to her, but Dominic hadn't been present for that. None of them aside from Blaire even knew who he was at the time they learned the information.

"The Celestial Conclave are our creators, child."

"The gods?"

"There are not many gods or a singular deity. The Celestial Conclave is made of several voices without a face. Shapers of our world and all who live and will live within it."

"That sounds like gods," Dominic said with a dubious look.

"They are not corporeal beings existing on physical planes like our planet, heaven, or hell, in the way Vasirian and humans imagine deities to be. At least, to the best of my knowledge."

Dominic rubbed his forehead then pinched the bridge of his nose. They'd all had the chance to process, so he needed his time as well.

"And they have told you things? They speak to you?"

"Through dreams and whispers. They are the source of my prophecies and revealed memories. Always have been." Her smile was warm as she patiently explained things to Dominic. Riley wondered if she would be so patient at four hundred years old.

Dominic blew out a breath and chuckled. "That's a lot to take in." He looked at the others. "Judging by your faces, you all knew about this?"

"Blaire told us," Riley said.

"Right. Well. Carry on."

Blaire patted Dominic on the arm, and he shook his head with an exaggerated pout. He reminded Riley of a puppy scolded in a corner.

"I have been informed of what transpired the day of the attack at Blackthorn Manor. Of what happened to you," she said, her eyes focused on Aiden. "In knowing this, I have also learned why Blaire's magic surfaced this time and saved you, child."

The air crackled with tension as everyone eagerly awaited answers. Blaire held both Aiden and Lukas's hands tightly as if she couldn't stand parting with either one of them.

The air shifted behind Riley and in her periphery Seth moved closer to her, but she remained silent and kept her hands to herself.

"Long ago there lived a Korrena pair. A human warlock and a Vasirian woman who married one another. They loved each other deeply. Their days were happy, and the woman was expecting a child in the coming months. With their marriage, they decided the man would transition after the birth of their child. But they never made it that far. When Rosendo Blackthorn called for the death of human witches and warlocks and pregnant Vasirian by those with magical blood, their lives were cut tragically short."

Blaire let go of Aiden's hand and covered her mouth. Dominic looked at the floor, clenching his jaw in anger.

"Similar to your father's plea," the Oracle continued, directing her gaze at Blaire. "The Celestial Conclave heard the desperate, final plea of two dying lovers." Her stare drifted between Aiden and Blaire. "A desire to find one another again."

"No way," Riley blurted, and Seth snorted a laugh behind her at her outburst.

The Oracle smiled at them with a knowing gleam in her eye, and Riley's stomach soured. She knew. The Oracle knew.

"Are you telling me that Blaire and Aiden are reincarnated lovers?" Lukas asked, confusion twisting his brows. He didn't sound angry, but a note of trepidation in his tone couldn't be hidden.

"Not entirely. They simply carry the magic of that couple's devotion to one another. The Celestial Conclave could not let their spirits carry forward, but took the essence of what made their connection special and placed it in the next generation, which is why Aiden and Blaire share such a deep bond with one another. The essence of that original love passed through the years before finding these two, though you do not need to feel threatened, child."

She looked at Lukas.

"This love is not that of romantic passion. This is a pure love made up of devotion and connection. It could be shaped however they wanted it, and they have found what suits them best. It is with that deep bond that Blaire could reach within herself and find what was necessary to save him."

"I can't even remember doing it," Blaire said in a low tone.

"Your magic protected your mind. With the emotional turmoil you were experiencing, if you were fully aware, your mind would break from the power unleashed."

The Oracle looked on as Aiden and Blaire looked at one another with varying degrees of awe and bewilderment.

"With more of the prophecy coming to pass, another key element was revealed to me."

"There's more?" Riley couldn't hold back the anxiety in her tone. What more could the Oracle drop in their laps?

The Oracle smiled at her. "Much more. Along the vein of reincarnation, you all share a connection that I'm sure you feel."

"What do you mean?"

"It was easy to fall into friendship with Blaire, was it not?"

"Well, of course. She's awesome," Riley said without hesitation. Aiden and the Oracle chuckled; Lukas shook his head as Blaire's face turned red.

The Oracle looked from Seth to Riley then back to Lukas. "You three found yourselves together very early, despite the many places in the world you could have been. Lukas's family is Finnish and left him at the academy in America. He could have easily been placed in the other academies, but would not have met you two, nor Blaire, had it happened that way. Seth, your brother and you ended up here with no family until your cousin moved to Georgia, despite your father living in Germany. Aiden and Riley, your mother stayed in Atlanta before moving down here with you both instead of joining your father and sister in New York."

"But she's a teacher at the high school branch," Riley protested.

"She is. But the point is, circumstance placed you here with the others. Finally, we have Blaire. Your parents moved from North Carolina because of family issues, and you found yourself right on our doorstep."

"So what does that mean?" Headmistress Velastra asked. "Circumstances are merely that. What are you implying it means?"

"I am not implying. I am telling you precisely what it means. Each of you has shared a connection that has carried through time since magic's existence. Fate has continued to draw you five"—she let her gaze drift over Lukas, Blaire, Aiden, Seth, and Riley—"to one another as friends, lovers, or family, and will continue to do so long after your current bodies return to dust."

Riley stood still in shock. The idea of what the Oracle suggested was unheard of, but she couldn't deny they all shared a deep bond that didn't fit the normal bounds of friendship. They were their own little family. Their new friends were always on the outskirts of their bubble, except for Charlotte. She fit in well, probably because she was already so close to Blaire, but they had to force her away or reveal their secrets.

Even Mera and Kai, who'd always been around, didn't fit the same, and Kai was related to Seth by blood.

Now it made sense.

"There is another. A sixth bound to you who isn't here."

Riley's head snapped up to look at the Oracle.

"Who?" Lukas asked.

The Oracle gave him a somber smile.

"She can't tell us," Blaire said with a shake of her head and a huff of laughter. "I recognize that look."

"I am afraid you are correct. But know the answer will reveal itself sooner than you expect. There will be no mistaking the sixth when their purpose is revealed."

"Talk about cryptic," Dominic said, laughing.

"Do not think I have forgotten you."

His eyes widened in surprise. "Me?"

"You may not be bound to these souls in the past, but you are bound to Riley's future."

The harsh, inhuman growl that ripped through the room surprised them all. Riley's spine straightened as a shiver of something unrecognizable shot through her. Molten whips of fury licked and lashed at her skin, making panic wrap itself around her lungs, stealing her breath.

All eyes were on a point behind her, and she realized it was coming from Seth. She was feeling Seth's unrestrained rage.

The Oracle sighed and held a hand up. "Calm yourself, child. His connection to her future is not in the sense you think."

Her words did nothing to assuage the hostility rolling off Seth in waves.

Not able to take it any longer, Riley spun around, and the downright glacial look in Seth's eyes as they stayed locked on Dominic chilled her. She didn't stop to question her next move, only stepped forward into Seth, wrapped her arms around his waist and buried her head against his chest in an attempt to soothe him.

It didn't matter that things were strained between them, or that they wouldn't bond. No. This was what they did. They always helped each other, and as much as it pained her, especially with the pull of the bond already strong in her chest, she would be his support. She'd never seen him lose control this way before.

Startled, Seth sucked in a sharp breath, but then relaxed and sank into her embrace, his arms coming up to wrap around her.

"Now that is settled," the Oracle said with a soft chuckle. "You share a connected future with Riley, should her present path progress as it should."

"What does that mean?" Dominic asked.

The Oracle looked at Riley and Seth. "If she achieves happiness, you will find what you seek, but it will not be immediate satisfaction. You must be prepared for the years that await, or you will miss what you truly want."

Riley had no idea what the Oracle meant, and didn't know what the others were doing, as she remained locked in Seth's arms.

She needed this.

She hadn't felt like herself because such an integral part of herself was missing.

He doesn't want a bond.

Riley took a deep inhale of Seth's calming scent and stepped back, looking up at him.

"Good?"

It was the only words she'd said to him since she kicked him out of her room and rejected their bond.

Seth's jaw muscle ticked, and he kept grinding his teeth, but he nodded.

Turning away, she had to take a deep breath to avoid bursting into tears, especially when the Oracle looked at her with pity.

29

Dark Reality

The shock of what the Oracle shared about their bonds settled heavy in the room, but Riley lacked the ability to focus after Seth's outburst. She wanted to run and hide in her room, but the Oracle pressed on.

"To the next reason I needed to bring you here…" Her gaze swept the room. "I spoke alone with King Adrian after he gave Dominic his instructions. His choice to send Dominic to the academy was wise, but while I have no extensive insight as to what is happening in the underground, I believe his presence won't be enough in the end."

Dominic crossed his arms, shifting his weight to his left foot. "What then? In the end what?"

"My vision is cloudy, but I urge you all to be vigilant. It won't be long before the rogues make a move."

"The council discussed the rogues before," Dominic argued. "Like with the black market drugs, we didn't believe the rogue state had much of a foothold in the Americas."

"Seriously?" Aiden asked, tone disbelieving, but lacking heat. "You didn't think one of the biggest countries in the world could be infiltrated by rogues?"

"Well, we knew rogues were over here, but not as organized as in Europe or Eastern countries."

The Oracle moved to stand in front of Dominic. "Do not stress yourself over it, child. Even Adrian was unaware how deep things went. But I am here to tell you now these rogues are organized and have controlled the criminal underground for quite some time."

"Even the humans?" Blaire asked.

"They aren't aware the rogues are Vasirian. They only see them as run of the mill gang members, mafia, and petty thugs—depending on geographical location."

Headmistress Velastra put her hand on her cheek as she angled her head, considering the Oracle's words. "Well, if that is the case, why are they only now posing a threat to us?"

"They didn't know about the prophecy. Until I shared what I knew with you all at the manor, I had not uttered a word about Blaire's role in our species' survival."

Dominic shifted. "So the leak is responsible for their movement against us?"

"I believe so."

"Hold up," Aiden said, getting the attention of the room. "If this prophecy means the survival of our kind, then why would they try to stop that? Why would they not also want to protect the one person who holds their fate?"

Riley had the same question, but with Seth at her back, and her emotions unstable, she found herself unable to speak up.

The Oracle turned and walked across the marble floor, her robe dragging behind her, the thin chains swaying with her movements.

She stopped in front of the window overlooking the academy grounds. "I wish I had those answers. I think this goes higher than the rogue groups."

Lukas stepped forward. "Higher than the rogue groups? Like what? The Order?"

"Whoever is pulling the strings of this movement controls even members of the Order, and the other leading factions around the world."

"That's impossible," Headmistress Velastra said, placing a hand on her hip. "The only beings who hold any power over them are the members of the Blackthorn Clan."

When the Oracle said nothing, continuing to stare out at the academy grounds, an eerie disquiet settled over Riley.

"You're kidding me," Dominic snapped. His usual cheerful demeanor broke as his facial features twisted into a scowl. "Are you suggesting members of the council—or worse yet—members of the royal family are responsible for the contract on Blaire's life and the attack on the manor?"

The Oracle turned from the window, and from the tight lines around her eyes and mouth as she stared at Dominic, the answer was clearly "yes" before the word passed the Oracle's lips.

The corruption they thought isolated to only the Order went deeper than they could ever imagine.

"I'm sorry, Dominic. I know it is difficult to consider that people you grew up with cannot be trusted, but this is the reality we must consider."

"Then why didn't they just order Blaire executed if that's the case?" Aiden asked, crossing his arms.

"I don't get it either," Blaire said. "The king has the power to do that, right?"

"He does. I do not feel Adrian is involved in this."

Headmistress Velastra's sculpted brows lowered. "Then who?"

"I don't have a definitive answer yet, but I have my theories."

"And?"

"Until I'm certain, I think it best to keep a wrap on that."

Lukas dragged both hands through his hair, gripping at the back of his head. "Are you kidding me? How is that okay? Just put a wrap on it? I want names."

The Oracle's expression softened with pity. "This is why I must keep it to myself. You cannot act on a hunch. You cannot even act on confirmation. If you are placed in Cresbel Asylum for an act of treason against the Blackthorn Clan, you'll never see Blaire again. You won't be able to protect her."

"Fuck!" Lukas kicked a wrought-iron candelabra, sending it clattering across the room, candles crashing to the floor and breaking. Blaire went to him and wrapped her arms around his waist, and he buried his face in her hair as he held her tightly.

"So let's assess what we do know and can process," the headmistress said, clapping her hands. "There is an active contract out to capture and exterminate Blaire to prevent the prophecy from coming to fruition."

The Oracle nodded.

"It is safe to assume that someone in the Blackthorn Clan is responsible for this."

Another nod.

"But not someone who wishes to get their hands dirty in the public eye like previous leadership."

Dominic paced the room until he sat with a heavy sigh on the marble steps leading to the dais, placing his elbow on his knee and rubbing one eye with the heel of his palm. "The Blackthorn Clan isn't small. You saw the size of the council in the ballroom. We're scattered all over the world."

Riley chewed the inside of her cheek. "Um… If the information about Blaire and the prophecy was leaked from the manor, it had to be someone present for the meeting, right? Like, that makes the most sense, you know?"

Seth cursed under his breath.

"Not necessarily," Aiden said.

"Huh?"

"The room could be bugged by a council member."

Headmistress Velastra looked at Aiden as if considering his words. "Even a staff member could have placed a bug for an outside party, if we're using that logic. This might not have anything to do with the clan."

The Oracle's downcast eyes told Riley that wasn't the case.

"So let's say for the sake of covering all our bases, they succeed in their plan," Dominic said.

Lukas growled.

Dominic raised a hand. "It's a hypothetical situation. One I will do everything I can to prevent, just like you. Calm down." He sighed. "You've said that Korrena bonds will grow weaker, Vasirian will stop finding their pairs at a greater rate until none exist, but you haven't explained the why—at least I don't think. Why can't we just continue to reproduce with compatible pairs or other lovers?"

The Oracle moved to the dais and sat in one of the empty chairs. Riley wondered if she was tired. She was four hundred but was nothing like an old woman.

"If Blaire dies, what makes our survival possible dies with her. The magic. It isn't only losing Korrena pairs and weakened preternatural abilities. Those abilities will fade to nothing, and when they do, our lifespan will be that of a human. When the magic ceases to be, those older than what is expected of a human body will crumble to dust as their organs and tissues age in minutes. There will be massive loss of lives. I will be no more. Those older will rapidly age. We will become susceptible to ailments we've never known."

Blaire gasped and looked at the headmistress and the Oracle. The headmistress might look in her thirties, but she was seventy-four years old. She wouldn't live much longer.

"As far as having more children, I've seen what is in store for our kind. The loss of magic will dry up all reproductive functions."

"What?" Seth's brows pulled together. "Are you saying we all become sterile—infertile?"

"That is exactly what I'm saying."

Dominic looked over his shoulder at the Oracle on the dais and the mirrored hopelessness on his face made her want to cry.

"I do not wish to frighten you all, but you must know what is at stake." The Oracle's eyes connected with Blaire's before moving across those in attendance. "Most Vasirian won't get to the point where reproduction will matter, though."

"What? Why?" Aiden asked.

"With our bodies losing response to the magic of our creation, becoming like humans, we no longer can consume blood. It would become poisonous to us."

"That makes no sense." Lukas shook his head. "Blood isn't poisonous to humans, and if we're basically humans…"

"We will not be humans. While many functions will be like the species, we will remain Vasirian. The magic will not disappear all in one go with Blaire's death. Remnants will remain, and our kind will exist on that for a short time. But as time moves forward, the blood will sour, and we will not be able to consume it. Without being able to quell that need, we will succumb to *sanguis manie* and perish. For younger Vasirian, this will be their fate when Blaire dies."

Blaire let go of Lukas and walked up to the dais. "It sounds like Vasirian who aren't older than elderly humans will live for a while. How long does it take?"

The Oracle's head canted to the side. "For the destruction of our kind?"

Blaire winced.

"I cannot say for certain, but my visions imply as little as the years you could count on one hand."

Dominic shot up from his seated position and stalked across the room to the door, pulling it open and stepping outside.

Riley understood his frustration. To be part of an organization where someone sought to end a life that would bring about the extinction of their kind would rattle her too. But she wondered what could be so important to warrant Blaire's death when it meant their extinction once the magic dried up.

"So what do we do?" Aiden asked.

"For now, you all protect Blaire. Right now, it is too dangerous for her to make the transition."

Lukas crossed his arms. "Why?"

"Until we can ensure there will be no interference in her transition and adaptation to Vasirian life, she mustn't follow through with what I suspect she desires to do now."

Blaire toyed with the leather bracelet Lukas gave her.

"But if she transitions, then that's that, right?" Riley asked.

"No, child. If Blaire is killed before fully connecting with her new self, the balance will shatter completely. It isn't as simple as becoming a Vasirian. She will be too vulnerable during that time, and hiding her away might not be enough to protect her from those who seek to destroy her when they know their time is limited after her change."

Aiden rubbed his face, cursing.

Of course this wouldn't be easy for them.

30

Conflicting Thoughts

With every heavy step of Riley's platform boots from the administration building, the tension from being in an enclosed space with Seth and other people faded. Steady inhales and exhales allowed the sweet spring scents of azaleas, magnolias, and jasmine to provide calming aroma therapy, further easing her discomfort.

The idea of making it back to her dorm room for much-needed peace and quiet to sort out her rampant thoughts after learning not only the reality of how dire the situation was for their kind if Blaire didn't transition—even though she couldn't right now—to the possibility someone in the monarchy was responsible for what happened to them, to how fate bound her to not only her brother but to her friends for all of eternity. It sounded nice, but she wasn't so lucky.

"Riley, wait!"

The tiny hairs on the back of her neck stood at the sound of Seth calling out to her. She turned to face him and was immediately reminded why she felt a desperate need to put distance between them.

She wanted to throw herself at him, latch on like a cat, and take whatever small morsel of treats he would grant her.

Maybe he was right. Maybe the Korrena bond distorted their behavior.

It sounded pathetic in her opinion, but the reality that she'd always acted that way with Seth couldn't be denied. The bond didn't change that.

Incomplete bond, she reminded herself.

An uncomfortable weight pressed down on her shoulders at the thought.

Seth caught up to her at the edge of the grove, but she glanced away, unable to meet his eyes and face the turmoil within.

"We need to talk about this," he said.

"What's there to talk about?"

"Oh, I don't know, the fact that I walked into your room and saw my mark on your skin and realized the signs had been there for months staring me in the face that you're my Korrena? You wouldn't even hear me out."

Riley winced and laughed meekly. "Ah, that." She crossed her arms, scratching at the backs of them. "What's there to say?"

"Listen, I've done some thinking since that night." He softened his voice. He moved over to one of the many stone benches lining the courtyard to sit shaded by a large palmetto tree. "Sit with me."

After hesitating a moment, she took the seat on the other end of the bench and hooked her fingers in the hem of her skirt, toying with the fabric.

Inhaling deeply through his mouth and exhaling sharply out again, he said in a voice void of emotion. "I don't want it like this."

"What are you talking about?"

She couldn't even feel his emotions through the weak, newly-forming empathic link. It almost felt like he purposely blocked her from his feelings, but that notion was ridiculous. Whatever he felt wasn't strong enough to reach her, that was all.

It happened with fully bonded pairs. They didn't have a twenty-four-seven pipeline to their Korrena's every waking emotion. The emotion needed to be strong, or important enough to the Korrena feeling them, for it to carry through an empathic connection.

"I've had time to think about what you said in the room. I had no idea how you felt, but after you pushed me out, I can't help but wonder… no, I can't help but *realize* one important thing."

"And that is?" She wasn't sure she wanted to hear it. Dread filtered in unbidden.

His gunmetal eyes met hers with a seriousness that made her stomach twist and chest tighten. "You only want me because of the bond. This isn't real. You have no control over it." He laughed without humor and carded his fingers through his hair, leaving it sticking up in different directions.

As the words fell from his mouth, a pit opened in her stomach, making her sick. Her heart raced, and pain sliced through her. The cruel words hurt, yet he continued. Could he not feel her pain?

"It's the only thing that makes sense to me with how vehemently you rejected me after saying you've felt things for years. I don't want you forced into feelings for me because of our biology, Riley. I care too much about you."

Of all the things she expected out of a confrontation with him, this wasn't it. He was way off base. His misconceptions and strong aversion to the biology of the bond skewed his perception of her feelings for him. She could understand why he would think that, considering she rejected him after admitting her feelings, but she needed to explain to him why she had. He deserved to know why this would never work. It had nothing to do with his stupid hang-ups about biology.

"Seth, you're wrong. I've wanted you since we were kids. Before we ever knew about the Korrena bond, I had a huge crush on you. And yeah, maybe some of that was destiny already working, but if I didn't want you, the bond wouldn't make me."

He shook his head, rejecting her logic. "You've always wanted a pair. Of course you would jump at the chance. And it's easier with me because I'm familiar." Sadness filled his eyes. "But you didn't take that chance with me in the end, because deep down you *know* it's just biology."

"Oh, piss off. It's leagues worse because it *is* you. You're one of the most pig-headed, unpredictable hotheads I know. And the fact that you know most everything about me—you'd think it makes this easier, but it doesn't. You're so against the Korrena bond… the rejection of that coming from someone I've shared my life with…" Her nails dug into her thighs before she began plucking at the fishnet material. "Seth, I'm not ready to lose you."

The admission stunned him, based on the slack-jawed expression he gave her.

"What? You'll never lose me."

"I… I can't do it," she mumbled.

"What are you talking about?"

"I can't be around you knowing you're my pair. It's painful in more ways than one. It's not like we can perform a blood ritual and break our bond, because we've never completed it. Besides, you saw what it did to Lukas! I don't think either of us wants to live like that." She squared her shoulders and looked straight ahead, saying the thing that had rolled around in her mind for days. "It might be better if I transfer to one of the sister schools."

"What?" Seth jumped to his feet. "Fuck that. No."

She glared up at him. "You don't get to decide."

"Like hell I don't!" he roared, and several students cast wary glances as they walked by. "You're my Korrena!"

"No." She sprang to her feet and pointed at his face. "You don't get to do that. Don't you dare play the mate card because it's convenient for you. This isn't a game."

His fists balled at his sides. "I'm not playing a fucking game!" The jolt of rage and pain ricocheted behind her ribs like out-of-control lightning, tearing up her insides. Oh, *now* his emotions wanted to break through when she attempted to be strong.

Riley threw up her hands. "I don't get you." She started ticking off points on her fingers. "First, you act like it's not real. And now? You think you can use it to keep me where you want me?" She scoffed and crossed her arms. "You've known me long enough to know no one controls me."

"Except you," Aiden said as he walked up, grinning at Seth. "You've always been able to get her to do what you want. She just won't admit it." His chuckle died as he took in the heavy atmosphere. "What's going on?"

"I can't do this. I'm out of here."

Before either of them could stop her, Riley sprinted for the dorms. She needed to talk to Blaire, her mother, *someone*.

"She's going to leave the academy—transfer."

The words fell from Seth's mouth as Riley ran away from him like a pack of ravenous hyenas were chasing her. The urge to chase after her made his skin tingle. But what would he do when he caught up to her? She didn't want his comfort, and for once in their lives he didn't know if he could give it to her.

"What?"

"She thinks I don't want her."

Aiden stared at him for a long moment and asked calmly, "Why would she think that?"

"Because of my reservations about the bond."

At Aiden's confused expression, Seth sighed. He hadn't told his best friend the truth yet. Aiden knew on some level. He'd suggested it was a possibility more than once. Taking a deep lungful of air, Seth confessed, "She's my Korrena."

"Congratulations, man," Aiden said with a broad grin that died after a moment, his expression turning contemplative. "If that's true, why are you at each other's throats?"

Seth dropped to sit on the bench and rested his forearms on his thighs. "She rejected me when I tried to accept it…so I told her the only reason she feels anything for me is because of biology."

Aiden balked. "What? Why would you say something so tactless?"

Seth squinted up at Aiden against the sunlight in his eyes. "Because it's true." He looked down at the cobblestone as he tried to verbalize his inner thoughts. "Riley wants her pair, and well, here I fucking am,"—he extended his arms wide as he sat back—"but she threw me away like I'm nothing." He scoffed with unrestrained bitterness. "It's gotta mean she's fighting what the bond is making her feel. She doesn't want it."

"Huh."

"What?"

"Well, you've been railing against it for years," Aiden said, taking a seat beside Seth.

"It's just… I wanted her to want me for me. Not because of biology. I didn't want to think what I felt for her all these years is because fate decided it for me."

"Seth…"

Seth looked over at Aiden. "The cruelest part of it all? I know now it isn't biology that made my feelings what they are. I loved her long before what science shows our bodies go through before awareness. I was ready to accept this because the pair-bond would only amplify what we could possibly have." He put his head in his hands, resting his elbows on his knees and the heels of his palms on his forehead. "But she rejected me."

"She's scared, probably." Aiden sighed. "Let me ask you something."

Seth tilted his head in his hands to look at Aiden.

"What has you convinced her feelings since childhood are any different from yours? Because I *know* she likely told you, if it's come this far. She's been devoted to you like you hung the moon and made the stars in the sky shine since before she could read." He laughed. "If you'd seen those stupid notebooks in her room growing up, you'd have known it. Silly hearts with your name. 'Riley Emerson' in cursive over and over like she was practicing for the future. She threatened me with castration if I ever told you."

Seth's eyes widened in surprise. He had no idea.

"That girl would follow you to the ends of the Earth if you asked her."

Seth swallowed down the emotion building in his throat. He had told Riley those positive feelings were biology because he genuinely thought that if she felt so distressed by the realization they were Korrena pairs, then that made the most sense. But the more he talked things through with her, and with Aiden, the more he realized how much his brain had worked against him to twist the narrative into something more palatable.

"You just said your feelings come from a time before biology could dictate it, Seth. Think long and hard about what that means for Riley's feelings and why she's truly scared and running from you."

Seth sat up and rubbed his chest.

"You have to understand her reservations of trusting your sudden acceptance, only for you to turn around and tell her that her feelings aren't real. That's cruel." He sighed. "I don't think you meant to be cruel, but objectively, it is."

He couldn't ignore the truth staring him in the face, and that was what it took for him to make sense of it.

Had he been the problem all along?

Was he the problem?

Was the only reason Riley wasn't in his arms and his bed at this moment because of his defiance against the Korrena pair-bonding process?

He was an idiot.

"That it took this long to figure all this out proves she deserves better than I can give her," Seth said with a subtle shake of his head.

"Stop giving yourself a pity party."

"I'm not."

"You are. You're entitled to happiness, and if you don't show her the truth and try, if my little sister leaves this academy because of this, I swear..." Aiden didn't finish his threat. He didn't have to. Aiden would curb stomp him and have every right to.

With new realizations, he needed to figure out the best way to convey to Riley how he felt and apologize.

He had so much to apologize for.

31

Advice

The seven-bedroom family farmhouse with white trim on the other side of Rosebrook Valley looked like it did the last time Riley visited her mother. The fresh smell of newly-cut grass filled the air along with the enticing perfume from the flowerbeds that lined the stairs leading up to the wraparound porch featuring crisp white railings and columns that matched the white trim of the tan home. Evenly-spaced baskets overflowing with flowers dangled from the edge of the gabled roof, adding to the inviting appearance of her childhood home.

Riley took a deep breath. She could do this.

"Are you going to tell me why we're here?"

Riley glanced over at Blaire and offered a hesitant smile. "Soon."

She hadn't told Blaire about Seth yet, and it was getting harder to keep it to herself. The moment she put words to the reality of things, she would break down, and she didn't want to have to weather that storm more than once.

Stomping up the stairs, Riley took a moment to steel her nerves before knocking on the door's large center window.

"Is anyone else here besides your mom?"

"Shouldn't be. The grass was cut recently, so maybe our neighbor's kid, but no one else knew we were coming besides Mama."

The door opened and Annie Easton beamed a bright smile that made the blue eyes she shared with her daughter light up.

"I was startin' to get worried y'all weren't gonna make it." She stepped back and ushered Blaire and Riley inside. "Come on in. Take your shoes off. I just waxed these floors. When you're done, come on into the kitchen. I made lunch."

Blaire slipped off her flats while Riley unzipped and put away her boots before they made across the hardwood floor of the foyer into the open concept kitchen where Riley's mother busied herself in the cabinets over the marble counters, gathering plates and setting them on the center island of the kitchen.

Fluffing her stacked black hair, she smiled. "Wanna eat in the dining room or here in the kitchen?" She squinted at Riley. "Baby, what is it?" She came around the island to where Riley had taken a seat on the high chair on the other side. Her small hands held both of Riley's cheeks, studying her.

That's all it took. The concern of her mother.

Riley took a shuddering breath and the dam broke.

"Mama!" she cried, collapsing forward and wrapping her arms around her mother's shoulders and burying her head in the crook of her neck as the tears flowed.

"Oh, honey, what's wrong?"

"I don't know what to do," Riley said through her sobs. "Aiden died. But he didn't. He's back. Seth… We… We're… I can't do it! Mama, I wanna come home."

"Hold on. Hold on, baby." Her mother moved to hold her at arm's length to get a good look at her. "What's this about Aiden? Honey, what's happened?"

Tears welled in her mother's eyes, so she had to say something.

Blaire circled around to stand near the two of them, and Riley looked at her helplessly. The confusion on her friend's face made her sad.

Annie pulled Riley close again as Blaire explained what happened with Aiden at Blackthorn Manor.

"Oh, my boy… my sweet boy," her mother said as she stroked Riley's hair. The emotion in her voice said her mother was crying as well, but Riley didn't dare look up from the safety of her mother's embrace.

"He really is alright now," Blaire said, moving to sit down again next to Riley.

But Annie pulled her into the same hug she shared with her daughter. Blaire sniffed, and the three of them held each other for several minutes before Annie stepped back, circled the island again, and used her apron to wipe her eyes.

"I've half a mind to whoop that boy for not givin' me details when he said y'all made it back to school from England. Is that's what's got you all emotional and needin' to visit, baby?"

Her mother pulled a casserole dish from the oven that looked like one of Riley's favorites. When she scooped a heaping spoonful of baked macaroni and cheese with chicken onto a plate, Riley smiled through her tears.

"No," Riley said with a sniff. Swiping at her eyes, she shook her head. "I mean, yeah. Some of it. You needed to know, but it's not just that."

"Seth?"

Riley looked at Blaire. How did she know?

Blaire answered her unasked question. “You said his name when you were crying.”

“What’s this about Seth? Is he okay?” Annie asked, taking a seat across from Blaire and Riley as they began eating.

“I guess… I don’t know.”

“What do you mean, baby?”

“He’s…” Riley choked on another sob that bubbled up her throat, and when Blaire’s hand closed over hers, she looked over. The serious look in her friend’s eyes that held both strength and support helped her to speak the truth. “We’re Korrenas.”

Her mother’s fork clattered to her plate, and Blaire’s hand squeezed.

“That’s wonderful news!” Her mother said, a hand over her chest as she swiped her eyes. But her face fell at Riley’s slow shake of her head. “What’s the matter?”

“I rejected him.”

Blaire sucked in a breath and Annie stared, dumbfounded.

“I’m sorry, but I must be hearin’ things. You did what now?”

Tears raced over Riley’s cheeks, probably making a mess. She needed to invest in waterproof makeup. She had never cried so frequently, and with reality as cruel as it was, a lot more crying was in her future.

“Riley, baby?”

Riley shook her head quickly and looked at her mother.

“Mama, he doesn’t want a bond—”

“He rejected you?” her mother shouted, hopping to her feet. “I will tan that boy’s hide.”

“No! Listen!” Riley held her hand out, and her mother sat down. “Seth has never liked the idea of a Korrena bond. He’s always thought it was biology's way of forcing us to want each other, where normally we wouldn't. He's been like that since before we knew."

Her mother hummed and then asked, "When did y'all figure it out?"

"While at the manor, in England." Blaire frowned at Riley.

Riley backpedaled at her accusatory tone. "It hasn't been long. I've just needed time to sort my thoughts. I'm sorry I didn't say anything."

"I'm not upset," Blaire clarified. "At least not about that."

"What then?"

Blaire sighed. "I'm just disappointed to hear you rejected him. I mean, I didn't grow up with you two, but I've been able to see something between you both ever since I started Blackthorn Academy."

"One-sided."

"I didn't think so."

Riley closed her eyes as fresh tears rolled down her face. Her mother gave her a tissue. "He came to me a few nights before we left and saw our mark on me."

"Where is it?" her mother asked.

She looked at her mother and pursed her lips. How was she supposed to know? Seth didn't tell her, and she never saw his— Gasping, she recalled the day at the pool when she accused him of getting a fresh tattoo, but he had no idea what she was talking about. Riley sat back and lifted her shirt, pulling down the edge of her skirt and pointing to the area of skin on her lower left abdomen above the pelvic region. "Here."

"The tattoo you saw on Seth that none of us saw?"

"Exactly!" Riley looked at Blaire, fixing her clothes. "I thought I was losing my mind. Turns out it was the first time I'd seen the mark appear. I haven't seen it since, but I wasn't looking for it either. I thought I was drunk."

Her mother *tsked* but made no comment. She had said a long time ago that while she didn't like the idea of her underage children drinking, she wouldn't stop them because she expected them to act like responsible adults—including accepting any consequences.

"Okay, so he came to you..." her mother encouraged, leaning forward on her elbows with sadness in her eyes.

"I was just out of the shower, and he came in without knocking—which isn't abnormal for us. I do it all the time. It was just the first time one of us wasn't dressed when it happened." Riley flushed. "I had my earbuds in, so I didn't hear him, so he scared me when I caught him staring. When I got mad, he came and kissed me, and I had to tell him it needed to stop, you know? It was too much for my heart to let it keep happening."

"Wait a minute, baby. What do you mean by 'keep happening'?"

"It's not the first, or even the second, time we've kissed." She didn't say more things had happened, but now that she thought about it, they shared a lot more physical intimacy than Blaire and Lukas had before they bonded, so it wasn't a surprise things between them grew out of control so fast. Physical intimacy helped the bond to grow. If they'd both known they were Korrenas to one another, it would have been crazy.

They didn't question Riley about the kisses or anything more, so she continued her story.

"He didn't understand, of course. But he asked me if I could feel him."

Blaire raised her eyebrows at the same time in shock. "Feel him?"

"Like, his emotions." She sighed. "It was his way of telling me." Her shoulders slumped. "I ended up pushing him away. Told him he couldn't do this to me after all these years. How I felt about him all these years." She looked at her mother with teary eyes. "Mama, he seemed like he wanted the bond."

"Then why did you drive him away?"

"I don't want him to resent me."

"Oh, baby girl…"

Blaire shook her head and absently rolled the napkin in front of her on the counter. "Then what was that in the administration building when the Oracle said Dom was in your future?"

"I couldn't stop myself. I felt his fury so strongly I needed to fix it. I needed to make it better." Riley looked at Blaire. "Seth has always been important to me. He will always be important to me. The Korrena bond doesn't matter. At that time, all that mattered was soothing away his anger."

Her mother hummed and sat back in her chair with an inhale through her nose, taking in the information as a quiet observer, disparate from her usual boisterous personality that Riley inherited.

"He stopped me outside of the administration building," Riley admitted.

Blaire perked up. "What'd he say?"

Riley looked at her. "He said he'd done some 'thinking,' and apparently in the time we've spent not talking got it in his head that the reason I rejected him is because the Korrena thing really is biology after all, and my feelings aren't real."

"Is he out of his mind? I really need to pay that boy a visit."

"Mama, please." Riley grumbled. "He's convinced I came to the same realization he always has. The bond is biology, and that I haven't actually felt these things, and what I felt isn't my own feelings."

"That makes no sense," Blaire said with a disapproving head shake. "Like, it doesn't even *sound* right to the ears."

"Imagine hearing the same thing from him! I ended up telling him I couldn't do it anymore and that I'm considering leaving the academy."

"You're what?" her mother screeched at the same time Blaire said, "Since when?"

"I haven't decided. But he freaked out. Started demanding that I couldn't because I'm his Korrena, but he had just told me all that other mess. Then he acts like he has a choice in the matter. I don't understand it." Riley met her mother's gaze. "Can I come home for a while?"

Her mother closed her eyes briefly as if composing herself while she took a slow breath, and then stood, moving around the island and pulling Riley into a hug. "No," she said after a moment of silence.

Riley pulled back in surprise. "What? Why not?"

"Because do you honestly believe separation is going to help?"

"Yes."

"Then you have a lot to learn about the Korrena bond. Baby, they put pairs in rooms together at the academy for a reason. Being physically apart is going to hurt you emotionally and physically, more so than the way the two of you pined for each other before your awakening."

Riley didn't know if she could handle that, but at the same time, the torture of being at his side and knowing who he was to her would kill her.

"This is what you're gonna to do. You're gonna march your pretty little tail back to that academy and give it some time." Her mother put a hand up to staunch Riley's protest. "You don't have to speak to him. Just go about your day like always. You both need time to process this. For some pairs, it's not a simple discovery and things work out—in fact, for most, it doesn't work that way."

"Don't I know it," Blaire mumbled.

"Don't be so quick to write that boy off. He loves you. I've always thought so. I know your brother thinks so." Annie cupped Riley's cheek, brushing away a stray tear. "I *know* you love him. You've loved that boy before you even knew what love was. I saw it. He owned your heart from the moment you saw him, and I honestly believe it goes both ways."

Blaire reached out and took Riley's hand. "If it helps, I don't want you to go anywhere. You were my first friend at the academy and have become my best friend. It wouldn't be the same if you moved home or went to another academy. I'll be there with you. I'll help you around him if it gets too rough. Just tell me, okay?"

Riley turned and hugged Blaire, closing her eyes.

She didn't know how she was going to face Seth, but she could give it time, like her mother said. Time for what, she didn't know, but she trusted her mother's judgment, even if she was kookier than she was herself. After one-hundred-eighteen years, her mother likely understood a thing or two about life. She would do well to heed her advice. And if Blaire was with her, she could do it.

She only had to keep reminding herself of that fact until she believed it.

Sitting on the edge of the marble fountain in the courtyard at the academy, Riley stared at the clouds moving across the sky. A spring storm was approaching, and the air smelled of impending rain. It looked like a night of hanging in her room with junk food and a romance novel was in her future.

Though, she considered trading out a romance novel for an epic fantasy where the women were badass and beheaded men who wronged them in the love department.

Riley laughed to herself at the silliness of it.

She didn't get the woman-scorned-becomes-violent trope. Probably because it went against what she would do in reality. What she wanted to do with this situation she found herself in. Run away. That was likely the big difference.

Where one woman chose fight, she chose flight.

A week had passed since she spoke to her mother, and Blaire had done an excellent job of keeping her occupied. Blaire even took her to her therapist to set up a few appointments to deal with the bad dreams she kept having about her brother's death. They'd gone to the movies a couple of times after school and ran Lukas out of the room to take over their space in case Seth came to her room on other evenings after classes.

Her mother said to go back to the academy; she didn't say Riley had to interact with Seth.

Of course, she'd seen him in the cafeteria. She pretended as if everything was normal. She even fired her usual barbs and jabs, but they weren't as convincing as before. Even if Seth couldn't feel anything through their unsealed bond, she wasn't into the usual banter. The others noticed it too and cast them wary glances.

Seth had likely already shared the news of their Korrena marks appearing with both Aiden and Lukas. Blaire wouldn't have told them. Riley had told Layla, Mera, and Kai one evening before she and Blaire went to the movies.

Kai was extremely upset with his brother. Which made sense. Kai took the bond seriously. That Seth threw the biology argument in her face when she rejected him angered Kai in a way Riley had never seen before. Riley had made him promise not to say anything, and with reluctance, he agreed.

"Hey you," a familiar voice called, drawing Riley's attention from her thoughts as the first rumbles of thunder sounded in the distance.

Dominic strode toward her in Blackthorn Academy's uniform of pressed black slacks, white button-down Oxford shirt, and burgundy-and-black plaid tie. He looked handsome. His icy-silver dyed hair coordinated nicely with the uniform. She grinned at the Doc Martin boots he paired with it.

While the paperwork was completed for him to join classes as of yesterday, they hadn't seen him because he spent the time settling into his dorm.

He sat next to her on the edge of the fountain. "Loonie for your thoughts?"

Riley snorted at the reminder of their awkward date. "Just thinking about the last couple of months."

"Care to elaborate?"

She wondered if she should tell him about things with Seth. Dominic liked her. Would it hurt him? She'd already told him how she felt about Seth. Besides, he would find out once he started joining them in the cafeteria.

Blowing out a breath, Riley kept her gaze trained on a cloud that looked like a fish and said, "Seth's my Korrena." When she got no response, she turned her head to find Dominic staring at her in amazement. "I guess you were right in your assumption of us, after all."

"Wow. That's…" He rubbed the side of his neck. "Wow. Congratulations."

"Yeah, don't do that."

"Pardon?"

"He doesn't want the bond, and I rejected it."

She laughed at the bewilderment on his face. It was all she could do to keep from crying whenever she talked about the weird standoff she and Seth had.

"But why?"

Riley gave Dominic the Cliff Notes version of what happened between Seth and her at the manor and the academy. She didn't go into the things they shared prior, or any intimate details, just the fact that they both saw the mark on each other and what Seth believed about how the Korrena bond worked. How her feelings worked.

She bristled remembering his implication that her lifelong feelings for him were nothing more than chemicals firing in her brain.

Dominic leaned back and whistled long and low. "That's a lot."

"Tell me about it."

"So what do you plan to do about it?"

"I wanted to leave. Go home, or maybe transfer."

"Wanted?" His brow arched. "So that changed?"

Her shoulders hitched in a light shrug. "For now, it has. Mama said I should wait to make a decision like that. I don't know why, but we'll see."

"Well, making rash decisions when you've been through what you have in the last few weeks isn't exactly advisable."

Riley nodded. She understood that, which was another reason she conceded to her mother's request to stay.

"I hope it works out for you two, though," he said, and Riley scoffed. "Seriously. While it would have been nice if it worked out between us, I believe the Korrena bond is a sacred thing, and if you want my advice…"

He paused and tilted his head as if truly asking first if Riley wanted it. She nodded in silent agreement. No one ever asked, they just projected onto her what they would do. The respect made her listen more.

"I don't think you should run from it," he said. "Let the pieces fall as they may. I think it might turn out differently than you expect.

Especially when you felt love for him before you knew."

Dominic stood and stretched as the first droplets of rain fell. "If you ever need to talk, I'm around." He dropped his arms and looked down at Riley with a sad smile. "I mean that. It's not just polite talk. I don't do that."

Riley nodded, wringing her hands in her lap. "I'll keep that in mind."

32

Truths

Thunder rumbled loudly outside as she lay in bed beneath her blanket, cozied up with her book and a bag of sour cream and onion chips, enjoying the occasional flash of lightning. The smell of the academy ground's flower gardens, blooming trees, and rain blew in through her open window, stirring the sheer black fabric hanging between her pulled-back blackout curtains. More snacks and candy sat on her nightstand under her reading lamp.

She hadn't worn earbuds, choosing to let the ambient sounds of the approaching storm be the soundtrack to her reading. It hadn't started raining yet. This was her favorite type of storm. Eventually the rain would come, but she always enjoyed the night air and the thunder and lightning leading up to the storm.

A knock at the door pulled her attention from a crucial part of her book. She really wanted to know what happened to the main character's friend who took care of her while imprisoned by the king. Though the king's right-hand dragon enforcer held most of her attention.

Bookmarking the page, she closed the book and padded across the floor on bare feet. Her breath caught in her throat when she pulled the door open to find Seth standing in the hallway.

They'd seen one another in the cafeteria, but she hadn't looked at him directly until now. What she saw cut her to the bone.

His hair was disheveled, as if he'd been running his hands through it repeatedly. Dark circles lay heavy beneath his gray eyes, making his discomfort stand out in notable contrast to his usual appearance. When he reached up and rubbed a hand across his jaw awkwardly, a faint tremor shook his fingers.

Turning her head to the side, no longer able to face the sight, she murmured, "You shouldn't be here."

"I should. I should have come sooner."

"Seth, just leave it alone." Riley moved to close the door before he could see the physical evidence of the pain he probably felt through their weak empathic link. She certainly felt something at the edge of her consciousness that was uniquely him, but she couldn't place the emotion.

Seth's arm lashed out and grabbed the door before it could swing shut. "No." He stepped into the room when Riley stepped back with rounded eyes. "I'm not leaving it alone. Not anymore. I'm not playing this game anymore."

"I'm not playing a game," Riley said with a glare. "None of this is fun for me, Seth."

He sighed, shoulders drooping. "You think it's fun for me?" He moved across the room and sat on the desk chair she didn't use as a clothes hamper, putting his elbows on his knees and face in his hands. "I'm fucking miserable."

Riley plucked the fuzzy area rug in the center of her room with her bare toes, unsure what to do.

In the past, she would make a joke and they would tease one another and fall into their happy normal, but that would never be possible again. Not only would that never be their normal again, but also being around each other had become awkward and uncomfortable. At the same time, *not* being around one another was downright unbearable now that they acknowledged the Korrena bond.

Clutching at how he discarded her feelings as nothing but biology, she asked, "Why do you insist on making this harder for me?"

His hands dropped. "I don't understand why it has to be hard. Why won't you just accept our bond?"

The floor shifted beneath her feet as his words threw her for a loop of confusion.

"Accept the bond?" she asked incredulously. "*You* don't want the bond!"

His lips tightened, his nose screwing up as if it pained him to hear the words.

"Seth, I might have been the one to push you out, but you've spent your entire life denying the entire institution of Korrena bonding."

"That was before."

"Before what?"

"Before I got a wakeup call."

Riley turned and paced a path across the room to the desk, tearing open a pack of jellybeans, popping some in her mouth—*ugh, chili mango flavor*—then pacing more, stopping to eat more with each turn as her mind swam, grounding herself by naming the flavors to corral her thoughts. *Apple? No, pineapple. Cinnamon. Kiwi.*

A wakeup call? That wasn't good enough. Was she supposed to fall at his feet because he had some grand epiphany he wouldn't even share with her? Swallowing her candy, she stopped and spun on him.

"I need more than that. You can't show up here after everything you said outside of the admin building and think that's enough to make me change my mind."

"I talked with your brother. I told him what I said. What you said. He made me realize how much of an idiot I am, and how my words held no solid foundation."

"I could have told you that," she quipped.

Seth released a self-deprecating laugh and shook his head. "I'm sure you could."

Her arms went across her chest, and she squinted at him. "And now?"

"Now?"

"Well, what does it mean now that you've had this wakeup call?"

"I want this," he said without hesitation. Steel gray eyes darkened as they connected with hers. "I want you. Now, tomorrow, a hundred years from now… I just want you."

Popping a few jellybeans in her mouth—*cotton candy, peach, and cream soda*—she moved to the window to watch as the rain poured in sheets, only noticeable when the lightning lit the courtyard below.

"I've wanted to hear that for so long," she whispered. "I would have given anything to hear those words. But now that everything has happened the way it did, I've also had more time to think. It made it easier to see things from another angle."

He stood from the bed and turned toward her. "What are you saying?" A dull pain hit her chest that wasn't hers. It made it hard to say what she needed to.

"Seth, you and I both know it wouldn't work." Her eyes burned as she tried not to blink for fear that tears would fall. "I'm not really what you want."

"What are you—"

"*Listen.*" She sighed. "I've said it before, and I'll say it again. I am nothing like the girls you mess around with. I'll never be like them. Not physically, and not mentally. I'm messed up in the head. I can't even finish a task some days without going on to three others. And some days? I can't even start the first one."

"Riley, I know that. But those girls—"

"Just listen to me!" She turned and took a long, calming inhale through her nose as she looked at a blurry Seth through her tear-filled eyes. "I'm trying to tell you I can't be what you need. You deserve something so much better than I could ever give you. You're amazing. All I want is for you to be happy. Taking care of me for hundreds of years doesn't sound like my idea of you having real happiness. There are plenty of other girls and women who want you and would be a better choice as a compatible pair than I would be as your Korrena."

There.

She said it without breaking.

Laid bare everything that plagued her mind in her week of avoiding him.

Seth turned away and stalked over to her desk, gripping the back of her desk chair as he hung his head forward, taking deep breaths. Rage twisted and floated in the air from him like a tangible thing, wrapping around her body and latching on tight.

When he turned to look at her, his face was impassive—a look she'd seen many times before. But the intense anger peeling off him in waves made it clear how easily he cloaked his actual emotions behind a mask… like she did.

"I don't deserve you? Do you have any idea how wonderful you are? How much I live to see you smile? How I would cut my heart out and serve it to you on a silver platter if it would make you happy?"

Riley sucked in a breath, and his jaw tightened as an uncomfortable expression crossed his features, a flicker of panic filtering through the anger. Her head tilted as she studied him with curiosity.

As quickly as the strange emotion came, it was gone, and he shook his head. "And you need to get it out of your head that another woman is right for me."

"But they are."

"No!" he yelled, and she flinched. "They're not. Let me make something crystal fucking clear for you, because you have been under the wrong impression for a very long time."

He stepped forward and pointed toward her door. "Those girls? I used all of them to fuck you out of my head. All of them! And guess what?" he said with a sardonic laugh. "It hasn't worked!" He rubbed his face so hard his skin was flushed red when he dropped his hand away.

"All I picture is you. All I've ever done is picture you. Every. Single. Time."

His words surprised her. One of her big arguments aside from what she voiced aloud was that along with her not being comparable to those girls, he chose to be with them instead of her. If he had genuinely wanted her in the way she wanted him, he wouldn't have been sleeping around. But if his words were true, it explained why he did it.

But did it?

He didn't have to sleep with other people. He chose that path. It sounded like he was blaming her for his decision to sleep around and his lack of enjoyment of it.

"I don't know what you want me to say to that. I didn't tell you to sleep with them."

"I know that. I just needed you to know. You think you don't compare, but Riley, I chose the exact opposite of you for a reason." His voice was hard and tense, hands tight at his sides in fists. "I needed to, but your face still haunted me. Do you remember the waitress from that Japanese restaurant who gave me her number? I know you do. You gave me shit for throwing the number out."

"I do." It confused her that he didn't keep it.

"Do you remember what she looked like?"

"No," she hedged, dragging the vowel out.

"Short. Petite. Black pixie cut. Big blue eyes." His head inclined forward. "Do you remember what I said about her when you asked if she was my type?"

"No. I don't know why I asked that, considering who you normally keep as company."

"*Kept*, and I told you that she was *exactly* my type." He shoved his hands in the pockets of his jeans. "You two could have been sisters. But she wasn't you, and I couldn't bring myself to ever go near another girl who looked like you. It'd kill me." He ground his teeth and huffed a heavy exhale. "Do you get it now?" His tone came out harsh with his final words.

"I don't know why you're angry with me," she said softly, unable to hide the hurt in her voice. "If you wanted me, I don't know why you didn't come to me." She looked up into his eyes. "You could have had me."

Seth's heart ached in response to the revelation. Her voice sounded soft and small—much like Riley herself. A sharp contrast to her usual boisterousness. The vulnerability in her words was palpable.

It would take more than placating words about how he viewed those girls who warmed his bed and he no longer wanted to think about. No, he needed something concrete to show Riley he meant everything he said about his feelings for her. That she could trust his words as truth. He'd almost showed his hands in his emotional outburst earlier, saying words so similar to what he put to paper that he feared she would recognize them.

Taking a colossal risk, he dug his phone out of his back pocket and began swiping through apps.

"What are you doing?"

"Proving my feelings to you."

"Seth, you don't need to—"

"Yes, I do. You don't trust in my feelings, and I don't blame you." He looked up from his phone. "Especially after I denied yours for me. Which I am so fucking sorry for it makes me sick."

"Sorry? But why?"

"Because I should never have said it. I was confused and scared. I couldn't understand why you pushed me away. I was grasping at straws to find a reason for it." He shook his head. "I landed on my theories of biology as a possible reason, and it reinforced everything I once believed about the Korrena bond, so I went with it. It was the stupidest thing I've ever done, and it's cost me everything."

He looked down at his phone, unable to meet the pain in her eyes any longer, and needing to find this for her so she could see for herself. Finding what he wanted in his email, he held his phone out for her.

Riley's small hands shook as she took the phone from his hands. The small brush of their skin in that moment made him want to wrap her in his arms.

"What am I looking at?"

"Read it."

She looked down at the screen and her forehead wrinkled, her brows puckering as her eyes narrowed. Her lips twisted to the side as she looked up at him. "I don't understand."

"Those are from my editor." He took the phone back and put it in his pocket. "More accurately, Emley Rison's editor."

"I don't… I don't understand," Riley said, that same tightness between her brows making her face scrunch adorably.

"It's a pseudonym. My pen name." He offered her a wan smile. "The author you've been so obsessed with."

"Okay, wait a minute. How did we go from that other stuff to this? Even my thoughts aren't that disjointed." She picked at the edge of her T-shirt. "Please explain what you're trying to say, because I don't get it, and I don't know if I have the spoons to try."

Seth nodded and reached for her hand. "Please come sit with me?"

She hesitated, but when she slid her hand into his, it felt like a victory. He led her to the bed and pulled her down to sit next to him on the edge.

"Emley Rison. Em and son? It comes from my last name: Emerson. And I took ley and Ri from Riley." He took a slow breath in then exhaled. Meeting her eyes, he said, "This recent series… Ryan and Shelby? They're us."

"What?"

"'*How could I tell her she owned my heart from the moment she punched me in the face as a toddler?*'" he said softly, quoting the last release. "It's true. I knew the moment your fist connected with my face that you were it for me. Long before I knew Korrenas were a thing. How I knew that as a child, I will never know. It was just instinctual. I was obsessed from that day on."

When Riley said nothing, her mouth parted on words she didn't say, he pressed on.

"When I turned sixteen, I felt the pull. Earlier than expected, I know, but I felt it, and it scared the shit out of me. I thought I was going crazy. You didn't show any acknowledgment, so I got frustrated, and that's when it first set in that biology played a cruel joke on us all." He looked down at the floor. "I spent my childhood and early teens pining for you, so when I didn't get instant gratification when I thought you were my pair, I allowed bitterness to move in. That disdain festered and rotted inside me until I thoroughly despised the idea of a bond." Taking a heavy breath, his gaze collided with hers. "If it wasn't going to be you, I didn't want it at all."

Riley took one slow, long breath as if composing herself. The real reason he abhorred the idea of the Korrena bond had to come as a surprise, but she deserved to know everything.

"Then, when you were finally the age our kind typically finds our pairs and nothing happened… Needless to say, I was furious. I turned to fighting. Sex. Anything short of drugs to forget. To run. I'm so sick of running." He dropped his head into his hands, elbows on his thighs. "So fucking sick of denying how I feel about you. How I've felt for you before I even knew you were born for me."

"Then don't."

"What?" He looked up at her, startled by the confidence in her voice.

"Don't run anymore. I'm right here. This is confusing to me too, but the one thing that's always been real and steady has been my feelings for you. Even through these awful few weeks, I've never stopped loving you. Never stopped caring for you. Never stopped wanting to make it better."

"I just… don't feel like I'm good enough, you know?" He rubbed his hands on the thighs of his jeans, getting rid of the sweat from his nerves from his confession. "I've done so many stupid things, and you could do better than me."

"Seth, I think you're the only one really capable of handling me."

He shook his head.

"No, I'm serious." She turned his hand and put a jellybean in it, popping one into her own mouth before dropping the bag on her desk and turning around to lean on the chair. "Not only are you the only one who can calm me down, but you're the only one who can get me out of my head. You ground me in ways no other person can. But there's more than that. I've known you were my person since we were little."

"Your person?"

"Yep. My person. My annoying, moody, hot as sin person."

"Hot as sin?"

Her eyes rolled. "Of course you'd choose that to focus on."

"You didn't exactly give me other positive things to focus on."

She snorted. "Fine." She started ticking off traits on her fingers like making a grocery list, and Seth's heart sped up with each point. "Smart, protective, loving, compassionate, loyal… should I keep going?"

"Please."

"Oh, piss off."

Seth laughed for the first time in weeks. For Riley to be comfortable again around him enough to banter made him beyond happy.

But hearing her tell him he was worthy, that only he could be what she needed, was the greatest gift outside of sealing their bond she could give him. He hadn't known how badly he needed to hear he was enough until this moment.

"Now, I need to know something."

He tensed at the severity of her tone. "Okaaay."

"I haven't finished the last book. Do Ryan and Shelby end up together?"

Seth's face hurt from the grin that spread across his face. "Thought you didn't like spoilers?"

"Yeah, well. Here we are. Gimmie." She giggled. "I can't believe you're Emley Rison! I have all your books!" She went to her bookshelf, waving to his entire bibliography. "You're really talented, and wow, can you write—" She jerked to a stop and turned around with wide eyes.

"I can write what?"

"Nope."

"Riley."

"Nuh uh."

"I still haven't told you what happens," he said, not above using what she wanted to get what he wanted. He grinned at the shocked indignation on her face.

"Fine! Spicy stuff! You write those scenes really good."

"That so?"

Seth didn't think her face could get any redder, but it did when she said, "I like them."

He chose not to embarrass her further by revealing those scenes were his own fantasies of what he wished could happen between them. Instead, he nodded and gave her what she wanted. "Yeah. Ryan and Shelby end up together. Married, a ton of kids, a dog, and cat."

"Yes!" Riley punched the air and danced around in a circle. She finally stopped and blinked at him. "What?"

"You're so beautiful."

Her face burned bright pink, and he wanted to pull her to him, but he needed to approach things delicately or it would be two steps forward and five steps back.

Did she understand he wanted that same happy ending? He wanted it all with her.

When she came to him when he held his hands out, he breathed a sigh of relief. Looking up into her eyes, he said, "I love you more than

I've ever loved anything in my life, Riley Easton." His hand moved up to her cheek, and she leaned into his touch. "Please say you'll accept this pairing."

33

Ready

Riley looked down at Seth, studying his face. As much as he tried to hide his uncertainty and fear, she tasted it on her tongue, and it ran over her skin like thousands of skittering bugs. He couldn't hide such powerful emotions from her in this moment. Their bond wasn't sealed, and the control wasn't established.

But it would be.

That much she knew.

Placing a hand over his, she nodded with teary eyes. "I'm ready."

"Thank fuck," he said, laying his head back with a groan. "I didn't know what else to do if you said no."

"Can't really top being my favorite author." She paused, and a smile tugged at her lips. "Want to know what really baffles me?"

His hands dropped, and he leaned back, resting his hands behind him to hold himself up. "Shoot."

"How in the hell are you an author when your texting is cringeworthy at best?"

Seth's bark of laughter made her stomach flutter. She missed the sound. "Just because I'm a writer doesn't mean I always have to be on." His head tilted. "I can be lazy with texting. Now, come here."

She squealed when he reached forward suddenly, snatching her around the waist, twisting, and dropping her onto the bed where he hovered over her, one knee between her thighs, the other foot still on the floor.

"Little warning would be nice."

"I *said* come here, didn't I?"

Riley rolled her eyes, but when he lowered himself to brush his lips across hers, as if to test if she'd push him away, her eyes slipped closed.

"I love you," he said, trailing kisses across her jaw to her neck as he climbed onto the bed entirely. "Please know I love you."

Worry tightened her chest. He sounded so unsure and afraid, and it was unlike him. She wanted his confidence back.

Seth looked down at her with hesitation when she pushed his shoulders to get him to lift away from kissing the side of her neck.

She cupped both of his cheeks. "I know, Seth. Trust me, I know."

He turned and kissed her palm.

Nodding tightly, she added, "If I didn't know, and didn't love you, this wouldn't be happening."

His Adam's apple bobbed with his swallow. The restraint he imposed on himself was obvious. She wanted to break the self-control he clung so desperately to.

He no longer had a reason to hold back. She was his if he wanted her. This wasn't a lesson in pleasure, or whatever else they chose to label what had been simple desire for one another that they were too afraid to admit.

"Seth, if you don't touch me, I'm going to start without you."

His eyes flew to hers, and a salacious grin crossed his lips. "So a couple of orgasms and you're all raring to go? An expert? Been handling yourself?"

"No, but..."

"I mean, if you really want to start yourself," he said in a teasing tone. He sat back on his heels. "By all means." He waved a hand forward. "Don't let me stop you."

She was going to slap him. "Seth, if you don't—"

Her words died the moment he fell forward and claimed her mouth, his body cloaking hers.

Seth's kisses started slow; an exploration of their mutual want for one another. He tenderly brushed soft lips over hers. The kiss wasn't like any of the others they shared. He kissed her like he wanted to savor her. The occasional brush of his tongue when he parted his lips to deepen the kiss made shivers pass over her.

Riley trailed her hands up both his arms until she held the back of his head, keeping him there so he couldn't stop kissing her. She never wanted him to stop. He bit her lower lip and pulled lightly, making her gasp. When he slid his tongue across the abused flesh, she moaned.

Her nails trailed over the back of his scalp, and his answering groan made her smile into his mouth, her other hand dropping to his neck to allow his head to move freely with hers as their kisses turned into a frenzied dance of teeth, lips, and tongue.

Seth settled between her thighs when she hooked her leg over the back of his leg.

Everything about the moment felt different from the times where they pushed the boundaries of their relationship with small, stolen moments of teasing, and passion-filled occasions where they couldn't hold back from one another. Riley realized now more than ever those moments were more than Seth simply helping her and her heart being too deep into it. His heart had been right there along with hers.

A tear rolled from the corner of her eye into her hairline.

Seth lifted his head, taking in her glassy eyes.

I've wanted you for so long.

His thumb brushed her temple. "I'm overwhelmed too." Lowering his head to her shoulder, resting his forehead against it, he inhaled. "Trust me, I've wanted this for as far back as I can remember. *Needed* it. Needed you."

She wrapped her arms around his shoulders and hugged him close, even though he kept his weight from settling too much on her upper body.

"I love you," Riley whispered against the side of his hair, and he shuddered. It was the first time she said it to him in the context she really wanted to. He knew it. She knew it.

Lifting himself up, he looked down at her with a renewed hunger in his eyes.

It was amazing how quickly things could shift from slow and emotional to frantic and needy, but her body buzzed with desire for him and what was to come.

When he lifted onto his knees and pulled his shirt off his toned body, she wiggled, working her own T-shirt over her head. Already ready for bed, she didn't have on a bra, but he liked her breasts before, so she didn't shy away from the absence of clothing in the lamplight. Even if she still felt self-conscious about not having larger breasts.

"Perfect."

Seth lowered himself to take her nipple into his mouth, swirling his tongue around the bud like it was his favorite dessert. The little sounds that came from her throat embarrassed her, but she loved the things he did that triggered those sounds. When his other hand twisted her other nipple between his index finger and thumb, her lips parted on a gasping moan.

Riley felt his grin against the flesh of her breast at her response. How was she to know she liked a little sting with pleasure? It was just another thing Seth helped her learn about herself and her sexuality.

He licked a trail across the valley between her breasts to lavish her left nipple with the same attention he had given the right. A gentle bite and tug made her arch into him, a strangled sound leaving her throat, her hand grasping the blanket beneath her at her sides.

"I love how responsive you are," he whispered against her skin before moving to the side of her nipple and grazing his fangs over her breast. "I live for every. Single. Sound." He punctuated each word with a light bite that had her panting.

"Please, Seth."

He didn't lift his head, only tilted his gaze up to meet hers. "Please, what? Tell me what you need, baby."

Riley pressed her lips together, and she frowned. She didn't know what she needed, but she needed something. Her body was lit up from head to toe with something driving her forward to fulfill its needs, but it wasn't only about sex and orgasms. She hadn't figured it out.

"You feel the pull?" he asked.

"Huh?"

"I feel this incredible desire to claim you. Fully. I think that part is our biology guiding us on what we have to do to complete the bond. Is that what you feel?"

She wanted to be one with him. Wanted to crawl inside him and never leave. Becoming pair-bonded would give her that soul-deep connection satiating that need.

"Yes," she whispered.

Seth trailed kisses up from her breasts, over her sternum, and back to her lips, where he didn't linger long. He sat back on his heels, his fingers looping under the edge of her pajama pants. She nodded when he looked at her, and then he pulled them and her panties off.

Moving to kiss down her body again, he nipped and licked at her skin until his head was between her legs.

"Remember when I said you smell like tiger lilies?" he asked, dragging his nose over her thigh, his breath fanning over her skin as he breathed out. She had no idea what he was talking about. "I think that's what my sugar cookie scent is to you, but it's tiger lilies for me." He bit her thigh, and she gasped. "I fucking love it."

Sucking on the skin of her thigh, he trailed the tips of his fingers through the wetness at her center, making her whine for more. "I don't think I'll ever get enough of how well you respond to me. You were definitely made for me. So good, so reactive." The sound she made at his words of praise made him smirk. "You like hearing that, don't you?"

Her eyes opened, and his irises glowed brightly at the edges.

Seth lowered his head and swiped his tongue over her clit. She bucked upward, but he pulled away. "You like hearing me tell you how much of a good girl you are, don't you?" She whined, and he flattened his tongue, dragging it through her soaked core to her clit, where he swirled around slowly. "You like being praised." His chuckle at her moan vibrated against her sensitive flesh.

She wanted to both kick him and beg him to keep going. His words were embarrassing, but they were true.

"Tell me," he said in that commanding voice that made her toes curl.

She pressed her lips together tightly.

"Riley." He held himself still over her, his breathing heavy against her exposed wetness. "Are you telling me you don't want to be praised?

You don't like being my good girl?"

She couldn't stop the broken whimper that fell from her lips at the question. She wanted it more than anything.

His dark chuckle told her he knew.

"Tell me," he demanded again.

"Yes, okay?" She huffed. "Yes, I want to be. I like it." Her arms crossed, and her face burned with embarrassment.

"Good girl. Now for your reward."

Not allowing her to slip into her thoughts or question his words, Seth sucked on her clit hard. Fireworks burst behind her eyes as she threw her head back on a scream. Her hands reached down and found purchase in the long strands of hair on top of his head, gripping tightly as Seth's true assault began.

He used his bent arm laid across her thigh to hold her down while he spread her apart with his index and thumb, giving him full access to her clit where he sucked, nipped, and licked until she became a writhing mess.

Riley yanked on Seth's hair, and he growled against her core, sending shivers down her spine.

Seth feasted on her like a man on death row, and she was his last meal before his execution.

Feeling the now familiar spark of blissful climax approaching, she tried to warn him, but her voice wouldn't work beyond moans and broken sounds she didn't recognize.

She was close. So close.

When she couldn't stay still, rocking her hips up to meet his face, he slipped two thick fingers easily into her, making her cry out his name as all thoughts and reason faded.

"Fuck, I love the way you call my name."

She wiggled her hips at his words, and he rose, leaning forward to brace his hand on the pillow beside her head. His piercing steel-gray eyes bored into hers, stealing her breath.

"I want you to ride my fingers, baby. Be a good girl and get yourself there for me." He moved closer, slowly moving his fingers in and out of her body, and whispered in her ear, "Use me." The last words were a growled command. Normally, his commands and tone remained calm and controlled, but the intensity he exuded, the words he said, and the growl that zipped down her spine were new. This new level of dominance was a side to Seth she didn't know existed, and she was so on board with it.

The things Seth did to keep her out of her head and present in the moment made every minute of what they shared more amazing than she ever imagined it would be.

Closing her eyes, she rolled her hips against the thrust of his fingers as need coiled tightly in her belly. She chased the feeling from when he licked her earlier.

"You're beautiful this way."

Opening her eyes, she looked up at him. She needed more.

Her gaze trailed down his sculpted body, taking in his intricate tattoos and smooth skin. When her eyes settled on his jeans, he brought the hand he wasn't using to tease her to unbutton and unzip them. Working them down with his boxer briefs to halfway down his thighs, he gripped his cock and gave it a long, slow stroke.

"This what you want?"

Riley couldn't answer him. Her nerves thrummed when her shaking hand reached for him. He let go of his shaft to allow her to do what she wanted.

She loved the velvety soft feel of his flesh despite the hardness. The contrast intrigued her.

Groaning, Seth laid his head back when she stroked him the way she had before, twisting a little near the head. She remembered he really liked that before.

"Fuck, yes," he drawled. "You're so good at this."

She preened under his praise, and when his fingers stilled inside her, she ground down against them.

"I can't wait anymore," he said, his voice raspy. He sounded as wrecked as she felt, and they hadn't even gotten to the big part.

Moving off the bed, he pulled his clothes the rest of the way off. Digging in his pocket, he pulled out his wallet and retrieved a small foil square she recognized.

Jealousy and sadness curled around her heart, and he stilled, lifting his head to look at her as a frown lowered his brows.

"What is it?"

She'd forgotten she couldn't hide the stronger emotions from him. Not this close to sealing their bond.

"It's stupid."

"Nothing you say is stupid," he said, moving to the bed and tossing the packet next to the pillow. "Tell me." He sat beside her, and she flushed at the sight of his erection so close without the heat of the moment distracting her.

Looking at the ceiling, she said. "Just had the stupid thought of how new that condom is."

"Hey now," he said, grabbing her chin and forcing her eyes to his. "It's been in there for months. I switched wallets and put a new one in there just to be on the safe side and haven't given it a second glance."

It was good he was being careful, but it didn't mean she liked the possibility he was prepared to sleep with someone else when he said he hadn't wanted anyone.

"Riley, there's only you. And if I'm being honest, I don't even want to use that with you. I've never gone bare. I don't want that between us."

Her eyes rounded. "What? But pregnancy." They couldn't contract and hold on to sexually transmitted diseases the way humans could, but they certainly could reproduce.

"Yeah, I'm aware." His hand pushed his hair back, and he laughed. "I want it all with you."

"Well, me too, but…"

"But you're not ready for that step?"

"A baby?"

"Yeah, maybe. I mean… you did want a big family."

"At some point. Not when I'm eighteen!" She laughed. "But I want it, someday." She then whispered, "With you."

Seth lunged forward, and she squealed with laughter as he pinned her to the bed. "You are so perfect. Everything I ever wanted." He lowered his head to kiss her chastely, but it quickly turned heated and all-consuming as their need for one another ratcheted up the inferno of desire burning in the room.

He moved to his knees and tore the packet open, making quick work of sheathing his cock and stroking it as he watched her with undisguised lust.

"Are you afraid?" A flicker of concern crossed his face.

She shook her head slowly against the pillow. "Just wondering how it'll fit. I'm small, and well, you're not, so…"

"It doesn't work that way. You can handle it. Your body was made for me, and besides, you're designed to be able to birth a child." The way he smiled down on her let her know he didn't judge her for her naïveté, and she loved him even more for it. "Thanks for the compliment though, but my dick isn't the size of a newborn." His exaggerated shudder made some of the apprehension fade.

She kicked the side of his hip with the side of her foot.

He laughed, and then his features turned serious. "I'll take it slow. If you need me to stop or want to stop at all, tell me. We do this at your pace, always. We do this together. This isn't about sex, Riley."

And boy, did she know it.

What they were about to do would shift the foundation of everything they'd ever been and would be to each other for the rest of their lives.

For the first time in forever, she didn't feel riddled with anxiety about the what ifs. She trusted that whatever came their way, Seth would be with her. He wouldn't let her fall.

She reached for him, and he met her halfway, bracing himself with one hand next to her head. She held that arm while he used his other hand to hold his cock and slowly ease into her.

Due to their conversation interrupting the moment, it stung at the beginning from not being as wet as she was earlier when they were all over each other.

"Doing okay, baby?"

She nodded, holding his arm to anchor herself as she breathed in and out quickly. She expected that sting to grow, and it made her anxious.

Seth's hand came up to hold the front of her throat and he used his thumb on her jaw to force her eyes to meet his. "Don't think about it. If you tense up and fight against it, it won't feel good. I'll stop if it's going to hurt you." His hand moved away from her neck, and he replaced it with gentle kisses across her sensitive skin. "I love you too much to hurt you."

Riley whimpered softly at the words that melted her heart, and that nervous energy fell away, and the sting that came with her tense muscles faded.

The feeling quickly morphed into a fullness and pressure that turned into absolute, toe-curling pleasure when he fully seated himself inside her.

"That's all of me. You did so good. So damn good. I'm proud of you," he soothed, leaning forward to kiss her forehead, cheek, then lips.

Tears rolled down her temples, and he kissed them away. She wasn't in pain. The tears had nothing to do with sadness. There was no way he didn't know.

"I love you," she whispered, and her arms came up around his neck as he slowly rocked into her after withdrawing. He groaned and his eyes rolled back.

"I never expected it to feel this amazing."

Seth stayed close to her body, allowing her to cling to him as he slowly made love to her, dragging lazy kisses over her jawline, across her neck, and over her shoulders.

Riley hooked her legs around his hips, and he put a hand beneath her backside to fit her to him tightly as he picked up the pace, his breathing becoming heavier against her skin.

His mouth slotted over hers and he licked at the seam of her lips until she parted hers and allowed him in. Their tongues dueled while Seth took her to heights of pleasure she never knew existed.

Moving his hand from her backside to trail over her body and grip her breast, he pinched her nipple in the way she responded well to before, and she arched against him, moaning into his mouth.

Her gums tingled, and she knew what she wanted, what she was allowed to have.

"Seth," she begged. "I need… I need…"

He lifted himself and looked down at her, still thrusting into her at a steady, but not too harsh, pace. He was being considerate of her again.

"What do you need?"

"More." She rocked up against him, grinding, making a garbled sound fall from his mouth. "Harder." She did the move again, and he groaned.

"Can you handle it?"

"Yes," she whined. "*Please.* Don't make me ask again." She put her heel on his backside and pushed him tighter against her.

Seth chuckled and placed his hands on both sides of her hips, rolling them against her and making stars dance behind her closed eyelids.

The possessive, firm hold on her hips was the only real warning before Riley discovered the true meaning behind "getting railed into the mattress." Seth seemed to take that phrase as a personal challenge, dragging his cock in and out of her at a punishing pace that had her gasping and arching her back, grasping at the pillows above her.

"It's too much… I can't… Seth!"

Seth groaned and rasped, "You can, and you will. You asked for this." He grunted. "I can *feel* you. You're burning up for this. For *me*." He growled at the last word.

He was right.

Even as the denial slipped from her mouth, she knew it was only the physical and emotional onslaught overwhelming her.

He knew it. His emotions blazed a path through their nearly sealed empathic link straight to her heart, so hers likely did the same for him.

"Isn't this what you wanted?" he said, the words rough and strained between thrusts, sweat beading his forehead and running down his chest and abs. He looked better than anything she could ever dream.

"Yes," she breathed.

"Do you want to come?"

He punctuated the question with a hard thrust that hit in a way that made her yelp in surprise, and he grinned and did it again. The intensity and depth of the move bordered on pain, but toed the line so lightly that pleasure overrode it. He repeated the move until she was writhing and scratching at his stomach and chest with her nails, leaving wicked track marks that would heal, eventually.

"Tell me, Riley."

"Huh?" She'd forgotten what she was supposed to say in the onslaught of his new move.

"Do you. Want. To. Come?"

"Please."

Seth's hand slipped between their bodies and began circling her clit as he rocked into her at a steady pace. No longer frantic, but rhythmic in a way that stoked a fire that grew deep within and expanded more and more until the familiar tightening in her muscles came shortly before she went over the edge.

"That's it. Be my good girl and come for me."

His words were the last piece to the perfect storm to send her hurtling over the edge into the abyss.

Quicker than she realized what happened, Seth had shifted them to sit on the bed and hold her in his lap, straddling him, her inner muscles still fluttering around his shaft.

"Bite me, Riley. Now."

Snapping out of her drunken haze, she realized what she needed to do. What she wanted. The idea she would get not only his blood, but his mark, made her orgasm linger.

His head tilted, and she drove her fangs deep into his skin, getting the first taste of her childhood friend's blood. She moaned as the sweet taste of candied blood coated her tongue, and she latched on, greedily pulling mouthfuls of his blood.

Seth jerked a few times, and she felt warmth where he spilled into the condom at her bite, before biting her on the soft patch of skin where the neck met her throat.

She rocked her hips against him, dragging out the pleasure as they drank from each other until the high settle enough they could stop.

Gently, Seth lifted her off his softening shaft and laid her on the bed. He quickly disposed of the condom and crawled back up the bed, pulling the cover over them.

Riley smiled sleepily up at him as he looked down at her from where he rested his head in his palm, elbow on the pillow.

"I can't believe it's done," he said softly, tracing the fingertips of his other hand over her face.

"Any regrets?"

"None." His brows pinched. "Well, maybe one." He chuckled at her confusion. "That we didn't do this sooner."

"Some of us are stubborn."

"Right. And you're completely open and willing."

"Of course."

"Glad to see being pair-bonded doesn't change your ego," he said with a laugh.

"Oh!" Riley sat up quickly and pushed the cover down, looking down at her stomach. "Look!" She beamed at him, happier than she'd been in ages.

Seth pulled the cover away from his body, revealing the matching symbol a replica of the one she now had. Black, solid, and permanent like a tattoo.

A mark that would never fade.

A symbol of their connection.

34

Childhood Dreams

Grabbing her messenger bag, stuffing her earbuds, phone, and an unfinished bag of jellybeans, Riley bolted for the door to her dorm. Pausing at the door, she looked back at the bed that belonged to her former roommate and sighed wistfully.

It wouldn't be only her room for much longer.

Headmistress Velastra held a meeting with both Seth and Riley earlier that morning, before Seth's first class of the day, to discuss the situation. Now that they were Korrena pairs, they would move into the same dorm room to put less stress on the mind and body as their bond grew. The closer proximity was designed to aid them in cultivating the sealed bond and progress at a faster rate compared to bonded Vasirian out in the world at large.

Riley's eyes took in the space.

She would need to change some things to accommodate removing the two smaller beds for the queen-sized bed to be delivered. With their claiming ritual complete, the headmistress made the concession, as was the case with other fully bonded Korrenas.

Eager to get to the cafeteria for lunch to see Seth again, she set the redecorating agenda on the back burner and darted out the door.

The entire walk through the dorm halls, across campus, and through the main building to the cafeteria was mostly uneventful, even if a few eyes tracked her; but when she stepped into the packed cafeteria, something was different.

As she made her way to the eight-seater round table in the back corner of the cafeteria where her friends were waiting, unease prickled her skin as more than a couple sets of eyes turned to her and whispers followed.

"Okay, y'all," Riley huffed, dropping her bag on the table. "Can someone tell me why I'm being looked at like I have the plague?"

"Word's out my brother claimed you," Kai said, a slow smile spreading over his lips.

"Yeah, but people don't usually get all bent out of shape when it happens."

Before she could sit, Seth snatched her around the waist and pulled her into his lap, locking his arms around her.

"Usually, a large part of the female population isn't clamoring for one of the pair-bonded's attention," Aiden said, and then paused. "Or at least a good time."

Seth laced his fingers through hers. "Told you that hasn't happened in a long time, and sure won't be happening ever again."

"Well, maybe they just want to see who finally got lucky enough to win you over?" Layla offered with a grin.

"She always had me," Seth mumbled, but Riley heard him, and apparently Blaire did too, judging by the way she looked at Riley with a huge smile.

"I find it interesting how fast word spread," Mera said.

Lukas glanced at her. "One of Seth's classmates cornered him in the hall. The one we met before that hit on him here at the table."

"Didn't you say she had given up on you but now her friend wanted to ask you out?" Aiden asked, and then tilted his head. "Or was it the other way around?"

Riley bristled, and Seth squeezed her hand, kissing the side of her neck.

"Her friend. She's given up. I told her I'm pair-bonded now, and I guess word got out." Seth shrugged and leaned down, nipping over the delicate skin of Riley's neck. He whispered in her ear, "To think I can do this whenever I want now." He punctuated his statement with a bite that pierced the skin with his fangs, making her gasp. He licked the blood away, and it reminded her of something.

"How come when you drank my blood those other times the wounds had to heal on their own if you've been my Korrena all along?"

"What?"

"He drank your blood?"

"He bit you?"

Riley looked up at Kai, Aiden, and Blaire in surprise. She wasn't sure who said what with how fast they spat their questions.

"Things had sorta been progressing before we sealed the bond." She glanced at Aiden uncomfortably. "Um. We kinda fooled around?"

Why did she phrase it like a question?

Whining, she tucked her face into the crook of Seth's neck, and he smirked.

"To answer your question… I never licked the wounds. My saliva touched them, but because I still drank from the open wound, they wouldn't close."

"Oh."

All Riley knew was that a Korrena's saliva could close the bite of their pair. They'd done it last night. With the emotional rollercoaster she'd been on for weeks, it wasn't a surprise she had forgotten the other times.

"Is there room for me?"

They all turned to see Dominic standing with a tray in his hands, a half-smile on his face.

"Nope," Seth said with a rumbling in his chest.

Riley covered Seth's face with her hand. "Ignore him. He's just speaking fluent asshole again." She looked pointedly at Seth. "We're friends. He knows about you and me."

Seth's eyes narrowed, and his jealousy slipped through their empathic connection. She sighed.

She didn't blame him, but he needed to lighten up and see there was nothing between Dominic and her. Sometimes actions spoke louder than words.

She asked Seth, "What if you behave, and I let you pick the restaurant next time we go out? Will that make you feel better enough to let this go?"

He always had something to say about the places she picked, but she didn't know if it was an actual aversion to the things she picked or just his teasing. Maybe both sometimes.

Seth snorted. "Oh my, how altruistic of you to think of me," he said with a roll of his eyes and a smirk.

"What can I say? I'm a giving soul."

Lukas pulled a chair from a nearby table and slid closer to Blaire to allow Dominic to squeeze in between him and Aiden.

"She's right, you know," Dominic said. "We make for better friends, and I don't interfere with Korrena pairs. It's a wonderful thing to have." He opened his blood packet. "I think whatever the Oracle told us is why I felt drawn to you," he added before taking a drink.

"But what does it mean?" Riley asked.

Dominic looked at her. "Not sure, but there isn't much we can do except leave it for now."

As much as she hated the idea, he was right. The Oracle didn't offer information if she couldn't provide it, and most times, the information she did give was cryptic at best. Something about messing with the natural flow of things and restoration of the balance.

In Riley's opinion, things would go a whole lot smoother if things were laid out in layman's terms. Event A needs to happen for Outcome B; avoid Event C or Tragedy D happens.

Easy peasy, lemon squeezy.

"I guess knowing someone in the monarchy is linked to your future isn't half bad. At least there's power at your back," Seth groused. His reluctant acceptance of Dominic in their lives and even the realization of the possible benefit eased her tension. Baby steps. Minor victories. She'd take it.

"I think a compliment might have found its way into that statement, but I can't be sure."

Seth glared, but the slight upturn to the corner of his mouth betrayed his amusement.

"I still find it fascinating what she said to you five," Kai said, sitting back in his chair and biting into an apple.

"Even more so that Blaire and Aiden are not only soul-bound like the others, but also bound in the heart." Mera shook her head. "It's disappointing to have missed that."

Blaire's mouth dropped, a horrified look crossing her features.

Lukas pulled her into a hug and kissed the top of her head. "She means when we met the Oracle and learned what it meant when you saved Aiden, not when it showed itself when he..." He frowned and let the words hang in the air.

Mera sat upright, her face paling. "I didn't mean that, no."

Blaire waved a hand. "The whole thing is just touchy. It wasn't easy."

"I wish I could see the magic," Layla said with a smile. "I bet it's pretty."

"It is, but we've only seen it under the worst circumstances. I don't know if it's possible to show itself any other way," Lukas said.

If it took death to bring forth Blaire's magic, Riley never wanted to see it again. Considering it'd only shown itself twice—first, when Blaire died, and then when Aiden died, it stood to reason that was when it would manifest.

Seth took her hand, the one she was using to tear at the hole in her tights, and held it in his warm palm, his thumb brushing circles over the top of it, distracting her.

"Want to go to the movies and have dinner later?" he whispered in her ear.

"Just us?"

"If you want."

She whipped her head around to look at him. "Like an actual date?"

"Sure."

Her heart gave a giddy flutter. To get another shot at a date, but this time with the guy she loved more than anyone, who also loved her back! If he didn't feel it through their empathic link, she was sure her face said it all, because he chuckled and slotted his mouth over hers in a very passionate, very public kiss that left her reeling when he pulled away.

"Well, then," Aiden said, clearing his throat.

"Get used to it." Lukas patted Aiden's shoulder the way Aiden always did to others. "Those two have been denying each other for so long, I'm surprised they're even in here."

Layla asked, "What do you mean?"

Lukas shook his head at her. "When you first seal the bond, it's hard to want to leave your bedroom."

Riley's face felt as red as Blaire's often looked. It wasn't uncommon for them to talk openly about the bond and the things that came with it, but now that she was part of that, she couldn't deny the wave of shyness that came over her.

"So it's all finished? Sealed and permanent?"

Seth looked up at Dominic from where he had been focused on tracing his fingertips over Riley's thigh. "Yeah, why?"

"Oh, no reason. Though I'm curious about your mark."

"What?"

"What your mark looks like, I mean."

Riley stood. "It's—" She squeaked when Seth pulled her back down, his hand covering her stomach possessively.

"I'll do it. It's too low for me to feel comfortable with you sharing."

She wanted to argue, but she liked the possessive gesture, and he actually bothered to explain his feelings. Feelings that made sense. It wasn't like she was wearing a bathing suit. He was right that pulling her clothing down in public would be more intimate.

Why hadn't she thought of that?

It was probably hard to express his vulnerabilities in front of the others to explain his proprietary move, so she wouldn't deny him the control. She liked it anyway.

Riley smiled at him, kissing his cheek. "You used your big boy words and not your fists for once… Color me impressed."

Seth scoffed and nipped her ear before sliding her off his lap and standing. Lifting his shirt, he exposed the small mark the size of a child's palm on the left side of his abdomen in the V near the edge of his jeans.

Kai put his arm over the back of Mera's chair. "I'm happy for you, little brother." He sighed. "I know we don't meet on the same wavelength, but I am genuinely happy for what you've found. It is a blessing. Cherish it."

"And to think it's with Riley, of all the possible people in the world!" Layla gushed.

Lukas laughed. "These two have been after each other for so many years it was starting to become embarrassing. It's good it finally worked out. The mark actually looks pretty cool."

"I like it," Blaire said, looking at Riley. "You'll have to show me how it looks on you later."

Aiden grinned at Seth. "Well, at least it didn't get lost in your existing ink."

A few girls glanced their way, and Riley resisted the urge to glare at them. They were curious, and she wanted them all to see that Seth was a marked man.

Hers.

To know the one thing she'd dreamt of since she was a little girl was actually hers made her heart soar.

He sat back down and pulled her into his arms again. She stole a baby carrot off his nearly empty tray and bit it in half with a *snap*, winking at him. He smirked.

Things wouldn't magically be better in their lives because they claimed one another. The trials of the Korrena bond were only beginning. Until they spent time developing their bond into something solid, they were going to stumble over difficulties like her best friend had.

Jealousy. Lost trust. Anger.

But they had their beginning.

They'd conquered the first hurdle by letting go of their reservations and embracing what they'd wanted since they were children.

Each other.

Like Ryan and Shelby in Emley Rison's books, Riley would get her happily ever after with Seth.

Finally.

It only took them fifteen long years to realize their love wasn't unrequited.

Final Note from the Author

Thank you for picking up (or downloading) my book and completing it. I hope you loved it as much as I loved creating it. I appreciate every one of you.

If you enjoyed this book, and the others, please consider leaving a written review. Indie authors rely heavily on the reviews of their readers to make it in the self publishing world, and sites like Amazon, use those reviews to determine visibility.

Stay in Touch

Join Stephanie over on Facebook in Stephanie Denne's Book Sanctuary Facebook Group! It's a place to discuss current works, future works, and interact directly with Stephanie.

https://www.facebook.com/groups/743979797516659

Social Media

TikTok: https://www.tiktok.com/@stephaniedenneauthor

Facebook: https://www.facebook.com/stephaniedenneauthor

Instagram: https://www.instagram.com/stephaniedenneauthor/

Newsletter

Sign up for Stephanie's Newsletter to keep up to date on the latest news around the Blackthorn world and future series, and get special sneak peeks at the writing process and chapter previews for future books.

http://eepurl.com/h_N5uP

About the Author

Stephanie Denne is an author of Paranormal Romance and Dark Fantasy for new adults and adults. The Blackthorn Saga marked her debut in the literary world.

Inspired by art and music, she felt the need to give life to characters that had been rolling around in her mind for 12 years. Never having written anything before, when she sat down and started drafting, she discovered she had a passion for the craft and the story naturally grew into something much bigger than she could fit into one book—much less a few, or even one series!

Born in the United States of America in the Southeast, Stephanie has now called Ontario, Canada her home since 2011. When not writing, she can be found reading her favorite stories, playing video games with her husband, painting with watercolor, or cuddling with her Golden Retriever. But not the cat—the cat has her own agenda.

Acknowledgments

To everyone who supported me through the creation of Ruinous Secrets, I want to extend a huge thank you. Navigating the world of self publishing as a rookie writer isn't always easy but having a strong support system from not only my husband and friends, but readers who have reached out to me along the way after reading book one and two of the Blackthorn Saga has been an exciting journey.

Thank you to my wonderful editor Kelly for helping me build and grow the world of Blackthorn. Helping me expand and be a better writer without squashing my voice, while maintaining patience and keeping me on track, makes our partnership one I will never forget. Thank you so much.

A huge thank you to my ARC team in helping me establish a footing for this book and give me advanced feedback. I take your words to heart and love seeing your reactions!

www.ingramcontent.com/pod-product-compliance
Lightning Source LLC
Chambersburg PA
CBHW020522310726
48979CB00014B/2171/J

* 9 7 8 1 7 3 8 1 0 1 4 1 2 *